Nowhere to Go But Tomorrow

Nowhere to Go But Tomorrow

Nelle Cooper

Fresh Ink Group

Guntersville

Nowhere to Go But Tomorrow

Fresh Ink Group
An Imprint of:
The Fresh Ink Group, LLC
1021 Blount Avenue #931
Guntersville, AL 35976
Email: info@FreshInkGroup.com
FreshInkGroup.com

Edition 1.0 2024

Cover art by Anik / FIG
Cover design by Stephen Geez / FIG
Book design by Amit Dey / FIG
Associate publisher Beem Weeks / FIG

Cataloging-in-Publication Recommendations:
TRA001080 TRANSPORTATION / Automotive / Driver Education
EDU029090. EDUCATION / Teaching / Materials & Devices
EDU029100. EDUCATION / Teaching / Methods & Strategies

Library of Congress Control Number: xxx

ISBN-13: 978-1-958922-93-4 Softcover
ISBN-13: 978-1-958922-94-1 Hardcover
ISBN-13: 978-1-958922-95-8 Ebooks

Introduction

Lapeer State Home 1948

A tall black wrought iron palisade fence separated the Lapeer State Home property from the M21 highway. Two matching gates attached to stone columns stood open at the main entrance. Beyond the gates, numerous three- and four-storey red brick buildings dotted the grounds. Trees of elm, oak, and maple shaded the vast lawns, the streets, and the drives. A group of children emerged from the school building for recess. Sounds of boys and girls at play blended with other less pleasant sounds, groans and guttural noises, high-pitched shrieks and cackling laughter. The residents of this small city exhibited a myriad of diseases and physical aberrations affecting their bodies and minds. There were children in wheelchairs, walking with crutches, or supported using canes, limbs in braces; there were the blind and the deaf, the seizure prone and others with deformities since birth. Among those with known disorders were the abandoned, and those conceived within this society. Here in this community of humanity numbering more than four thousand lived the employees, their families, and the children of the "Home."

"Suffer the little children …
to come unto me for, of such is the kingdom of heaven."

Matthew 19:14 (KJV)

"I don't remember the time of the year or the day of the
week, but I remember the day my world collided with
reality, and I learned what it meant that I lived at "The
HOME." That day, my life shattered and left me with
broken pieces of empty."

Kaye Maureen O'Shay

Chapter 1

1948

"This is the Missouri Trail." Teacher Timmons pointed to an area on the pull-down map. She was interrupted as the map zoomed up the wall, whirled into its canister, and finished with a loud bang.

Eight-year-old Kay O'Shay snapped to attention.

Miss Timmons droned on. "The pioneer families traveled west across the Missouri River to have a new life. Some stopped on the way and settled to make farms, but others traveled on westward." Her finger traced a line across the retrieved map just as the school bell sounded to end the day. "Tomorrow we're going to do something exciting," she continued. "We're going to ride on a wagon like the pioneers." Her smile and encouragement bounced around the room.

The children slapped on their desks and squealed anticipation.

"Kay, would you stop by my desk before you leave?"

"Yes, ma'am." Her homework was done. Sometimes kids say things and get other kids in trouble. Not knowing what Miss Timmons wanted scared her.

The "walking children," those who could walk without help, clattered toward the door. Kay approached Miss Timmons's desk and waited as the teacher helped the remaining children clear their desks. Attendants brought in wheelchairs and assisted those who needed help. The children struggled to perform any act of independence. As the last child left the classroom, Miss Timmons returned to her desk.

"Kay, thanks for waiting. I found a book you might enjoy reading. It's very popular with girls your age, and it's about what we're studying in class—the migration of the American people as they settled the West."

A chapter book—she'd never read a chapter book before. Kay couldn't wait to get back to her cottage and start reading. Maybe if she read it aloud to Jessie, the staff wouldn't give her other tasks to do.

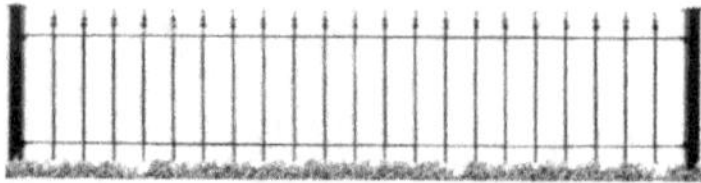

Kay huddled in the closet. A single light bulb glowed overhead as she turned the pages of her first chapter book. Her toes cramped from the cold; her fingers grew numb. The book slid onto her lap. Several questions brewed like a storm. She touched her face, her eyes, her ears, her nose and mouth. On her feet were the clean and matched socks she wore every day. Some of the children had family who came to visit. If no one came to visit her, that must mean she didn't have a family—or at least if she did, they didn't want her to live with them.

Tears rolled down her cheeks. The book had opened a window, leaving her with shattered pieces of empty. A family! That girl had a family. Struggling to stand, she retrieved the book, turned off the closet light, opened the door, and walked to her bed. She pulled the curtain back from the window. As far as she could see to the left and right, the moon cast shadows against the black, ever-present and always ominous fence. She had never envisioned a life outside the Home. Pain twisted in her stomach as she clenched her fists and decided she would take that book back to Miss Timmons tomorrow and not discuss it. Miss Timmons would inspect it and pronounce it returned in proper condition. Kay had not made a mark in the book. But the book had left its mark on her—an unforgettable mark.

The next morning, Kay left for school early. It would be best to get it over with before anyone arrived.

When Miss Timmons entered the room, Kay was seated at her desk, the only student in the room.

"You're early this morning," Miss Timmons said. "You returned the book." She picked it up and fanned the pages. "You must have read all night to finish it so soon."

"No, ma'am. I didn't finish it," Kay announced as she approached Miss Timmons's desk. Anger and frustration propelled her forward.

Miss Timmons continued stacking papers on her desk. "That's an award-winning book. Most girls enjoy reading it."

"Do you know where I can find *my* ma and pa?"

Miss Timmons paused, her shoulders slumped, and she looked up.

Kay listened to the sounds of her own body as it inhaled and exhaled, but she refused to cry. She continued her questioning stare as Miss Timmons's face paled, her eyes sad and searching.

No answer came forth. Kay's anger burned from within.

"Can you tell me why I live behind a fence? In that book animals lived inside a fence, a corral." Kay's words tumbled out like a snowball rolling downhill. "Why am I living inside a fence? What did I do? Why do I live here?"

"Kay, I'm sorry about the book. I didn't think about how you might feel. I thought you would enjoy reading about girls and their lives in the wilderness because we're studying history. I hurt you and I'm sorry." She paused as if to consider the situation before continuing. "I don't have the answers to your questions. If you're too upset to stay in school today, I'll write a note and you can return to your cottage."

"That wouldn't change anything. No one there will answer me! Someone knows. Somebody in charge. And someday I'll find out."

Someday I'll find out.

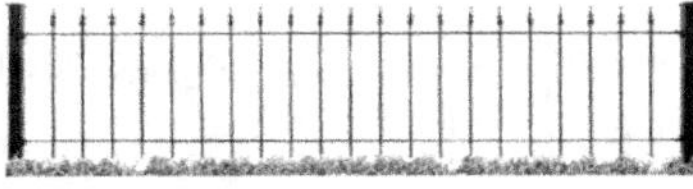

Seth Thomas stood nearby as Kay grasped the flagpole with her hand and walked a circle around it. The older boys played catch away from the smaller children.

"Why do you walk like that, Seth?"

"Who?"

"You. Isn't your name Seth?"

"No! Well, yes, but everyone calls me Toe."

"Can I call you Toe?"

"Maybe."

"Last year and the year before you came the first day of school, but you didn't come back. We could be friends if you came to school." He was nine and kinda cute. His black hair curled out from under his ballcap and his crooked smile made that deep dimple in his right cheek. Only when he walked did he look strange, like an old man gimping along.

Kay placed her hands on her hips. "I've seen you play ball and you run good. So, Toe, why do you walk like that?" Maybe if she told him how he looked it would help him. She liked to help people.

He leaned forward and shouted at her. "Like what?"

"Like this." Kay bent her neck, positioning her head level with her chest as her feet propelled her forward. Looking down, she swung her upper body and head from side to side as if searching for something on the ground.

A ripple of laughter erupted from some of the other kids. Kay had Toe's full attention. He was staring at her, his face scarlet, eyes blazing in anger. The bell rang to end recess, so the children ran back toward the school.

Toe bolted from the playground.

Kay paused, then ran after him. "I'm sorry, Seth . . . Toe! Really, I am!" She called out again from the border of the playground. "The rules, I can't go any further. If I do, I'll be late. I can't break the rules." He hurried down the road that led across the railroad tracks and on to the barns at the farm. His head was down, his body leaning forward as if heading into a storm.

"Boys!" Kay stomped her foot. She just wanted to help him. When he walked, he looked strange, all humped over, and she liked to help people.

Maybe he didn't know how he looked when he walked. She tried to show him. If he knew how he looked, then he wouldn't walk that way anymore. But, he got mad.

Just like a boy to get mad.

Chapter 2

1949

"Jessie, let's go outside and see the pretty leaves." Kay had finished her chores. She placed Jessie in her stroller, tucked in her doll, and headed for the door. "We're going over to the swings!" she called out to the attendant in the dayroom.

Kay pushed Jessie's stroller in the direction of the swings. A crew of working men raked rows of leaves toward the street. A young boy came from behind her, racing toward the playground; but as he got closer an older boy in the crew flipped his rake around, whisking it between the young boy's legs, causing him to stumble and roll on the sidewalk.

Kay raced to lift the child up, then scowled at the big boy. "Why did you do that? That was mean."

He turned to face her, his eyes filled with hate. "Shut up!"

The younger boy ran away.

Kay backed up toward Jessie's stroller. "It's you. I know you."

He started toward her. "I said shut up."

A man shouted from the street. "Tony, get to work!"

Kay's knees trembled; she turned Jessie's stroller around, afraid to pass by the angry boy. On the way to their cottage she remembered the first time she saw Tony. She had tried to forget, and her efforts had been successful—until she saw him today.

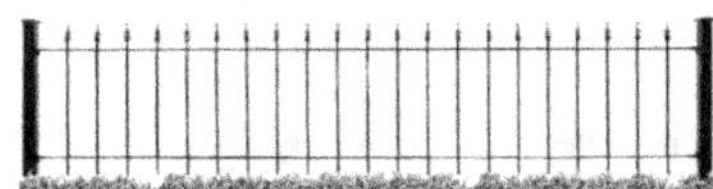

1948

Last year when Kay was eight, the regular aide named Peters stopped her as she returned from school. When Peters started her shift at three in the afternoon, she smelled like flowers. Her white uniform looked spotless with her hair knotted at the back of her neck, but by the end of the shift her uniform appeared dirty, her hair looked like an occupied bird's nest, and she smelled like the children.

"I have to take this to the Castle," Peters said. "You can go with me if you want to. You'll have to wait outside. Can you do that?" Her voice commanded attention, but her eyes crinkled into a smile.

"Yes!" This was the second time Peters invited Kay to do an errand with her.

"Can I say hello to Jessie first?"

"Sure." Peters nodded. "I'll wait here at the door."

Kay ran to check on Jessie in the dayroom. She rescued her favorite stuffed toy from the floor and laid it in Jessie's arms before returning to Peters.

It was exciting to go on an errand, especially to the Castle.

Peters asked, "Have you ever been to the Castle, Kay?"

"No, I've only seen it."

"That's where the important people work, the doctors and administrators. I'm not sure why they built a castle, but it's interesting, isn't it? It's built out of natural stone on the front and red brick on the sides and back. It's *four* storeys high." Peters spoke of the four storeys as lofty as a mountain. "Do you like those circle-shaped towers on the corners?"

Kay took note of each area of the castle as Peters called her attention to it. The towers had windows on every floor. The tops of the towers had a ridge above the windows and the roof went up to a point.

"The towers look like they're wearing hats," Kay observed.

"Yes they do." Peters laughed.

Kay counted five chimneys towering over the roof. Wide steps ascended to the porch.

"This is called a portico." Peters pointed to the stone arches over the driveway. "A car can stop under the roof and the people won't get wet if it's raining. Do you know before there were automobiles people came here in horse-drawn carriages?"

They climbed the steps together. "You wait right here." She pointed toward the top step and entered the Castle door.

A car turned from the highway onto the drive toward the Castle. All the motor vehicles moved slowly inside the fence, more slowly than they did on the highway. The car was black and white and had a round red light on top. Kay knew about police cars because something happened at the gate one day and the guard told everyone, "Go back to your buildings. The police are here now."

Kay scurried down the steps and around to the side of the building. She had to be near when Peters came out. Shrubs pressed against the walls of the Castle and crowded onto the sidewalk. Kay eased in between the bushes, the branches scratching her arms as she watched. A door opened on each side of the car. Two policemen appeared. One opened a back door on the car and pulled out a boy. The man's fist gripped the shoulder of the boy's shirt.

She tried to understand. The boy looked skinny and tall—too old for the schoolboy's cottage. He couldn't be bad—if he were, the guard wouldn't have let him in. The guards keep the bad people out.

"No!" the boy yelled, wrestling against the policeman's grasp. "No. Take me to jail!" He screamed louder, "Don't leave me here. I'll never get out." He twisted again, jerking against the policeman several times until he had freed himself. He ran toward the highway.

Kay stepped out from between the shrubs to watch. He was fast; they wouldn't catch him.

"Stop him! Stop that boy," one officer yelled to the guard at the gate.

The guard saw the boy and ran toward him. As they neared each other, the boy dodged left, then right. The guard countered, right then left, and lunged. They tussled and tumbled around in the dirt. The policemen shuffled down the drive. One policeman knelt as the other men held the boy. The policemen stood; each man grasped the boy's shirt and trousers, carrying him toward the Castle as he struggled. With his hands secured behind his back, his body jostled between the two men as they walked. His head bobbed up and down, level with their knees. His shoes dragged in the dirt behind him.

"No, no!" he called out. Kay could see he was crying. Sobs shook his body. Tears rolled down his dirt-stained face. When they reached the steps, he raised his head and stared at her. Then his face twisted in rage and his eyes went wild with fear. Beads of sweat ran from his forehead and streaked his face.

Kay didn't know what was happening. She trembled with fear.

The boy continued his stare as he twisted against the men, pleading for help.

Kay's feet stuck to the sidewalk; she couldn't move.

"You can't *ever* leave, you know that?" the boy screamed to Kay.

One policeman's gaze followed the direction of the boy's stare. When he saw Kay, he thumped the boy on the head with his fist. "Shut up!" he bellowed.

Peters appeared. "Kay, Kay, where are you?" She clomped down several steps and looked at the policemen and the boy. She followed the boy's stare and spotted Kay. "We can go now. Come along." Peters reached for Kay's hand.

All the way to her cottage Kay thought about what the boy had said. Peters didn't offer conversation. That boy said she couldn't ever leave. She had always been sure she lived here because the people outside the black fence were mean. She knew some of the workers went home after work, but others lived in rooms at the cottages. The gate kept the bad people out. Now that boy said she couldn't ever leave, but what could he know? He'd just arrived. Kay returned to the cottage, bewildered and confused. She climbed the stairs to her room, then curled up on her bed and wept.

Peters didn't follow her, nor did she inquire later that evening why Kay was quiet.

Kay had so many questions that night, she couldn't sleep. The next morning, birds started singing before the sun came up. Who would tell her the truth? She'd find someone she could ask, someone to tell her the truth, and she wouldn't cry.

At school the next day, she wanted to ask her teacher, but kids were acting up, and one got sick and puked. At recess Kay played on the swings alone. She wouldn't think about it anymore. It couldn't be true. She would grow up and become a lady and she wouldn't live here. She'd have a beautiful house with flowers and gardens where she would drink tea like ladies do.

The bell rang and children scurried up the steps. Kay's questions consumed her.

"Time to come inside, children," the teacher called. "Kay, did you hear me?" The frustration of her morning sounded in the tone of her voice.

It didn't sound like a good day to ask the teacher.

"That was a fast trip to the swings. Guess you didn't want to miss supper?" Peters was sailing out the door toward the employee dining room. "Where's Jessie's doll?"

Kay glanced at the stroller. Jessie was banging on the tray and her doll was gone. Kay searched the porch and front sidewalk. The crew was still raking and gathering leaves. They were well past the swings, but Kay wouldn't go out there now. She patted Jessie's arm. "I'll go back after they leave, Jessie. I'll get your doll. Don't you worry."

Worry is what Kay did—worry about what that boy had yelled, that she could never leave. Sometimes trying not to think about something helped, but it was harder not to worry. Two old women readied their buckets to mop the floor. They must have lived here a long time. She knew they couldn't leave. They were like Jessie, but they could walk.

Toe hated folk dancing, but the band instructor remained firm: to play in the band Toe must also dance. "The dance teacher," the band instructor said, "needs boys who can follow directions and understand rhythm."

The folk dancing class lasted six weeks. Every Friday after lunch, the schoolchildren followed their music teacher, Mrs. Trett, to the parade ground.

Standing on the temporary stage, the music teacher blew her whistle, commanding attention. "Tomorrow lots of people will come to see you perform. After, there will be a party with wonderful cookies and juice. I want you to pay close attention so the visitors can see how nicely you dance."

Several attendants assisted arranging the children into two lines, a row of boys and a row of girls facing each other. Mrs. Trett urged the two lines to move forward, forming one line, alternating boy/girl boy/girl. The attendants scurried about, guiding the children into place.

Toe scanned the group: there was that girl Kay, the one that made fun of him at the first day of school. Kay maneuvered through the group, pretending to help the other children until she stood beside him. He didn't look at her, but he could feel her there.

Mrs. Trett directed the children—four-forward and four-back— to form circles.

Kay reached for Toe's hand, but he hesitated.

An attendant grasped Toe's hand and said, "Hold her hand like this," as he slapped Kay's hand into Toe's.

Toe felt her hand slide into his. He lifted his head and pulled his shoulders back to reach his full height, pleased to see he now stood more than a head taller than Kay.

The attendant hurried on to other groups assisting them to form circles.

Toe forced a frown about the dancing, but when Kay looked up at him and smiled, well, he forgot he was angry.

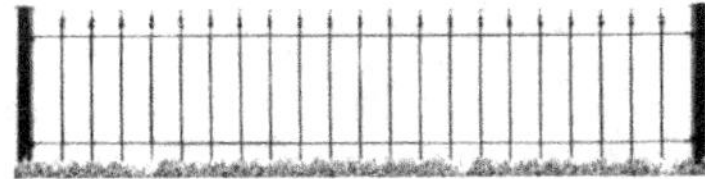

The day of the Maypole celebration, cookies and juice appeared after the folk-dancing exhibition. Toe watched Kay serve juice to the younger children. Then she carried a cup over to him. "Thank you for dancing with me," she whispered as she handed the cup to him. His fingers circled the punch cup as he avoided her gaze. She made him nervous.

Every reply he thought of sounded dumb. "Your hands are soft," he squeaked.

"I'm sorry I hurt your feelings that day at school when I talked about the way you walk. I said I was sorry but you didn't hear me."

Toe turned away, afraid she would see he was still upset.

What she did was mean.

"Don't leave again. Please." Kay stepped around to face him. She looked up to see Mrs. Hannot heading toward them, shaking her finger; Kay could read her lips from across the lawn.

"No boys! No talking to boys."

"I'm going to check on Jessie. Meet me at the pine tree behind third base. There's so many people here they won't notice," said Kay before running to Jessie, narrowly escaping the wrath of Mrs. Hannot.

He watched Kay remove a piece of paper from Jessie's mouth, then offer her some juice and a cookie. He followed the path toward the barns until he was out of sight, then circled back toward the pine tree behind third base. He climbed up the tree, avoiding the sharp needles, and eased the heavy boughs away to perch on a limb.

Kay struggled with pushing Jessie's wheelchair toward the ball diamond. Her hands slipped off the handles when she hit a rut in the outfield. She arrived at the tree and turned the wheelchair toward the diamond. In line with third base, they faced the parade grounds. In the shade of the pine tree they were within clear view, watching the party below. "Are you there?" she mumbled, keeping watch for Mrs. Hannot.

"Yup," he said from within the tree.

"We can't talk to boys."

"Yeah, I know."

"Can you talk to girls?"

"Nope."

Kay giggled. "It's okay; nobody's watching." She paused. "Why did you run away that day? I said I was sorry."

"You were making fun of me. Why did you do that?"

"I thought I could help you."

"I don't need your help."

"I said I was sorry."

Toe did want to talk to her. He wanted to tell her she was the first girl who ever talked to him, but he wasn't sure he should risk it. Maybe she'd make fun of him again. He decided maybe it would okay just to share a little, and as he started to talk, his story began to unfold through the boughs. "Stan walked like that. I called him Dad."

"Did you know your dad?"

"Do you?" He could not hold back the sarcasm in his voice.

Kay's reply was almost inaudible. "No."

He wished he hadn't sounded mean. He was starting to say dumb things around her. He took a deep breath and continued. "Stan was good to me. He said I was smart and he taught me how stuff works. I wanted to be like him." He paused. "I didn't know anything was wrong with the way I walk until you said that. After, I heard someone say Stan had a bad fall and it bent his back so he was crooked."

Toe wasn't sure she was listening, but he could hear her breathing.

A few moments passed before Kay broke the silence. "Why do they call you Toe?" Her whisper was gentle like the purring of the barn kittens.

"When I was little I fell a lot. My foot, this one." He edged around the tree and stuck out his right foot. "See? It's bent. It still won't walk me straight. They said I fell over my own feet. That's when they started calling me Toe and I've been Toe ever since."

"You should come to school. How will you learn if you don't come to school?

"I'm gonna have a farm someday. I need to learn about farming, not nouns and verbs. I read a lot of books . . . probably more than you!"

"What books do you read?"

"Promise you won't laugh?"

"Promise."

"I read about a guy who built a cabin and lived in the woods. His name's Thoreau. I read any books I can get. I read Shakespeare, too."

"Shakespeare? Isn't he really old?"

"Yeah, he's really old." Toe coughed to smother his laugh. "And he's really dead."

"How did Stan teach you about stuff?"

"He was the manager over at the cottage where I lived. First, he got me paper and pencils and taught me how to draw. He could draw anything. Then he put a canvas down in the corner of his office and brought me stuff to take apart—alarm clocks, broken things with parts. He let me use his tools, too. When I got something apart, he would help me put it back together. He said if I learned how things worked, I could fix 'em. We worked on motors, too."

"Motors? Like cars?"

She sounded impressed. Now he had her full attention.

"Yeah, during the winter after supper we'd work on 'em. We got 'em running, too. We had to take them outside and set them on blocks to start them. Toe's voice trailed off. "I wanted to be just like Stan except one morning he wasn't there, and he never came back. I started getting into trouble, and when I got into fights at school, they sent me to the barn to work. I've been there ever since."

Toe worried he'd said too much. He hadn't planned to tell her all that. And all he wanted at that moment was to change the subject. He didn't want to talk about Stan anymore. "Is Jessie your sister?" he asked.

"No, I take care of her. I wish you'd come back to school." Kay was relentless.

"I do all right. I know a lot and I read. We'd better go. I got chores to do."

"Thanks for talking to me. I'm really sorry. I didn't want to make you feel bad. It's just when you walk nobody can see your face 'cause you look at the dirt."

She sounded honest. She might be a kind person; look how she cared for Jessie.

Toe dropped to the ground. From inside the tree, he lifted a pine bough away and peaked through, smiling. The bough slipped and whipped toward his face. They both laughed as he swatted at it. He pulled the bough back again. "Miss Kay?"

Kay turned to face him. Her brown hair glistened in the sunshine.

His gaze halted as he studied her emerald-green eyes with their copper ring around the iris. The bough fluttered in his hand. "It'd be real hard to stay mad at you—real hard."

Mrs. Hannot called from the parade ground. She fluttered her arms like a mother hen attempting to gather her chicks. Kay started back down the hill, pushing Jessie's chair.

He couldn't see her face or the smile he hoped she wore, but as he watched her walk away she was singing, "I'm looking over a four-af clover that I've overlooked before."

Jessie made happy, laughing sounds as her chair bounced over the grass like a carnival ride.

Toe raced back toward the barns as if his feet had wings. Maybe school wouldn't be so bad after all.

Chapter 3

1950

Kay awakened from her sleep to the two odors that remained constant: human sweat and urine. Three o'clock in the morning, no air moved inside the room, and not a leaf fluttered outside where the large oak and maple trees shaded acres of two-storey brick cottages. On the second floor, beds lined the walls in dormitory style. Pairs of tall windows interrupted the expanse of the green walls. Despite the heat, the windows remained closed. Over the years they had accumulated layers of paint, or someone had nailed them shut. The doors at each end of the room had screens. The space between the steel-framed single beds required placing one foot directly ahead of the other, similar to walking a narrow board or a sidewalk curb.

Kaye watched as the workers lifted several children off of the floor and placed them in their beds, and covered them with their blankets. She knew some of the children crawled off their beds during the night and others fell. Her nights were filled with the sounds of sleeping children. Some snored, some murmured in their dreams, some had seizures, and some cried out in their sleep. Attendants cared for their toileting and diaper changes. Over the years, Kay knew the sounds and breath rhythms of each slumbering child. She recognized which child was safely sleeping and which child had entered a danger zone. She considered herself the unofficial custodian of their care. Employees came and went, but she remained vigilant.

Lotzie and Benke were kind people who had worked the night shift together for years. Lotzie walked with a limp and Benke brought in cookies after her day off.

They chatted as they went about their tasks.

"We got more people working here than any place in the county," Lotzie stated. "That's a fact."

"Who's got time to count workers?" Benke pushed the mop bucket into the closet.

"I mean people getting paid here. There's more than anywhere else. Ouch! I smacked my shin into Mazie's bed again. There's just too many beds in here. No wonder we got so many on the payroll, they's stackin' kids in here like cordwood."

"I heard the payroll is up into the thousands. My cousin Gertie says they can't build buildings fast enough and she should know, her workin' in the Castle and all."

Lotzie went on with her unhappiness. "Yah, those folks in the Castle, they know 'bout everything 'cept how to change a diaper and wipe up slop. They so busy having meetings and deciding 'bout who goes where and when. Then they sit around and think of new rules. I'd like to tell them a thing or two."

"Are you going to grumble all night?" Benke asked.

"I might." Lotzie sat down on a bed and rubbed her shin.

"You're assigned the infirmary all next week."

"Nothing different. I just don't have to climb one flight of stairs."

Nighttime was restless. Time moved in an eerie pace at night, punctuated with sounds that would seem strange to a visitor.

The morning light filled the eastern sky; the whistle of a freight train sounded at each of the three successive gate crossings and chugged east, shaking the ground with rumbles that echoed around the buildings and through the trees. Kay listened to the rumbling rhythm, imagining the cars of the train rocking from side to side. This one was long, car after car thundering east. Everyone said the trains that went toward the sunrise were going to the water and those toward the sunset to the big city.

Kay eased her body away from Jessie, who remained asleep and continued to suck her thumb. If Kay turned her back as she put on her worn robe, maybe she could transfer Jessie into her own bed before

Hannot realized Jessie had slept with her again. At age five, Kay had moved from the little girls' cottage to the girls' cottage. The other workers didn't care where Jessie slept, but Hannot was the building supervisor, and she didn't hide her agitation at either Jessie or Kay. Sometimes she came in early to see if she could catch the night staff not following orders. When Hannot was not there, Lotzie and Benke came into the room together singing, "Oh what a beautiful morning." But, today they didn't sing. Kay understood. Hannot had a rule against being happy anytime, but being happy in the morning invited "Hannot's wrath," as Lotzie called it.

At six, both workers entered the dorm. "Okay, girls. It's a new day. Let's get started early, while it's cool."

Hannot followed behind, carrying her clipboard and making check marks on the page as she passed the foot of each bed, stopping to lift the sheet and peer under for any evidence of dampness or soiling.

"Here's a list of appointments for the girls. I'll leave the clipboard on the door of my office. Make sure everyone going for a medical appointment has a bath this morning. I have a seven o'clock meeting. See to it that all those children have their teeth brushed after breakfast and make sure their shoes are on the right feet." Then louder, Hannot said, "The correct feet."

Benke and Lotzie turned away to prevent Hannot from seeing their smiles. Sometimes the children, who knew their right foot from their left, would fumble and fumble trying to put both shoes on their right foot. Kay mourned for the children who tried so hard to be obedient. It was unkind to give confusing instructions.

Hannot remained in the middle of the room and summoned her day staff of four together with the night workers. She cleared her throat.

"Attention, attention everyone. The state inspector will be here at ten with observers. They will select two patients at random. Those patients will have a physical examination this morning, and their charts reviewed by the committee this afternoon. The day shift will be involved with arranging the activities. Two staff from the night shift will remain one hour over to help with morning care. The rotation list is posted." She continued her instructions amid the cacophony of noises erupting from the awakened girls. Squabbles started, blankets stretched in tugging wars, and pillows sailed through the air. Kicking children required supervised separation.

Kay straightened the sheet on her bed, smoothed her blanket, and dressed quickly. Although privacy was unknown, she remained modest. She pulled Jessie onto her lap and began to dress her. Kay slid into her shoes and picked up Jessie's shoes from the floor. If she could get Jessie outside before Hannot observed them, perhaps she could eliminate one episode of Jessie losing control today;. Jessie was terrified of Hannot. Kay placed Jessie's hairbrush into one of her shoes and rushed toward the door, but Jessie jerked in her arms. Kay watched horrified as the hairbrush sailed through the air across the room. *Thwhack!* It struck the middle of Hannot's back.

The room silenced. Hannot picked up the brush and stormed across the room; the floor echoed her heavy footsteps. Kay wrestled to corral Jessie's flailing arms before they could strike her in the face. Jessie had awakened from Hannot's voice.

Trying to distract Jessie, Kay stroked her arms and used her sing-song voice, "We're going to have a good day today. See your pink dress. How nice you look!"

"Don't you start with me, Jessie May," Hannot shouted. "I'll whomp you with this!" She waved the hairbrush in the air in front of Jessie's face.

As the air passed Jessie's face, her body to tensed. She arched her back and started to kick. Jessie reacted to anyone who'd frightened her and she always reacted to Hannot.

"That's mine, Hannot." Kay reached for the hairbrush. "She didn't mean to hit you. She wanted me to help her get pretty"

"Well, little Miss Jessie has a fine way to ask for help, now doesn't she?" Hannot glared.

"I'll help her… Shush, Jessie." Kay carried Jessie to the bathroom.

Jessie was small but strong. Her chronological age was ten. She had short, powerful arms and legs. She could not see or speak. Some said she could not hear. On those occasions, Hannot never failed to mention: "She can hear the words "ice cream.""

Kay was the only person who could get near Jessie in the morning. Jessie struggled to remain asleep as long as possible. Any efforts to awaken her were similar to disturbing a sleeping bear. Jessie's curly hair remained a snarled mass because she wrapped it around her fingers and chewed on it. Jessie and lice were frequent companions. Keeping it short only frustrated her.

Kay and Jessie waited in line to use the bathroom, then for a towel, and finally to wash. Every step required waiting in line.

"There's too many people in this building," Benke said. She picked up the pillows from the floor. Speaking louder, she called out to Hannot. "When are they going to give us more staff here? Where did the day shift go already?"

"They went to breakfast; they've a busy day ahead," Hannot called back.

"Well, my shift last night wasn't glory land," Benke mumbled.

Kay found a stroller and placed Jessie in it. If she could just get her outside…

Hannot appeared, waving the newspaper in the air, and stopped in front of Kay.

"You get back into the room! You know you can't leave until you're told." Her rampage continued toward Benke. "I don't think you need more help to read the newspaper all night and sleep. There's blankets in that room, too."

Kay rubbed Jessie's shoulder, hoping the physical contact would keep her calm. "We're going to the kitchen to pick up the milk. I'm assigned milk this week. Jessie wants to help. We'll be right back." Kay maneuvered the cart around Hannot.

Benke stepped in. "Hannot, what time is Hazel's appointment at the clinic?"

Hannot checked her clipboard.

Benke motioned with her hand, telling Kay to keep going. Kay hurried out the door. She'd thank Benke later.

This was the only cottage Kay could remember. She knew many of the workers in several of the buildings. New people hired in all the time, but often their employment was brief. Some residents had lived in this building longer than Kay, and some arrived after. This was her family. She made every effort to know each and every child, what they liked to eat, what they would not eat, what amused them, and especially what upset them. She knew how to manage their tantrums, and how to gain their cooperation. A few required physical management by the workers. Kay watched carefully and learned what was safe and how to hold an over-excited child. She knew which workers to avoid and which to trust. She knew the safe areas to walk and play, and she learned to avoid the unsafe areas. She knew all the rules.

She also knew where she could go to see Toe.

Toe stayed away from old Crocker. He was the supervisor of the Bad Boys cottage. He was six-feet-six, a brawny man even for his age. He had forearms as big as most men's biceps and fists like boxing gloves. Toe heard it said, more than once, that "Crocker's boys look at Crocker every morning before they take a breath."

"Hey, Toe, Crocker is a comin' toward the barn." A worker called out. "What yah bet he's after somebody?"

"He's got a boy by the shoulder of his shirt, sort of a-shuffling him along," another reported.

"Come out here, Toe. I gotcha an early Christmas present."

Toe watched the boy cower under Crocker's massive grip.

"I can't get no sense in this boy and I can't beat on him, cause that makes no sense, neither. He's big but he's too young to be in my building. Green said maybe you could get him a-workin and get some of the fightin' outta him." He sighed. "See what you can do."

When Crocker released his hold, the boy wobbled on his feet, straightening his legs to stand upright as he glared at the men.

Toe braced himself. *I'm going to have to fight him right off the start.*

The boy clinched both fists tight and pulled in his chin, preparing to duck a blow. "Nope." The boy belched a sound that came from deep in his abdomen.

"His answer is always 'nope.'" Crocker sneered. "He don't even know what's happening and he says 'nope.'"

Crocker dusted off his hands and turned toward the tracks, the direction he had come from.

"Hey, Crocker, what's his name?" Toe called.

Crocker looked back and shouted. "It don't matter, cause he don't answer." He gave a chuckle. "His papers say Ben. The boys call him Big Ben. I ain't ever seen a boy his age that big, but we grows 'em all different here. All he wants to do is fight. He's yours now, Toe." Crocker walked away and didn't look back.

Toe wasn't sure what to do. The other men were snickering behind him.

"That ba-boy c-c-can f-fight, I hear," Earl stuttered.

Ollie came toward them from the horse barn. "Go back to your milking."

Toe reached up to move his hat and scratch his head. Ben ducked.

"Whew! Boy, what am I gonna do with you?" Toe made a fist of his right hand, opened it flat palm and smacked it into his left hand, shaking his head. "No fight, no hit!"

Ben watched Toe, his own hands still fisted.

Again, Toe released his fist and smacked it into his palm, shaking his head and saying, "No fight."

Ollie scolded. "You can't stand out here all night playing _rock-paper-scissors_. There's cows to be milked. Get to work."

Hal Green, manager of the dairy herd, pulled up in his pickup truck. "Hello, Toe. I see Crocker's been over. He talked to me a few days ago." Mr. Green looked Ben over from head to toe. "I think he's big enough to work. Crocker says he's only a boy. What do you say, Toe?"

"I don't know howhe can work if he's always gonna have his fists doubled up. He can't even lift a milk pail like that."

"Well, take him into the barn and show him a cow. If he can make a fist, maybe he can milk." Mr. Green laughed.

Toe shook his head. "Come on, Ben."

When Toe reached out to urge Ben toward the barn, he started swinging, pelting Toe in the back. Ben's bulk was no match for Toe's agility. Toe took the boy to the ground in one quick motion and sat on him. "Stop it." Toe tried to pin Ben's strong arms as he continued swinging. "It ain't gonna do you no good. I'm bigger, faster, and meaner. So stop it," Toe yelled between gasps.

Ben continued trying to twist free. His eyes widened in terror.

Toe touched Ben's lips with his first finger and pressed.

Ben's eyes widened and his arms stopped flailing.

Toe snapped his fingers next to Ben's ear.

Ben made no response. His eyes did not flinch. He was deaf.

Toe lifted himself off Ben and pulled him to his feet.

Ben's eyes tracked Toe's every move. Toe walked into the barn,. Ben was one step behind. Several times that night when Toe turned suddenly he bumped against Ben. Once he almost spilled a whole pail of milk.

At suppertime, Toe moved his hand to his mouth several times; Ben nodded and rubbed his stomach. Toe showed Ben where they could wash up and they sat down at the table together.

But Toe couldn't figure it out. Every bowl of food handed to Ben he passed on to the next man. Even if he didn't like the food, he must be hungry.

All the men filled their plates and started to eat. Ben continued to wait. After the men finished and started to leave the table Ben began to fill his plate. The food was cold and there wasn't a lot left. Toe watched. When Ben finished, he carried his plate out to the kitchen and proceeded to help clear the table. With the table cleared, Ben started to wash the dishes. Mrs. Tubbs, the cook and house mother, patted his arm and swatted at him with her dishtowel. It was the first time Toe had seen Ben smile.

Ben followed Toe everywhere. He would do anything Toe directed, but he wouldn't leave Toe's side. Toe didn't mind; he enjoyed having someone to look after. Toe moved his own mattress onto the floor that first night for Ben because there weren't enough beds.

Saturday night was bath night. But Toe couldn't convince Ben to take a shower. Ben would just shrug his shoulders and gesture that he had washed up. The following Saturday Mrs. Tubbs had had enough.

"That boy takes a bath or he sleeps in the barn. You see to it," she demanded.

Toe took Ben out to the barn, pointed to the gutter, and pinched his own nose. Then he pointed to the gutter and pointed to Ben's nose. Ben nodded. Then Toe pointed to the gutter, then to Ben, then to his own nose. Ben appeared surprised. Toe pointed to the water and mimicked washing his face. Immediately Ben began to wash his face in the cow's drinking cup. Toe laughed until his sides ached as he pulled Ben away from the drinking cup and led him toward the bath area. Ben refused to go in until Toe grabbed a towel for himself.

In the shower, Toe saw the dark red scars and marks in various stages of healing on Ben's back and legs. He began to understand more about Ben's world; he wanted to both weep and be ill.

Just a boy, they said. As big as he was, he was only a boy.

No wonder he was always ready to fight.

Across America, baseball emerged to become America's sport of choice. Teams formed in communities, factories, and sandlots everywhere. Home Boys occupied the ball diamond whenever they could spare time from work. The State Home teams played both the community teams and the local high-school teams.

Toe played catch with Ben and taught him to play ball. One Sunday, Ben stepped in for an absent player and joined Toe's team on the ballfield. He'd only play the shortstop position so he could be near Toe at first base. Ben's humor was infectious. He would open his mouth wide, shake his head, and slap his thigh, leaving the audible laughter to the others.

Ben was Toe's first true friend, and Toe only needed one friend until that girl showed up.

For the last two years, Toe had escaped school by getting into a ruckus the first day, absconding with a few books and not returning. He found the school library and during the winter months he always carried a book or had one tucked nearby. No one cared that he didn't go to school. He was known as a good worker, and there was a lot to do.

Ben changed things.

Toe wanted to help Ben learn to read and write, but how if he couldn't talk or hear? He wasn't sure how much Ben could see because he squinted all the time. There was only one way for Ben to have a chance.

That fall, 1950, when the first day of school arrived, Toe and Ben sat side by side in the schoolroom. Toe was glad to see Miss Timmons. She had taught here for several years. Although he came only the first day of the fourth grade, she remembered him. He liked her and hoped she'd be fair.

She asked the children's names and wrote them on the board. When she came to Ben, Toe answered for him.

Miss Timmons rebuked him. "Seth, Ben can answer for himself."

"He can't, ma'am. He can't talk."

Her eyebrows arched halfway up her forehead. "Who sent him to school?"

"I brought him, ma'am. You're a good teacher, Miss Timmons,.I think you can teach him." Toe grimaced and whispered. "He can't hear much, either."

Some of the children giggled; others mimicked the sounds of humor.

Miss Timmons smacked her ruler on her desk and sighed. The room silenced.

She moved down the row of seats until she stood in front of his desk. "Seth, will you be coming back tomorrow?"

He gulped. "I got a lot of work; there's still the corn to put up."

Miss Timmons peered over her glasses. "The only way Ben can attend school is if you attend every day. You miss one day and Ben is out. Do we understand each other?

Ben, observing Toe's face, stood to leave. Toe tugged on Ben's shirt urging him back into the chair.

During the day, Ben became distracted and restless. Miss Timmons and Toe worked together, encouraging Ben to color or draw. The second day, Miss Timmons placed a bench at the front of the room and asked Toe to bring Ben forward and sit with him as she taught the first grade. She pointed to her mouth and at Ben, encouraging him to watch her lips. She pointed to the letters of the alphabet, then pointed to her lips as she said the letter and spoke words. Ben's eyes never left her face.

The next day when Ben entered the classroom and went forward to sit on his bench, Miss Timmons had moved a desk in place of his bench. Now Ben could learn to write the letters. Ben slid into the desk wearing his biggest smile. He wanted to learn.

She was helping Ben. Now he had to stay.

During the year, Toe read every book Miss Timmons offered. Both Toe and Ben passed to the next grade. Miss Timmons restated her conditions for the next year.

"When you complete the sixth grade you'll go to work in one of the buildings. There they will teach you a trade. Have you thought about what trade you want to learn, Seth?"

"I'm gonna be a farmer. I'm good with the farm."

"Carpentry is a fine skill. You're good with math."

"No thanks, ma'am. I'm a farmer."

Miss Timmons fanned her gaze over the other students. "It makes me sad you cannot further your education." She returned to her chair behind the desk.

Farming is what he did before and after school, and farming was what he wanted to do his whole life, but he had to think about Ben.

Toe decided one more year in school wouldn't be so bad. Besides, that girl Kay would be there, too.

Chapter 4

1952

Kay circled the building known as the Girls' Hospital. The building was twice the size of the cottage buildings, three stories of red brick, rows of windows on each floor. Elevated up several steps, each entrance had access to the lower level. If she found the hospital or even the right floor, finding the room Jessie was in would be difficult. Kay stood behind a big tree and watched people come and go. A man came out and lit a cigarette.

Kay pulled a piece of paper from her pocket. She had written a note, hoping someone would read her plea to see Jessie even if they wouldn't hear her.

"I'm supposed to take this message to the hospital. Do you know where it is?"

"It's up that way." The man waved a hand indicating, up the steps, the glow of his cigarette lighting the way.

Fear and concern for Jessie pushed her up the steps and toward the building. She pulled open the door to see a male attendant seated at his desk.

"Please, let me see Jessie. I feed her. I can help. She'll eat for me. Please." Kay stood at the hospital door, pleading.

The attendant surveyed her, his mood unrelenting. "We don't let the kids in here. Git along." He picked up his newspaper, shaking the pages into obedience.

A car pulled up and two women emerged wearing black winter coats with fur collars. The attendant immediately left his station, eager to direct the driver to the parking area and assist the ladies.

Kay hovered near the entrance. When the hospital door opened and another attendant came through pushing a cart with boxes and supplies, Kay scurried toward the door.

When the attendant turned the cart toward the ramp, one wheel thumped into a crack in the threshold. She tugged and pushed to free the wheel. Kay held the door for the distressed attendant as she maneuvered inside unnoticed.

Milky white walls surrounded her. Holding the paper and walking as if on an errand, she passed several rooms, unsure where to go. Where was Jessie? How could she find her? Determined, Kay entered a room and passed from bed to bed. Reaching the end of the row, she heard someone enter and tried to hide behind one of the curtains that surrounded a bed.

"Can I help you?" A crisp voice behind her snapped the words. Kay trembled and leaned against the wall. Now she'd get thrown out of the hospital. It'd be bad when Hannot heard about this. Kay came out from behind the curtain. It was Nurse Higgins, the nurse who came to their cottage when someone was sick.

"Hello, Nurse Higgins…" Kay's words tumbled out. "I know I shouldn't be here, but I'm looking for Jessie. They brought her to the hospital. I told them she was sick. I take care of Jessie. I want to tell her not to be afraid. Can I see her, please?" Kay's hands trembled. She clinched her teeth and swallowed, pushing back the tears. It was never good when someone broke the rules and today she had broken several rules.

"Children visitors are not allowed." Nurse Higgins did not look at her but regarded the hall. "Do you have a cough, are you healthy?"

"I'm real healthy and I don't have a cough. Can I see Jessie?"

"Follow me. This is a one-time thing, just this once. And don't come back. This could get us both in big trouble."

They entered area with four beds clustered. Each bed had a clear plastic tent over the crib. Kay didn't see Jessie at first. Nurse Higgins led her to the third bed.

"These are oxygen tents. The children in this room have respiratory problems. The oxygen helps them breathe and helps their lungs work better." Jessie lay under a tent, her face pale, perspiration beading on her forehead. Nurse Higgins placed something over Kay's nose and mouth and tied it in place behind her head. "You should wear this so *you* don't get sick."

Jessie's thick matted hair pressed against the pillowcase, while some moist curls spiraled around the edges of her face. Kay pressed against the bed, sneaking her left hand under the tent and along the fabric tying Jessie's hand down. She couldn't reach Jessie's fingers, but if she moved further up the bed she risked Nurse Higgins seeing her touching Jessie. There was probably a rule about that.

Tears filled Kay's eyes. She should have come earlier. They've tied her down. *Oh Jessie I'm so sorry. You must be afraid.* Jessie lay quiet, her eyes closed, with dark circles underneath. Jessie's wrists were red and raw. She must have pulled and pulled against the pieces of cloth they'd used to tie her arms to the bed rails. She was wearing only a diaper. A worn and faded pink blanket covered parts of her body. More knots of cloth circled her chapped and bruised ankles.

"Please, Nurse Higgins, can I touch her?"

"You better not. Whenever someone touches her, she struggles."

"Is she eating?" Kay moved along the bed to stand closer to Jessie's head. She inched her left hand up until she touched Jessie's fingers, tapping them in their familiar game.

"She bites, that one. She tries to bite anyone who tries to feed her."

"I always feed Jessie. I've fed her for a long time. Can I try?"

Nurse Higgins observed Jessie wiggling and responding. Her glance followed down Jessie's arm where she saw the blanket moving up and down. Nurse Higgins touched Kay's shoulder.

"It looks like Jessie knows you. I'll get some applesauce. We had some left from her lunch tray." Nurse Higgins returned with a cup of applesauce and a spoon. She lifted up the side of the tent and Kay moved inside. Nurse Higgins watched Kay stroke Jessie's face. After she moved the backside of the spoon across Jessie's lips, Kay filled the spoon half full with applesauce and slid the food into Jessie's now open mouth.

"I'm here. It's time to eat." She crooned the words over and over until the applesauce was gone. "I have to go now, Jessie. I'll come back to feed you again. Shush, shush little one." Kay patted Jessie's arm with three strokes.

Jessie breathed a sigh and turned her face away. Kay tapped on Jessie's fingers. Jessie tapped back without turning her head.

Kay moved outside the tent while Nurse Higgins tidied up. Two other nurses had entered the room. They had tried to feed Jessie earlier and pelted Kay with questions.

"Why did you tap her fingers?"

"Who taught you to stroke her lips with the back of the spoon?"

"How come she didn't try to bite you?"

"Am I in trouble?" Kay asked the nurses.

Nurse Higgins put her hand on Kay's shoulder and smiled.

Kay took a deep breath. She felt safe.

"Sometimes, she does bite me, so I wear socks on my arms." Kay pushed up her sweater sleeves to show the scars of old bite marks. "These were before I used the socks. She doesn't mean to bite. Jessie can't see or talk, but she can hear. She knows when Hannot comes into the building and I think sometimes she hears too good, that's why she gets afraid. I use the tapping game and she knows it's me. She knows I won't hurt her. She remembers everyone who has hurt her."

The taller nurse moved forward. "What's your name?"

"Kay O'Shay."

"Kay, do you live in the same cottage with Jessie?"

"Yes."

"Kay, I'm Kitchenmaster. They call me Nurse Kit. I'm in charge of the hospital. I'd like to speak to your cottage supervisor. If I could make arrangements for you to come and feed Jessie, would you like to do that?"

"Sure. I take care of Jessie. I told them Jessie was sick. She was hot all over, and they brought her here right away. Is she getting better?"

"She has to eat to get stronger, but she refuses to eat. I'll send a message by courier. You can stay for a while longer as long as she's calm."

"Will you take those knots off her arms and legs? She's just afraid."

"Maybe soon. Where do you work?"

Kay replied without taking her eyes off Jessie. "In the folding room at the laundry. I don't go to school anymore. I finished the sixth grade."

"Do you like working with the children?" Nurse Kit removed a blank piece of paper from Jessie's chart and started to write.

Kay paused to answer respectfully. "Yes, but I don't always know who they are." Kay tugged on the blanket and struggled to cover Jessie.

Nurse Kit peered over her glasses with a quizzical expression. "You don't know who they are?"

"No. They're everywhere, every size and every age. Do you know which ones are the kids?"

Nurse Kit cleared her throat. "I see what you mean."

The other nurses left the room chuckling. Why did they think what she said was funny?

Nurse Kit continued. "I'm going to talk to Lucy Heusted over in the nursery and see if she could use your help. Do you think you'd like working there?" Nurse Kit finished writing her note, folded it, and placed it in an envelope.

Kay smiled. She was not in trouble after all.

Nurse Kit turned to her. "What's your building supervisor's name?"

"Hannot, the supervisor is Hannot."

Nurse Kit wrote "Hannot" on the envelope and gave it to a courier at the door. "Take this to cottage #29, and hand it to the supervisor.

She returned to move a chair next to Jessie's bed. "You may sit here, Kay. Call if you need anything." She reached down and untied Jessie's left arm. "Be sure to wash your hands before you leave."

For the next five days, Kay arrived at every mealtime to feed Jessie. The last day Jessie was in the hospital another nurse stopped by.

"Are you Kay O'Shay, the future nurse?"

Kay blinked, unsure how to reply or whether the woman was teasing.

"I'm Nurse Heusted—Lucy Heusted. I've heard about how you've nursed Jessie back to health. Nurse Kit said you'd like to work in the nursery. Is that true?"

Nurse Heusted smiled with a friendly face, but her ink-black eyes were serious. She looked younger than many of the other nurses in the hospital. She wore her dark brown hair up under her white nursing cap. Her bronze skin glowed a soft warm color.

"I answer to Nurse, Nurse Lucy, and to Nurse Heusted." She chuckled. "Nurse Kit tells me you'd be a good helper over in the nursery. When you stop by tomorrow morning, I'll introduce you to the staff and some of the children. There are lots of things you could do to help and, from what I hear, you have a knack for working with the children."

"I'd like to try. Do you really think I could be a nurse someday?"

"Miss Kay, perhaps you've already started. Do you know where the nursery is?"

"I've heard of it, but I don't know where it is. Is it over by the other girls' cottages?"

"No. It's in the other end of this building."

"It's that big."

Nurse Heusted and Kay stepped aside as a group on a tour passed by.

Kay listened as the guide explained the building. "This building is called the Girls' Hospital. It has seven units. This end is the hospital. Much patient care happens on the west end of the main level." The tour moved on.

Nurse Heusted continued, "Come to the back door at the other end of this building tomorrow and wear an apron if you have one. If you can do the work, we'll order some cover aprons from the sewing room that will fit you. Our work can be messy. See you tomorrow."

Kay returned to her cottage, relieved she didn't have to work in the hot steamy laundry anymore. Maybe someday she could even be a nurse.

She walked, holding her head high to keep her imaginary nursing cap in place and humming, "Oh what a beautiful morning, oh what a beautiful day. I got a wonderful feeling everything's going my way."

Best of all, Jessie was coming home tomorrow.

"You hear that?"

"What? Toe listened. He and Louie were hoeing and working their way along each side of a row of beans.

Louie was one of the older men. His skin was deep-tanned from working in the sun. He wore his hair shaggy and gray. He didn't know how old he was and nobody ever said. Louie was lean and bony and prided himself that younger men could not keep up with him in the fields or in a ballgame. It was his tales of adventure that brought entertainment and caused consternation from the others.

Louie pointed toward the set of railroad tracts that bisected the state home separating the front cottages from the farm and the back cottages. "The rails." He continued hoeing. "They sing. I seen the rails call a man and he never leaves um. It's like the sea calling a sailor."

"Rails don't sing. I sleep so close to those tracks the only thing they do is shake my teeth loose every night, one train after another."

"Oh no, ya don't want to miss the call. I heard it when I was young and I went to lots of places. Yes sir-ee. The cities I seen...."

"Louie, you lived here your whole life. You probably ain't even seen downtown Lapeer."

"I sees it, those cities. I sees 'em when that train sings down those tracks. You ever put your ear on the tracks and hear 'em sing?"

"No, I ain't, and I ain't gonna." Toe's hoe dug deeper. "I ain't that dumb."

"Don't you be making fun of me. I ain't talkin' to you no more." Louie turned his back to Toe.

"Good, now I can get my work done since you stopped talkin'." Toe moved on.

Louie peeked around his left shoulder. "You ain't gonna sleep tonight. I told you the curse, the 'Song of the Rails.' It happens that fast. You hear about it, then you think about it, and pretty soon you wants to hop any old train and go," Louie said wistfully.

"The trains that go to the blue water, that's the only place I want to go."

"It'll take you there. It ain't nothing, you just hop on and ride along."

"So why don't you?"

"Oh, I thinks about it. I dreams it, that's all I need. But you, it's callin' you, that whistle, and those singing wheels. It's callin' you, Seth... Thomas..." Louie spoke Seth's name in a singsong voice.

Toe shook his shoulders. "Louie, you get real spooky sometimes."

Louie's words came out through the single hole of his nose and mouth. His face had a one-side look. If you saw only the left side it looked like most any face, but the right side was skin over flat bony skull, as if he had run real fast into a wall or the Maker just didn't finish him.

Toe didn't sleep that night. He heard every train that passed through—the rumbling, the whistles, and the slap-roar of loaded, speeding freight cars. As Louie had foretold, those sounds crept inside Toe's thoughts, but all the guys knew Louie wasn't right in the head.

Chapter 5

1953

"Trent, are we going to the ballgame tomorrow?" Kay tried her best not to sound too excited and hopeful.

"It's on the schedule, but I'm hoping it won't rain." Bea Trent smiled at Kay. "My feet are telling me its gonna rain."

From the day room they heard singing.

"Hinkey-dinky-parley-voo!" Smitty, an afternoon aide, sang as she zigzagged back and forth around the girls, tapping on each girl's head as she passed. The girls laughed, some boisterously, and others smiled even in their shyness. A couple girls lifted their arms. They wanted to dance, too. Kay laughed as she watched Smitty standing in the middle of a large circle bending and waving her arms like a big bird.

"Everybody sing!" Smitty beckoned. "It's first your right, then your left and parley voo." Her arms extended in alternating motions. "Go all the way around, go all the way around, go all the way, all the way, all the way around." Smitty twirled, and several girls pounded their tables; others clapped as Smitty sang.

Kay stepped into the circle and extended her arms. "Show me, Smitty."

Smitty looped her right arm through Kay's and they twirled. Then Smitty bowed to Kay and they hooked their left arms, turning in the opposite direction. "Hinkey, dinky parlee voo."

"For ever more!" house afternoon supervisor Briggs roared. "Stop this commotion! Look here, Winnie spilled her milk. You best parlee voo your work." The room silenced. The few minutes of Smitty's fun was worth the price of Briggs's scolding.

From the alcove, Kay heard two other afternoon workers talking.

"Smitty's going dancing tonight," one said.

"Well, she's warmed up now," the second replied.

"If she keeps up that sashaying, it's going to get her a man grabbing at her every night and a passel of rug rats. Then we'll see how she dances."

"Let her have her fun while she's young."

"Well, I say it's that fun that got us working in the likes of here, bone-tired every night and still poor."

"Oh, Bea, you're not poor, just down."

"You want my assignment?"

"No, I did my three months, it's your turn."

"Maybe I don't want a turn." Bea Trent was kind to the girls even when she was tired. She walked with a limp, often saying her feet were talking.

Briggs tromped down the hall. "Quit your staring at Smitty and get these kids cleaned up. Wheelchair pushers, stand behind the chair assigned to you. If we don't get going, the picnic'll be over before we get there! Kay, you lead with Jessie."

Briggs didn't have to tell Kay twice. There would be ice cream at the picnic and ice cream was the best part of summer.

If Briggs thought everything went well today, there was even a better chance they would be able to go to the ball game tomorrow. Two teams played on Sunday; the younger boys played at noon and the older men played at four. Kay hoped to get to the early game because there was a chance she would see Toe watching the other team play. Sometimes the boys and/or men would trade their barn chores so they could stay and watch some of the later game. Games were played every night of the week all summer. The baseball diamond was surrounded on three sides by hills that provided a natural place for viewing, and later in the day there was some shade.

She might get away to talk with Toe near the tree where no one would see them together. Being seen together could mean big trouble. Kay was unsure what would happen to Toe, but for her it could mean being shut in the pantry by Hannot.

"Perversion!" Hannot would shout whenever she had to take a girl to task for being with a boy. Sara Jane was in the pantry a lot, but she didn't care. She just got down under any ole bush with any boy or man. The staff always found her 'cause she giggled so loud.

A chance to see Toe might be worth the risk, but Kay didn't like breaking the rules.

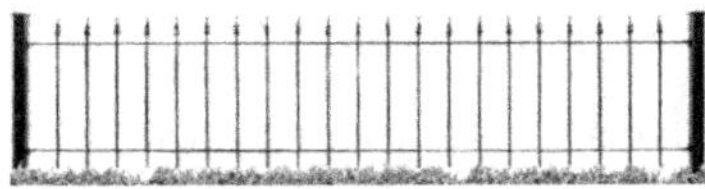

1954

Toe opened the choke on the lawnmower and pulled the cord. It obediently hummed into action. He pushed in the choke and grasped the lever to engage the drive wheels. The mower jerked forward in front of the Castle as Toe clutched the handle, his feet racing to catch up with the self-propelled mower, trying to control the direction of the machine.

Toe dashed back and forth across the grass. As he made his third pass, Dr. Helmsley waved his arms from the porch, urging him to stop.

Toe shut off the mower. "Am I doing something wrong, sir?"

"I've been watching you from my office." Dr. Helmsley waved his hand toward the upstairs windows. "If you continue to walk that fast, I'll have a heart attack."

Toe noticed the man's trimmed mustache, three-piece suit, and gold watch chain suspended from his vest pocket. Sensing an opportunity to test wit with a learned person and unable to resist his impulse for entertainment, Toe slid his tongue around the inside of his lower teeth. *He thinks I'm just a dumb home kid. He's got us all pegged. Maybe it's time for a little fun.* Toe wiped his brow with his forearm.

"I'm not walking fast sir, it's my long stride. It just looks like I'm mowing fast because the lawn mower wheels are small. It's a law of physics--

like large and small gear ratios. You know about physics?"

The administrator flushed. He gestured his hand for a handshake.

"Dr. Helmsley. I'm the new administrator."

Toe rubbed his right hand on his pants and returned the gesture. "Seth, Sir. My friends call me Toe."

"I've been here three weeks, Seth… Toe. I don't think I've seen you mowing lawn before."

"No sir, I work in the dairy barns."

Dr. Helmsley glanced in the direction of the barns, his expression puzzled. "Why are you here mowing lawn?"

"I got into trouble when I fixed the separator." Toe mumbled and shuffled toward the mower, eager to get away from the man's scrutiny.

"You fixed the separator?" Dr. Helmsley repeated, following him.

"Machines that don't work are useless. I think if a machine has a purpose, it should work. So, I fixed the separator. You know about cows?"

Dr. Helmsley smiled. "No, I don't, but you could probably teach me."

"Yes sir, I could do that." Now they were getting somewhere.

He liked this Dr. Helmsley. The man was important and humble, a rare combination. He understood the game.

"Let's step over into the shade and visit for a minute." Dr. Helmsley wiped his brow with his handkerchief. "Have you lived here long?"

"The legend of my family is in the hallway of the Castle, Sir. It's the principle by which you schedule your day."

"And how is that?"

"The hall clock. It's a Seth Thomas clock and I'm Seth Thomas. He was an engineer. He designed mass production. Folks here get upset 'cause I fix things. They call me a tinker. Guess it's just in my blood. I think a thing should work. If it's broke, fix it. Don't you think so?"

"Hmm…" Dr. Helmsley stroked his chin. "Are you in school?"

"No, sir. I work the herd. I follow Thoreau's kind of thinking… Let me ask you, sir, would you rather have your lawn mowed by someone who read about how to mow lawns or someone who had done it?"

"Did Thoreau say that?"

"No, not exactly." Toe grinned. "Thoreau was talking about a boy smelting ore to make his own jackknife, or a boy who listened to lectures about smelting ore and got a jackknife from his father."

"I see." Dr. Helmsley smiled, indicating he was amused and enjoyed the conversation.

Toe fidgeted. "With all respect, sir, I can't be here a-jawing, I got work to do."

Dr. Helmsley turned to go back to his office and paused. "Just a minute, Toe—Seth? What happens if you don't get your work done in time?"

"Toe's fine sir. You can call me Toe." Toe looked with suspicion to his left and right and lowered his voice. "I won't get supper." He reached for the mower handle.

Dr. Helmsley placed his hand on Toe's arm. "Toe, if you ever need food you come here and speak to Mrs. Tibbens, my cook. She'll give you food."

Toe grabbed the mower handle. "Gotta go, sir."

Dr. Helmsley stopped in the foyer and surveyed the hall clock. He opened the door and studied the clock face. There, above the number six he read aloud, "Seth Thomas." The boy was right. The script was small. How did he know that name was there?"

He turned to the receptionist's desk. "Mrs. Porter, can you tell me why that boy is here?"

"What boy?"

"The boy who's mowing the lawn. He said his name was Seth and they call him Toe?"

Mrs. Porter appeared annoyed. "I saw him. I would guess he has a club foot, the way he walks."

"A club foot?" Dr. Helmsley sat down in a nearby chair. "Do you know he can quote Thoreau and explain gear ratios and physics?"

"I hardly think that philosophy will get him into the Lord's realm, when his time comes." Mrs. Porter removed several folders from her desk and proceeded to file them.

"Did you know that is a Seth Thomas clock?" He gestured toward the hallway.

"No, I never paid attention. I just wind it every Friday."

"I wonder how he knows. This name is printed so small. When would he have seen this clock?"

Mrs. Porter clicked her tongue. "Don't underestimate anyone here. Everybody and anybody seems to know nothing, anything, or everything."

Dr. Helmsley left the lobby, entered his office, and returned a few moments later.

"Mrs. Porter, do you know if all the buildings have Seth Thomas clocks?"

"Are you of a mind to need to know that right now?" Mrs. Porter shuffled through the mail on her desk and handed him a fistful of message slips.

"No, I was wondering, that's all. Would you please obtain Seth Thomas's file for me? I want to know if we are housing someone who understands physics and mechanics simply because he has a club foot."

Chapter 6

Nurse Lucy watched fourteen-year-old Kay rocking back and forth in the rocking chair, holding Roma, touching her face and playing with her hands. Kay's shoulder-length brown hair swung back and forth as she rocked. Her striped apron twisted across her lap, covering her plaid dress. The bottle bobbed around Roma's mouth as she lurched forward and waved her hands, frustrated and hungry.

"She won't eat, Nurse Lucy. I've tried."

Nurse Lucy lifted Roma from Kay's arms, suspending her in the air. "Oh look, my little one's stuffed up. She can't breathe or eat. Here, I'll show you." Nurse Lucy opened a jar. "This is camphor. I'll put a tiny bit under Roma's nose. That should help."

"Did you see the big truck parked in the street?" Kay leaned closer to the window.

"Yes, Dr. Helmsley's family is moving into their house today."

When Nurse Lucy sat down, her white uniform made a crinkling sound. She crossed her legs. There was not a mark on her white shoes. She must polish them every night, Kay thought.

"What's he like?" Kay asked, glancing askance toward the house and the van.

"Oh, he's nice! I met him at the Welcome Tea. I think he'll bring some new ideas to the Home. He wants to offer more education to the children."

"That's good, isn't it?"

"Well, it's a double-edged sword."

"What's a double-edged sword mean?"

Nurse Lucy ignored Kay's question. "Look, hold Roma upright this way so the air can go up her nose and the milk down into her stomach. Otherwise she can't swallow."

"Oh, I can do that." Kay returned to her chair, propped a pillow behind her elbow, and held Roma upright. She sang, "Jesus Loves The Little Children," one of the songs Nurse Lucy had taught her.

"You might be selected to go on to school, Kay. Nurse Lucy returned to her diaper-folding task. "He said he's considering sending some students to Lapeer High School. My supervisor mentioned she had a girl working in the nursery who was a very good student. She told him the girl had continued to study on her own to finish eighth grade and took the examination, too."

Kay's eyes grew large. "High school! Not me. I'm staying right here. Jessie needs me and I have this job. I finished the eighth grade because Mrs. Timmons gave me books and helped me. I'm not going out there."

"Kay, you could go to high school and maybe someday be a nurse."

"Hannot says I'm a home girl and I won't ever be anything else. And a home girl is a home girl. She says everybody knows that."

"Don't you want a family and a home of your own someday?"

Kay stared at Nurse Lucy, stunned that she would ask such a cruel question.

"No!" Kay shouted loud enough to startle Roma, who began to wail. "Hannot says I've lived here too long and if I have children they'll look like the people who live here 'cause I caught the disease from being here." Kay pointed toward the unit with those babies that were called the water-head babies. Sometimes she watched them being cared for. Their heads were so large it frightened her. Those babies lay in their cribs and their eyes followed the movements of their attendants. Kay had not worked there because they needed special care. There were so many children with so many problems, rows and rows of cribs and beds. Even little Grace, who had to be placed on a bed of cotton because she was so frail, a kind and loving child whose delicate body failed her.

Kay scanned the children. "Nurse Lucy, do you know why I'm here?" Kay played with the corner of Roma's crib blanket. "It doesn't matter anymore because I know I can never leave."

"Who told you, you could never leave?"

"Nobody had to tell me. I heard if you run away they will try to find you and bring you back."

Nurse Lucy stopped folding diapers and looked up, "Surely you know those are rumors. There are working girls that leave. They live and work for a family. Some children are adopted."

"I wasn't adopted." Kay laid Roma in her crib and stepped over to the window. Anyone could see the old people. Nurse Lucy must see them, too. The teacher at school didn't talk about anyone going to high school. Nurse Lucy didn't say things that weren't true, but going to high school and someday being a nurse seemed like a dream.

The moving van pulled out onto the highway, leaving a man and a woman on the porch. Three children clustered around them.

"Nurse Lucy, won't it bother them living behind that tall black fence when they don't have to?"

"No. They can leave any time they want." She moved a stack of diapers onto the changing area.

Kay arranged Roma's favorite blanket around her and paused at Jonni's crib to change her diaper.

"Nurse Lucy, I'm sorry you can't have a family."

"Who said that?"

"I just thought."

"These *are* my children. Isaiah says enlarge your tent. Guess my tent is filled with God's special babies."

"Yeah! How could anyone not love our babies?" Kay snuggled her chin against Jonni's cheek.

The other two attendants left the area, giving Nurse Lucy the chance to ask about Toe.

"In the meeting with Dr. Helmsley, one of the other supervisors mentioned a boy named Seth. He said they call him Toe. Didn't you say something about a friend named Toe?"

"He's not my friend. He got mad at me in the fourth grade and he still acts kind of mad at me sometimes."

"I thought you went to watch him play baseball during the summer."

"I do, but that doesn't mean he likes me."

"Why did he get mad at you?

"I just asked him why he walked funny. He looked at me like he didn't understand what I meant, so I showed him."

"And how is that?"

Kay slumped her shoulders, dropped her head down, and moved across the room with a slouching gait.

"Does he really walk like that?"

"Yes! I told him to look up and stand up straight."

"Maybe there's a reason he walks that way."

"No, I've seen him run on the ball diamond. He can run. He walks funny. The other kids laughed and he got mad and left school. He would have left anyway. He used to come the first day of school every year and then get sent back to the farm, but that changed."

"Maybe you should apologize."

Kay ignored that comment.

"He did come back to school because of Ben. He finished the sixth grade. I didn't do anything wrong. I was trying to help him. If he wants to be mad and doesn't understand, I don't care." Kay tried to control the emotion in her voice.

"Ah, but you do care." Nurse Lucy smiled.

"Oh, boys! I have to leave and take Jessie to the clinic. They're going to clean her ears or something. Are you coming to the party next Saturday?"

"The one to welcome Dr. Helmsley?"

"Yes. The band is playing and the folk dancing class is dancing. Is it okay if I leave now?"

"Sure. I'll see you at the party next Saturday if I'm working."

The boys arrived early, ready to warm up their baseball muscles, stretching their arms and legs. Their breath clouded white when they exhaled in the crisp spring air. The clear sky promised a good day for baseball.

"Eh-bidden-baddish-baddeh," Freddy cheered as if it was the bottom of the ninth as Toe stepped up to the plate. A speech problem didn't daunt Freddie's desire to cheer for his team. The Home boys didn't need an opponent to have fun playing baseball. They didn't need a ball, a bat, or a glove. They could imagine a game and go through the motions. Today was different: the pitcher took a step forward, turned back, spun around, and wound up, pitching a hard fast curve ball. Toe stepped into his swing, whirling the bat in time to catch the ball before it dropped.

"Ith-ith's-ith's a goner." Freddy cheered as he hopped up and down.

Blacksmith Bart Eherty scanned the field. The players shuffled their feet to claim their space. He was the coach for several reasons. First, he could physically handle the players on his team and if necessary he could handle several at a time. The boys had seen him do it, too. Second, he loved baseball as much as the boys did. Some had wagered that he loved it more than his hammer. He was a strong man—lean, but tough as leather. He worked all day between his forge and his anvil. He could swing his hammer with the ease of another man swatting a fly.

He had pulled together the best for today's game, the annual preseason game with the Lapeer High School Varsity Baseball team. They would play another game at the end of the season. That game would be well attended and the varsity would win. He always felt he let the boys down, but somehow they understood. No one liked it, but it was better than not playing at all. The preseason game would be an all-out effort. Only a few spectators of Home residents and employees would be sitting up on the hillside today.

The conversation between the coaches for this preseason game was always the same. The high-school coach wanted his new team to learn that success comes with effort and team play. If the final score humbled his team, he'd be okay with that, it was only preseason. This game was Coach Eherty's to win and he believed his boys could. The homeboys played all year round. They raked leaves off the field, they shoveled snow off the base lines, and they played in rain, mud, snow, and sleet. They loved the sport. Sunday afternoon at the State Home was about baseball. Here, spectators or no spectators, the teams played throughout the day.

The high-school team played only during the spring season, certainly a disadvantage. Healthy and eager as they were, they were no match for this ragtag team of ambitious boys and men who had little else to enjoy and lived to play ball.

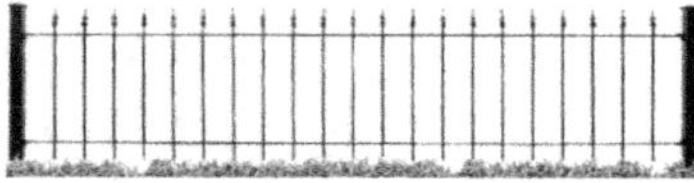

Coach Eherty was pleased, for today they all had shoes. Five boys had thin, old ball gloves, padded on the inside with rags. He opened a burlap bag and pulled out seven new gloves and passed them out. The boys' eyes opened wide. "I need these back after the game. They're mine. If I get 'em back, I'll bring them to the next game." The boys nodded. Some could hit, some could run, and some could throw and catch, but five players could do all three. They ranged in age and size approximating the opposing team.

Freddie circled behind the players, patting their backs, calling each by name, and repeating, "Play hord-goud team." His stocky body with short arms and legs made it hard for Freddie to play against the varsity team. But, his small stature did not prevent him from being the most spirit-filled cheerleader any team could desire. His chatter was his offering, and every player played harder when Freddie cheered.

Toe pulled off Freddie's ball cap and tousled his hair. "Now, Freddie, this could be a long game. Just cheer when we are up to bat so you don't lose your voice. We need ya, buddy."

Freddie grinned a full smile. "Toe, you tha-mack 'em and I'll yell."

"Pay attention!" Coach Eherty yelled. The boys circled around him.

Coach grabbed the ball Buck was tossing to Frank. "Listen up. We can win this one. We got a good team. There'll be no fights. I don't care what names they call you or what they say. *No fights!* If anyone starts a fight or swings back, I'll walk off the field and forfeit the game. That means you all lose. You'll be losers if there's any fighting."

"If they start it, can we finish it? I can smell 'em already," Harry mumbled from under his oversize ball cap.

"If anybody fights, the game is over and we lose! They'd like the game called because after we play our first inning they'll know we can win. They know the rules, no fighting. So if they see you're beatin' 'em, they'll try to get you to fight. Do you want to play ball and win or do you want to fight and lose?" Coach Eherty waited for an answer. He called each player by name and waited for a reply. He started with Harry. When the last name was called, a cheer went up from the team.

"We play to win."

Coach Eherty's words rumbled through the dugout.

"There's water in the water barrel. You had a good warm-up. Now run to the outfield and back. They should be here by then.

Ben jogged beside Toe, nudging him and pointing toward the hill. Toe shook his head, trying to focus on the game ahead. Ben tugged Toe's sleeve and pointed again, motioning toward first base. On the hillside, to the left of the big pine, Toe saw the girl sitting on the grass waiting for the game to start. She came. Beside her sat the girl in her wheelchair, wrapped in a blanket. It sure would be nice if she stayed and they had a win.

His team passed third base for the second lap as several cars pulled off the dirt road. Baseball players tumbled out, wearing new uniforms, every player carrying a glove. They jogged toward the dugout like a herd of antelope, their movements graceful, rhythmic, and confident. Coach Eherty watched. He knew they had the advantage. His team didn't always win the preseason game, but this year they would. This year his team was different. They had both skill and heart. A team, starting the season, would not match their love of the game.

"Coach, look at 'em!" Toe said, observing the team of uniformed players as they ran onto the field.

"Toe, there ain't no uniform in the world that can make a baseball player or a team. It takes more to win and this year we've got it. We're gonna win this one. They're gonna leave here a little dirtier than when they came, if I can keep my boys from starting a fight. You're first batter, Toe. Set the example. Don't let 'em get to you."

Their pitcher was on the mound. As Toe left the dugout Ben handed him a bat. Toe approached the batter's box.

The pitcher yelled, "Come on, 'boy.' Swing that bat. Try to hit one off me."

The catcher chirped behind him, "Hey, we got a boy with a bat, can't hit, and can't run."

Toe shook off the comments. He dug his crooked toe into the dirt and took the first pitch, then the second. The chirping continued.

From their dugout Freddie called, "For me, Toe! Hith one, for me!"

Toe stepped into the pitch, the bat cracked against the leather, and the ball whirled into the outfield, over the fence.

"Home run!" announced the umpire.

Freddie jumped up and down, inching toward the baseline between third and home to greet him.

Toe nodded at Freddie as he ran by. After touching home plate, Toe turned to the catcher. "Did ya bring another pitcher?"

The catcher jerked off his mask. The umpire grabbed his arm.

Toe raised both his arms into the air as his teammates charged from the dugout.

"I thought you boys came to play ball," Toe called out.

"Day kin pay ball or bring it on," Freddie yelled, shaking his fists.

Coach Eherty jerked Freddy back into the dugout and followed Toe inside, patting him on the shoulder.

The game was on and his boys were here to play.

Kay turned her back to the tree. "You won, 21 to 4! That was great!"

"Yeah, the guys had a good bat today." Toe's voice came from somewhere in the tree. "I think their pitcher was new. He'll get better as the season goes."

"Well, so will *your* team." Kay could hear him moving around among the limbs and imagined him resting against the trunk with his feet propped up on a branch.

The ball diamond was empty. The next game would be at four, but no one was warming up yet. No one would see them. To anyone observing, it would look like Kay was resting in the sunshine on a pretty summer day, with Jessie sitting in her wheelchair in the shade.

"Do you have to go do chores?"

"Not today. I traded yesterday for today with Joe. He had a horseshoe tournament."

"So you can stay a while."

"Yeah, if no one gets suspicious of two girls sitting in the grass under a talking tree."

"Toe, you stop making fun! You know I worry."

"That you do, Miss Kay."

"I can't stay long, Sunday school is tonight and I always go." Kay twirled a piece of grass in her fingers. "I heard the auction is coming in the fall. Will they sell your cow?"

"Not this year, maybe next."

"I'm sorry. It seems like nothing stays here but us."

"Something bothering you?"

"I keep thinking about that boy they brought that day, how they put those things on his arms and dragged him in. How he looked straight at me and told me I can't ever leave."

Toe thought a moment. "I wonder if Thoreau would have gone to Walden Pond if he had lived here."

"What?"

"It's a book I read. This man goes into the woods and builds a cabin near a pond and he lives in it. He writes, too—interesting things."

"You just changed the subject."

"Yup, I hoped it'd work."

"It didn't. I want to know if it's true that we can't ever leave."

"Why, how does knowing help anything? We work. We take care of animals and do chores and we take care of each other." Toe sighed. "Kay, some say we can't leave, that there's only one way out and that's back there."

"Back where?"

"The cemetery. It's back there, in the woods."

"No, you don't mean that. Are you telling me I can't leave when I grow up?"

"Look around. Where do you think the old people come from? They got old here."

"How do you know?"

"The men talk. They say some men get hired out to farms. They have to work hard on those farms. You gotta have a place to go to leave."

Kay hoped it wasn't true. She'd heard that too. She didn't want to believe it, but she knew Toe would never lie to her.

"Are you going to stay?"

"No. I'm going to have my own farm with a dandy herd of Holsteins, a red barn or two, and a white house for my family."

"How you going to do that if you don't leave?"

"I'll leave. When the time is right, I'll leave. But first I got to make you laugh. Did you see the guys in our dugout cheering? There's no way not to laugh when you watch Freddy. Here, this is for you." A Milky Way candy bar tumbled from the tree and landed near her feet.

"You just did it again. You changed the subject."

"Yes, Miss Kay, I did. Because I just won a ball game and I'm feeling good about that and I don't want to think about why most people here don't leave. Ask yourself—where would Jessie go?"

Kay's eyes filled with tears. She stood up and tucked Jessie's arm inside the wheelchair. "I'm glad you won your game. I'm going to go now."

"You do that and be sure you smile while you eat that candy bar. I worked hard for that."

Kay tossed the wrapper over her shoulder and up into the tree. "Thank you, Toe," she said with a chunk of candy in her cheek. She walked toward her cottage. Thoughts of spending her life here created so many questions and filled her with dread. Even if she had a chance to leave, she would never leave Jessie.

Kay saved a small piece of the candy bar for Jessie, who waved her arms in delight at the sweet taste. A bite of the chocolate candy bar melted on Kay's tongue.

Tony, an old man with one eye, shuffled past her.

Toe's words echoed, *Where do you think the old people come from, they get old here.*

Toe could fight and he could play ball... but she knew he always told her the truth.

Chapter 7

"Kay, come to my office," Hannot called. Her icy command echoed down the hallway.

Kay handed Jessie her doll and rushed toward the summons. When she arrived at the office door, Hannot, without turning toward her, motioned a pointed finger toward a wooden chair. She had on a dress and matching pumps, the way she dressed when there were meetings all day.

"Sit there. I have some paperwork that says you are to attend high school, starting next Wednesday. Did you know about this?" Hannot tapped her pencil on the desk.

"No ma'am. I heard rumors about some kids going to high school, but I didn't know who was going."

"Well, if this don't beat the band. We get someone who can follow orders and do some work around here and they send her to school. What on this green earth could be the reason to send you to high school? All you'll ever do is housekeeping work. You sure don't need high school for that."

Kay hesitated to answer. Hannot had her own ideas of punishment. It didn't matter what a girl did or didn't do. She could always come up with a reason for punishment. Kay had learned it never went well to reply, but it didn't go well not to answer either. "I don't know ma'am."

"You don't know," Hannot mocked as she crossed the room and closed the office door. She studied Kay, her eyes moving from Kay's head to her feet. "I know, you, you think you're so smart. I'll just call you Miss Smarty Pants. How'd that be?"

"Yes, ma'am."

"It says here high school starts at 7:45 and the bus will take you to school. Do you know these names?"

Hannot read several names. Kay recognized them all, especially the name Seth Thomas."

Toe's going? He hates school! Maybe he thinks he can play baseball all day.

"Albright will to take you to the sewing room to get measured. You're to get a new dress and a new skirt and blouse. Albright will pick up two sweaters and a coat at the store downtown. You're to meet her over at the school building tomorrow at noon. The teacher will give you pencils and paper. If you're old enough to go to high school, you're old enough to get your smarty pants self over to the school by noon. Understand?"

"Yes, ma'am." Kay hesitated. Hannot could blow up real fast or just get mean and ugly, but she had to ask. "Please don't separate me from Jessie."

Hannot smiled. It wasn't a kind smile. "Don't you worry about Jessie. You just run along and get your ed-u-cation!"

"Please, let us stay together. I'll take care of her."

"Not running off to school in town, you won't. Like I said, these papers say you go to high school. I can't do anything about that, but you and Jessie, I'll do as I want. Now go on, and get out of my office, Miss Smarty Pants."

Nurse Lucy placed a clean diaper on Hollis. She rolled him to the left, then to the right, and giggled against his neck, making him laugh.

Kay had been quiet since she arrived today. She waited until Tommie; short for Thompson, an aide, left the nursery dayroom and Kay started asking questions. "What's high school like? Is it someplace high and far away?"

"No." Nurse Lucy tucked Hollis back into his crib and stifled her amusement at Kay's literal translation. Sometimes she neglected to appreciate the reality of Kay's world. Her days, weeks, and years were spent with others who think in concrete and literal terms.

"It's not high like on a mountain, Kay. It means higher education past eighth grade."

Nurse Lucy washed her hands, tidied the counter, and continued pouring milk into bottles, placing the nipples inside and twisting on the caps.

"The school is just up the road toward town. Years ago people didn't go past the eighth grade. Rich people sent their children to private schools or had private tutors. When more country schools became available, people wanted their children to go on in school, so they started high school to prepare them to go to college. It's just another step in higher education. Probably that's why they used the term high school."

Kay placed the bottles into the refrigerator. "Did you go to the high school? The one where they want to send me?"

"No, I went to one farther away, nearer my home up by Capac."

Kay joined Baby Baxter on his floor mat. "Did you like it? Going to high school, I mean?"

"Yes, it was a lot of fun. There were football games and the band, and lots of different classes. In high school, you go from classroom to classroom. The teachers stay in their room and the students come to them."

Kay played with Baby Baxter, moving his arms and legs to exercise them.

"I hope you'll go to high school, Kay. I think you'll like it."

Kay continued to exercise the baby and didn't reply.

Nurse Lucy fed Sophia as she rocked in the chair next to the window.

"I don't want to go… I'm afraid."

"What do you have to be afraid about? A few of your school friends are going. I think there are six or eight in all. At the staff meeting they said four girls and four boys.

"I'm afraid if I go Hannot will move me to the older girls building. She's always threatening to. She calls me Miss Smarty Pants. I'm afraid what will happen to Jessie if they move me away from her. She's my best friend and she trusts me. Besides, I don't need to learn more. Hannot says I already know too much for a Home kid."

Nurse Lucy placed her hand on Kay's shoulder. "I'm sorry you're worried about Jessie, but it would be wrong for you not to go. If Jessie could tell you herself she'd say go. I know she would. And you don't know too much. Kay, that's not true. This is a wonderful opportunity. Don't you see? It could help other girls, girls who are younger. Because you went to high school, they may be able to learn more. You're a pioneer!"

Tommie returned from her break and said, "Are you talking about them sending some Home kids to high school? It's the talk in every building. Land a mercy, did you ever hear such a thing?"

Nurse Lucy turned to face Tommie. "Tommie, would you like to tell Kay why she shouldn't go to high school?"

Tommie gulped like a fish and stopped talking.

Kay waited.

Tommie muttered, "They's just…"

"Yes?" The anger Lucy had restrained about Hannot ridiculing Kay spiraled with her reply.

"I's got a feeding to do."

Nurse Lucy stood. "You tell Kay why she shouldn't go to high school or you apologize."

Tommie smoothed her apron.

"Heusted, you know." Tommie searched Heusted's face for a reprieve and finding none, she turned to Kay.

"You's a good girl, Miss Kay. I didn't mean no harm to you. It's just something that ain't been done before. But you go if'n you's want to."

"Thanks, Tommie." Kay smiled at the woman.

Nurse Lucy knew Tommie was just repeating gossip, it wasn't like her to be unkind. "Kay, you run along now and go feed Jessie her lunch.

I'll see you tomorrow." Turning away from Tommie, she whispered, "Don't let Hannot upset you."

Toe passed three new brick buildings under construction and jogged cross-lots between the school and other buildings. He couldn't use the roads, they'd be too slow and he was going to be late for his 4 o'clock appointment if he didn't hurry. He couldn't be late to a meeting at the Castle. What could they want? Who wanted to see him? He considered all his activities for the past few weeks. He was sure nothing he had done constituted a visit to the Castle. With all the new folks coming and the new construction, Dr. Helmsley hadn't had time to be concerned about the farming operation. He probably wouldn't remember they'd met last spring when he was mowing lawn and that he got into trouble for fixing the separator.

Toe dashed around the corner of the laundry building, dodging between loaded and empty laundry carts, but someone stepped in front of him. She was carrying a bundle of folded diapers piled higher than her head. He crashed into her at the same instant he saw her. She fell backwards onto the ground, her laundry flying.

Ben, always two steps behind Toe, grabbed for the girl's hand and helped her up. Then he shook his finger at Toe and made a fist.

Toe blinked and ducked in time to miss Ben's swing.

Annoying as it was, he could always count on Ben following behind him.

"Sorry, ma'am," Toe grunted as he bent forward.

"You should be, Mr. Seth Thomas, and I am not a ma'am. My name is Kay."

Toe raised his hand to grab Ben's arm before he could take another swing. He touched his own lips twice with his first finger and nodded toward Kay. Ben dropped his arm back to his side, satisfied Toe had apologized.

"Kay?" Toe was puzzled.

"Don't turn your charm on me after knocking me to Timbuktu." She watched his mouth form that one-sided grin that produced a deep dimple and made his eyes twinkle.

"You grew up!"

Her voice was impertinent: "I watch you play ball every Sunday." She gathered the loose diapers into her arms.

"You do? I only saw you at the first game."

"Well, I've been there every Sunday."

"Ollie says to stay away from girls. He says to stay away from them that's okay and them that ain't. He says getting caught messin' with girls, can get a guy twitched."

"Twitched? What's that?"

"I'm not sure, but I got an idea. Sometimes a guy gets to hitting and fighting and one day he leaves and when he comes back he don't even know where to pee. Ollie says he got twitched. Sometimes Ollie says twitched when he talks about the herd. I'm not sure but I got an idea. Anyway, I ain't messin' with you."

"Well, I ain't askin' you to. I'm askin' you to be polite—you don't know about that."

"I don't want to be late."

"You could be a gentleman and help me."

"I can't, I've got an appointment at the Castle. Ben'll help you." He tapped Ben's shoulder, pointed to the diapers and then to Kay. Ben took the load from Kay's arms as she reached for another piece of laundry, folded it, and placed it on the stack Ben was holding.

Toe raced on toward the Castle, ashamed he had not even asked if she was hurt, yet grateful for Ben.

Toe entered the Castle. He'd heard a lot about it but had only been inside the front door once. It smelled of lemon oil and fresh tea biscuits. He had imagined how it would look. There was a large oak desk just inside the door where a woman sat, a dining room off to the right, a long table with at least a dozen high-backed upholstered chairs, mirrors in heavy gold-colored frames, paintings, patterned rugs with fringe on the dark hardwood floors, and an open winding stairway leading to the upper rooms.

The woman at the desk smiled. "Your name?"

"Seth Thomas, ma'am." Toe lifted his ball cap and ran his fingers through his hair, tousling it up into a stack.

"And who are you here to see?"

"I don't know, Ollie just told me to be here at 4 o'clock."

The woman sorted through several notes on her desk. The telephone rang. Then someone came in for a report. She answered their questions and pulled out a note on yellow paper. "Oh, here it is. You're here to see Dr. Helmsley and Mr. Kent. I thought they were going somewhere to a meeting."

She buzzed the intercom. "Seth Thomas is here."

"Send him in please," came the reply.

"First office on your left."

Toe rubbed his sweaty hands on his pants. He wondered if he was supposed to shake her hand. She didn't stand up, so he went down the hall to the office.

Dr. Helmsley stood when he knocked on the open door. He looked all business—not like he did that day when he came out to see the lawnmower.

"Come in, Seth." His voice was deep and resonated in the dark-paneled office. He spoke as if he intended everyone in the room to pay attention. He was intimidating in his ink-black suit and dark striped tie.

"Seth, thanks for stopping by." He reached to shake Toe's hand. "We met last spring, you may remember, when you were mowing the lawn. This is a big day here at the State Home. You're helping us start on a new goal. You know Mr. Kent, the high-school agriculture teacher?"

Toe nodded to Mr. Kent, and followed Dr. Helmsley's gesture to sit down in the chair opposite his desk. Mr. Kent occupied the other chair. He was dressed in a blue short-sleeved shirt and casual pants, his body occupying much of the chair, his long legs folded back at the knees. He was equally tall toes-to-hips and hips-to-head.

"Hi, Seth. I came by to schedule some visits for the agriculture classes in the fall. I was talking to Dr. Helmsley about the prize-winning herd you have here."

Toe nodded. "Yes, sir. Finest in the county and maybe the state."

"Dr. Helmsley said he has not visited the farm program yet. I told him to arrange it soon." Mr. Kent smiled.

Toe relaxed in his chair. They wanted to talk dairy herd. He could do that.

"Yes, Dr. Helmsley, we sure would like to have you come down to the farm. You'd be proud if you saw how hard we work and how nice the herd is."

"He tells me his wife grew up on a farm in Alpena," Mr. Kent said.

Toe flashed a quizzical look at the men.

"Alpena's in Michigan, Seth." Dr. Helmsley smiled.

"Oh." Toe squirmed in his chair. "I've only been here."

He watched the two men exchange a glance.

Dr. Helmsley took the lead.

"That's what we want to talk to you about." Dr. Helmsley turned to Mr. Kent.

Mr. Kent cleared his throat.

"Seth, I've been coming to the farm here at the State Home for three years. I've watched you grow up, to become active in the management of the dairy program. I believe you have potential beyond what is offered to you here. I spoke with Dr. Helmsley, and we want you to come to high school."

Toe looked down at his shoes. They stared back at him, brown, scuffed and worn, the broken laces knotted in several places. These were his best, his only real shoes. He took a slow, deep breath.

"I'm not sure you know what a Home boy is out there." Toe motioned toward the highway. The tenor of his voice was low and deep, with the resonance of one who had experienced more than fifteen years of life. His words flowed so easy he wasn't sure he was speaking them. He looked at the teacher. "It's nice of you to offer. But, that's not something I want to do. I'm a Home boy."

Dr. Helmsley took the lead. "Seth, we thought you might have some reluctance. So we've decided you will go to high school."

Seth shuffled his feet, and looked Mr. Kent in the eyes. "Can I tell you how it is?"

"Sure, Seth." Mr. Kent leaned forward, intent and waiting.

Toe sat down. "With all due respect, sir, the boys from high school come here and I show them around. I tell them about the herd and the operation, but you don't hear what some say when you walk away. There's always one that will poke another, and call me a retard, or boy, or say something like, "Not bad management for a barn full of idiots." Toe looked down; his voice changed to a whisper. "I don't do nothing, I don't hit 'em, I don't say nothing back, but I get real mad inside and I can't wait for them to leave. I can't go to school with those boys. Sooner or later, I'd have to fight 'em and shut someone's mouth. Then I'd either be back here in trouble or maybe in jail someplace. No thanks! I don't belong in high school."

Dr. Helmsley cleared his throat, moved his chair back from his desk, and stood up.

"It's not an option for you to decide. You have potential, and with the proper education you could have a successful vocation. I have reviewed your school records and discussed this plan with your former teacher. If you need any tutoring with your high school classes, she's offered to help. As a reward for your work in the farm program, Mr. Kent has offered to arrange transportation for you to school after milking in the morning and a return ride back after school. You won't ride the bus with the other students. Mr. Kent will be your overseer. Your education will be an extension of the agriculture program, and you can remain involved in the farming operation here as long as you maintain your grades. If you decide to do less than your potential at high school, you will not be eligible to work on the farm."

Dr. Helmsley stepped around his desk, pulled up a chair, and sat down beside Toe.

"Seth, this is the first phase of a new program to help residents reach their full potential. For some it will be self-care, but we believe there are others who are capable of independent living and gainful employment. We are pursuing this endeavor with our best students first."

Toe stroked the arms of his chair, moving his hands back and forth on the smooth polished walnut. "You're telling me I can't say no." Toe's gaze met Dr. Helmsley's.

"No, is not an option. Seth, I'd hoped for your cooperation. This is about so many more people than the students we've selected. I'd hoped you would see that."

"I don't want to go," Toe said, determined. He imagined what his days would be like, filled with ridicule and mocking. His stomach knotted. They've never lived here. They'd never understand. His anger boiled from deep within. "I know how it works here, Dr. Helmsley. I've seen it all. I've seen what you do to men. If you can't break 'em you twitch 'em."

Dr. Helmsley's face paled. He regained his composure. "Seth, I'm trying to give you the opportunity for an education."

Toe struggled to control his raging thoughts and hold his tongue. He took a deep breath. He knew about the coal yard, the steam engine room, and the slaughterhouse. The bad work.

"If it's the only way I can stay working in the dairy barn, then I guess you've got me."

Pictures of inevitable fights whirled through his mind. If the staff determined he was unmanageable they could assign him to the bad-boys building. He squirmed in the chair. "If I try… and it doesn't work can we talk about this again?"

Dr. Helmsley's Adam's Apple bobbed up, then down. He looked at Mr. Kent. "Yes, Seth, if you try your best and it doesn't work we can talk again. I'm sorry to end our meeting but I have another appointment. I'm sure you have more questions. Ask Mrs. Porter to schedule us another appointment soon. I'll try to answer your questions then."

Dr. Helmsley reached up to the coat rack and removed his hat. "I'll follow you out, Mr. Kent."

Mr. Kent stood. "Seth, would you like me to drive you back to the barns?"

"No thank you. I think the walk'd do me good. Besides Ben's waiting outside." Toe checked the window. "Yup, he's waiting."

Mr. Kent approached. "I don't see anyone."

"You won't." Toe motioned with his hand. "He's there, behind that third tree."

Toe rubbed his sweaty hands on his pants as the men reached out to shake hands.

Leaving the Castle, Toe's thoughts rushed to Ben. They didn't care about Ben and keeping him out of fights. All they cared about was that they could say they sent some Home kids to high school. Desperation and powerlessness fueled Toe's anger. No choice! They would take away everything he had worked for and they could do it. If they wanted to do something for him they could leave him alone.

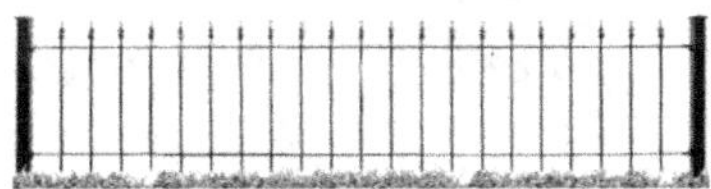

Kay left the nursery and ran back to wait on the path that led from the Castle toward the barns. She wondered if Toe's appointment at the Castle had anything to do with high school. From behind the lilac bush, she watched Ben standing beside an elm tree. Toe came out on the porch of the Castle. With his long stride, he took the flight of stairs two at a time. Kay waited near the path, hoping he would tell her why he was there.

As he passed the third elm tree, Ben came out from the shadows and fell into step behind him.

When Toe passed the lilac, Kay asked, "What happened? What did they want?"

Toe continued his stride and circled the large bush. Kay struggled within the shrub to come out the other side and walk a distance from them. She could hear Ben's heavy breathing.

"You didn't get hurt when you fell, did you?" Toe asked.

"No, not much. I skinned my arm. Why did you have to go to the Castle?"

Ben huffed and puffed behind them, his labored breathing accented by his stomping footsteps.

Toe pounded his fist into his hand. "I gotta go to high school. I told them no, but they said they would take me away from the farm if I refused. That's my life, my cows, my herd. What the heck will I do at high school but look like a fool? A fool from the Home!"

"I'm going." Kay spoke hoping it was loud enough for him to hear. "It says in Proverbs, 'The fear of the Lord is the beginning of knowledge but fools despise wisdom and discipline.' You won't be a fool if you seek knowledge."

Toe stopped so abruptly Ben crashed into him.

"That's in your book? That Proverbs thing?" Toe grabbed Ben by the shirt and moved him out of the way to look at Kay. "What? You're going to high school?"

"I am, and so are four other kids who finished the eighth grade. Miss Timmons helped us study and we passed the exam. We're riding the regular school bus. It'll pick us up in front by the gate every morning and bring us back after school."

Toe surveyed the area. No one was near. He stepped farther away from her and kicked at the dirt.

"I work hard and this is the thanks I get…I'm not riding the bus. The ag teacher's picking me up after milking in the morning and bringing me home after school. They got it all worked out." Panic crossed his face. "I gotta go. I don't want anybody to see me talking to a girl."

"See you at high school!" Kay fluttered a low wave and ran back toward her cottage. Now she could stop worrying about stuff that might happen at high school.

Toe would be there.

Chapter 8

"Nurse Lucy, come 'ere." Kay called from beside Rachel's crib, her voice hushed and urgent.

Lucy Huested approached the crib, stroked the child's head, and then passed her hand over the child's eyes.

"She's passed, Kay. Her suffering is over."

"I just checked her. She was pulling on her blanket."

"I know you checked her. It's okay! You run along, or you'll be late."

"Can't I help you say goodbye?" Kay rubbed the tears from her eyes.

"You don't have to."

"I want to. Please?"

Nurse Lucy and Kay bathed the small thin body and wrapped her in her favorite pink blanket.

"It never gets easier, Kay," Lucy said, tears rolling down her cheeks. She wrapped her arm around Kay, pulling her to her side as they gazed at the child.

"I don't understand how I feel, Nurse Lucy. I don't want her to have to live the way she lived. But I'll miss her. She had such a happy smile, even if it was crooked."

"Kay, we have to accept life and death by faith. I don't have the answers; I can only say I know the one who does."

"Let's sing her goodbye together."

Nurse Lucy smiled, and started to sing just above a whisper: "Jesus loves the little children, all the children of the world." Kay joined in. When they finished singing, Kay returned to her cottage.

Kay was late. She was sad about Rachel. Sometimes the work at the nursery tore at her heart, but other times seeing a child's joy at simple pleasures was so gratifying. Tonight she wanted her bed. She entered the cottage by the service door, passing the pantry toward the back stairs, when she heard Hannot's voice. The staff must have had a meeting. Several workers were gathered in the office and the door was ajar. Kay hoped she could pass by the door without making a sound. If Hannot saw her, she'd confine her to the building and certainly punish her in front of the others for being tardy. Kay scurried up several steps before hearing her name. Then crouched down in the shadows to listen.

"I don't think Kay O'Shay's back from the nursery yet," said Becker, the night attendant.

"Shay's okay! Shay's okay!" Hannot repeated again and again between gusts of laughter, slapping her leg with her hand. The other workers joined in with titters and giggles, responding to her excited humor. "I declare! Tears are running down my cheeks."

"What do you mean, Shay's okay!" Becker asked.

"You don't know about our Kay? Now there's a story. The guard found her in a basket on the doorstep out by the gate. He brought her to the hospital and I was covering that morning. We thought she was about a day old. That would make her born on St. Patrick's Day. That foreign doctor, Huggerolie something or another, you could hardly understand him. He was trying to be so American. He looked that baby all over, handed her to the nurse, and said "Shay's okay." I was doing the paperwork and when the nurse finished bathing her I asked, "What do I write for a name?"

"Kay O'Shay," she said. I thought she was quite clever, myself. Certainly O'Shay was a good Irish name for a little leprechaun born on St. Patty's day."

"What about her parents?" someone asked.

"Shay may be okay, but Shay's got no parents. Shay's abandoned, but Shay's okay!"

The only laughter she heard was Hannot's boisterous cackle. Relieved she didn't hear the others join in, she climbed the stairs, clutching her broken heart. Abandoned! In a basket! She was nothing. The only thing she had that was her own was her name and now that was joke.

Several days passed before Kay could talk to Nurse Lucy about what happened the night Rachel passed. Nurse Lucy sat in a rocking chair and with a sigh eased off her right shoe. Kay continued to fold diapers.

"Nurse Lucy, did you know my name is a joke?"

Lucy rubbed the red area on the side of her foot.

"Why would you say your name is a joke?"

"My name *is* a joke." Kay was nearing the threshold of a tirade. "When I went back to my cottage yesterday, after Rachel passed, Hannot was telling the whole staff my name is a joke. Everyone was laughing. She's so mean. I hate her."

"Hate isn't good."

"I hate *her*."

Lucy slid her foot back into her shoe and walked into the workroom. Kay followed as anger overruled her judgment. "I want to talk about what happened."

"Kay, don't bring ugly words into the nursery. This work is hard, our children need love, and they don't need people to bring in the *ugly* of the world."

"Hannot's mean."

"That only affects you if you let it."

"How would you feel if your name was a joke?"

Nurse Lucy started preparing formula. "I know you're upset."

Kay explained what happened, all the things Hannot said and how the others laughed. "So you see? My name is a joke. I'm a joke. I have nothing. No one wanted me, not even my own mother!" Kay couldn't stop the tears. Her body trembled with anger and pain. She wanted to run, but there was nowhere to go. No one cared.

Nurse Lucy called another nurse over.

"Mo, we are going to lunch now. There's only Jay Jay to feed. We'll be back at one."

Kay didn't pull away when Nurse Lucy put her arm around her and gave her a hug as she picked up her lunch box.

"Come on, Kay. Let's go to lunch."

Behind the building at a picnic table Nurse Lucy opened her lunch, removed her *Bible*, and placed it on the table.

"Kay, I believe God names his children. If you read the *Bible* you'll see several places where God gives a person a different name. Sometimes people change their names. When I married, I gave up my maiden name and took my husband's name. God changed Jacob's name to Israel and Abram to Abraham, Sara to Sarah. In Revelation 2:17 it says, 'He who overcomes, God will give a new name.' Do you like your name?"

"It's all I've ever known, but it's short. I think Kay is too short for a name. It's a letter of the alphabet, not a real name."

"Lots of people use only initials. F. Scott Fitzgerald, an author, was one. You're starting high school in a couple weeks. In high school, the way you sign your name is the name they will call you. You can change your name at high school. You can sign it K-a-y or K-a-y-e. If you keep the Kay, it will remind you God helps his children overcome difficulties. Every time you write the K to begin your name, you will remember God will help you overcome."

"I don't understand all that." Kay's thoughts turned to her lineage. "Do you think I'm Irish?"

"Do you want to be Irish?"

"Can I tell them I'm Irish, too?" Kay chuckled. "Yes, I do want to be Irish."

"There are lots of lovely Irish names like Katherine, Patricia, Maureen."

Kay's eyes brightened. "Won't I be breaking a rule somewhere if I change my name?"

"Oh, yes rules!" Nurse Lucy patted her *Bible*.

"Well, keep the Kay O'Shay here and maybe dress it up a bit at high school. There are fewer rules about things like that at high school."

"I like Kaye with an e, or Maureen …O'Shay. That sound's pretty, don't you think?"

"Without a doubt! Kay, you are a child of the living God. He created you. Show Him how grateful you are for the wonderful gifts He has given you. Look around! Don't you see how you are blessed? All the things you can do! Why, you're even going to high school. That has never happened to anyone here before."

"I'm so scared."

"Hey, Huested, it's past one," Mo called out from the window.

"Lunch is over." Nurse Lucy picked up her lunch box and *Bible*. "We have work to do, Miss Kaye, with an e, Maureen O'Shay."

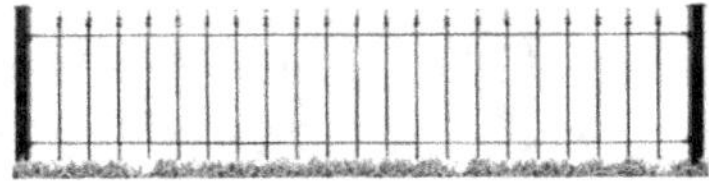

Toe listened to the rumors, but he didn't believe it until the day Mr. Green paid him a visit.

"Hi, Toe. I wanted to come by and tell you boys that I've decided to retire. Mother is gettin' tired and we're goin' to head up North. Got us a little place up there where I can do some fishing. I'll miss you boys, but I know you'll take good care of the farm and the herd. Is Ollie around?"

"He went to see the blacksmith about the bull-pen bars. He'll be right back," answered Toe, suppressing his questions.

"When we told cook we were leaving," Mr. Green continued, "she began planning a picnic. Can you boys pull a wagon around by the kitchen? She'll hand out the food. I think she's cooking up a little party with cake and ice cream."

"Mr. Green, we're gonna miss you," said Toe, but what he wanted to say was, *We can't do this without you. You're the one that keeps it all together.* It wasn't the day for that, with Mr. Green being so happy and Mrs. Green looking so pretty in a new dress.

Cook had prepared a cake and three crocks of iced tea. She opened a cask of ice cream, too.

"Boys, this is your new herdsman," Mr. Green said, his arm around Ollie. "Mr. Olinzski's worked hard here at the farm, and now it's time for him to get his reward. I know you'll all work for Ollie as you did for me. After all, it's all about our prize-winning herd. Right, boys?"

A shout went up from the men. Ollie pranced around the wagon, patting guys on the shoulder and telling them how good it would be to be the boss!

Toe cringed. It wouldn't be the same with Ollie in charge. He worked for his paycheck and bossing the men behind Mr. Green's back. That's what Ollie cared about, money for the things he wanted to buy—like liquor—and the bossing. He was shorter than most of the men, a full head shorter than Toe, and he enjoyed ordering the men around and calling them names. Sometimes he pushed too far and caused fights. Now Toe would have to watch Ben even closer. He'd seen Ollie try to egg Ben into throwing a punch at him. Ollie was still quick with his fists and feet. Testimony from Ollie that Ben attempted to attack him would land Ben in a real bad way.

A few months after Ollie took over, Toe joined Homer on his way to the barn to check on his cow that was due to have a calf. While they waited, Homer unrolled his newspaper and sat down on the milk stool. Toe fluffed the straw around some of the cows and cleaned a little, and then set up the cans and pails for morning. Still restless, he pulled out the box of cards and the ledger where Mr. Green kept the herd records. Each cow had an ear tag with numbers for identification. Toe thumbed through the cards of the five cows he managed. Ollie had not entered any information since Mr. Green retired. Toe checked every card— two hundred of them. No recording had been done for almost three months! The quarterly report would be due at the end of the month. He put the cards back in the boxes, helped Homer deliver the calf, and went back to bed. He tossed and turned, too restless to sleep. The more he thought about the herd and those records, the more he wondered why Ollie had not kept them updated.

The next day he asked Homer for the sports page of the newspaper he always carried in his back pocket. He took the paper to the barn. He had an idea.

"Hey, Ollie, look what it says here about Charlie Gehringer." Toe thrust the paper toward Ollie, who would rather talk baseball than eat.

Ollie tossed the paper back to Toe. "You read it to me. I forgot my glasses today. I'll listen."

They exchanged a look, one they each understood. Toe rolled up the newspaper and handed it back to Ollie. "Here, I got work to do, you can read it later."

Toe knew his answer. Ollie couldn't read or write. No recording on the herd to date; someone would find out. He didn't like Ollie, but he loved the herd. It would be a mess to backtrack and sort out the breeding schedule for a herd so large. Toe knew what he had to do.

Night after night, he worked on the records. He pulled production sheets and recorded the estimated breeding schedule. He left the breeding record empty until he could be sure exactly which bull had been used. Each man knew his assigned cows. Toe worked every evening for three weeks, careful not to let anyone know what he was doing. He finished the night before the quarterly was due.

After milking two days later, Mr. McDonald, the manager of the agriculture program, came into the barn. "Ollie, where's your report?

I came to pick it up. You told me it'd be on my desk yesterday. I've got summaries to submit!"

Ollie laughed. "Oh, McDonald. Hey! That's funny. Old McDonald had a farm!" Ollie laughed, slapping his knee. "How important is paper? The proof is in the pudding, my Grannie used to say. Look at the herd. It's doing fine."

Mr. McDonald walked over to the wall cabinet. "Mr. Green kept all his paperwork in here." Ignoring Ollie, he pulled out the first box and opened the accompanying ledger. Ollie started toward the silo. "You wait up, Ollie, I might have a question."

Ollie returned, cussing under his breath and yelling at the men working in the barn as they continued watching. "You guys get out of here and stop your gawking. If you can't find work, I'll find work for ya."

"What's your problem, Ollie? Why couldn't you send this over when I asked for it?"

Ollie squirmed. "I—t's been real busy here in the barns."

"Well, I'm glad to see that even as busy as you've been the records are in order." He tapped the box and the ledger. "Good job, Ollie! We can verify every production record now."

Ollie's eyes opened wide as Mr. McDonald's finger slid down the columns of figures. He removed the ledger. "I'll have this back to you tomorrow afternoon. Sorry for the interruption. Again, good work. Mr. Green would be proud." He slapped Ollie on the shoulder and left the barn.

About a week later Ollie came into the barn chewing on a stalk of timothy grass and leaned against the wall near where Toe was milking.

"So you think you're real smart, Mr. keeper of the records." His voice sneered. "You stay out of my way, you and that pile-of-crap Ben you call your friend. You tell anyone and I'll fix him real good. You know I can."

He spit a wad of tobacco juice in front of Toe's shoe and left the barn. Toe clinched and unclenched his fists as Ollie's pickup roared out the back drive. Ollie tooted his truck horn twice, a signal, commanding the attandant to open the gate.

Toe knew he had to make sure no one saw him keeping those records. Ben's safety was on the line.

Chapter 9

The man on duty at the guardhouse nodded toward the children as the school bus hissed to a stop. The bus door folded in the middle and opened. The children stood, frozen in place, their eyes wide in amazement.

The bus driver called out his orders without a greeting or a smile. "You kids sit here in front. Our next stop is the high school." Kay urged the children forward. She didn't want any mistakes today.

Once they were all seated, the bus driver lurched from his seat and stood to glare at the students in the back of the bus. "That's it!" he barked and continued his stare until the children were silent. He retook his seat and the students remained quiet as the bus rumbled one more mile.

All five of the children who boarded the bus at the State Home remained in the front two seats, as stiff as if they had been posed. Kay glanced at Margo, whose straight black hair glistened, falling against her shoulders, her heavy bangs covering her eyebrows. Her skin tanned deep from the summer sun. Margo did ironing and day work on Saturdays for a lady in town who insisted she take Margo shopping when she found out Margo was going to high school. Margo looked like the other high school girls in her plaid skirt and red cardigan. Kay saw a couple of girls in a seat across the aisle point toward the red socks Margo wore with her new saddle shoes. She hoped Margo didn't see them laugh.

Leah cowered behind the notebook she held in her left hand. Schoolwork came easy for her, but strangers made her fearful. Her right arm twitched sporadically; some of the aides called it a seizure. Without warning Leah's right arm would thrust straight up or away from her body and freeze in that position for several seconds. She was delicate-featured and looked younger than her age of fifteen. She wore a new print dress with a narrow leather belt.

Gary liked school, but he particularly enjoyed meeting people. His almond- shaped crystal-blue eyes danced with excitement and matched his winning smile. Gary did not know a stranger; he considered everyone a friend.

Johnny's words came slow because he had a stutter. He seldom talked. He had large feet and hands. Johnny would probably be a big man someday, but at fourteen he had not yet started to grow.

All the children's shoes had been polished until they were shiny. Kay wondered if the leather was that shiny or if it was the polish. The students knew each other well because they had been in classes together even before attending the seventh- and eighth-grade study classes to prepare for the eighth-grade test. All of them had passed. That accomplishment, combined with a new administrator's policy, brought them here today. Her thoughts churned from feelings of excitement to learn and… not wanting to be here at all.

The bus driver eased the large vehicle around the horseshoe drive in front of the two-storey red brick high school, rolling to a stop. Kay smoothed her new skirt and rechecked her white blouse to make sure the buttons were all properly fastened. The brakes on the bus hissed. The door opened with a *swoosh*. Crisp early morning air freshened the confined pungent odors of fifty excited children.

"The five," as they came to be known, were the first to exit the bus. Clusters of students huddled together in groups of three or four on the sidewalk. Some chatted, a few pointed and giggled, and some covered their mouths and whispered between themselves.

Leah's arm thrust into the air. She struggled to pull it in toward her body. She regained control of her errant limb, anchoring it across her chest with the other arm. Observing students gasped while Leah pressed the knuckles of her hand toward her mouth, seeking comfort.

Kay read the card pinned to Leah's jacket. The first line contained her name followed by a list of room numbers indicating her schedule.

Kay had removed her own card and placed it inside her notebook. She refused to go out in public with a card pinned to her sweater.

Struggling to suppress her own fears, Kay spoke to Leah with all the assurance she could muster. "I'll help you find the way to your room, Leah. It's okay, I'm going inside, too." She urged Leah toward the door. "And you know Toe. He's coming later after chores. We'll all be here together. You'll see."

A woman emerged, waving her arms as four students tripped along behind her. She spotted the five grouped together.

"Hello, students! My name is Miss Wilson and we're going to help our new students find their rooms. It's such a big building." She lifted Margo's card and read the room assignments. "Marie, you will go with Margo."

Then she turned to a boy. "Duane, you go with…." She looked at the tag on Gary's jacket. "Duane, you go with Gary. Who do we have here?"

The teacher lifted Leah's tag. "Leah, that's a lovely name. Leah, this is Helen. She'll be with you today to help you. Dan, you go with Johnny. Oh, I should have brought another student. I thought only four were coming."

She assessed Kay standing slightly in front of Johnny, shielding him. Kay had noted the dark circle on Johnny's pants and the stain moving down his left leg. He had wet his pants as he stepped off the bus.

"Excuse me, Miss Wilson." Kay stepped closer, speaking so no one else could hear. "Would it be all right if Dan took Johnny to the restroom before school starts? He has clean pants in his book bag. I came here last week, so I know where the classrooms are. I could take Johnny to his room and my first hour is upstairs next to the library."

"Yes." Miss Wilson's glance passed over Johnny and onto Gary, followed by a nod. One student host shy and Johnny's accident left her grasping to maintain her authority. "And your name is?"

"Kay O'Shay, ma'am.

"Miss Kay, you know all the children?"

"Yes, we attended school together." She's angry with me, Kay thought. All I did was try to help Johnny.

"At the Home?"

"Yes." Maybe she wouldn't have her for a teacher.

"Let's go inside. We don't want to be late the first day."

The eight-foot oak doors opened and the foyer swallowed them. Dark oak woodwork glistened. The morning light blazed through the panels of glass in the doors and transom windows. The terrazzo floors shimmered, reflecting a mirrored coating of wax. The foyer smelled like warm sugar cookies and reminded Kay of the whole orange she received on Christmas Day—the deep rich smells of good things. Kay tucked the aroma of the foyer in her mind; these smells would always be a reminder of her first day of high school.

Miss Wilson waved the children and their guides toward their destination and motioned Johnny and Dan toward the boys' restroom.

Nurse Lucy had not faltered in her campaign encouraging Kay to go to high school. On her day off she took Kay to the school for a tour. They had walked her entire schedule, finding all the classrooms, cafeteria, and her locker. Kay was not convinced she should go to high school, but she was grateful today that she knew where to find her rooms.

Kay waited in the hallway until Dan and Johnny emerged from the restroom. Johnny was hugging his book bag; Dan's disgust remained evident.

Gary remained near Kay. They followed Dan and Johnny upstairs to the second floor. Gary walked as fast as his short legs could carry him. His round face framed his happy smile, a smile that welcomed anyone who would respond. He had so many friends at the Home. Dan reached the second stairwell and gestured down the hall. "Go that way. Third door on your left," he said, before vanishing in a mass of students descending the stairs.

Johnny entered the correct classroom and Kay hurried to position herself behind Gary, concerned he would be swallowed up in the crowd of students. She touched his shoulder and leaned down near his ear. "Your first class is at the end of this hall, and your next class is in the room next door. I'll come back and take you to your third class, which will be third hour." Kay hoped Gary would make friends here. Once they got to know him, they would like him.

With her thoughts on Gary, she hesitated at the door to the classroom. Several students rushed through, pushing Kay and Gary back into the hall. Gary pressed against her and struggled to stay upright. Kay held onto the doorknob and braced her legs against the wall, shielding Gary against the tide of students. The first bell rang and the students scurried to their chairs.

Gary smiled at her and entered the room, the last student in. "Thanks, Kay, see you later. Study hard." He waved goodbye to her. That was Gary, little Gary with the big heart, always caring for others.

Kay wondered how she could study, knowing what might be happening to the other kids. She hoped Leah would be okay, she was so shy. Her thoughts rushed to Johnny, hoping Johnny didn't have another accident. He'd already used his extra pair of pants. Her worries carried her to Margo's new red socks. No girls were wearing colored socks, only white. She wanted to watch over the Home kids , but they were in different rooms and classes.

Kay was still three classrooms away from her first class, room 214, when second bell rang. The hall emptied. At the door of room 214, she turned the knob and the latch released with a click. Every pair of eyes turned toward her. A hush fell over the room. Her first day, her first class, and already she was in trouble.

"You are tardy!" shouted the teacher standing behind a large desk. He was short and shaped like a mushroom with shaggy gray hair and bushy eyebrows that feathered over the top of his glasses. His crumpled gray suit sagged on his body like sections of an abandoned newspaper.

"I was helping—"

"I've heard every excuse. Sit down." He waved his hand toward the only vacant chair.

"Mr. Kennedy, she came on the bus from the Home," someone offered.

Kay couldn't tell who spoke. She hurried to the chair desk, not looking at anyone and swallowing her tears.

"Well, that's one I've not heard before." He chuckled under his breath. "Sit down," he said as the students tittered.

He wrote *Mr. Kennedy* on the blackboard and rapped his pencil on his desk.

He began roll call, looking at each student when they answered, pausing to put the face and name together. "Kay O'Shay."

"Here, sir," Kay answered.

"O'Shay. That's a good Irish name for a lass. What is your full name?"

Kay lifted her chin. Now she would tell everyone. "My name is Kaye, with an e, Maureen O'Shay."

"Welcome Miss Kaye with an e Maureen O'Shay. Yes that's a pure Irish name if I ever heard one. I believe I may have some O'Shays in my own ancestry."

He rubbed his chin.

"Kaye with an e." He smiled. "Means fire in Greek, and Maureen is Irish for Mary, and you finish with an O'Shay. It doesn't get any more Irish than that."

No one was tittering now. Kaye relaxed in her chair, no more tears to swallow.

Before third hour Kaye rushed back to Gary's classroom. He stood outside the door, waiting for her and holding three heavy books. Kaye removed the books from his arms.

"Did the teacher give you a locker?"

"No, nothing locked."

Kaye pulled a card from her jacket pocket. Did the teacher in your first hour class give you a card like this? It has a number on it."

Gary searched his pockets. Kaye opened the inside covers of the book on the bottom of the stack and found the card in his first hour book.

"Here it is. I'll put your books in my locker now and after lunch we can find your locker and put your books in your locker." Kaye understood how literal language and behaviors resulted in confusion for the kids of the Home. She had grown up with that fact. She hoped Gary understood there were two lockers; one would be hers and one his. She'd explain what a locker was later.

She walked with him to the outside of the building. Another student passed her carrying a music stand. "Are you going to the band room?"

He turned toward her and looked at Gary. "Yes." His reply was halting.

"This is Gary, could you show him where the band room is? He has band next."

"What do you play?" The boy looked at Gary, bewildered. His expression questioned whether a person that small could play in the band.

"Drums, te-dum, te-dum!" Came Gary's reply. He flipped his hands as if they held drumsticks.

"Come on." The boy smiled. "Really, you play drums?"

"Yes sirree! Wanna do a challenge?"

The boy laughed. "No. I play tenor sax."

Gary gleefully accepted his guide as a new friend. He waved goodbye to Kaye, "Bye, Kaye. Work hard."

After class, Kaye waited at the entrance for Gary to return from band. He was smiling and carrying a pair of drumsticks.

"They're mine, Kaye. I played real good, too."

"I'm sure you did, but we have to hurry so I won't be late. Now you're going to go to Gym." They rushed down the hall together.

"I know him." Gary puffed out the words as he trotted beside her.

"No, it's not a Jim that you know. It's g-y-m, where you go to exercise and play games."

Gary looked sad. "Not a Jim I know?"

"No, it's different. I don't know why it's called Gym but it's different. Here we are now. When you're done, you go down these stairs and the cafeteria is right there. That's where you'll eat lunch. I'll meet you there. Okay?"

Gary eyed the stairway and the massive oak doors, then tapped his drumsticks to the side of his head and said, "Okay, Kaye, I got it."

Kaye couldn't help laughing at his humor. Gary stood just above her waist. She didn't pat him on the head although she was tempted to, as so many people did. She knew how he felt about that. Sometimes he would immediately kick the person in the shins. That was the only time he ever had an outburst or showed any anger.

After fourth hour she had to stop at the bathroom. She rushed into a stall and closed the door. Several girls were giggling and talking about their hair, complaining about the teachers and gossiping about other girls. As she emerged to wash her hands, she stopped in alarm. Someone was looking at her. She looked frightened. The other girls left, chattering on their way. The door closed and the room silenced. Still Kay could not move. She reached up to touch her face. The other person touched her face too. She touched her lips, her hair, and the same result. Another girl came in and used the restroom. She washed her hands in one of the many sinks, stood for a moment, and adjusted her hair. Kay stepped back and looked at the wall in front of the other girl. Someone was looking back at her, too, and they looked exactly alike.

Kaye couldn't help herself.

"Excuse me. Um. Do you know her?"

The girl paused, continuing to dry her hands on the linen towel.

"What do you mean?"

"Nothing."

"No. You asked if I knew someone?"

Kaye drew in a deep breath. "Do you know her?" She pointed toward the second girl on the other side of the sink.

"You're kidding, right?"

"Yeah, right." Kaye tried to fake a laugh.

"For a minute there you had me going. I thought maybe you were spooky or something, asking me who was in the mirror."

"In the mirror?" Kaye eyed the wall again.

"The mirror." The other girl tapped the image, clicking it with her pink fingernails. "The mirror."

"Of course. The mirror."

"You look pretty in that color red, Kaye."

"You know me?"

"We have second hour together. I come in here before lunch and make sure my makeup is fresh and my hair is right." She preened in front of the mirror and adjusted her skirt and sweater.

Kaye turned toward a mirror facing her. A smile crossed the anxious face staring back. Yes, she did look good in red. *It was the first time she had seen Kaye Maureen O'Shay.*

At lunch she found Gary. He was already seated at a table, eating and laughing with two other boys. Kaye searched the cafeteria for Toe, just a glimpse of him. It would be nice to know he was here. She carried her tray to a table and sat alone. There were two lunch periods; Toe must have been assigned the second period, or he didn't come to the cafeteria.

After lunch she went outside to get away from the mass of students in the hallways. The huge maple trees cast shadows over the lawn. A few students were sitting on a knee-high concrete wall across the street, smoking cigarettes. Others were seated on the grass, talking. Kaye searched for Leah and Margo. Leah was seated under a tree, reading a book. Margo was walking with two other girls toward the library. She had seen Johnny with Duane in the cafeteria. Kaye took a deep breath. Everybody was doing well but her.

"I thought you wanted to go to High school," came a familiar voice behind her, followed by a chuckle.

Kaye spun around to face Toe.

"You're here! I'm glad to see you." Her eyes consumed every detail. He was wearing a blue plaid shirt and new blue jeans. His shirtsleeves were rolled up. The muscles of his tanned arms were rippled and taut like ropes. His thick dark hair, short from a recent haircut, twisted and tried to curl. His eyes sparkled with mischief and his smile revealed that deep dimple in his cheek.

"That's a nice greeting, Miss Kaye with an e Maureen O'Shay."

"How do you know my new name?"

I heard it during roll call in math class."

"I didn't see you."

"I sat in the back. I gotta go, my next class is at the other end of the building, in the basement. It's auto mechanics; I hope we work on real cars. Look, everyone's going in."

Several groups of students filled the sidewalks, returning to the school.

Toe gave her a wink and rushed off toward the north doors.

Kaye held her breath. He winked. At her! He's happy we're here. She'd see him tomorrow. There was so much happening—and so far it's good.

Kaye's day progressed on schedule until her route to eighth hour took her past Leah sitting on a window ledge in the stairwell, her knees tucked up under her chin, arms tightly encircling her legs. If she stopped to talk Leah off that ledge she'd be late to class again. Kaye was sure twice in one day would get her in trouble. Panic captured her, but she couldn't leave Leah there. The hallway was emptying and the doors of the rooms were closing. She'd have to pay the price.

"Come on, Kaye's here. It's time to make new friends," Kaye coaxed.

Leah started to ease herself down from the window ledge with obedient reluctance. Kaye took hold of her hand.

"It's going to be fine. By tomorrow you'll have several new friends. You wait and see." *Liar Liar, pants on fire*, Kaye mocked herself. She hadn't made any friends. The girl in the restroom said she looked nice in red. But, she did say something about Kaye acting spooky. No, she hadn't made a friend.

The moment Leah's feet touched the floor, Mr. Kennedy appeared on the landing. "Can I help?"

"Mr. Kennedy, Leah's afraid and if I take her to her class, I'll be late again.

Mr. Kennedy scowled.

"Were you helping Leah when you arrived late for my class this morning?"

"No, sir. Yes, sir." Kaye's words wrestled out. "I helped Leah, then I helped Johnny."

"I was told each student would have an assigned escort. Leah, come with me and we'll go to the office and find out who is supposed to be assisting you. You can't sit here on the windowsill. Miss O'Shay, please commence to your classroom."

Kay caught herself before she tried to correct Mr. Kennedy regarding Leah's helper. The time spent to clarify the oversight could make her late for class.

"Thank you, sir. Be brave, Leah." Kaye grasped the oak handrail and rushed down the two flights of terrazzo stairs. She had to make it into the classroom before the second bell. This teacher might not be as forgiving as Mr. Kennedy. She arrived in English class, sliding into a chair near the door as the second bell rang.

"Good afternoon, students. My name is Miss Turkle. 'Quoth the Raven, Nevermore.' Can anyone tell me who wrote that line?" Miss Turkle closed the classroom door. The room silenced.

A frail, pale girl sitting in the front row near the window shuffled her feet and raised her hand. "Is it from a poem by Edgar Allan Poe?"

"Very good. You are correct." Miss Turkle explained how her classes both first- and second-semester English would include classical literature.

A moan passed around the room. She took roll and each student removed a book from the table at the front of the room when their name was called.

She continued to explain her assignments and noted several authors' names on the blackboard.

The school day ended. Kaye had overheard only a few remarks about the "Home" kids throughout the day, but for Kaye, each remark felt like the sting of a hornet. It didn't matter to people *why* you lived at the Home. You were there and one of them; that said it all.

In every class she presented herself as Kaye Maureen O'Shay, adding the e to Kay. It worked just like Nurse Heusted had said, and adding the e to her first name made it seem even more like a name and not a letter. It gave her a sense of accomplishment. Her name was now her own, one she had created. Mr. Kennedy liked it. He said a name "aptly rendered to an Irish lass."

She liked the sound of that.

The bus pulled up to the front of the building. All the members of "The Five" boarded and sat in their assigned seats. Kaye and Margo sat together in the second seat looking more like good friends than they ever had before.

"Did it go okay for you, Margo?" Kaye asked.

"If I liked being called an Indian, it was fine."

"Sorry. I got called names, too. I hope it stops."

Kaye waited. She'd never asked Margo why she was at the Home. Were they friends now? Friends who could trust each other? She ventured, "I got left…How did you get there?"

"Train." Margo was looking out the window at the cars passing the bus.

"Why?" Kaye asked softly, trying not to pry, yet curious. Many of the kids had obvious reasons they were at the Home, and if you couldn't see the reason it was understood you didn't ask.

"'Cause I'm Chippewa… 'Cause my mom got sick… My brothers came, too."

"You have family here? Oh, I wish I had someone."

"I haven't seen Tom since the day we arrived, and Ahmok went to school for a couple years. Then I heard he went to the farm to work. If I don't see them, I guess I don't really have any family. Where're you from?"

"Like I said, I got left. That's all I know. Now you know all I know."

"Sorry."

Kaye looked at Margo. "I'm glad you're going to high school, too. It helps."

Margo nodded.

The bus screeched to a halt at the front gate. The guard left his station and approached the bus, exhibiting an important strut. Was he new? Kaye hadn't seen him before.

"Straight to your cottages," he shouted, and waved his arm toward the buildings. "Don't dally."

The students piled out. Leah was humming a song, Gary carrying his drumsticks, Margo smiling with a new confidence, the insults of the day behind her. Johnny chattered about having different teachers and lots of books.

Kaye was the last one off the bus. She caught the guard smiling and appraising Margo as she walked away. Kaye could not help the feeling of alarm that swelled within her. His smirk. Tomorrow she'd tell Margo to stay away from him. But, what would she say? That the guard had watched her?

Kay rushed toward her cottage; she could not contain her excitement. She wanted to see Jessie and tell Nurse Lucy about her day.

Kaye hugged Jessie. "I'm back!" she called out to the staff. "I'm taking Jessie for a walk." She pushed Jessie's chair toward the nursery. Nurse Lucy was exiting. Jessie was making giggling noises as her chair rumbled over the bumps.

"Nurse Lucy, I'm back."

"Hello, high-school girl."

"Did you know my name means something? Every word of my name means something."

"Is that what you learned at high school? I was sure it would be algebra or chemistry." Nurse Lucy laughed at Kaye's excitement. "By the way, you look very nice. Very high-schoolish!"

"I learned about those things, too, but I told each teacher my name is Kaye with an e, and my history teacher, Mr. Kennedy, said it means 'fire' in Greek. He said my second name Maureen means 'Mary' in Irish, and my last name O'Shay is a very old Gaelic name."

"It sounds like you had a wonderful day. Aren't you glad you went? I have to hurry home; my husband likes his supper before six."

"Bye, Nurse Lucy!"

"Bye, Kaye with an e!"

Toe did not return to general math class the next day and the teacher did not call his name. When Kaye opened her locker, a folded piece of paper fell to the floor. She picked it up and stuffed it into her notebook. Refusing to risk opening it in class, she waited until lunchtime to use the restroom. There she could read it and throw it away. She would not risk anyone finding a note to her from Toe.

> *H, i Kay with an e,*
>
> *I got transferred to algebra so I won't see you in math class. Work real hard and you will do well. I know you don't like numbers. I like the ag class, not sure about the other stuff. Don't know if I'll stay in high school. You keep going, the other kids need you here. My locker is #44 on the main floor. You can slide*

a note through the holes at the top if you want to write back.
T..................................

With an s, and an e, and an h.

It took three days for Kaye to compose a note to her satisfaction.

Hi, T with an s and e and an h.

Don't you say anything to me about you not coming back to high school. I have to know you are here, too. It would be awful without you. I hope you read Proverbs chapter 2. It's all about wisdom. That's why!

K with an e

Several days passed before she saw Toe again, although she snatched each note that fluttered out of her locker. Kaye was in the biology lab on the second floor when she saw several boys getting off a bus. They were wearing matching blue jackets with an emblem on the back.

They're called Future Farmers, boys who want to farm someday.

"Those are the boys that study ag," Joan said. Joan was working at Kaye's table.

"What's ag?" Kaye asked..

"They're farm boys who want to farm someday. They go on lots of field trips, too. No girls! Guess girls don't farm." Joan extended her fingers and checked her nail polish. "I don't know anybody who'd want to." She cleared off the table and put their Bunsen burner away.

"Future Farmers, huh?" Kaye was still thinking about the farm Toe told her he wanted someday, when Joan interrupted with an air of importance. "It's like this: there's city boys and farm boys."

"Are they different?"

Joan sighed. "Kaye, as different as night and day."

"Is it a bad different?"

Joan sighed again. "It depends if you like to dance." She grinned. The bell sounded and class dismissed. "We'll talk about it tomorrow."

Kaye returned to the window. Toe was talking with the Ag teacher and neither of them looked happy.

Oh, Toe, don't mess this up.

Ollie could be evil sober, but he was a mean drunk.

Toe stepped out from between the two Holstein cows, carrying a full pail of fresh milk.

Ollie came toward him, thrusting the pitchfork and yelling.

"Ollie!" Toe shouted, kicking his left leg up toward the swaying fork, knocking Ollie off balance.

Clay rushed up to grab Toe's pail of milk, staying clear of Ollie's fork.

Toe wrestled the fork from Ollie's hands, grabbed the collar of Ollie's shirt, then dragged him outside and around behind the barn where the straw stack loomed like a gold dome. He dropped Ollie onto the ground. Toe struggled to control his temper. He wanted to push Ollie's stinking face into the dirt and kick his behind. The tines of that pitchfork could have gone clean through one of his legs. It could have crippled him for life.

Toe held the pitchfork in his right hand, pressed his foot on the side seam of Ollie's pant leg, then plunged the pitchfork through the floppy pant leg all the way to the shank, all four tines of the fork, pressing it deeper into the earth with his boot, pinning Ollie to the ground. Toe dragged his hand through his thick black curly hair, pulling the sweaty curls into tangles of black spirals. He needed to calm down. He'd let his temper overwhelm his judgment, but he hadn't hurt the man. Toe could fight clean with the best of them, but Ollie was different. Ollie was an angry, crushed man, too stubborn to overcome his weakness. Toe delighted in outwitting educated snobs, but a weak beaten man needed no one to add to his misery.

"I'll get you, Toe!" Ollie shouted, struggling to pull the fork out of the earth and dislodge his trapped body. He slumped to the ground, his eyes closed.

"Sleep it off, Ollie. I can't get my work done if I have to be watching for you trying to stab me with your pitchfork."

"Ollie's a mean one," Clay mumbled. He had carried Toe's pail of milk outside and followed him behind the barn to watch what happened.

"Yeah, but we can't let him hurt us. He just gets out of his head sometimes. He don't even remember. You just gotta watch him. We can't get two-hundred cows milked dodging a pitchfork!" Toe removed his hat and wiped the sweat from his brow.

Jimmy moved ahead of Toe, washing each cow's udder. The sounds and smells of the barn eased Toe. The work went faster without Ollie around. Ollie didn't drink every day, just once in a while, but when he did he went crazy.

A cow turned her head to watch, then made a moaning sound.

"Yes, Cassie, I'm a milking ya." Toe stroked the cow's hindquarter, pulled up his milking stool, and started striping milk from the cow.

He smiled as his bare forearms moved in alternating rhythm. His shirtsleeve cuffs, always unbuttoned, ended at his mid forearm. They stayed cleaner that way. His pant legs, too, hovered above the top of his work boots. He loved the sound of the milk streaming into the pail, the rhythm of the work, the warmth of the barn, and the peace of a cow in the stanchion, chewing her cud.

"Cassie, I'll just lighten your load a bit. You sure are producing like a prize dairy cow."

A radio played down near the milk house. No one really listened to it unless the ballgame was on. Two black and white kittens tumbled in the alley, hoping for a squirt or two of milk from a nearby udder.

That night Toe read more pages of *Walden* and wrote in his journal.

Thoreau understood solitude and the peace that comes from simplicity. Did he have dreams? I only know how to work, and work is all I'm intended for. I read books and learn about math and engines. I get excited about other possibilities. I look at the old men here and wonder, Will I grow old here, too? I like the farm and the dairy operation, but when I think about Kaye I want more. Can I only dream? Next Saturday night one of the attendants is bringing a record of Shakespeare. I've read Shakespeare and I'm excited to hear someone speaking it. —T

When Ollie awoke, he unbuckled his belt, slid his suspenders off his shoulders, removed his truck keys from his pocket, then shimmied out of his green work pants. He stumbled to his pickup and climbed inside. Driving toward home, he was halfway home when he looked down at his underwear, unsure what had happened and how he lost his pants.

Chapter 10

Kaye entered the home economics room to see Margo standing at the window.

"Hi, Margo. Is something wrong?"

"No, I guess not."

Margo's ink-black hair shone in the afternoon sunshine. Her tawny skin accented her cheekbones, and not a blemish hampered her complexion. Kaye envied Margo and wondered what it would be like not to have freckles. As they both gazed out the window, they shared the view of a line of yellow buses and kids playing baseball on the ball diamond. The backstop towered and a fence circled the outfield. Cars in assorted colors dotted the parking lot.

"Did you look at these?" Margo fingered the heavy drapes. "Do you know there are homes with drapes like this at the windows? Beautiful drapes, not curtains made out of bed sheets."

Kaye touched the woven gray threads of the fabric. The deep burgundy threads that created the pattern of ascending spirals felt smooth and silky.

The bell rang and the girls hurried toward the chairs arranged on each side of a long table.

Seated, Margo continued to study the pattern and texture of drapes. Kaye contemplated the kitchen units, four kitchens each with a white four-burner stove, a white refrigerator, and sink. Each kitchen had a table and a set of four chairs that matched the table colors. It looked like a pretend kitchen.

"Good afternoon, ladies. I'm Miss Briggs." She tapped her pencil on the table. "We have so many things to discuss today. I'm sure you're all excited to learn the skills of Home Economics."

"I'm excited, all right," Margo whispered to Kaye.

Some of the girls moaned and rolled their eyes as the teacher explained the class.

"We will begin with an orientation of Home Economics. I'm sure many of you have helped your mothers and grandmothers in the kitchen, or made clothing or worked in the garden. Home Economics includes a vast array of the skills required for successful homemaking. Every student brings a variety of ability and interest to class. However, I have planned a curriculum that will expand your skill levels and your interests. Our first eight weeks will focus on basic culinary arts and our second half of this semester will include an introduction to textiles."

"First," Margo's commentary continued, "we're going to cook, then we're going to sew."

Miss Briggs persisted. "This week we will begin our cooking unit. First, we will make a roux. It's a fundamental recipe for any kitchen. Around the world, cultures prepare a form of roux. The French call this *Béchamel.*" She wrote the word on the chalkboard. "It was first referenced in a cookbook in 1651 during the reign of King Louie the 14th." She wrote the information under the word *Béchamel.* "I suggest you take out a paper and note some of this information."

She frowned as some of the girls mumbled and groaned, but soon everyone was writing notes.

"There are so many uses for a roux." She continued writing in three columns, first a list of the items they would need, second the terms for the method, and third the many ways for using a roux in food preparation.

Margo leaned near Kaye. "She's talking about gravy."

"Hush. Don't get us into trouble. I think it's more than gravy."

Margo waited until Miss Briggs turned back to write on the blackboard, then leaned near Kaye. "Whatever you call it or do with it, it's gravy." Margo would not allow any French word to intimidate her.

"Margo." Miss Briggs turned around and faced them. "Are you familiar with *Béchamel?*" Several of the other girls tittered.

"No, ma'am." Margo's pencil started moving in soft sweeps on her paper.

The cooking assignments went well for the girls because the directions were very precise and complete. All week they studied the ingredients, the method, and the uses for a roux. They studied the application of a roux in different cultures and how the quality of the ingredients changed the flavor and product. On the second Friday each group of girls made a roux and followed a different application for its use in a meal.

"Yep, it's gravy," Margo announced when the fourth group prepared their roux with sausage and served it over biscuits.

"I want a kitchen like that," Kaye told Margo.

"Where are you going to put a kitchen like that?"

"In my house. Someday."

"Yeah, you and King Louie the Fourteenth. Kaye, this is pretend. It's all pretend, so they can say they tried to educate us. Don't be deceived. We're from *The Home*."

Kaye didn't answer Margo that day. She continued to visit the Home Economics room and soon gained Miss Briggs's favor. She spent every spare minute in the room that held her dreams. She pored over books of home designs and floor plans, pictures of interior rooms decorated with art, varieties of curtains and drapes. She studied stacks of magazines about fashion, furniture, and gardens.

Following Miss Briggs's syllabus, the second unit was textiles. The girls moved to the other end of the room near the sewing machines. Margo and Kaye had worked in the hand-sewing rooms at the Home so they were familiar with a needle. In their cottages during inclement weather and winter days, the young girls worked on embroidery, cross-stitching, knitting, and crocheting.

Miss Briggs appeared surprised to learn they knew much more about sewing and clothing construction than many of the other students.

As young girls Kaye and Margo learned about sewing from doing mending and hemming in the sewing room. There the more experienced women used the sewing machines. They were eager to learn in Home Economics class they would have access to patterns and they would be taught how to sew on the machines. Miss Briggs opened up a large book of clothing patterns. Margo ignored the book and sketched her own ideas, sketches of dresses and beaded jewelry designs.

One day Miss Briggs examined some of Margo's drawings. "These are beautiful, Margo. You have an eye for design. There's a prom in the spring. You could design a dress to wear to the prom."

One of the girls at the table snickered. "Miss Briggs, you have to have a date to go to the prom."

Miss Briggs flushed.

Margo understood the implication. "I like to draw and I'm not going to the ball," she sneered back at the girl. "I'm not Cinderella."

Miss Briggs examined another drawing. "Margo, this one is lovely. It could be a clasp for an evening bag. It could also be enlarged and applied on the bodice of a dress."

The room hushed. Miss Briggs paused for a moment.

"What would you girls think of planning a fashion show? We could have it in the spring. We'll model the clothing we make, and mount a display of Margo's drawings. We could invite guests and maybe serve punch and cookies. Yes!" She smiled and tapped with her pencil. "The cooking classes could make cookies. We could invite your mothers or grandmothers or a friend. If each of you would commit to make a garment appropriate to your skills, we could make this happen."

Kaye noted her teacher scanning the room of students, assessing the possibility of her vision. Half the class appeared interested. Kaye evaluated the rest of the students. She wouldn't get the other girls interested by focusing on Margo.

"Margo, I want you to continue sketching and keep all your work. I'll talk to the Future Homemakers club about planning a spring tea event. I have two senior students who need a project to achieve advanced level recognition in the F.H.A." In response to a few puzzled stares, she removed a pole from the closet and unrolled it.

"This is the FHA banner. There's a national organization for students interested in Home Economics. This poster explains we meet here in this room once a month. There's also a state and a national conference. Anyone in Home Economics class can come to the meetings.

Kaye leaned near Margo. "Look, it's during lunch hour and on the first Wednesday of the month. We could go."

Margo turned toward Kaye and raised her eyebrows.

Miss Briggs replaced the banner in the closet. "You have two weeks to choose your pattern and have your fabric here. Now let's get back to the basic skills of sewing."

Miss Briggs's enthusiasm and Kaye's positive attitude fueled a fire in Kaye and Margo. They began to think of possibilities. Margo stopped talking about pretend. She looked at those drapes with a gleam in her eye. Kaye kept thinking about the kitchen unit—*someday a home of my own, somehow.*

Kay with an e

Meet me at the tree at three on Saturday. Don't bring Jessie. I want to show you something real special. —T with an S and an e and an h

The note fell from her locker on Friday at noon. Kaye worried all night what would happen if someone saw her walking toward the ball field. She had to think of a reason to go over to that area. Toe would be disappointed if she didn't show up. Visiting hours started at one and lasted until four. There would be visitors milling about, pushing wheelchairs and walking with the person they were visiting. Toe would be watching for her. From his spot in the tree he would be able to see her walking in his direction. A basket. She could carry a basket.

Anyone seeing her might think she was off to deliver something.

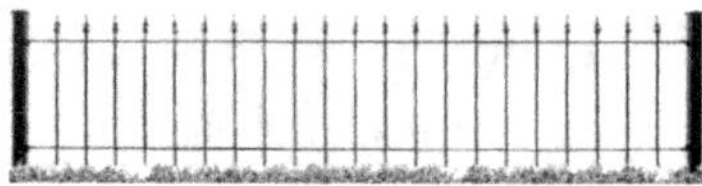

Kaye passed by the tree, then circled around and back to the other side of the tree.

"Hey, thanks for coming." The branches rustled above her head. The boughs swept to the ground on the front side, leaving an open space inside near the trunk of the tree.

"How's school going?" His voice didn't hide his excitement that she had come.

"It's all right… Toe, do you think I'm pretty?"

"Kay with an e, are you asking me or are you wanting me to tell you the truth?"

She smiled. She knew his dimple was deep and his eyes were dancing. "You're teasing me and it's not funny. Do you like high school?"

"We take field trips in ag. Hank and Mike are fun. Nobody here cares if we like it!" His voice took on an edge and the words came out in a sneer. "We just do what they tell us." He obviously didn't want to talk about school.

"If you knew Jesus you'd know He loves you. He cares."

"Kaye, that stuff may be fine for you, but I've met a few *Bible* thumpers and I'd rather trust a rattlesnake. At least they rattle and warn you. Some of the meanest guys I know quote the *Bible*. No, thank you."

"They're just wrong. Jesus doesn't want them to hurt you."

"He don't stop 'em." He didn't want to talk about that stuff either.

Kaye sighed. "They're evil, there's evil people in the world."

Toe grabbed a limb. All at once his legs were dangling in front of her. He lowered himself to the ground. Kaye brushed the falling pine needles from her hair.

"Wanna see my cow? She's a top producer. She just had her calf."

"What's her name?"

"I call her Agnes."

"I can't go to the barn. I'm a girl. Somebody'll see me and tell."

"That's why I brought this."

Toe pulled a feedbag out from under a pine tree and opened it up.

"Here, put these on."

He handed Kaye a plaid shirt, a pair of bib overalls and a baseball cap. She held the pants up.

"What if someone sees me?"

"Put them on over your clothes and don't talk. Don't say anything. Nobody'll be in the barn for another hour. They're eating ice cream at the parade grounds. Come on."

Kaye slid her feet into the pant legs and pulled on the shirt as Toe kept watch. She stepped out from under the protection of the pine boughs. Toe pulled the straps over her shoulders and buckled them.

"Stuff your hair up under the cap."

"There's not enough room."

"Then tuck it inside your shirt."

Kaye pulled her hair tight and tucked it inside the collar of her shirt, then buttoned the top button. She popped the ball cap on her head, pulling it low on her brow, and tilted her head down.

"Toe, we'll be in a world of trouble if we get caught."

"That's your job. Make sure we don't get caught," he laughed. "I thought you trusted Jesus!"

"I don't think Jesus wants folks to do dumb things."

He clutched her hand. "It's not dumb, it's my prize cow and her calf. I raised this cow." He pulled her out from under the big tree and let go of her hand. "Walk slow and stay a little away from me." He turned his back to her and started toward the barn.

They followed the road away from the grove, past second base, across the railroad tracks down by the potato field, staying in the shadows of the buildings until they reached the dairy barn.

"Toe." A man's voice called out. "What you up to?"

"Checking my calf, Mr. Green."

"Who you got with you?'

"This here's Toby. He's a friend from school. His Dad's at the harness shop. He wants to see my cow and calf."

"Don't be late for chores and get him out of the barn before four."

"Yeah, I'll do that."

Mr. Green climbed into his pickup and drove away. The dust curled from behind the tires, forming clouds.

Kaye held her breath until he was gone, then started to cough.

"Who was that? I told you we'd get caught."

"You got your feathers all ruffled and you're clucking like a fussing hen. He's gone and we're not in trouble. That's Mr. Green, he doesn't even work here anymore. He stops by sometimes. C'mon." Toe opened the gate of a small pen. Across the pen, a black and white calf wobbled on four spindly legs and struggled toward them. Toe cupped his fingers. "Here, do this and she'll suck your fingers."

Kaye hesitated. Toe clutched her hand and thrust it toward the calf. First it licked Kaye's fingers. Then it started to suck. "Yuk! Her tongue's bumpy and she's slobbering."

"Yes, she's a dandy." Toe pulled Kaye's hand away. Using his knee, he pressed the calf away from the gate and closed it behind them. "Mama's in here."

The barn smelled of animals, and the sun shining through the window cast a glow on the mounds of fresh golden straw around each cow. Kaye thought of the fairy tale about spinning straw to gold. Several cows stood in their stanchions, gazing at her with their big eyes.

"They're looking at me."

"Well then, I'd say they're smart cows." Toe grinned at her. "They're chewing their cud. Come over here. I'll introduce you."

Kaye circled the large animal and appeared in front of the cow.

Toe said, "Agnes, this is Kaye with an e. Put your hand near her nose." Kaye moved her left hand toward the cow.

"Not that one, the other hand."

"Will she bite?"

"No," Toe replied indigently. "See what she does."

Kaye paused and moved her fingers that the calf had licked toward the cow. Agnes murmured and moved forward, sniffing Kaye's fingers. She began to lick them with the largest tongue Kaye had ever seen.

"Yikes!" Kaye squeaked.

"Shhhh!" Toe gestured with his palm toward her.

"That's a big tongue."

"Top producer for three years in a row."

"That's good, right?"

"They don't get any better. C'mon. We gotta get back to the tree. We can cut behind the wagons and take the path toward the potato field and cross the tracks there.

"What happens if a train comes? Someone will see us for sure."

"If a train comes, we'll hop on it and r-i-d-e to the blue water."

"You're crazy, Seth Thomas. A person could get killed doing something like that!"

"We better get a move-on." He hurried her along.

At the tree grove Kaye slid in between the big hanging branches and into the pine sanctuary. Stuffing the bib overalls and shirt into the bag, she emerged *Kaye the girl*. "That was scary but fun. Agnes is a nice cow and she has a pretty baby."

"Like you said, no need to be afraid if Jesus is in your heart. It's a calf, not a baby cow."

"Toe, don't tease. It's not nice."

He stepped toward her, she edged back, he leaned in to kiss her, and she ducked.

"Seth Thomas, you be a gentleman!"

"You know I am, Miss Kaye with an e. See you at school."

Chapter 11

"Nurse Lucy, do you know there's a pattern for anything you want to sew?"

"Sewing is not something I learned to do."

"Didn't you have home economics?"

"Yes, but let's say sewing was not a focus of my attention in high school. I made an apron. Certainly not one anyone would wear."

"Miss Briggs, my Home Ec teacher—they don't say the whole thing, just Home Ec— she lets me come to the Home Ec room whenever I have any extra time. I straighten things up and I look at the pattern books and magazines. I showed her some of my stitches and she likes my needlework. Do you know Margo and I are the only ones in our class who can do all three—embroidery, knitting, and crochet. Margo wouldn't tell her but I told her we know how. Margo said it would be better if I didn't act so happy about Home Ec. The way the girls groan and complain, you'd think when they get married they'll have a housekeeper and hired help to run their houses."

"Maybe they will."

"There aren't that many that are rich. I wouldn't want someone keeping my house and making my family's clothes. I'm going to do that myself. I'll know how, too. I'm going to have my own home someday—after I become a nurse, a real nurse."

"Speaking of homes, did anything more come about your moving to the older girls' cottage?"

"No. I pray I won't have to leave Jessie. She's losing weight because I'm not here to feed her. I'll be off for Christmas vacation soon, and she'll get to eat then."

"Are you saying she doesn't get fed?"

"I'm not sure."

Kaye saw the fire in Nurse Lucy's eyes. She couldn't afford to have Lucy go to Hannot ready for battle. Hannot might use any excuse to move Kaye to another building. She didn't like Kaye, but Kaye knew her caring for Jessie made their work easier.

"She probably won't eat for them. Mornings are hard for her and she gets…"

"Upset?"

"She's a real fighter sometimes, but I can calm her down. We play a hand game. It works. Are you working Christmas?"

"Of course. I always work Christmas. If you want to work there will be lots to do."

"I'll be over after I feed Jessie. Thanks, Nurse Lucy."

Kaye wanted to tell Nurse Lucy about Toe but wasn't sure she should. She knew everything would change if Hannot found out.

"Heusted…should I call you Nurse Lucy or Heusted?"

"I answer to either. It doesn't matter."

"I don't want to be disrespectful. I like to call you Nurse Lucy because it reminds me that someday I could be a nurse."

Lucy smiled and patted a stack of diapers. "You would be a fine nurse."

Kaye checked the area for listening ears. Both the other workers were in the infant nursery.

"I have a friend."

"Well, I told you you'd make friends at high school. Keep up the good work."

"Uh-huh!"

Nurse Lucy didn't understand. That was probably good.

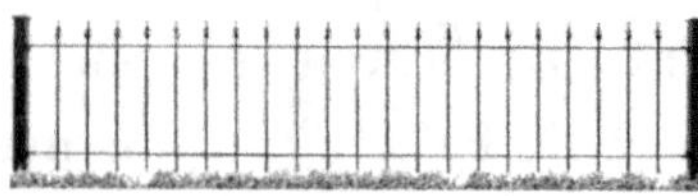

After Kaye left the nursery, Nurse Lucy continued her work, but she couldn't stop her churning thoughts.

Sending residents to high school sounded like another experiment? The questions always remained about the capabilities of the children. Is it wrong to encourage them to dream and hope for a future? They are vulnerable and society has a lot of expectations. As a nurse she understood the challenge from several perspectives and she understood the underlying desire to help them achieve and the workers' concerns. She cared about Kaye and the others going to high school. Kaye often spoke of their dreams. Graduation from high school would be an accomplishment. Yes, she knew there were residents of the Home who had gone off to the military and fought in the war and she knew there were others who would spend the rest of their lives here. Some residents were now seventy and eighty years old.

Kaye had no family to help her or encourage her dream to go to nursing school. It would be hope that would sustain her. It hurt to see the dreams in a young person's heart and know the reality of them being dashed. It's not kind. Kaye speaks about faith and hope. Lucy thought about King Herod who tried to kill hope when he tried to find the baby Jesus. God makes a way when there is no way.

Lucy Heusted cradled a child in her arms and bowed her head. "Lord, helping Kaye become a nurse is something only you can do, so I'm going to pray that you will find a way. Thank you. Amen.

"Shush, Shush little one. You're with me. I'll take care of you. Shush, Shush!" She sat down in the rocking chair. "Your mama is home with empty arms." When I go home I'll have empty arms too. Help me forgive." Her thoughts were too heavy to carry another day.

"Lord, help me.

"Shush, shush little one." The rocking chair creaked and the child slept.

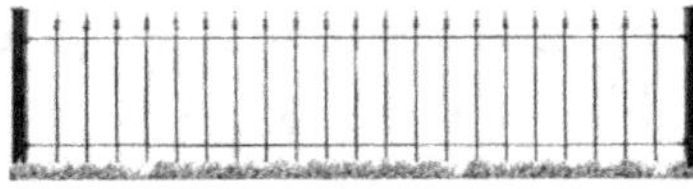

Another note lay in the bottom of her locker. Kaye clutched it tight in her fist so no one would see it. It was like holding a lit match. She could hardly wait to open it in secret.

Kaye,

See you on Christmas Eve. You will not get a chunk of coal, because I am sure you have been a good girl.

T

She tore it up into tiny pieces and flushed it down the toilet. As much as she wanted to save every note, there was nowhere safe to hide them. She had kept only one note--the one about meeting him to see his cow. That note she had folded as flat as she could and placed in under the insole of her right shoe. She also had a sale bill from the cattle auction in her notebook. Toe had left that in her locker, but she could have picked up one of those anywhere. Kaye was sure it was a picture of Agnes on the sale bill. She hadn't had a chance to talk with Toe since the sale. They had seen each other in the halls but without any classes together there should be no gossip to get back to the Home. Toe had been busy with the auction and all the ag activities and his workshop classes. Workshops were the only reason he stayed in school. Kaye knew how he loved to fix things.

Thanksgiving holiday gave way to Christmas. Families and visitors started arriving after Thanksgiving, and choirs from the local churches that came to give concerts. Several groups put on plays, the band gave a holiday concert, the folk dancing group performed, and the school children put on a Christmas play. Throughout the season most of the cottages had a Christmas tree. Sometimes it came out of a closet only when everyone was seated. Then it went back into the closet. Other cottages placed their tree on top of the piano, but there was always a risk someone would climb up to touch it and knock it down. The children made miles of colored chain from strips of paper. Kaye worked with the children in her building to make the chains and stand guard against anyone eating the mint-flavored paste. Even Jessie liked the smell of the paste.

For several days Kaye worked on a pillowcase doll for Jessie for Christmas. She tore off the hem, wet the material, and rolled it into a ball, letting it dry to form a head. She re-hemmed the skirt and embroidered flowers around the edge. She stitched a face on the head and embroidered gold curls around the face. She would have preferred yellow yarn for hair, but Jessie would probably suck and swallow it, so she compromised with tight embroidery stitches for the curls. At least she had a gift to give. Some visitors brought gifts of fruit and toys. The toys were not substantial and the parts were unsafe, so they disappeared almost as fast as they arrived. Food baskets had to be removed or monitored because the children would consume the pits, skins, and seeds. Kaye grew up watching for the children's safety; it was the way she lived and she protected her family—her family in her building.

Cook made treats through the holidays, putting everyone in a happy mood. Christmas Eve Kaye attended the church service held in the auditorium that afternoon.. She saw Toe as soon as she entered. He was on the stage, playing his cornet. Gary was there too with his drumsticks, and Leah with her flute. Kaye didn't have enough time for band practice although she loved to play. Watching them she could imagine her cornet in her hands, her fingers pressing the lever keys. The girls and boys chorus sang and after the preacher spoke, the service closed with everyone singing "Silent Night."

Toe didn't see her. She wanted to wish him Merry Christmas.

She returned to the cottage with a greater sadness than she had ever felt. Not seeing him at all was easier than seeing him and not being able to talk. When she stepped outside of the chapel Hannot was watching her.

"Cheer up, little miss sunshine. It's Christmas. Why the long sorry face?"

Kaye fought back her tears and turned away. How could Hannot know what it's like to live here? To care so much about someone you can't see or talk to. How could she ever know?

On Christmas day, Kaye fed Jessie and hurried to the nursery. Nurse Lucy had told her if she could come on Christmas Day it would be a big help as so many workers shifted hours and would be off during the holiday.

Lucy Heusted always worked during the holidays ."These are my children, of course I will be with them on Christmas."

There were remarks by other workers about why Lucy didn't want to be at home with her husband, but she dismissed them as nonsense. "He's a grown man," was always her reply.

When Kaye entered the first room in the nursery hungry children were waiting to be fed, soiled diapers needed to be changed, and the bathing had not yet started. Lucy's sleeves were rolled up to her elbows and Kaye saw only two other attendants. They worked through the morning as visitors interrupted the routine and the tasks, sending the children into restless behaviors. Lucy sent the other workers to lunch and handed Kaye a box hidden in a diaper.

"There was a package leaning against the door when I arrived this morning. It has your name on it."

Kaye took the package and glanced around to make sure the other workers had not returned. She opened the corner of the diaper to see a rectangular box wrapped in burlap with a burlap bow, probably an old feed sack. A tag hung from the bow:

To: Kaye O'Shay from Santa.

Kaye smiled. It was Toe's writing.

Nurse Lucy couldn't hide her eagerness. "Well, open it! Let's see what Santa brought."

Kay removed the folded burlap, and inside was a wooden box. The wood was so shiny it glistened. She turned it over. "There's no lid." She shook it. "There's something inside."

Nurse Lucy took the box from her and turned it over. "Oh look, the lid slides like this." She handed the box back to Kaye, who pushed the lid farther back.

"It's a sewing kit." Kaye removed a pair of embroidery scissors, a paper holding a needle, three skeins of embroidery floss—red, yellow, and blue —a pincushion made of rolled strips of burlap that looked more like a tiny ball.

"I guess Santa knows you like to embroider."

"I guess he does." Kaye grinned. "I better wrap this back up." She hurried to encase it in the diaper. A real Christmas gift made for her. Scissors and needles? Joy turned to fear, and her stomach churned.

"Nurse Lucy, I can't take this back to my cottage. I'd have to turn it in to the office and if I do…" She paused. "I might never see it again."

Kaye understood the risk. If Hannot knew this was hers and a gift from someone. There would be no peace until she found out who was the giver. Kaye would never tell. Never.

"Nurse Lucy, could you take it?"

"Are you sure you can't have it?"

"Yes I'm sure. If I lived at the big girls cottage maybe I could, but not living in the cottage with younger kids like Jessie."

"No, I won't take it." She patted Kaye's arm. "But I'll keep it for you."

Kaye sighed. Maybe… maybe someday she would have it back.

"You haven't opened your gift from us."

"You brought me a gift?"

"Yes, it's in my car, I have to wait until my lunch break. Let's take our break together."

"I have to go feed Jessie. I'll come back after I put her down for her nap."

When Kaye returned Nurse Lucy handed her a long box. The other workers came to watch. Each carried a child. Their work didn't pause for gift giving.

Kaye read the card:

To Kaye, from the nursery staff.

Merry Christmas.

She opened the box to find two new skirts, a pair of new blouses, a couple of sweaters, and penny loafers with four pair of white socks. As Kaye removed each item she became more overwhelmed. She controlled the tears that threatened until she lifted the shoes. Her shoulders began shaking. "You did this for *me*? All of you did this for *me*?"

"For you." Nurse Lucy patted her shoulder. "We wanted to do something special because you're working so hard every day and going to high school."

Kaye folded the clothes up carefully and placed each item back into the box. "Thank you."

"You're welcome," they chimed together.

She circled the group giving each worker a hug, even the reluctant one who didn't hug back.

Early New Year's Eve day, Kaye arrived at the nursery the same time the milk delivery arrived. Toe appeared from behind the milk cans.

"Milk for the babies?"

"Yes, sir, we need milk for the babies." Kaye glanced around to search for anyone observing. She could trust Nurse Lucy but there was no one she knew who didn't gossip both truth and lies. She moved up next to the building into the shadows.

"How come you're here?"

"The delivery man wanted today off, and I said I'd bring up the early delivery." He removed a milk can from the cart.

"Thank you for the sewing kit."

"How did you know it was from me?" He removed the second can.

"You're my Santa," she giggled.

Toe ducked into the shadows and reached out to pinch her cheek.

"That I am," he whispered. "Did you read the lid?"

"No, was there something on the lid?"

"On the underside of the lid."

Kaye couldn't hide her disappointment. "No, I didn't."

"Well, now you know it's there, you can read it."

"Yes, I will. You were careful, and didn't write anything that can cause trouble?" She couldn't tell him she didn't have the box. He'd think that she didn't like it.

"Nah! You worry too much. I wrote it in Latin."

"Toe, I can't read Latin!"

"If I tell you what it means you'll get upset. I know you. Better that you wonder."

"That's not kind."

"Something wrong?"

"No, but I have to go inside. Somebody will be looking for me. Happy New Year, Toe."

She couldn't tell him the truth. Now she'd never know what was written on the inside of that lid.

Chapter 12

Nine days since Christmas. Nine long days of no notes and only once has she seen Toe. Kaye sprinkled powder on a diaper and drew a heart with her finger. She missed seeing his quirky smile with the dimple tucked into his cheek. He always found something to tease her about.

"Nurse Lucy, why is everyone so crabby? It's still Christmas."

"There's lots of reasons; the kids get excited when there's changes in the routine, or when visitors are around, and the staff quarrel about the schedule. Then there are the children who go on leave with their families for a day or two. It upsets them; even the ones who understand and want to go, know it will be different."

"I hope the families understand." Kaye snuggled Heidi against her as she rocked in the chair.

"Sad to say, some do not. When the child misbehaves, they take that as a confirmation the child should not be at home." Lucy could not hide her concerns.

"If they went home more often then it wouldn't be strange," Kaye mumbled as she tucked a clean blanket around the sleeping child.

"We cannot know the heartbreak of the families, Kaye. We must never judge them. Our task is to love the children and care for them. It's a privilege we've been given. I appreciate how you've worked extra this week. It's especially helpful because you know so many of the children."

"I know them all." Kaye placed the child from her arms into her crib.

"Yes, you do." Nurse Lucy smiled back at Kaye's insisting stare.

"Did you enjoy Christmas vacation?"

"I missed seeing the kids at school. I didn't think I would." Kaye smoothed a towel she was folding.

"Have you seen the carpenter?" Nurse Lucy was careful no one was around who would hear her comment.

Kaye grinned. "No. No carpenters until school starts." She shouldn't talk with Nurse Lucy about Toe. Someone might hear. "Did you know I'll have new classes when we go back? They call this a semester break."

"Yes, I forgot to tell you about that."

"No one tells us anything. It's like here, except here we have the rumors. There, everybody else knows." Kaye fumbled with a safety pin. "I have the same English teacher but it's English number two."

"What other classes do you have?"

"Home-Ec, I asked for that. I hope I get Miss Briggs. There's one other teacher, Mrs. Martlow, she's older. I have math, history, biology, gym, a study hall and, oh, I think it's Spanish. I don't know why I need that. But no way was I taking Latin. Toe has Latin and it's really hard." His name slipped out before she thought. Oh well, what of it? He's one of the students, and everybody knows he's going to high school, too. That didn't explain why her cheeks felt so warm.

"I think Spanish would be easier. It sounds like you'll be busy. Have you joined any groups?"

"They don't want us in their groups."

"Kaye, I'm sorry it's hard. I'd hoped you'd make some friends."

"I guess I've made a couple. I'm glad Margo's going. She knows how to handle things. One girl threatened to fight her in the bathroom, and Margo stepped toward her, then walked right on past. The girl just stood there. No one said anything. I think they thought Margo would beat her up. Margo's really strong, and when she gets that look in her eye, the one that says she's not afraid of anything, nobody's sure what to expect. They call her Pocahontas behind her back. Nobody bothers her since that day, and nobody bothers me when she's around."

"Has anybody threatened you?"

"No, they just say mean things about being a retard when I walk by or when I'm helping one of our kids. I pretend I don't hear them."

Nurse Lucy sighed. "Life shouldn't be made harder, high school's hard enough."

Kaye twirled a diaper and snapped it toward the cupboard. "Nurse Lucy, do you know what it means to say, 'live like a dog?' That's what one of the school kids said to Johnny. He said, 'How can you expect him to be smart when he lives like a dog out there?' After he said that, I went right up to him and asked what he meant by that. He said, 'It means living behind a fence and being fed scraps.' People don't know what it's like here. They just guess. The people who live here live in a house, sleep in a bed, and eat regular meals. This is our home, we live here. At first, I was afraid to go anywhere else. Then I found out that I probably wouldn't ever leave. Now they send me to high school. It's so confusing!"

Nurse Lucy laughed. "I think you have the right idea, Kaye. Don't try to figure it out. In this life we're offered many surprises. It's good that we know Jesus and he's with us in every situation. Here we can pray and sing to the children and help them have a better day."

"I'm tired. Is it okay if I go now?"

"You start school on Monday?"

"Yes."

"I work Tuesday so come over as soon as you can and tell me about second semester."

Kaye nodded and left. Two more days and she'd see Toe. She must think about what to say if he asked her about the sewing box, she couldn't tell him the truth. Not telling him the truth made it hard to look forward to seeing him. Her stomach churned. She always tried to tell the truth.

Kaye snuggled into her bed, but when she took her second deep breath, Jessie was beside her, her arm wedged under Kaye's and her head pressing against Kaye's shoulder.

1955

Kaye placed her schedule in the inside cover of her notebook. She couldn't believe her good fortune, another semester with Mrs. Turkle! Earning an A last semester proved she could do high school English. Kaye circled around the open door and panicked. The only empty seat was in the next to last row— beside Toe. Last semester, they decided by mutual agreement not to acknowledge each other when they passed in the hallway. It had not occurred to her that Toe might be in one of her classes. She smoothed her skirt and slipped into the chair. The bell rang and Mrs. Turkle stood up from her desk.

Sonny hissed from behind them. "Keep the retards together." The boys who tagged along behind him snickered. Sonny was a known bully who took delight in picking on shy or poor children.

Toe clenched his fists so hard he snapped his pencil. Kaye covered a new pencil with the palm of her hand and slid it across to the edge of her desk. Toe picked it up without looking at her.

Mrs. Turkle called the roll. "I'm glad to see some of my last semester students." She smiled at Kaye and began to explain the course. "This semester we will meet some of the authors of classic literature and we will discuss their literary styles. There will be a quiz each Friday and a paper due every four weeks. We will study several authors." She pointed to the black board where she had listed the focus of the class:

1. *We will study about the period when the authors wrote.*

2. *Explore the meaning of their work.*

3. *Study the impact of their work as it relates to modern society.*

4. *We will also begin an introduction to the works of Shakespeare.*

Sonny began to complain. "I don't get this. Why do we need to know about someone who's been dead that long?"

Several students chuckled, encouraging his challenge.

Mrs. Turkle turned to Kaye. "Miss O'Shay, do you understand the assignment?"

"Yes, I think so."

Turning to Sonny, Mrs. Turkle said, "Sonny, if you would like to remain after class, perhaps Kaye can offer you some assistance with the assignment."

"Ain't no retard Home kid helping me!"

Before Sonny could take a breath, Toe bolted from his chair and spun around; chairs tumbled and students scattered as Toe grabbed the front of Sonny's shirt, sliding him up the wall until his feet dangled helplessly off the floor. Toe and Sonny were eye to eye.

Sonny's switchblade knife opened with a *click* and echoed in the silent room. Toe switched hands like a magician, placing his right hand on Sonny's throat, grabbing Sonny's right wrist with his own left hand, and squeezed. Everyone watched Sonny's face deepen to a brick red as he gasped for breath. The knife fell to the floor.

Toe loosened his grip as Sonny's color faded to pale.

Toe continued to face Sonny. "If you ever insult Miss O'Shay again, I will pop your head clean off yer neck." Toe shook his hand causing Sonny's head to bob twice. "Apologize to her!" Toe loosened his grip, allowing Sonny's feet to drop to the floor.

As soon as his feet touched, Sonny lunged for his knife.

Toe's left boot slammed down on Sonny's right wrist, pressing hard. Sonny remained bent in half and cursed. He released the knife. Again, Toe clutched Sonny's shirtfront and slid him up the wall. At that moment, Mr. Weston, the principal, appeared in the doorway.

"Apologize to her," Toe demanded once again.

"Yeah!" Sonny glared at Toe.

Mr. Weston stepped into the room. "Boys, come with me!" His voice boomed. "Right now! Both of you!"

Kaye tried to watch everything, Mrs. Turkle, the other kids, Sonny's friends, Toe, and Mr. Weston. A fight, exactly what Toe said would happen. He didn't fight but that wouldn't matter. It'd be called a fight and he'd be expelled or worse. Maybe Toe wouldn't be allowed to come back to school. Sonny and his friends might get mean and beat Toe up. Kaye shuddered. They all depended on protection from Toe. Even if he didn't get expelled, he'd be in one fight after another until everything he had said would happen, happened. It wasn't fair. This was all her fault. She wanted to stay calm, but it was so frightening. Her stomach knotted in anguish as she waited.

Sonny went out into the hallway. Toe handed Mr. Weston the knife and followed Sonny toward the office.

The kids in the classroom moved their chairs back into rows and Mrs. Turkle continued.

At the end of class, Kaye gazed out the window. Sonny was sitting on the low brick retaining wall across the street, smoking a cigarette. Toe had not returned. Her fears multiplied. If the principal called Dr. Helmsley, Toe could lose his job in the dairy barn. Kaye folded the note she intended to slide into Toe's locker. It read, *I'm sorry.*

Out in the hallway, some boys wearing leather jackets mumbled they would get even for Sonny. But no one said anything to her. She passed Toe's locker, sliding the note between the louvers. There was no note in her locker.

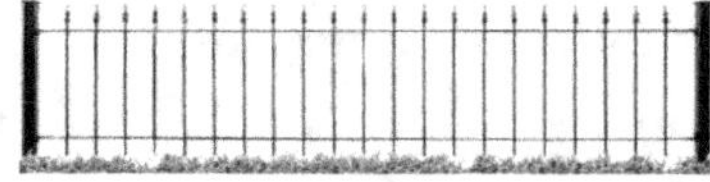

The next day Toe stepped in behind her on the way to second hour. "Kaye, don't turn around. Everything is okay. He was real nice. Don't worry. Did you read the box lid yet?"

"The box lid?" She feared he was suspended or worse and he wanted to talk about that box lid. She forced herself to stare at the floor and not say the things she had worried about. She shook her head.

There must be a way to find out what Toe had written on that box lid. Everyone feared Sonny's gang except Toe. Another fight and he'd be expelled for sure, and he wanted her to read Latin.

<h1 style="text-align:center">Chapter 13</h1>

The incident with Sonny didn't end with the trip to Mr. Weston's office. Instead, the rivalry with Sonny's gang continued with remarks in the hallway about the farm boys having "cars so slow they couldn't outrun a tractor," calling them "rural rutters'" and "mule pushers."

"If you guys want to go to the prom, you better leave home in February to get there by May."

"Your dates don't know whether to wear buckskin or carry a flashing caution light."

"A farm boy can't dance because their boots are sticky."

The threat of a rumble continued until they agreed to settle it with a drag race.

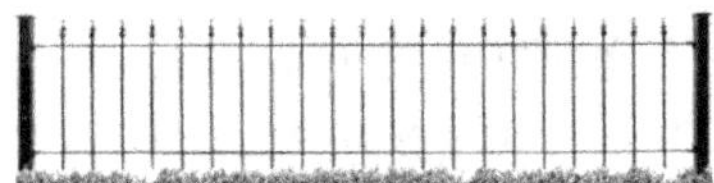

Kaye twirled Jessie's braids around her fingers, standing with her back to the pine tree. "Do you know how worried I've been?" she said into the pine boughs. "All you say is it's fine. I don't know what happened."

"If you calm down, I'll tell you. I explained to Mr. Weston we didn't have a fight because no one took a swing. Mr. Weston decided to take Sonny's knife, suspended him for two days, and told him not to bring another knife to school. I stayed in Mr. Weston's office for the remainder of the hour."

"Don't you realize how worried I was?" Kaye asked.

"You waste a lot of time worrying. Mr. Weston and I had a fine game of cribbage."

"You what?"

"We had a game of cribbage. I beat him too." Toe laughed.

125

"Well, that's just swell, but what are you going to do about the drag race?"

"Oh, you heard about that?"

"Everybody's heard about that, it's all over school! The girls are all talking about it. Those jokes about going to the prom with farm boys are getting ugly. They're saying the farm boys need to ask their dates in February because their tractors are so slow. Then there are the jokes about them getting the chores done in time to take a bath and how all the farm boys can't dance because of something about their boots. It just goes on and on."

Toe couldn't stifle his laughter over Kaye's provocation.

"Toe, everything's a mess and it feels like our kids are in the middle. Can the farm boys win a drag race?"

"No, I don't think so. They can't win a drag race because no one has a car that can compete with Sonny's. They say it's the fastest car in three counties."

"So, that's it? No race?"

"As far as I know—which half do you want?" Toe produced a Mounds bar, displaying both halves.

"You're silly, they're both the same."

"Are you sure?" Toe's question was firm, but then he laughed, tossed her a piece, and ran down the other side of the hill toward the barn.

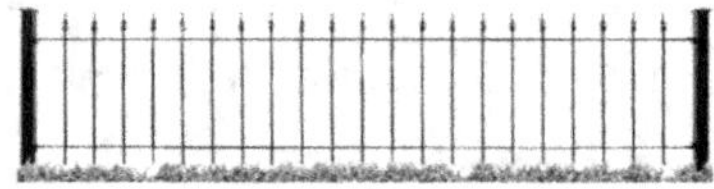

A pickup rolled down Farm Lane, the dirt road alongside the railroad tracks at the back entrance of the State Home. The driver pulled up to the gate.

"Hey, mister! Can we see Seth? He works in the barn."

"Seth?" The attendant pushed his hat back on his head.

"Yeah, he goes to high school."

"Oh, you mean Toe." He turned toward another man. "Hey, you run over to the barn and get Toe. Tell him some boys are here, and they want to see him."

The boys waited in the cab of the pickup. Soon Seth appeared jogging toward them.

Mike Trott and Hank Dempsey climbed out of the pickup. He recognized them from school. They were farm boys from north of town. Mike's dad had a dairy farm. Mike talked about their farm and was active in the ag group. Hank worked on his dad's farm because it was expected, and his dad needed him.

"Seth, we wondered if you could help us."

"You're not talking about that drag race, are you? I don't have a car."

"We got a car." Mike rubbed his jaw and kicked at the dirt.

Toe studied the boys. "It's not enough to have a car, you have to have a car that can win."

"That's why we're here."

"The guys in auto-mechanics class all say you know engines. Mr. Cossack, the teacher, says so too. We have a car. It needs a little engine work to win, and we want you to help us get it ready."

"I can't just go off and work on a car. I work here!" Toe gestured toward the barns. "Where'd you guys get a car?"

Hank pulled at a piece of oat grass, broke it in half, and stuck the sweet stem into his mouth.

"It's like this. It's about more than a race. Those guys are insulting our girls about dating farm boys. My brother Bud got drafted just after he bought his 54 Ford Custom. It's parked in the horse barn. He's in basic training at Fort Knox. If he knew what was going on here, he'd want us to use his car."

"You can't mess with an engine in a guy's car because you *think* he would want you to. I can't be a part of that."

Hank tossed the oat stem into the grass, his exasperation fuming. "He's in basic training, I *can't* call him and ask."

Toe turned to walk away. "Besides, I don't go to the prom. Mr. Cossack said his Uncle Bill used to race cars. Why don't you go talk to him?"

"Used to race cars. Seth, he's an old man. He's gotta be forty." Hank pressed on.

"If I can get Bud's okay, will you work on the car?"

"I'll think about it. You make sure it's all right with him."

"We don't have much time. The challenge is for the Friday before the prom."

"That's two weeks. Let me know what you find out."

"Toe," came a shout from the barn. "Get back here and quit your jawing!" Ollie was stomping toward them waving his pitchfork.

Toe turned away from the fence. The pickup was throwing up a cloud of dust by the time Ollie reached the gate.

"I'm hearing you're talking to fellers about cooking up a drag race. Don't forget you works for me, and you ain't going anywhere but this here barn."

"That's right, Ollie, I works for you." Toe reached for Ollie's pitchfork. "Here, I'll carry that back."

Ollie adjusted his hat and resumed his usual swagger.

The following Saturday Mr. Dorman was covering for Ollie. He stopped by after chores.

"Hey Toe! A man by the name of Cossack called and requested Seth Thomas to work for him today. I told him okay, from nine to four. He'll be by to pick you up."

Toe shrugged. He'd never been allowed day work before.

A red pickup pulled up to the back gate at nine. The driver gave Seth a big smile and said, "Those buddies of yours can be convincing." Toe climbed into the cab of the truck.

Hank was straddling the floor gearshift. "My brother said go ahead and use his car."

Toe eyed him with curiosity. "I'm not sure we can beat Sonny's car. The guys in auto-shop class all talked about his engine."

Hank interrupted, bubbling with enthusiasm. "We drove Bud's car over to Uncle Bill's tool shed. He's letting us use his machine shop. It's the best around."

The pickup rolled down a country road, the driver and the three boys bouncing against each other. They turned into the driveway and stopped at the toolshed. Hank pulled each door open. Parked inside stood a waxed and spotless 1954 black Ford custom sedan. Toe's gaze moved from the car, around the walls of tools and workbenches.

"I've never seen a shop like this." His eyes wide with excitement. They worked throughout the day. Guys ran to the parts stores and brought back food.

Uncle Bill made a telephone call to Mr. Dorman: "I'm gonna need this boy for a couple more hours. I'll bring him back by nine tonight. Say, can I pick him up about seven tomorrow? We gotta get the work done before the rain. Yeah! Thanks."

By Sunday night they had a few minor changes left to complete. They all agreed Seth was the best engine man they knew. Even Uncle Bill said the engine sounded real nice.

They knew the quarter mile time for Sonny's car and they were sure they could beat it, but they didn't have a driver.

"Seth," Hank called out, and the others nodded.

Wiping his hands on a rag, Seth replied, "I don't even have a driver's license. I'm not driving."

"You drove it in the timing test."

"That's different, it's testing. No, I'm not driving."

Sandy, Bud's girlfriend, stepped up in front of the hood twirling the fuzzy dice she'd removed from the rearview mirror, announced, "I'll drive."

"Uh, no." Hank grabbed the dice from her hand and leaned near so only she could hear. "I'm gonna be in enough trouble when Bud finds out about this. Don't you say a word."

"If you let me drive, I won't tell," Sandy teased.

"When we win, the whole town will know and I'm sure the news will travel all the way to Fort Knox with or without your help. No! Bud'd really kill me if I let you behind the wheel."

The whole town did hear about the race coming up, but no one knew what car the farm boys planned to use.

When Hank's dad came out to the Cossack farm, the boys lifted the hood.

"You boys are gonna get somebody killed in that. Hank, are you sure Bud told you it was okay to load this car up for sport?"

Hank eyed Toe. He had lied to Toe, but he didn't want to lie to his dad.

"Dad, Bud would be the first one in line to fight if he ever heard what they've been saying about the farm boys.

Hank's dad nodded. "You better be sure. That's all I got to say.

Uncle Bill walked around the car, using his shirtsleeve to rub a spot here and a spot there.

"Uncle Bill, will you drive for us?" the group chorused. His eyes gleamed as he gazed at the car.

"She sure looks stock. You've done a great job on it. Let me take it out and I'll let you know."

He was gone about fifteen minutes, returned with a smile on his face, and waving a checkered flag in his hand. A shout went up from the group.

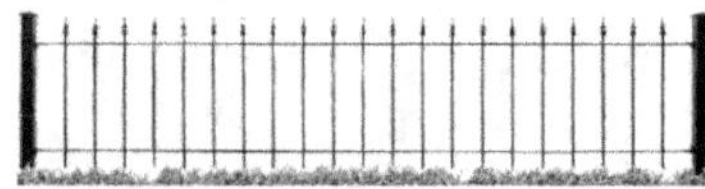

Sonny and his pack of greasers continued their harassment throughout prom week, certain the farm boys could not come up with a competitive car. By Friday night the local cars were cruising Main Street, waxed and shining, hubcaps glistening, whitewalls without a mark. Mufflers bellowed powerful chugs. At eight o'clock every car left town and headed for Dally Road.

Some kids placed road-closed barricades at both ends of the mile.

Cars lined up in the hay field shining their lights the length of the quarter mile and the finish line. There were kids sitting on the roofs and the hoods of cars. High school students were everywhere. Sonny turned off the highway. Guys scrambled to move the orange barricade for him to pass. He rode with his arm angled out the driver's window and one hand on the steering wheel. The car rolled down Dally Road past the anxious observers. The road was used so often for racing someone had painted the start and finish lines with permanent paint. The car rolled toward the starting line like an adder moving through deep green grass. Sonny took a long drag on a cigarette and tossed the butt out the window.

The crowd shifted their focus from Sonny to a black Ford custom turning from the highway onto Dally Road.

It was a few minutes before someone called out, "That's Bud's car."

"That's nothing. It's a stock box," Sonny yelled as several of his gang called out jeers.

Uncle Bill pulled up shy of the starting line. Hank and Mike jumped from the car and removed the caps from the straight exhaust extensions on each side. The crowd on the strip came to life when Uncle Bill revved the engine and rolled up to the painted marks.

Sonny's head whipped to the right to see the car that pulled up beside him. His face paled and his forehead beaded with sweat. He glared at Uncle Bill, spat out the window, and grasped the steering wheel with both hands.

The crowd hushed on cue as they watched a boy step between the cars. He raised his hands high above his head and yelled out, "On the count of three." He counted "One… two…three." Both arms lowered abruptly. Tires squealed and blue smoke rolled across the blacktop. Sonny's car danced as his engine roared and his tires searched for road to grasp.

Uncle Bill released the clutch and pressed the gas pedal with the precision of a skilled driver maneuvering to gain the maximum out of first gear.

Sonny's crowd started a mocking chant. "He's gonna blow that engine. He's gonna blow it."

At his tachometer's red line, Sonny shifted into second gear with a lurch and a thrust. He lost fractions of a second, as Uncle Bill roared past.

When Uncle Bill caressed the clutch and gas pedal into second gear, he moved a bumper length into the lead.

Sonny had used up his advantage in first and second gear.

In third gear, Uncle Bill finished the quarter mile winning by half a car length. Sonny left the strip, his tires screaming.

The farm boys claimed their victory.

He was not there for the race, but the fame of Seth's mechanical skill spread far and wide. He refused to accept any credit, but everyone knew Uncle Bill's machine shop could only do so much and to soup up an engine you need the engine man, a good machine shop, and an experienced driver.

The taunting stopped for the Home kids. Through Toe, they gained a new status.

On Sunday night at 8 o'clock, Hank waited in the living room with the whole family for Bud's weekly call from Fort Knox. Dad made Hank answer the phone.

"Hey, Bud, it's Hank. I oh…"

"Go ahead, tell 'im!" Dad's command was firm and not without anger.

"I ah, we sorta pepped up your car and we drag raced Sonny Travis." Hank held the receiver away from his ear waiting for the cursing he expected to hear.

When no sounds emerged he placed the receiver back to his ear.

"What'd you say?" Hank waited, unsure what to expect, then he began to nod.

"Yeah, we won. You bet your boots we won." Astonished, Hank gasped for breath. "Yeah, man," he started to laugh uncontrollably "Yeah, we sure did!"

His dad grabbed the phone.

"Bud, you there?"

"What'd you say?" Hank's Dad started to chuckle. He said, "If you hadn't won, he'd have come home and beat you all up. He says he's in shape to do it, too."

"Hey, Hank, he wants to talk to you." Dad handed Hank the phone.

Hank listened intently.

"What'd he say?" Dad asked.

Hank cupped his hand over the receiver. "He says, "nobody drives his car until he gets home!"

Hank removed his hand. "Hey, I promise you, Bud, it's back in the horse barn. Nobody'll drive that sweet car until you're home, that's a promise."

"Bye, Bud, and thanks. See you in a couple weeks."

Hank hung up the receiver grinning like a kid.

Ollie came into the barn drunk. So drunk he could hardly stand up. Toe pulled him back to his truck, pushed him inside, and locked the door. Then he watched as Ollie slid down onto the floor, found an empty bottle, hugged it, and passed out.

"Sleep it off, old man," Toe said, and walked back to the barn.

After chores, Toe went out to the truck and checked on Ollie. He continued to sleep. Toe went to his cottage to check in with Mr. Groves, the night shift attendant.

"Now I can check your name off and everybody's in. Get to bed, Toe."

"Mr. Groves, I gotta a cow having a calf tonight. I need to check on her in a couple hours. Will you be up?"

"No, I won't be up. I just said everybody's in bed. I saw Ollie's truck parked out there; he can check on her. You go to bed."

"Mr. Groves, Ollie has lots of work to do tonight with the records and all, he asked me to check on her."

"I said, Ollie's here and he'll check on her. Go to bed, Toe."

Toe waited in his bed. He heard the clock downstairs strike eleven, then twelve. The house was quiet. He crept down the stairs and tried the door. It was locked. He tried the back door. The back door was locked too. He could hear every pitch of snoring men. He pulled out his jackknife, tinkered in the keyhole until it made a twirl sound and clicked. He turned the knob left, slid the door open and headed for the barn.

The cow was in hard labor and moaning. It didn't look good. He wouldn't be able to get the calf out alone. He ran to the end of the barn, grabbed the rope, and dropped it beside the cow. Then he ran out to Ollie's truck and banged on the door.

"Ollie, get up. I need your help. Its number 84. The calf's hung up. Wake up, Ollie! Wake up!"

Ollie opened the truck door and stumbled out swinging both fists. Two empty liquor bottles tumbled to the ground behind him. "You no good stupid fool. Leave me alone. I ought to pound the crap out of you just for being stupid."

"Ollie, stop it!" Toe pleaded. "I need your help!" Toe struggled to wrap his arms around Ollie as he grappled to restrain his flailing arms. Then he picked him up, carrying him sidewise like a log on his hip, and headed for the cow trough. He plunged Ollie's head into the cold water. Toe's usual restraint lost the battle with his anger, and he dunked Ollie into the tank a second time. Ollie came up sputtering and swinging.

"What the Sam—"

Toe held Ollie upright. Ollie was cursing and wiping the cold water off his face with his sleeve.

"You're an imbecile, Toe," Ollie said speaking through his shirtsleeve, then he started laughing an evil hysterical laugh. "Just like your mama.

You don't even know who your mama is, do ya? You stupid fool! She's over in the nursery. Her name is Jackie. Your daddy raped an imbecile and here you are thinking you're so all high and mighty."

Toe grabbed Ollie by the front of his shirt and threw him into the water tank.

Ollie was sobering up. He scrambled out of the tank cursing and struggling. He continued to fall as his unsteady legs and intoxicated body failed to respond to any efforts toward coordinated activity.

Toe could hear him stumbling and banging onto the earth as he tried to follow him.

Toe rounded the corner and ran down the alley of the barn. He saw the cow first, and then the gutter filled with blood pumping from the cow. The calf half protruded from her body, one leg and a rump. Toe rushed to the cow's side as her breathing diminished, then stopped. He held her head and wept. Ollie stumbled down the alley carrying a pitchfork.

When he saw Toe at the cow's side he yelled.

"You killed her. You stupid imbecile. You killed her. Why didn't you come and get me? Don't you know…. That's a prize cow. Stupid, you're stupid."

Toe stood. Ollie lifted the fork. Toe cocked his fist. A crack sounded as it connected with Ollie's jaw, knocking him out cold as he fell into the blood-filled gutter.

Better to walk away. Better to walk away. Toe looked down at Ollie's clothes covered with water from the cattle tank and now soaking up blood from the cow.

Toe knew it was better to leave the barn now. He couldn't be sure what he'd do if he stayed.

Chapter 14

"Thanks for coming."

"I can't stay. It's too cold today for Jessie."

"Yeah, Ben's waiting down in the dugout. Did you hear about the drag race?"

"No, what happened?"

"We won, hands down. Our car…"

Kaye struggled to restrain her impulse to pull down a branch to look up into the tree. Toe's words spilled out in bursts of excitement. It would be fun to see his smiling face and shining eyes.

"That machine shop of Uncle Billy's was something. There were tools of every kind."

"I'm glad you won, they won. I have to go back."

"Kaye with an e, Thanks for coming!" A package of fruit-flavored gum sailed out of the tree and landed near her feet.

"Thanks, Toe."

"What's wrong? Is something wrong?"

"Nothing you can change."

"What? Tell me?"

"It's the stupid prom." Kaye fussed around Jessie, tucking in her wrap and picking up the gum with a fluttering gesture. "I've heard about it for weeks. Their dresses. Their hair. Now it's over, and I'm still hearing about it." Her voice grew soft. "I'll never go to a prom."

He heard only fractions of each word.

Kay moved Jessie's chair away from the tree.

Toe landed with a thud on the ground behind her.

"Stop, Kaye."

"You stop! Don't you see what you've done? Get back before someone sees us." Kaye's voice shrieked as she strained to keep it in the range of a whisper.

Toe grabbed a limb, swinging his leg over it and perched again in the tree. "Talk."

"It's more." Kaye turned to her left toward the hospital. "Jimmy thinks he's going to be a famous drummer and play in a big band. Margo talks about going to New York to be a fashion designer, like the ones in the magazines. What will happen to them when they find out nothing is going to be different? That we will all live here!" She could no longer hold back the tears, the evidence of her suffering.

"Come here, come inside the tree. Kaye, please, Jessie's okay."

Kaye pushed Jessie's chair toward the backside of the tree and ducked into the seclusion provided by the pendulous boughs.

Toe eased down to the ground to stand near her. "I know how you feel. I helped the guys win a drag race. The boys brought me a jacket of my own as a thank you. I can't wear it. I have to leave it at school. Last week I lost number eighty-four, when she was calving. It was awful and she was a beauty. Ollie blamed me. I hate Thursdays. Every week Ollie works Thursday night shift. He picks up his chicken feed at the mill, then comes to work and stays til after midnight. When he's sober he works hard but when he's not.... The names he called me, the things he said." Toe pounded his fist against the trunk of the tree.

A breeze coursed through the tree, offering a gentle hush.

Kaye touched his arm. "I'm sorry, Toe."

"Kaye—"

She interrupted him. "So, what do we do, just keep acting like puppets when they pull our strings?" Kaye moved her arms and legs as though a puppeteer manipulated them.

Toe reached up to knock down the pretend strings. "No. We'll keep going until we figure it out. Anyway, you're too young to go to the prom."

"I'm fifteen."

"You're still too young. Next year, I'll take you to the prom." He pulled her against him. "If there's any way, I'll take you to the prom. I promise."

His breath was warm against her hair. He pressed his cheek against her forehead and held her in his arms. Her thoughts raced between exhilaration and fear, this man-boy who pulled her to him with so much confidence.

He jerked back. "Ben's waving, somebody's coming. I gotta go."

Kaye broke away, kneeled, and crawled out from under the boughs and huddled on the ground near Jessie's chair. Her breath came in gasps as Toe ran down the backside of the hill toward the potato field. She clutched her coat around her. But the fears of being discovered did not diminish the joy of Toe's arms holding her.

Kaye pushed Jessie's chair toward the nursery. She would circle back to their cottage from the far path.

Seth Thomas had made her a promise and held her in his arms.

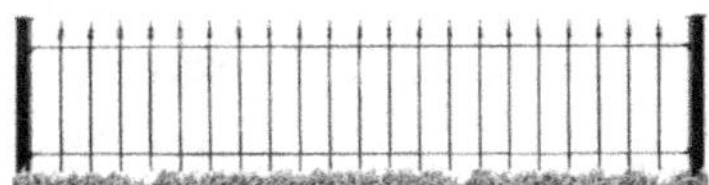

Monday at school Kaye's thoughts turned over and over about Toe's embrace and their stolen moments together. She knew when she saw him in English class she'd blush. If she thought about the class and the assignment, maybe that would help. After each class she checked her locker, but no note tumbled out. Maybe he was being nice yesterday. Perhaps he felt sorry for the other kids when she told him of their dreams. Maybe he was sad about #84 and needed someone to hold. It could not happen again. She couldn't let it happen again.

Kaye saw Margo in the hallway. High school had its troubles for Margo, but she seemed to know how to handle them. She was pretty and tough; she didn't even respond when some of the kids teased her and called her Margo-Pocahontas. In American history class one of the boys called her Margo-Sacagawea. Kaye thought he was flirting until she watched Margo move in, her face inches from his. With her eyes glistening and her jaw set.

She said, "You're a good history student. It's prudent that you know about American Indians." She hovered over him. "It may save your life someday."

The boy's face paled as he backed into his chair. Kaye stifled her amazement. If he was flirting with Margo or making fun of her, the odds had just reversed, and he now understood the wisdom of fear. He had just encountered his first strong woman.

The story of Margo's threat passed through school with the lightning speed of gossip. Within minutes they were talking about what kind of knife she carried and if she really scalped people. The rumors both alarmed and amused Kaye.

Thoughts of Toe were still racing through Kaye's mind as she sat in home economics class, unaware of Margo beside her, until she nudged Kaye and spoke.

"Kaye, can I tell you a secret?" Margo whispered as the teacher handed out sheets of information about clothing construction.

"Girls, be sure you put these in your notebook. You will notice the words underlined. These terms will be on the exam." Mrs. Briggs continued to circle the room placing the pages in front of each student.

"Sure. What's up?" Kaye whispered.

"Do you know Sonny, the boy that sits on the wall across the street and smokes cigarettes?"

"Yeah." Kaye waited for Margo to go on.

"He likes me."

Kaye turned to see Margo roll her eyes and kiss her fingertips.

"Are you…." Kaye's reply was more impertinent than she intended.

"He's not a boy, he's a man. He gave me a cigarette today. Besides, you've got Seth."

Fear gripped Kaye. "That's a secret!"

"Girls, quiet. Pay attention," Mrs. Briggs scolded.

Margo wrinkled her nose, wrote a note, and turned it for Kaye to read: *"I mean he really likes me."*

Kaye nodded at Margo and pulled the paper near to write back. *"Be careful. Rumors can be dangerous."* She turned the note back to Margo.

At that moment Mrs. Briggs snatched up the note, read it, and threw it away. "Please do not waste my time with your romances." The other girls giggled. The thought of girls from the Home having a romance appeared entertaining to them. Kaye winced from anger. Margo ignored their mirth, pulled a page from her sketchpad, and proceeded to draw a picture of her riding in Sonny's car, waving a tomahawk out the window.

What Margo had said, jolted her. Margo had to know about Sonny's gang and what could happen if school rumors went back to the Home.

For Kaye and Margo, the school year ended in a mutual silent agreement.

June passed into July. The farm work required every hand to be available and the cooking and preserving required as many as possible in the kitchens. Summer brought added work to every facility. Working people ate heartily, and the summer weather brought visitors.

The fourth of July was celebrated with the parade in town and the band from the Home also marched in it. Lunch in the picnic area at the Home followed the parade, and employees and residents enjoyed the traditional ice cream social with fresh strawberries. There were games for the kids. The chorus sang and folk dancers danced. The ball game was rained out that afternoon and rescheduled for the following Sunday.

It had been several days since Kaye had seen Toe. Ben brought milk to the nursery a few mornings but Toe didn't come. After the first ball game on Sunday and the crowd started to disperse, Kaye pushed Jessie's chair up the side hill toward the big pine tree.

Jessie banged on the arms of her chair, disturbed by the rough ride. Kaye stopped to linger and stroke the pine boughs. She knew Toe would be here if he could. Her restless thoughts teased her mind. The sun had moved on to the western sky. It's too near chore time. She patted Jessie's arm. "It's okay Jessie. I just wanted to hear the birds. Can you hear the birds? If you are real quiet, you can hear them."

"That Jessie can't hear nothing. What're you doing way up here?" Hannot was stomping up the hill.

"I like to take her outside for walks."

"She don't know. You get back down to the buildings and stop wandering around near the woods. You hear me?'

"Yes, ma'am," Kaye murmured.

Hannot turned and trudged back down the hill waving her arms and yelling orders toward the other attendants and children. Her bowed knees caused her uniform to flop in white waves around her legs.

"Round up your kids, get them rounded up," she yelled at everyone under her command.

Kaye smoothed Jessie's hair and tucked the blanket around her. Clouds moving across the sun had chilled the air.

"Do you know how blue the sky is when I am with you?" Toe lay on his back between the trees looking at the sky.

"How long have you been there?"

"About two seconds. Good she didn't see me, eh?"

"You got that right. Besides, you're silly. The sky is always blue." Kaye tucked her feet up under herself and leaned against the stroller.

"No, sometimes it's gray." Toe turned toward her. "But it's always a beautiful blue when I'm with you."

"It was a beautiful day." Kaye smiled at Toe and touched the sleeve of his shirt.

"You choose, it's your turn." Toe removed the wrapper from a candy bar and laid the cardboard tray on top of the wrapper.

"Toe, it's a Mounds bar, it's already divided. This is our third Mounds bar and our seventh candy bar picnic." Waves of fragrance from wild honeysuckle encircled them.

"Someday, we'll go on a real picnic. When we get to the water, we'll have fried chicken." He licked his lips.

"Boys always think about food. Are you still hungry?"

Toe lowered his eyes to the candy. "You choose, one piece is always bigger. That's a mathematical fact, and besides, I love you, Kaye O'Shay."

Kaye paused, her hand over the two pieces of candy bar. She looked up, moving her eyes from his chest to his chin, then to his face. He did love her. She was only fifteen but there was absolutely no doubt.

"Kaye, will you marry me?" Toe spoke the words quickly, reaching out to touch one of her fluttering curls.

She sighed, picked up a piece of the candy bar, and placed it on his lips. "I don't know when or how, Seth Thomas, but yes, I will marry you."

He reached out for her hand. "I really want to kiss you."

"I really want you to, but we won't, will we?" She attempted to press the candy between his lips.

He snatched it away. "For you, Miss Kaye O'Shay, we will do everything proper, and someday I'll build you a house. We'll have a family of our own. I'll work hard, Kaye. You'll be proud you married me. Everybody says I'm a hard worker. I want to work for us. All I need to know is that you want to be married to me. You won't ever be sorry… I'm going to kiss you."

"No, you promised." Kaye jumped up and squared her shoulders. "You will be a gentleman, Mr. Seth Thomas, just like you promised."

Ben galloped up the hill pretending to be a cowboy riding a horse, and then he galloped down the far side.

"You gotta go. I think Hannot's coming back."

Kaye scurried to push Jessie out from behind the tree and toward the buildings. Hannot was cutting across the clearing again, waving her arms.

"I'm telling you, girl, you can't be out here wandering around. I told you to get back to the cottage an hour ago."

"Yes ma'am."

"Is there some attraction out there I need to know about?"

"No ma'am. I found a cocoon and some pinecones." Kaye held out her empty fisted hand.

"Put those sticky things down. You'll have pine pitch all over your clothes."

Hannot pushed Kaye's shoulder trying to force her to hurry. "I'm going to the kitchen. You go along."

Kaye's feet glided down the hill and Jessie's chair seemed to float, too.

She was going to marry Seth Thomas.

Chapter 15

The first day of school was chaotic. New freshmen arrived from numerous one-room country schools spread over the county. Many harbored the same glazed look. They were overwhelmed with the complexity of class schedules and the sea of students. The six students from the Home returned to the brick building with the familiarity obtained through having a previous year of experience. Last year's concerns now exchanged for new worries. Every one of them shared the same concerns. Would the advancing classes be more difficult? If they worked hard, could they continue at high school and someday graduate?

Kaye didn't see Toe the first day. The combination of her schedule and making sure the other Home students found their rooms and lockers and books required all her spare time between classes.

"I did it, Kaye! I made it to second chair flute!" Leah scurried past Kaye on her way to class.

"Good for you. I knew you could do it!" Kaye wanted Leah to enjoy school. During the summer the band instructor at the Home had worked with Leah in private lessons. The individual instruction had proved beneficial. It became evident that the more Leah concentrated on her flute the less likely the spasms of her arm occurred.

Later in the day Gary tugged Kaye's sleeve. The hallway was crowded, and Kaye hadn't noticed him edging up beside her.

"Kaye, wanna meet for lunch?'

"I'm sorry. I can't today. Why don't you sit with me on the bus after school and you can tell me about your day."

"Terrific, Kaye, there's going to be lots to tell." He clapped his hands together and rushed on, his short legs carrying his happy little body through the mass of students.

Margo and Sonny strolled along the hallway, oblivious to anyone else. They were laughing and talking. Kaye didn't want to think about their future, but she couldn't help it. For two volatile people like that, they were certain to have a difficult romance—if one at all. They might one day hop into Sonny's car and be gone. Then Sonny would have committed a crime and Margo would be a runaway. Secretly Kaye was concerned that some bounty hunter would try to find Margo and get the reward, even though Nurse Lucy said that was gossip and a rumor, that it was not true.

Between seventh and eighth hour, Kaye opened the door of her locker and a note tumbled down.

> *K with an e.*
>
> *Can you shop for flowers tomorrow during lunch?*
>
> *S*

Kaye rushed to the restroom to destroy the note, flushing it away. Shop for flowers, shop for flowers, over and over Kaye tried to understand what Toe meant.

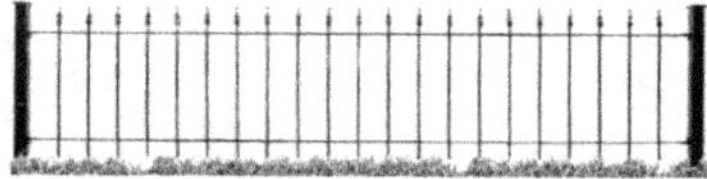

After school, the bus circled the driveway. Gary chatted about his day and tapped out a rhythm on his math book with his drumsticks. As the bus turned the corner, *Wilkins Flower Shop* sign came into view. The stone building was located north of the high school, on a side street. She'd been there once, when they'd ordered a corsage for Mrs. Briggs for the fashions show last spring, and she'd gone with Margo to pick it up. If Toe meant the flower shop, it would be away from the high school and away from the other kids who walked downtown during their lunch hour.

Gary asked a question, startling Kaye from her wandering thoughts.

"I'm sorry Gary, what did you ask?"

Johnny raised his hand. "Kaye, I'm a biology helper. I clean up the lab during my study hour. Mr. Ponteski says, 'Johnny, you are a good helper.'"

"That's wonderful news, Johnny! What did you ask, Gary?"

"I asked you if you had seen Seth. I wondered if he came back to school."

"No, I've not seen him. But I'm sure he came back to school."

"That's good for you cause he's your boyfriend, huh?"

Kaye panicked. "No, Gary, Seth goes to school, and he lives at the Home. That's all."

Gary snickered, his hand covering his mouth. "Everybody knows." Gary made a heart in the air and wrote *S T and K O*. He rolled his eyes and giggled.

"You're being silly. You better stop if you want to sit with me."

"Okay, Kaye, I was teasing you. I guess you don't think it's funny, huh?"

"No, saying things about boyfriends is not funny, Gary."

The next day Kaye left the school building at lunchtime and rounded the corner of the flower shop. The windows facing the side street had sheer tieback curtains showcasing flowers in vases on display and flower arrangements in teacups. Toe was waiting at the far end of the porch. When she was near enough to hear, he said. "Follow behind me. We're going up the hill."

Kaye followed, near enough to talk yet far enough behind to avoid suspicion of them being together. Toe entered the gates of the cemetery, and when he was sure no one was following, he turned around to face her.

"Hi." He smiled at her. How she had missed his smile! His face was tanned darker than she had ever seen it. His blue shirt was open at the neck. His chest and shoulders were wider, and he was taller.

"Hi."

He looked around, restless, cracking his knuckles.

"Is school going okay?"

"Yes. Is it okay for you?"

"I like some classes. The other ones are for fodders."

"Fodders?"

"Yeah, fodders. People who don't want to work."

"There's a lot of kinds of work."

"Farming is the only work I want. My herd and my milk production."

His cows again. "Do all farm boys only think about cows?'

"No." He laughed. "Some think about chickens and others about pigs."

"Oh, stop teasing."

"What to Home ed girls think about?"

"Well, it's not cows and pigs."

"I'll bet it is."

"I say no!"

"You study about how to cook them."

"That's different."

"How are the other kids doing?"

Just like Toe to be concerned about the other kids. Kaye walked around a tall monument, reading the names.

"They're doing well. I worry about Margo. She's flirting with Sonny, and I think he's trouble with a capital T."

"Yeah, I heard about that." Toe laughed. "I think Sonny has met his match in Margo. I'd wager she could whip him. And I bet he knows it."

"I don't think… well I don't want to talk about them."

"We can probably meet here on Mondays if you want. It doesn't look like anybody is around. Are you still my girl?"

"Once a week? I get to see you once a week?"

"Better than nothing."

"Will you still leave notes in my locker?"

"Every day. What do you do with them?"

Kaye wanted to say she kept them, put them in a special place so she could unfold them, read them, refold them, and put them away. That she held them in her hands and thought of him and all the things she wanted to tell him. And that she wanted him to kiss her. She put her hands to her rose-colored cheeks.

"I rip them up into pieces and flush them down the toilet as soon as I read them."

Toe pulled her hands away from her face as tears welled up in her eyes. "It'll be better someday. It's hard now because we're young. Someday I'll write you a letter you can keep, and you'll write me a letter I can keep, and someday all this will be history."

"I'm not sad. I'm happy. It's my eyes that lie."

"Yeah, sometimes my eyes lie too." Toe paused.

"We gotta go back. You leave first and I'll wait a bit, then I'll go. You go back the way you came, and I'll go between the greenhouses and through the ball field. See you next Monday." He kissed the tips of her fingers, pressed both her hands together, and held them between his.

Kaye focused her eyes on the sky. She could not look at him. She didn't want to leave. He let go of her hands and stepped away. She touched the monument to steady herself. The stone felt cold and damp.

"Seth Thomas, I am forever your girl," Kaye whispered, then forced herself to pass through the black gates and leave their granite garden. But she wasn't sure what it meant to be his girl. All they had were Monday's flushed notes, and promises.

On the bus Monday morning Kaye shared her Saturday experience with Margo.

"Saturday wasn't like I thought it would be."

"Oh, you did day work." Margo pulled a nail file from her notebook to fix a ragged nail.

"Yes. One of the doctors asked Heusted if she knew of someone who could help his wife Saturday and she recommended me. He put in a request and picked me up at the gate at 9.

"What did you do?"

"I thought you ironed clothes, so I figured I'd iron. But that woman kept me running all day. I went from one chore to another. She didn't let me finish anything. She wanted me to clean a room, and then she wanted me to play with the little girls. Then she sent me to the bathroom to clean it. Once she stopped me in the middle of something to go outside and pick a bouquet of flowers for the table. In the afternoon she had a couple women over for tea and introduced me as her hired girl. She said, 'The Home girls are getting better, the new director is trying to educate them.'"

Margo interrupted. "You shoulda told me you were out. I coulda helped you. It's not always easy. You've gotta know a few things."

"Well, I don't need to know now. I'm not doing that again." Kaye stared ahead.

"Some folks pay good. You learn. You don't do good work for the ones that don't pay. They won't ask for you again. You'll figure it out."

"I said I'm not going back."

"That's a good job, working for a doctor's wife. Every man is not, well, some you have to stay near the missus. When did she count the silver?"

"How did you know that?" Kaye searched Margo's face. "I felt dirty, like a thief."

"I've been working out since I was twelve. That's almost four years, weekdays and summers. The only ones that don't count the silver are the ones that don't have any."

"They can have their lace curtains and their blasted silver. They all deserve each other."

The bus rolled up in front of the high school and the door creaked open.

"It's okay, you'll get used to it. Let's talk before you work out again."

"I won't! Ever!"

<h1 style="text-align:center">Chapter 16</h1>

Toe searched in the Home store for a gift for Kaye. He wanted something special. Nothing could make her prettier to him. Thoughts of her filled his days and his nights. The warm summer nights he lay in his bed knowing if he tried to see her it could mean trouble for both of them.

More people were arriving every day. He'd heard the staff grumbling. Every existing cottage housed more than the allotted capacity of one hundred and more cottages were under construction. The farm cook complained there were too many mouths to feed three meals a day. Toe's mind returned to the task at hand. Something for Kaye.

There were lots of things in the store at the Home, items of wood and leather. There were hand-made lace items, knitted scarves and mittens, embroidered items, and objects made of pottery and metal. There were less expensive items too, small trinkets and toys. But nothing attracted him. Besides, he didn't have any earnings.

Ollie refused to let him accept any day work to earn money. He said, "You don't smoke so you don't need any money. Besides, those old farmers are afraid of you, you're big and strong. They think if you're in here you're probably ticked in the head and you could hurt somebody or kill them, maybe somebody in their house. They want scrawny guys they can push to work hard and ones that look like they don't eat much."

In despair, Toe left the store and returned to the dairy barns that loomed at the end of the road. The men were gathering; it was time to start the milking.

A dark blue car pulled past him and glided to a stop at the back gate. The driver rolled down his window to talk with Ollie who was leaning up against a nearby tree and chewing on a piece of timothy grass. It was Mr. Clyde and his wife Mabel. Toe walked by the passenger side of the car. His shirttail fluttered behind him, always too short to stay tucked in, his shirtsleeves rolled up to his elbow revealing his muscled and tanned forearms. He heard Mr. Clyde offer his customary small talk.

"Hey Ollie, how's production? And how's that new bull?"

Miss Mabel snugged tight against her car door. She rolled her window down and called to Toe.

"Hello there, do you milk the cows too?"

Toe turned to face the car. "You talking to me?"

"Why, yes I am." She smiled. "Your arms look strong, like you do a lot of work here."

She's a blinking her eyes like she's got dust in 'em. "Yes ma'am, I do. There's a lot of work to do."

"I'm sure there is. Tell me about the herd. Is it really the best?"

Toe didn't want to boast but he never missed an opportunity to tell anyone who would listen about the merits of the herd. "Yes, ma'am, they're a mighty fine herd. The *best* in the state if you ask me."

She gazed up at him, threading her fingers around and through the strands of a beaded necklace.

Ollie frowned at Toe over the roof of the car and interrupted their conversation. "Toe, open the gate. Mr. Clyde's on his way out."

"Miss Mabel, pleased to see you today." Toe tapped his forehead, nodded, and then opened the gate.

Miss Mabel smiled but it wasn't a happy smile. It left him a bit unsettled. Toe wondered why folks were uneasy around him. He wished they'd laugh and joke like they do with the other guys. But she seemed suspicious. That's it. She acted like she knew something, something secret.

When Toe arrived at the barn the men were chuckling and taunting.

"That Missus of Clyde's, she's a looker," said one of the men.

Toe ignored their foolishness, started milking, and drifted into his own thoughts. Ollie entered the barn, kicking at the straw and mumbling to himself. Ollie could be really mean sometimes. Doc, who took care of the horse barn, said, "Ollie gets thirsty, that's what makes him mean." That didn't make sense to Toe. There was a tin cup and plenty of cold water in the milk house.

Ollie knew a lot of things. Toe wondered if he lied about knowing stuff he didn't know. Doc said, "Ollie's cat has a long tail."

They were almost finished milking when Ollie returned to the barn. His mood had changed, and he started teasing.

"Toe, I thought ole Mabel was either going to pull apart those pearls on her neck or chase you straight to the hay mow."

"Ollie, you talk nonsense. Is that what was on her necklace? Pearls? I thought they were beads."

Louie passed between them. "Yeah, Toe, them were pearls all right, they come from oysters. A grit of sand gets into the oyster shell and that oyster turns it into a pearl. It takes a while, but they come out real pretty, like something that don't belong and turns out to be something special. When I was in the merchant marines, I saw lots of them pearls at the ports on the China Sea."

"Louie, you ain't ever been to the China Sea."

"Toe, you don't know for sure, do ya?" Louie grinned and spat tobacco juice into the gutter.

Toe thought about those pearls. He thought he understood what Ollie meant about Mabel and the hay mow. He didn't need trouble like that. Besides he had a girl. But he and his girl were like the pearls Louie talked about. *They* didn't belong here. If a grain of sand could become something special, there was a chance that he could become something. And Kaye, she was special already, but he hoped someday they would have their dream.

That night, as Toe worked on his homework at the kitchen table, he asked Cook, "Cook, do you know about pearls?"

"I thought you were doing your homework."

"I am. I was just wondering about pearls."

"If you don't have pearls in your homework, you don't be needing to know about them." She wiped the last pan dry and placed it under the sink.

"I saw Miss Mabel today and she was wearing pearls. I don't know if I can believe Louie, he was saying something about an oyster and a piece of sand."

"I don't know about a piece of sand, but I know what the Good Book says about pearls."

"What's that?"

"Well sir, in Proverbs it talks about wisdom being the pearl of great price. And in the gospel in Matthew, it talks about a man searching for fine pearls, and on finding one of great value, he sold all he had and bought it. So, I guess they are valuable. What got you so interested in pearls tonight?"

"They were pretty, that's all."

"You won't find many pearls around here. You best get your homework done and get to bed."

"Yes ma'am."

At high school the next day, a girl was wearing a blouse she said she made in home economics class. She twirled around to show her friends, it had pearl color buttons down the front. They were creamy and white, round on top. They looked like those pearls Miss Mabel was threading through her fingers yesterday.

Toe stepped into the home economics room during lunch.

"Mrs. Briggs, my name is Seth Thomas."

"Well, hello, Seth. Now what brings you to the home economics room?

"You don't know me, but I was wondering if you had any pearl buttons for sale? I'm looking for one round on the top."

"I have a few buttons left from projects."

"Yes, Ma'am. But do you have a pearl button?"

"Let me see." She opened a cigar box of assorted buttons and scooped out a handful pouring them into a pile onto her desk. She pushed them around, sorting them with her forefinger, finding a cluster of pearl buttons. "Anything there you can use?"

"I don't have much money, Mrs. Briggs. How much does a pearl button cost?"

"Seth, these are left over. I don't think there are any that match. There's nothing they could be used for excepting to replace another button. You can have one. Just pick out what you think might work."

He sorted through the pile of flat buttons until he found a round button that looked like a pearl if you didn't look too close and see the shank on the back. "This one's nice."

"It's yours if you want it."

"Thanks, Mrs. Briggs."

"You're welcome, Seth. Do you need a needle and thread?"

"No ma'am this button is not a sewing on kind of button." He rolled it through his fingers. It felt creamy and smooth as he slid it deep into his pocket.

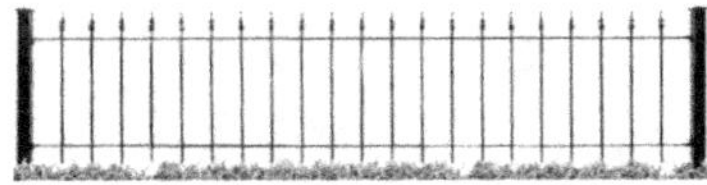

At the barn that night while he milked the cows Toe searched for something he could braid into a band or cord to hold the pearl. He wanted to make a necklace for Kaye. The strands from the hay rope would be too rough. He looked at the twine. It was too course and brittle. The cord from the feedbags was cotton and broke too easy unless they were thick. He left the dairy barn captured in thoughts about strings and twine. Doc walked into the horse barn leading one of the mares. She swung her tail, knocking Toe's hat off his head.

"Jumping jiggers! Hey, Doc, Doc!" Toe called. "Doc, can I have some horse hair?"

"Toe, what'd you want with horse hair? It's as itchy as all get out."

"No, Doc, I want horse *tail* hair. White horse tail hair! 'Bout a dozen nice long ones would be fine."

Doc put the mare in her stall, looked at Toe, and shook his head. He motioned for Toe to follow.

"The whites are here. They all look white, but they have color. I'll cut a bunch and you can sort out the whitest." He took out his pocketknife and slid his hand along the mare's flank talking to her as he moved. He fanned his hand out over her tail, separated several strands, and lifting the topmost away, cut some strands from underneath with his knife.

"What you gonna do with this here horse tail hair? Are you tying fishing flies? You know some are lighter than others, they float better."

"No, Doc," Toe said, grinning. "I'm fishing, but I don't want to catch no flies. Thanks."

Doc shook his head. "Toe, you always up to sumptin. I'm a wondering what you gonna do with horse hair but I don't wanna ask, in case I don't wanna know."

Doc chuckled and closed the stall gate behind the mare.

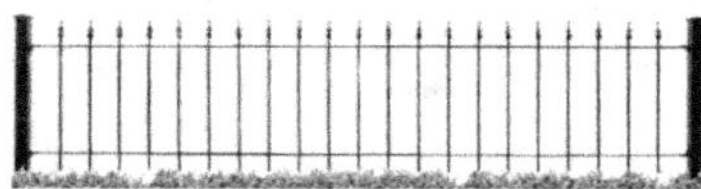

Toe worked hours perfecting the pattern. He used strands of grass to design a flat woven cord. He sorted the horsetail hair until he found a couple that were translucent. He covered a board with feed sack material and used fine wire nails to create an intricate pattern. He carried the horsetail fibers out into the sunshine to sort for color and to see if some would catch sun and reflect the light more than others. He used a file and filed the edges of the button shank, and, folding the hair in half to mark the center, he threaded it through and started weaving each way from the button. He worked on the braiding evenings at the day room table as he listened to the recording of Shakespeare's *Romeo and Juliet*. One of the college student attendants had brought in a copy of the latest recording made by RCA in 1950.

When the necklace was long enough, he used the technique Doc had taught him to repair the hay ropes. The ropes had to move smoothly on pulleys, so they had to be joined without burls of ridges. The ends were woven into each other; the transition from one to another became perfectly smooth. And the tug from each end tightened the splice. He finished it late on Sunday, and Monday morning he wrapped it in the lush green of a Milkweed leaf, tied it with a cord, and inserted a sprig of blue wild aster. He carried it to school in a brown paper bag.

At lunch hour it began to sprinkle. The leaves were shades of brown and gold. Some still clung to the trees. Others had surrendered and covered the walk with slippery copper foliage.

Toe waited until they reached the flat gray stone to the left of the gate and handed her the sack.

"I made you something."

Kaye removed the leaf bundle from the sack, unwrapped it, and passed the cord through her fingers until she held the pearl in her hand.

"Hold it to the light," he instructed. "Well, there's not much sunshine today, but in the light the cord almost sparkles."

She stroked her cheek with the button, and then rubbed it with her fingers.

"This is lovely, Toe. It's smooth and creamy white. Did you make it for me?"

Toe shuffled his feet. "I did make it for you, but it's for us too. Do you know about pearls?"

Kaye looked up into his eyes. He found it very hard to remember what it was he wanted to tell her.

"The pearl?" she asked.

"Yeah! I didn't know about pearls until I saw a lady wearing a necklace of pearls and I learned about how they're made. They cost a lot of money, the real ones. They're a precious jewel. Oysters make pearls from a piece of sand that gets into their shell. The sand, well, it shouldn't be there, but the oyster makes it into a pearl. It's like us. We don't belong where we are but we can become something special. That's why it's for us."

He reached down, removed the necklace from her hand, and slipped it over her head. Their eyes met. It was the closest they had been since that day he held her under the pine tree.

Kaye pulled away. "Toe, someone could be watching."

"Let them watch."

He kissed her forehead.

"I'll wear it always, Toe. Thank you."

1956

"Kaye, you can't bring another child into the nursery. We have to protect the children from infections," said Nurse Lucy.

Kaye moved Jessie's wheelchair forward and back in a rocking motion.

"I know, but I wanted you to meet my Jessie. I wanted you to see her, so you'd know who she is." Kaye pushed Jessie's leg down and tucked her dress around her legs.

"Hello, Jessie," Nurse Lucy whispered and touched Jessie's arm.

Jessie lunged forward. From behind the chair, Kaye grabbed a handful of Jessie's hair, holding firm, to prevent her from biting Nurse Lucy.

Oh, don't act bad Jessie. Please let her like you.

Nurse Lucy drew back and scowled at Kaye. "Well, now I've met Jessie. Return her to her cottage and hurry back. We have work to do."

"Yes, Nurse Lucy." Kaye whirled Jessie's chair around and struggled to push it along the sidewalk and back to their cottage.

Immediately upon her return to the nursery, she approached Nurse Lucy.

"Do you think Jessie could come here to live? I mean could she be on the list. You know, somehow?"

"No, Kaye, she's fine residing in the cottage where she lives."

"She's not, though. I'm going to high school and she's only eating supper. I have to leave before breakfast and I'm not here for lunch. I know she's not eating because her clothes are so loose. She's getting thin. She doesn't walk at all anymore. Besides, I have to know she'll be cared for when, when—" Kaye stammered, until the words spilled out. "When I die."

"Kaye, my goodness, you're too young to die! Don't talk nonsense." Nurse Lucy laid a diaper under Thornton, pulled it up between his legs, pinned it in place, and pulled a pair of pants up to his waist.

"I think I am." Kaye's eyes filled with tears. "Nurse Lucy, it's all red." She sniffed and rubbed her nose. "I'm bleeding and I'm dying. It hasn't stopped for three days."

"Kaye, how old are you?"

"I'm sixteen."

"Um," Lucy placed Thornton onto a mat and took Kaye's hand. "Honey, you're not dying, you're a woman now. That's all. When a girl grows up her body changes. It's just your body changing."

"When will it be changed?" Kaye's eyes scanned her body.

"It'll happen every month. Women folks call it their monthly."

"Every month, and I won't die?"

"Did you ask your worker for some pads to wear between your legs?"

"No," Kaye said horrified. "I didn't tell anybody. I heard Maude say if Jessie starts bleeding, they'll take her to the hospital and fix her. I don't want to go to the hospital. She said they'd take her parts. What parts are they talking about, Nurse Lucy?"

"Only parts she won't need. Don't you worry about that, I'll get some pads for you."

The next day, Kaye worried all afternoon at school; someone would discover her secret. She worried that she would leave a spot on a chair, or everyone would know when the cramps got so bad, they pulled her hands to her stomach. It didn't seem right that she would bleed and that it was normal. Other people bled and died. At least Nurse Lucy didn't make fun of her. If she used pads from the nursery no one at the cottage would need to know. It wasn't right to have to go to the hospital and have your parts taken if it was an ordinary thing. Either it wasn't normal and she might die or it was normal and if Hannot found out she would see to it that Kaye was sent to the hospital to lose her parts. She didn't tell anyone at her cottage.

She didn't want to meet Toe on Monday, she feared bleeding more because she walked all the way to the cemetery. No, it wasn't worth the risk. He'll just have to understand sometimes she can't come.

Her worries loomed larger now. Everything she had heard about this bleeding was filled with stories and fears. Remarks about smelling bad from the blood.

Her concerns about Jessie were well founded. Not being there to feed her three meals a day was evident in her diminished frame. Jessie was sleeping more and didn't enjoy being outside as much as she used to. Any bumps with her chair caused her to flail her arms and rock her head in pain.

Kaye's list of worries continued to grow as she feared for not only herself but also Margo and Toe.

Margo careening around town with Sonny at lunchtime and now everyone was talking. It wouldn't be long before that would get back to the supervisor of her building. They may not let her finish school even if her grades are good. Sonny wasn't a good person, but he treated Margo nice, and she was happy.

Toe always had something troubling him; something he was trying to pretend didn't matter. He shared his concerns about the herd and

Ben. His grades were good on his last report card. He studied a lot, but he didn't have a study hall.

There was no one who understood what all this bleeding meant for her.

She had to find a way to get some vitamins for Jessie. Nurse Lucy always said a dose of vitamins couldn't hurt.

Chapter 17

"Your going to school ain't working for the rest of us. You're only here to milk morning and night. The rest of the time you're huddled over a book or doin' something for school." Ollie poked at the hay in the manger with his pitchfork. "That Ben, he's always in the other barns. He only comes in here at milking time."

"I told him to keep busy when I'm not here. He took me out to the potato field and showed me where he had hoed. The other men say he works hard."

"I don't like his work and I don't like your going to school. You're so high and mighty. Maybe I should put Ben in lockdown for a few days."

"What he'd do?"

Ollie snorted and spat, "Well, I haven't decided yet. But I'm sure it'll be something real bad."

"Ollie, don't do that."

"Somebody's got to do the work and you're going to school." He sneered, twisting his mouth at the word *school*.

"Are you saying if I quit school Ben 'll be okay?"

"You might get that idea. I'm not sure that's what I said." Ollie rubbed his chin.

After Ollie left the barn, Ben came out from the box stall where he had watched. He could read lips so well he knew everything Ollie had said.

Toe tried to study that night. He worked on his English paper. Each page ended up in the wastebasket. He couldn't tell anyone what Ollie had said. He knew Ollie could get both him and Ben in trouble. If he quit school Mr. Helmsley would be mad and so would Mr. Kent, the ag teacher. If he kept going to school Ollie could lock up Ben and that would destroy him. He couldn't take being locked up.

Toe didn't sleep that night. He wanted to believe Dr. Helmsley would protect Ben, if he told him the truth. If he didn't, Toe didn't want to think of the consequences. Even going to school the next day, after what Ollie said, could leave Ben in danger. He had to stay near to protect Ben. He had to find a way to quit school. A way Dr. Helmsley would believe.

Ben rolled over and sat up on the side of his bed. He could see Toe was not in the bed next to him. He found Toe in his closet studying. He tapped Toe on the shoulder and picked up the geometry book. Ben had been working on the problems with Toe each night. Ben pointed to the book and shook his head. Then he lifted his hand up, palm open.

"You're right. If I stop going to school, you stop learning too. But I don't want you to get hurt."

Ben raised his arms and flexed his muscles, in a gesture of strength. Toe laughed.

"Yeah, you're strong all right, but Ollie has power."

Ben tapped the book with his fist. He picked up Toe by the front of his shirt and put the book into his hand. Then thrust him back down into the chair.

"I know, you're right. But it's a risk." Ben left the closet, his decision made. Toe dropped his face into his hands. Ben had just said he could face whatever was necessary for his friend to go to high school. The price of friendship was not too high for Ben, but Toe couldn't stop his own fears. The price was too high for Toe; he couldn't risk Ben being destroyed. He would find a way to protect Ben or quit school.

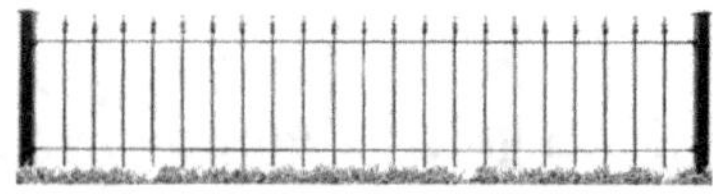

The wind whipped the icy sleet against her face and her thin coat grew heavy as it absorbed the water. Kaye's feet were wet and caked with ice as she walked. Battling against the first severe winter storm of the season, she willed her body forward until she reached her building.

"Child, get out of those clothes. I say, that working at the nursery after supper is not necessary," Alwerk, a part-time attendant, sputtered.

Kaye removed her coat and boots. "They were short of help due to the storm. I told Nurse Lucy I'd come back after supper. Is Jessie okay? She wouldn't eat any supper?"

Before anyone could answer Kaye ran up the stairs.

"Kaye, come back!" Alwerk pounded up the stairs behind her.

Kaye stopped in the middle of the room. Jessie's bed was stripped down to the blue ticking on the mattress cover. The bare mattress carried one message.

"Where's Jessie?" Kaye screamed. "Where's Jessie?"

The other girls awakened, and some started to cry in response to Kaye's screams.

Alwerk tried to calm her. "Kaye, honey, it was Jessie's time. You know it happens." Two other workers came running up the stairs.

"No, you should've taken her to the hospital if she was sick! Why didn't you do something?"

"There was nothing we could do honey. She slipped away. She just went to sleep."

"You didn't check her?" Kaye was shouting, her voice echoing around the room. "I can't stay here!" She ran down the stairs, grabbed her coat and bolted out the door before anyone could stop her. Her tears mixed with the sleet freezing on her cheeks. Hollow. She felt hollow. A part of her was missing. The part that snuggled against her every night. The part that woke her, played with her hair, and understood so much more than anyone thought. Jessie. Jessie was gone. Nothing remained that said Jessie had lived there. That Jessie had laughed and played here. Or that she had a friend named Kaye.

Alwerk watched from the doorway. Kaye was going into the nursery. She would send someone over to get her.

Kaye's mind tried to refuse the information. Her body operated by moving forward wherever it would take her. The castle loomed on her right. Would she die if she lay down in the snow? It sounded good to die and be away. All the promises of the hereafter had to be better than hurting this much.

Pictures of everything about Jessie were dancing in her mind. Leaving her to go to high school, working in the nursery, Jessie's doll she made for her, the one toy that never left her side, the box of ribbons Kaye kept to put in Jessie's hair. At once Kaye stopped, halted by the words she could not speak.) Had Jessie died of intentional neglect or unintentional, the result was the same.

Her eyes were red from crying, her hair tousled and wet from the raging storm. The back door of the nursery banged shut behind her. Nurse Lucy appeared, responding to the loud noise. Seeing Kaye in disarray, she rushed toward her.

"Kaye, what's wrong?"

Kaye fell into her arms and between sobs told of her sorrow. "It's Jessie! She… she was fine when I came back after lunch."

"No, no, Kaye. I'm sure no one harmed Jessie." Nurse Lucy stroked Kaye's wet hair and guided her to a chair. "You know, breathing problems can come on fast. Kaye I'm sorry, try to tell yourself she's in a better place."

"I don't want her in a better place! I want her here. I want her with me!"

"Try to think about how God would look at this situation."

Nurse Lucy continued trying to calm Kaye until she could no longer avoid her duties.

"I'll call someone to walk you back to your building."

"No, please no. I'll go back now. I'll be okay. I'll hurry."

"No, don't go out into the night alone. Wait a few minutes, I have a relief nurse coming. When she gets here, I'll drop you off at your cottage on my way home."

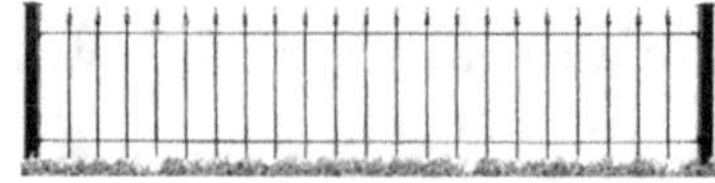

When Kaye arrived back to her building, everything was in an uproar.

"Where have you been?" Deters, the part-time night worker, was shaking her finger at Kaye. "I've had workers looking for you. You didn't eat any supper either."

"I ran over to the nursery; I left my homework there." Kaye rubbed her eyes to push the tears away.

"I fail to see how high school is going to put you on easy street anytime soon," the worker grumbled. Deters had the most amazing ability to know everyone's business, and although she was usually harmless, her remarks tonight struck Kaye as unkind.

Kaye sat down on the bottom step and closed her eyes. "I can't go up there."

"You don't have to just now."

"No, I mean I don't want to go up there at all."

"You can sit in the day room for a little spell. Then go up. You know folks pass." Deters lowered her voice. "That's how it is. When you're ready I'll go up with you."

"I can't look at Jessie's bed and know she's never coming back."

"You know she was doing poorly."

"No, she was getting better, she was taking vitamins, and she had gained some weight."

"You sit for a bit; I got work to do and you're slowing me down."

Every time Kaye closed her eyes that night, she saw Jessie. Jessie, playing with her pillowcase doll. Jessie eating candy. Jessie afraid. Jessie laughing. The pictures circled through her mind. She kicked against the covers tucked in at the foot of her bed. They were bunched up. She moved her feet right, then left, hooking something with her toe. She pulled it up to her hands. The pillowcase doll. Someone had tucked Jessie's doll into her bedding. Kaye hugged the wad of fabric against her and sobbed into her pillow. This was not what Christmas should be. Christmas was about birth, not death.

At least she had Jessie's doll to hold.

Chapter 18

1957

The first two weeks of school were complicated with ice, snow, and freezing rain. The buses skidded off the roads. The kids glided from the bus toward the school and back again on the ice-covered parking lot. The buses arrived late, classes were disrupted, and students continued to enter the classrooms until late into the morning.

The notes Kaye and Toe removed from their lockers were brief and provided little information. She couldn't tell him about Jessie. What would she say? "Hi, how are your cows? Jessie died." No, she wouldn't tell him until they could talk. That would have to wait until the weather improved and they could meet again at their granite garden, as he called it. Until then they shared the only time they had together in English Literature class 11 a.m. to 11:50, each day. Toe occupied a chair in the far row, next to the windows, and Kaye a chair in the next row beside him.

Mrs. Peters tapped her pencil three times and the classroom quieted. "We will continue our study of Shakespeare. I hope you remembered to prepare as I suggested over the holiday. Many of you found *Macbeth* a challenge. Today we begin reading *Romeo and Juliet*, Scene Two. Please take notes. There will be an exam on Fridays covering the portion of the play we read each week."

Pages rustled and books tumbled off desks, girls giggled, and boys groaned. Kaye glanced at Toe. His attention was gone as he gazed out the window.

He's probably thinking about his cows. Maybe he just wants to be somewhere else, somewhere outside. Wherever he is, he's lost in his desire to escape.

Toe excelled in his classes without any fanfare and if he completed this year successfully, he would graduate in June. Kaye was disappointed graduating did not make him happy. She sighed. His cows. All Toe thought about were those blasted cows, their production records, and their breeding schedule. Kaye noted the room had turned silent. She had missed something. She glanced up to see Mrs. Peters peering over her glasses at her, the other students waiting for her to reply.

"Yes Ma'am?" Kaye answered, unsure of the question.

"I asked if anyone in the room had attended a play written by Shakespeare."

The room remained silent. Kaye was sure Nancy Mercer had probably attended a Shakespeare play. Last term, she said her family went to Detroit to see a play. It would be unlikely anyone else had attended such an event.

Ann Barker raised her hand. "Shakespeare is a little, ah, difficult to understand."

"Apparently generations of well-educated people didn't think it's so difficult. I will explain the scene and the situation."

Mrs. Peters turned to the blackboard, drafted an outline of the play, and continued to lecture with her back to the students. She droned on, as some students attempted to copy her outline, others passed notes, completed math assignments, and otherwise ignored the instruction in process. When Mrs. Peters finished writing, the blackboard was covered with lines and words. Sentence diagrams. Kaye traced the key words drawing connecting lines on her paper, intrigued. What an interesting way to look at a work of literature.

Mrs. Peters turned around to see the classroom obviously not engaged in her efforts. Annoyed, she walked down the row of seats next to the windows. She observed Seth's closed textbook on the desktop. Her eyes followed his view down the street. He was her best student, and he was not participating.

"Seth," she asked, "would you like to read for us?"

Seth turned his gaze from the window to her, his composure intact. Then he fixed his stare on Kaye. His dark eyes twinkled, and his dimple pierced his cheek. He placed his clasp and folded hands on his closed book and began to recite.

[]"But soft what light through yonder window breaks? It is the east, and Juliet is the sun." His voice was almost a whisper; not a sound intruded on his recitation.

"Arise, fair sun, and kill the envious moon.

"Who is already sick and pale with grief,

"That thou, her maid, are far more fair than she."

Mrs. Peters stepped back, startled. She leaned against the window casement, her eyes moving from Seth to Kaye as he continued.

"Be not her maid, since she is envious

"Her vestal livery is but sick and green

"And none but fools do wear it; cast it off.

"It is my lady, O, it is my love!

"O, that she knew she were."

Kaye felt every pair of eyes upon her as Seth continued his gaze without falter.

"She speaks, yet she says nothing; what of that?

"Her eye discourses; I will answer it.

"I am too bold, 'tis not to me she speaks.

"Having some business, do entreat her eyes

"To twinkle in their spheres till they return.

"What if her eyes were there, they in her head?

"The brightness of her cheek would shame those stars,

"As daylight doth a lamp; her eyes in heaven

"Would through the airy region stream so bright."

The bell rang and no one moved.

"That birds would sing and think it were not night.

"See, how she leans her cheek upon her hand!

"O, that I were a glove upon that hand,

"That I might touch that cheek!"

The second bell rang. Toe picked up his book and left the room. The other students followed in silence. Mrs. Peters did not dismiss the class. She did not speak. Kaye took a deep breath; her mouth was dry, and her cheeks felt hot. Oh, what had he done? They would all be talking now. The other kids would hear the gossip. It's out. They had no secret now. She stood, gathered her books, and headed for the restroom. In the hallway students mingled and whispered as she passed.

"He knows that whole thing. All that old way of talking."

"He could probably recite the whole play."

She turned the corner near the restroom. Toe was ahead and entering the stairwell when Buzz Markel called out. "An idiot that can quote Shakespeare!"

Kaye turned in the direction of the remark. Buzz shifted his shoulders and snapped his gum. The other boys standing nearby laughed a nervous snicker as Toe passed them on the landing.

Kaye wanted to talk to him, but Toe took the stairs down toward the lower-level rooms. There would be no excuse for her being in that area of the school building.

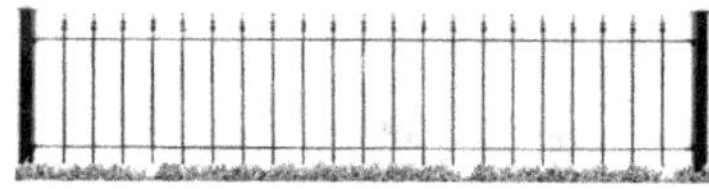

Mr. Kent entered the classroom to see Seth seated, his elbows on the table, his fists clinched, and his shoulders trembling. Mr. Kent placed his hand on Seth's shoulder. "I'm sorry Seth, I heard what happened. Mrs. Peters almost broke her hip getting to the office to see Principal Weston."

"I'm done here. I'm a farmer. I don't belong here. I told Dr. Helmsley this was a dumb idea. I got caught up in a stupid play."

Mr. Kent closed the door and sat down.

"You couldn't be more wrong, Seth! You just proved beyond a doubt, this is exactly where you belong. You try to hide your mind, but you can't. It won't let you, and that's a good thing! You're old enough to look at the people teasing you, or giving you counsel, and decide if they are the kind of people worthy of your respect. Several of those boys are failing their classes. Do you want to fit in with them? Seth, you can be a farmer, and you would be a good farmer. Probably a very successful farmer, but I'd be shortchanging you if I didn't interfere. You, young man, are going to college. You are going to see what is out there in the world. You finish college and then if you want to farm, I'll buy your first cow. How about that for a deal?"

"I'll always be a Home kid, Mr. Kent. I've never lived anywhere else. That'll never leave me no matter where I go. When they find out where I came from, they'll decide what they'll let me do." Seth rubbed his face with his hands and pushed them through his hair, standing his black curls into spirals.

"Maybe that's how you feel inside but on the outside people see a young man, a gifted young man with ambition. Tomorrow you'll return to Mrs. Peters's class because now you know the truth. You faced it today. The people who said you couldn't, they've lied to you. Don't be an angry man, take the truth and become the person you're intended to be, Seth. Mrs. Peters is meeting with the counselor after school today. She's already drafting a recommendation for you to continue your education, and I have no intention of buying a cow to the likes of which you're accustomed."

"College costs money. Mr. Kent, I've never even had a dollar. Seth gestured toward his worn shoes with the knotted laces. "If I had some money, I'd buy a pair of shoes. They cost a lot less than college."

Mr. Kent stood and patted Seth's shoulder. "I understand what you are saying, but shoes are easier to come by than an education. It's called a scholarship, Seth. Let Mrs. Peters and Mrs. Jennings the counselor take care of that. If anyone can find money for college, those two women can. You just keep your grades up and we'll see what happens."

"I say twenty-five lines of Shakespeare and now I have to go to college!"

Seth picked up his books. He thought of Kaye walking to the bus with the other kids from the Home. Kaye, the ever-vigilant Mother Hen. He hoped Hannot would not hear about him saying a poem to Kaye in English class. He should have thought before he spoke. The recording he had listened to through the holidays had blazed a path in his mind and it came out of his mouth. The beauty of the words and the thoughts just flowed. All the nights he listened to those words and thought of her, and there she was beside him today. He had made a fatal mistake. He had risked them both, and no one here at this high school would understand. His stomach churned. No note could say what he wanted to tell her. If he said he was sorry it would sound as if he didn't mean those beautiful lines, but he did.

If she decided never to see him again it would be his own fault.

The next day, Toe didn't come to English class.

Kaye went to her locker after fourth hour concerned Toe had quit school. He had not mentioned a field trip. A note tumbled to the floor. She clutched it in her fist, slipped on her coat, and hurried outside, waiting to open it when she could be alone. Toe must have come to school and skipped English class.

Kaye

Please meet me.

T

Surely the kids at school were talking about her and Seth, and it wouldn't be good if anyone saw them alone together. Everything told her it was a risk to go. She hesitated momentarily. The snow was falling in a fine powdery dust and the wind swirled it into circles. She rushed past the flower shop, her coat tangling around her legs as she passed through the gate and up the hill.

Sonny's car chugged past; the dual glass packs echoed. Probably Margo was cuddled up next to him, sharing his cigarette.

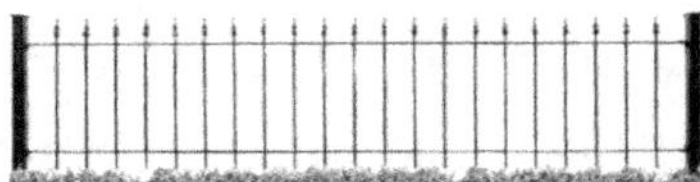

Halfway up the winding two-track drive, Toe stepped out from behind a towering dark rose monument, the one with the name *Bentley* etched deep in old English lettering. Their usual spot. The urns on each side were covered in wet, velvety green moss.

He was nervous. He twisted his hands and cracked his knuckles.

"I'm sorry I upset you." The words tumbled out. He wanted to tell Kaye he didn't mean to embarrass her or to cause her to worry. That he had listened to the recordings of Shakespeare all winter and every time he heard those words about how Romeo felt about Juliet, he thought of her and how much he wanted to tell her how her eyes sparkled when she laughed, and her hair glistened in the sun.

Kaye turned away.

"Are you crying? Please don't cry. I tried to explain."

"It's not about the poem. It's everything." She turned to him, her eyes red and her face filled with pain. "It's Jessie."

"Is she sick again? In the hospital?"

"No, Toe, she passed. She's gone."

"Oh, Kaye!" He wanted to hold her but paused. She reached for his hand.

"I loved hearing you recite, but don't you understand that caring about someone just leads to hurt? I loved Jessie. She was the baby sister I never had, and now she's gone, and it hurts so bad. Don't you see that how we feel about each other can only lead to … Oh, Toe, we can't ever have our dreams! We can't ever be together, and I care so much about you!"

He reached out and pulled her to him. No words passed between them as she cried, her face pressed into his jacket, the dark blue corduroy making ridges against her cheeks.

"Here." Toe handed her his handkerchief, and she wiped her eyes.

"I don't know where they took her. Might she be back by the woods?"

"Kaye, don't think about that. Think about how much she loved you and all you did together. That doll you made her and the tapping game you played. Think about the good things."

"I try but the thoughts of her being cold and alone… It hurts so much. What's going to happen to us?"

"We're going to have a home and a family, a nice dairy herd of Holsteins, and a house and barns. How's that for a start? I've even decided on the names for my sons."

"What?" Kaye looked up at him, her eyes still wet.

"Yes, ma'am. Winston and Albert, and my daughter's going to be Ada."

"Seth, you can't be serious. I'd never let you name our children those names. You can name the cows. That's all. Besides, our daughter will be named Jessie." Kaye paused; the moment of joy from Toe's teasing vanished and her eyes filled with fear. "Do you think we could have…" Her voice trailed off. "I mean, if we had children do you think…?"

"You mean, could they be like Jessie? Do you think Jessie's parents were expecting Jessie? Things happen. You didn't read the carving on the box, did you?"

"I told you I can't read Latin. Toe, but if Ollie won't let you work outside of the Home, how did you have the money for the things in the sewing box?"

Toe turned away.

"You didn't steal those things, did you?"

He faced her. "No, ma'am, I did not. I did make the box. You've never asked me what it says."

"All right." Kaye took a deep breath. "What does it say?"

"It says, *Omnia vincit amor.*"

"That helps." Kaye looked away, lifting her hand, palm open.

"Don't you want to know what it means?"

"I thought that's what you were going to tell me! Sometimes you can be pure exasperation. I said I don't know Latin."

"In your heart you know what it means, even if you don't know Latin. It means, 'Love conquers all.'"

"And that's supposed to help."

"It does. Don't you see, to know you loved Jessie and she loved you, *that's* what's important. That she never gets locked in a closet or punished again for something she did because she was afraid. We will be together. We are together now. How we love each other, that's what's important."

"I wish I had your faith." If only she could believe him.

"You're the one with the faith. Remember me? I'm the simplify guy. I follow Thoreau. I like the woods and the simple life. Maybe it's your faith that'll get us through."

"I'll miss Jessie forever, and I think I'll be afraid for us forever too."

"Say this after me, *Omnia vincit amor*."

"*Omnia vincit amor*."

The roar of Sonny's car echoed on the street below as he zoomed toward the school.

"We're going to be late!" Kaye wiped her eyes again and handed Toe his handkerchief.

"<u>Omnia</u> <u>vincit</u> <u>amor</u>," she said. "I want to believe."

"<u>Omnia</u> <u>vincit</u> <u>amor</u>," Toe answered. "Believe."

Chapter 19

"Kaye, would you check Jackie's chart and see when she's due for her lab tests? I think it's Monday, for her blood count. She's anemic most of the time." Nurse Lucy resumed changing Sally's diaper and giggled into her neck playfully. Sally gurgled with pleasure.

Kaye passed through the nursery and into the office. First, she telephoned the kitchen clerk to complete a food order before picking up Jackie's chart. She turned to the order section.

"It's next week, Nurse Lucy. I'll put it on the wall calendar." She noted the lab test on the wall calendar in the square for Monday.

"Thanks, Kaye," Nurse Lucy called out and continued with her work.

The nursery quieted, as many of the children slept after their morning feeding and bath. Kaye thumbed through the chart pretending she was a real nurse reading it. She found the histories interesting, but the lab tests and medical reports she didn't understand. She tried to read the physician's observations and their orders.

She folded back the history section of Jackie's chart, seeing her age as thirty-six.

Status/diagnosis listed as Infantile/imbecile.

Verbal-parroting only.

Presents with severe visual and moderate hearing impairment.

Ambulatory with adjusted gait.

The chart stated on her initial assessment when she came at three years of age she could walk. Kaye eyed Jackie lying in her bed in a fixed fetal position. It was hard to imagine how tall she might have grown. Her knees now pulled up against her chest and her hands down to her toes; she had to be lifted from her bed to her chair and even then, she remained in fetal position. It took two attendants to bathe her, and she cried out when her limbs were adjusted to accommodate for proper skin care. She weighed only about sixty pounds. Kaye paged on through the history.

Gyn. and Obstetric assessment-Mature and Developed female.
At age 21, birthed a male child, March 10, 1939
Traumatic Vaginal delivery.
Hysterectomy - post-delivery.
Recovery-normal. Infant transferred to institution nursery.
Family notification pending.

Nurse Lucy entered the office. Kaye looked up from the chart.

"Did you know she had a baby?"

"Who had a baby?" Lucy washed her hands and dried them.

"Jackie had a baby. Here!"

Lucy removed the chart from Kaye's hands.

"Kaye, these charts are confidential. You may read them but nothing within them is to ever be discussed with anyone. Do you understand? Our children have a right to their privacy. It's enough they're exploited with the residents from medical schools, nursing school students, and anyone who is interested gaping at them. They're treated like an exhibition. They're people, Kaye, and we are trusted to protect them as much as possible." Her voice cracked. "They're God's children, the work of His hands, and He entrusts them to our care." Her words softened and she turned away.

Kaye understood what Nurse Lucy was saying. Kaye too felt the pain of the student observers' disdain for the children. How they observed but did not see. Those students did not know they were children who wanted to be held and loved. Children held hostage in bodies that betrayed them. Victims of some circumstance no one could explain. There were children who understood in their own limited way they were being discounted. Those students could never understand the hug of someone like Jessie or discern the meaning of Jackie's moans. Every time another group passed through, Kaye wanted to scream, "Go away."

Kaye returned to the nursery. Nurse Lucy's words "the work of His hands" echoed in her mind. She maneuvered through the cribs to Jackie's. Her thin emaciated face was flesh over bones and she had raw areas on each facial cheekbone. Her gray-blond hair so thin it barely covered her scalp. She seldom opened her eyes and lay however she was positioned, often moaning a repetitious pattern of sounds. Kaye covered Jackie's feet, pausing to look at them, so thin and curled up. She stroked Jackie's back and the sounds she made changed to a moan. Her moans might be the only way she could communicate. Kaye had never cared for Jackie. She was always assigned to the younger children, those she could exercise doing arm and leg movements. She wanted to pick Jackie up and hold her, perhaps rock in a rocking chair with her. But Jackie was too fragile, even changing her position caused great pain for her. Instead, Kaye picked up Joni, a dark-skinned child, carried her to the rocking chair and began rocking her. Tears rolled down Kaye's face as thoughts of Jackie having a boyfriend and a baby went through her mind. The chart said no one visited and she had not left the institution since her admission. Yet, she had a baby. Kaye changed Joni's diaper and tied a soft pink ribbon in her hair. Jonie made chirping sounds, reaching out her arms to touch Kaye's face. Black curls twirled around her head and tumbled down her shoulders. Kaye traced the folds of her face, dried the crease under her chin, and wrapped her legless body in a blanket. She placed Jonie back into her crib and moved on to care for Bedda.

Nurse Lucy called from the nurses' station. "Kaye, it's time to leave. I'll take care of Bedda. You run along."

"I can't ask you a question about Jackie, can I?"

"Only if it's about her care."

"It is sort of."

"No, Kaye, it's not our business. It is not proper to discuss it."

"I just wondered…"

"Wonder, but don't ask me any questions."

"Yes, Nurse Lucy. See you tomorrow." Kaye returned to her cottage to finish her homework. Nothing took her mind away from the lonely nights without Jessie. Her restlessness produced a fitful sleep. Questions about Jackie and her baby boy filled her mind, questions with no answers.

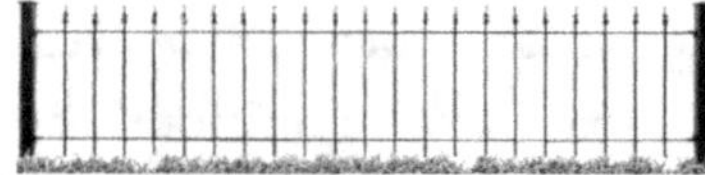

"Saturday, I'll have birthday cake for supper."

Kaye circled around the dark black stone with the name *Smith* in letters so damaged they could hardly be discerned.

"What kind of cake?" Toe asked.

"I don't know, probably green. Cook likes to make green food on St. Patrick's Day. I hate having a birthday on St. Patrick's Day. Every year for my birthday I eat corned beef and cabbage. It stinks."

"Yeah." Toe laughed. "It stinks cooking, it stinks when you eat it, and it stinks when the guys fart cabbage."

"Toe!" Kaye shouted at him. "Don't talk like that!"

"I can't say fart?"

"No, it's not a nice word."

"There's a nice word— for fart?"

"You stop that. You're just being crude and trying to annoy me."

"It may be crude, but what else do you say?"

"Pass gas. That's polite talk."

"Sure, that would go over good at the barn."

"You're not at the barn, and present company is excluded from barn talk." Kaye cast him a scowl.

"Do you get a birthday present?"

"Uh huh! I get something new every birthday. I keep it special. I can still wear last year's blouse and skirt because I stopped growing. Do you have birthday parties in the boys' cottages?"

"Sometimes Mrs. Avery, the dairyman's wife, she tries to have a cake for each guy on his birthday. But she's sick a lot and needs help to bake. Ben's started helping her."

"Do you get a present?" Kaye sat on one of the stones with her back to the street in case anyone was watching. Some of the school kids came around the corner to smoke but none of them walked into the cemetery. Toe paced toward a headstone near the drive and back to where she sat. He had been restless since she arrived.

"Kaye, when you go back to the cottage from the nursery, does someone walk with you?"

"No, I go alone."

"You should have someone walk with you."

"Toe, it's not like I'll get lost. I know the way."

"It's not that. It's just not safe. Some guys say things. I worry about you. I don't want you to get hurt. I've told you before."

"I won't get hurt," Kaye scoffed. "I'm a big girl."

"That's what I mean, Kaye. You're a grown woman. The women attendants walk around in twos. Haven't you noticed?"

"No, I never thought about it. I know what you're saying. If I must leave the nursery after supper, I'll have the nurse call the safety shack."

"NO!" Toe shouted.

"Shush, Toe. Someone will hear you." Kaye sounded alarmed.

"Don't call the safety shack!" Toe reached out to touch her sleeve. "Listen to me. One guy is, well, he's not a good person. He brags about… Just don't call the safety shack. You ask someone from the nursery building to walk with you back to the cottage. They know the rules. If no one can walk back with you, stay there until someone can. Promise me." He was squeezing her arm now.

Kaye pulled away. "That hurts, Toe."

He released his grip. "I'm sorry, Kaye," he whispered. "Promise me."

"I promise."

"And happy birthday, Kaye."

They could hear Sonny's car approaching.

"Toe." Kaye paused. "When's your birthday? I'll make you some fudge."

"It's already passed. March tenth, nineteen-thirty-nine."

She stopped and turned in his direction. "Toe, where were you born?"

"Where were you born, Kaye?" he snapped in a sharp reply.

It was the first time Toe had ever spoke to her in anger.

"I don't know."

Kaye's thoughts shook her to the core, as they bounced from lack of knowledge about her own birth to the notations on Jackie's chart. Her stomach wrenched and she felt hollow inside. Toe was visibly upset and angry. Her head whirled. People can be born on the same day. It happens.

"If you don't know where, then it doesn't matter." Toe started down the hill. "Remember what's important."

They parted, walking in different directions. Kaye headed toward the flower shop and Toe disappeared between the greenhouses.

Kaye heard the second bell ring as she approached the school building. She went directly to the office of the school nurse. Not only was she late, she also felt ill.

Chapter 20

Kaye held the pearl button and stroked the braided cord that twined through it. She wrote a letter to Toe, re-read it, and tore it up. Four angry pages would be too many to slide through the vent in his locker door. She couldn't hand it to him either. He might stop right there in the hallway and start reading it, and other guys would grab it. She didn't know how to tell him what she wanted to say. Writing it didn't make any sense, and if it didn't make sense to her she couldn't expect him to understand.

The day Toe confirmed his birthday, the date and the year, and then became so angry, her thoughts about him changed. He had proved he only cared about himself and what he wanted. If she were his girlfriend, he wouldn't keep this from her. She wouldn't be his girlfriend. Not anymore. Her mind whirled to thoughts of the children in the nursery. She cared about them, but she would never risk knowingly having a child like Jackie. She had exercised them, bathed them, and cared for them. She loved them as if they were her own siblings. Each child was special. Maybe it would happen anyway. She didn't know her own parents or why they gave her away.

Kaye wrote the necessary note. She would face him and break up. He could keep his secret, but it wouldn't include a future with her.

T

See you at the garden.

Kaye

That would do. The next morning, she would slide the note between the vents of his locker before class.

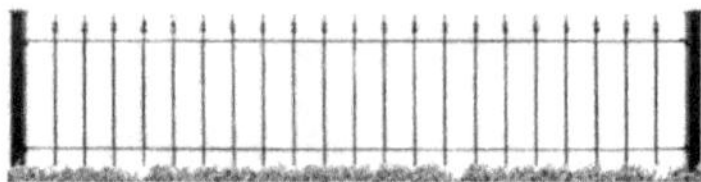

Kaye was standing behind the tall monument, waiting for Toe to arrive, rehearsing her speech.

"Hi, girl, you're early. You beat me."

"I left before the second bell. I wanted to be here early."

"You did?"

"Yes, I've got something I want to tell you and you have to understand."

"You don't want me to be a farmer?" He reached out to touch her cheek and she ducked away.

"What has that got to do with anything?"

"You're always saying, the cows I take care of aren't my cows, so I thought you didn't want me to be a farmer."

"No, I'm sure you'll be a good farmer. It's more than that."

"What could be more than us having our own home and our farm?"

"Toe, I don't want to be your girlfriend anymore, not ever."

Kaye pulled the pearl button necklace from around her neck, lifted it over her head, and handed it to him.

He folded his arms across his chest and refused to take the necklace.

"Just like that?"

"Yes." She pulled his hand forward and put the necklace in it. "What else is there? Without me you can go to college. Leave the clearing of land to the men who can only do labor, the Bens of this world. Someone points toward a stump, and they dig it out. You can do so much more. Don't you see machines, airplanes? Your mind races to explore the things that are coming. You must go on, you must try. You would never be happy without taking the opportunity to go to college."

"Your problem is your damn rules. Put down your rulebook and look at me and tell me you don't love me. Your rules don't honor God, they protect you from love! My love. For another thing, there's me, and what I want! Or doesn't that matter to you?"

"No. I've decided. Goodbye, Seth."

"Kaye, did I do something? Are you mad about the Juliet thing? What did I do?"

"Nothing. I'm going back to school. I won't come here anymore."

Toe grabbed her arm. "You can say what you want, and you can do what you want but don't ever give me back this necklace. It's ours. It's our hopes and our dreams. You don't have to wear it, but you have to keep it. Promise me you'll keep it."

Kaye blinked to hold back her tears. Toe slid the necklace over her head and looked into her eyes.

"You're hurting me. Let me go."

"Why are you doing this? Kaye, I love you!"

"No you don't. There are only two things you care about, and they are you and your cows. I'll keep the necklace because I had dreams too and you know them. You want to ignore them. Someone's going to find out about us sooner or later, Toe. Don't you see? It's no use. We can't go on pretending. Everything we fear is real and it can destroy us. Even if—"

"How did I ignore your dreams? What fears?"

"I know!" she shouted, astonished she had said something she had not intended to say. She struggled against his grip. "Let me go." She turned away from him and ran towards the school.

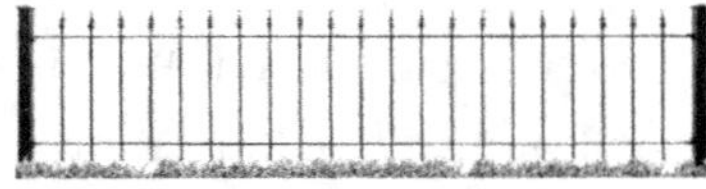

Toe remained in the cemetery as Kaye ran past the flower shop. He did care about the herd. He had worked for years in the barn, and he was working hard at school. What he wanted he wanted for them. She called him selfish when she was the one always talking about the kids in the nursery. Kaye had changed since Jessie passed. She was different, but he couldn't make her see how different if she wouldn't talk to him.

"Stubborn Irish girl anyway," he mumbled.

Kaye returned from school, her feelings of deception and anger gushing from a broken heart. She suppressed tears of anguish, changed her clothes, put on an apron, and prepared for work in the nursery. On her way out, Hannot was standing at the door.

"Kaye, I didn't see you come in. I want to talk to you before I leave today. Come into my office." The heels of Hannot's shoes echoed rhythmic thumps on the hard wood floor.

Kaye followed. Could anything make this day worse? She'd avoided Hannot since Jessie's death, knowing anything she said could mean trouble.

Hannot opened her office door to a clutter of papers, folders, and assorted items she had confiscated. She removed a stack of boxes from a chair and motioned for Kaye to sit down. She circled behind her desk, backed into her office chair, and nodded her head.

"Where was I? Oh, yes, Kaye O'Shay." She paused and smiled a menacing smirk.

"I received approval yesterday for your transfer to cottage twenty-five. I made the request after Jessie passed. I should have done it before, but you seemed so determined to live here with her. Not that she even knew who you were. I have some paperwork to complete, but everything is ready to go. Your things will be transferred tomorrow. I had to assure the supervisor *everything* was done." Hannot shuffled papers on her desk, stacking and rearranging them, looking for a specific page.

"Here it is. I was sure it was here. Now, don't drink anything after midnight, Kaye, you have an appointment at the hospital tomorrow. Pretty little thing you are. I heard you got yourself a feller." She smirked at Kaye and continued reading down a list and checking off boxes with her ink pen.

Kaye's mind whirled. Hannot had found out. Someone must have reported seeing them. They'd been careful and never walked together anywhere. Sometimes on Sundays, they met behind the ball diamond to share a candy bar. Kaye brushed her hand across her bodice, down her stomach, smoothing her apron across her lap. It was her body. She started to tremble. This could only mean one thing. After tomorrow she would never have a family of her own. Cottage twenty-five, that's Margo's cottage. It was too late to talk to Margo. Kaye shuddered. She didn't want a deformed child, but she might— someday— want a family of her own. After tomorrow, she wouldn't have a choice. There had to be a way to stop this from happening but there was no one she could trust. Her thoughts were interrupted by Hannot's grating voice.

"You won't be going to school for a day or so. When you go back, take a note from the cottage supervisor. I don't think they care much at high school if a Home kid misses a day or two, but they probably have their rules too." She snickered. "Oh yes, we are ed-u-cating the children," she said, fluttering her fingers and laughing aloud. "Would you look around at the progress we are making, educating the children." She sighed. "That's all. Make sure your things are packed tonight." She checked the clock. "I'm on overtime fussing with all this. Get along now."

Responding to Hannot's command, Kaye's body followed as her legs propelled her from the office, her mind churning to understand. She was numb from head to toe. She was an object, something shuffled around by other people who made decisions for her, not decisions for today but decisions that affected the rest of her life. People who didn't know or care what she wanted.

Kaye left her cottage praying Nurse Lucy would be working the afternoon shift. She passed Lucy's car parked in her usual space and hurried toward the back door. Kaye began preparing bottles, seeking a task that required repetitive action, little thought, and busy hands. She and Nurse Lucy wouldn't be able to talk with the other workers around. Kaye would have to wait until the others went to supper.

Nurse Lucy bustled into the kitchen. "I'm hungry, I'm going to first supper. This week's menu said Thursday—roast pork dinner." She hung her apron on a peg by the door and headed for the dining hall.

Tommie, an aide, placed several bottles Kaye had prepared into the refrigerator.

"My feet hurt and my back aches so bad. These kids are gonna break this old back for sure."

Kaye wished Tommie would be more loving to the children.

"Nurse Lucy says these are all God's children and we are to care for them as the very children of Jesus."

"Well, I dare say, some of Jesus' children have a few parts missing."

"Nurse Lucy says Jesus loves all his children and he loves us for caring for them."

"You care for'em and you love on'em. Me, I do this work for my paycheck. On Friday, I say to that Dr. Helmsley, 'Today, you and I are even.'"

"Nurse Lucy says—"

"You stop that Nurse Lucy says stuff. If she wants to think she's a nun that's her business. But I say, do your work and receive your check on payday, that's it."

"Why do you say Nurse Lucy's a nun? What's a nun?

"It's one of them religious Catholic ladies that wears a white thing around their neck and face and a long black dress."

"No, you're being silly. I heard those ladies marry Jesus. Nurse Lucy's married to her husband."

"She'd be happier if she was married to Jesus," Tommie mumbled.

Kaye jumped to Nurse Lucy's defense. "Maybe Nurse Lucy loves on the children like she does because she can't have any of her own."

Tommie turned to face Kaye. "Who told you that? She can have children, she won't."

"Tommie, don't you be gossiping to Kaye." Dot, another aide, turned toward Kaye and said, "Don't listen to her jabber."

"I ain't a gossiping. I know it to be a fact." Tommie sat down in a chair and slipped off her shoe.

Dot tidied up the changing table. "She doesn't need to be a-knowing any of your facts."

Tommie jumped up. "Kaye, go grab a bucket and a rag. Lulu Bell just made a mess."

Kaye brought a bucket of water and some rags. As she mopped the floor Tommie washed Lulu and put her in a clean diaper and gown.

"Tommie, can Nurse Lucy have children?" Kaye asked in a whisper, not wanting Dot to hear.

"Not the way she's a doin' her man, she can't."

"Huh?"

"Well—" Tommie glanced around for Dot and not seeing her she continued. "It's like this. A little while after they got married, that man of hers, he did a little ala-mand-de-left with another woman, and she got in the family way. He begged Heusted to forgive him and promised he'd never see the woman again. Heusted stayed with him. I hear she goes with him when he goes to see his boy, but Heusted vowed she'd never give him *their* child. And that's the gospel truth why she don't have children."

Kaye continued to feed Bobby and was still thinking about what Tommie had said when Nurse Lucy returned from dinner.

"Tommie, do you and Dot want to go get some supper?" Nurse Lucy glanced around. "Kaye, when are you eatin' tonight?"

"I don't want anything to eat tonight," Kaye said, and continued to rock Bobby.

"Not eating. We know what that's a sign of, don't we Dotty?" Tommie started singing. "You'll never know, dear, how much I love you."

Dottie cast a glance in Kaye's direction, "Yeah, it's more likely a sign that she's lost her appetite cleaning up around here." They were laughing as they left for supper.

"Not hungry, Kaye?" Nurse Lucy asked. "The roast pork in the dining hall was really good."

"No. Nurse Lucy, tell me something."

"Sure, what's going on? Something at school?"

They continued working down the rows of cribs, exercising arms and legs and repositioning children as they talked.

"It's Toe, the boy I told you about. He lied to me. I didn't think he would ever lie to me. We had a fight and he's mad at me. Then I came home from school and Hannot says I'm moving to the older girls' cottage but I have to go to the hospital first thing tomorrow morning. And I can't drink any water after midnight. Then she said I won't go to school for a couple days. If she had told me ahead of time, I could have got my assignments at school and wouldn't get behind. I work hard at school, and she laughs about ed-u-cating the Home kids." Kaye mimicked Hannot causing Nurse Lucy to stifle a chuckle by covering her mouth with her hand.

Kaye's speech was rapid, and she continued to watch the door. "We don't have much time to talk, but that's not what's most important. What do you think the hospital thing is about?"

"I can't be sure."

"I think they're going to take my parts! My baby-making parts. Will they do that?"

"I can't say for sure."

"I don't want babies." Kaye lowered her eyes, then her look passed over the cribs surrounding them.

Nurse Lucy paused. "Lots of people have beautiful babies." She changed the subject. "Now, about this boy. Maybe you don't understand what he meant. If he lied, I'm sure he had a reason. Maybe it was to protect you. I'm sure if you talk it over you can find a way to forgive him."

Guilt assailed Kaye. By refusing to meet him, she had left no possible way for them to talk. Now Nurse Lucy was telling her it was her responsibility to forgive. Forgive him for his deceit. Kaye's fear and rage continued to mount. She took aim at the one person in the world she trusted. Her face grimaced and her body trembled with fury.

"You care about these babies, right? You tell me we're all God's children. You tell me to forgive someone I trusted, who lied to me. You stand here and you know they're taking something from me they have no right to take, and you won't help me. I thought you were my friend. You're just like them. You don't care about me."

Her voice was trembling, and her breath was coming in bursts.

"You tell me to forgive but you don't forgive. You don't have children because you won't forgive. You lie too. You lie to yourself and that's worse than lying to anybody else." Kaye pulled off her apron and threw it toward the laundry hamper.

Tommie and Dot were standing at the door as Kaye thundered past.

Dotty waved her arms pretending to clear the air. "What was *that* about?"

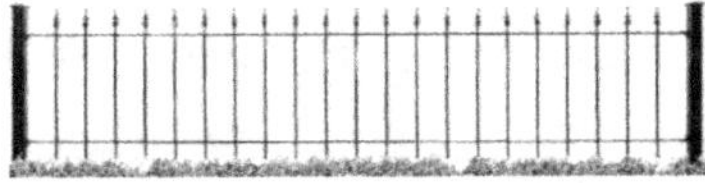

Kaye ran back to her cottage, entered through the back door, climbed the stairs, and flopped on her bed. Her arms and legs ached, and her head throbbed. Everything and everyone in her world proved Kaye O'Shay was nothing, not worth caring about, a joke left at the gate one morning in March; a prisoner of the institution that fed and clothed her, a slave to the master that had no face or name, a master who could cut her body, a master who could make her work until she died, a master she could never overcome.

From her bed, Kaye heard Dockery's uniform rustle as she passed each bed and made a mark on her clipboard. The afternoon shift were younger workers, the midnights were sometimes women whose children had grown. Dockery fits the second variety. She grumbled about getting old, and she disliked the younger women. She especially disliked young pretty girls. She leaned near Kaye, "Hannot talked to you, right? No water."

"No water," Kaye murmured back and slid down under her blanket. "I'll pack in the morning."

Dockery turned off the light and left the room. Patti called down from two beds away.

"They don't hurt you bad at the hospital Kaye-Kaye. Sometimes you get ice cream. Don't be scared."

"Go to sleep, Patti." Kaye tried to sound like a big sister. She was not okay. Nothing was okay.

Thoughts raced through her mind. Her head continued to pound. She heard the hall clock strike every fifteen minutes and waited for the night shift. Therese would be here at 11 o clock. When Therese worked, sometimes she would let Kaye get up and play rummy or canasta in the office. Kaye would go to bed late and no one ever knew. One time an attendant almost caught them, but Kaye saw his shadow pass the window in time for her to dive under the desk just before he opened the door. *Therese's my friend*, she thought. *She'll tell me the truth about this appointment.*

Kaye listened for the hall clock to strike 11:30, then walked downstairs toward the office. She could hear two voices, Dockery and someone she didn't recognize. She listened from behind the door.

"Therese'll be late tonight. She was sick all day, but she'll be here by two," the voice reported. "Our cottage is quiet tonight, so I said I'd cover for a couple hours.

Kaye turned to go back to bed when she heard her name.

"Hospital…Kaye O'Shay."

"I told the supervisor there'd be a price to pay for that romance."

"Kaye's involved in a romance?" Dockery asked.

"Yeah. That's why the little medical tour tomorrow. You know that would be nipped in the bud before she'd come to our building."

"You have to do something to stop'em. Folks are bringing kids from the outside in so fast, we can't afford to start makin'em here." The attendants moved on with their tasks and their gossip.

Kaye struggled back to her bed, a lump growing in her throat.

The clock struck twelve, then twelve-thirty. Kaye could not allow her eyes to close. She had to leave. Somehow, she had to run. There was no way to be sure Therese would help her, and if she refused, there would be no alternative. She had to decide now. She got up, added another layer of clothing, and waited. At one o'clock she carried her shoes and crept down the stairs in stocking feet. The fill-in aide and the safety guard were laughing and playing gin rummy in the dayroom. Kaye could see their stocking feet tangled together under the table. She moved past the archway and down the hall. As she passed Hannot's open office door; a brown folder lay angled across the corner of the desk. Stepping into the room she read the name, *O'Shay, Kaye*. She slid the folder under her sweater, clutched her brown coat tight, and moved cautiously through the pantry, out the back door, and into the night. With some luck, she had an hour before anyone would check her bed. She must get away before they began a search. The punishment could be severe if she were caught. Fueled with anger, she had been accused of doing *things* with a *boy*, her disappointment in Nurse Lucy, and her broken heart over the loss of her first love, she covered the grounds, running from shadow to shadow until she reached the railroad tracks. Lying in the tall grass, she waited for the guard to pass. He was swinging his lantern left, then right, as he walked beside the tracks. Her thoughts went to Jessie. She could never have left Jessie. But somehow, tonight, she knew she had Jessie's permission to go. But there was no place to run. The trains went too fast to ever catch one of them. If she tried to walk out the gate the guard would stop her.

One window of the barn glowed with light. Toe said sometimes someone had to go to the barn at night. He told her if he went with the building supervisor, he worked on the production records while they waited for a cow to calve. Maybe he was inside. Kaye circled around the corner of the barn.

Ollie's truck was parked away from the barn, and she could see bags in the back. It's Thursday. Toe said Ollie picked up his chicken feed on Thursday.

She had to hurry.

Chapter 21

Several days had passed since Ollie's threat to punish Ben if Toe didn't quit high school. Maybe Ollie was drunk when he said it. Toe watched Ollie for any signs that he remembered. He told Ben to be extra careful and to never be alone with Ollie if he could help it. Kaye hadn't been the same since Jessie died, but the way she acted and the things she said today made no sense.

Toe flipped through the production records. Each record was up to date.

"Ben," Toe called out, and then chuckled as every man within hearing distance turned and Ben continued on his way. One of the men pulled on Ben's sleeve and gestured toward Toe. A smile lit up Ben's face. *He's like the jolly green giant of Jack and the beanstalk,* Toe thought to himself. He told Ben to wait outside, that he wanted to talk to Ollie alone after chores. Ben nodded.

Ever since Ollie had told Toe it wasn't working with him going to high school, Toe had worked on a plan. He would teach Ben the system of recording for the herd. That would make Ollie dependent on Ben, and if he mistreated Ben, Ollie's incompetence would be exposed, and he would lose his job.

The same way Toe shared his high school classes with Ben he shared his method of recording the information on the herd. Separate manuals for health records, breeding records, production records. Ben proved to be an excellent student.

After several evenings of work, Ben had a complete grasp of the system. He not only understood it, but he also improved it, reducing some of the duplication.

After his argument with Kaye today Toe was ready to take on Ollie. Tonight would be the night Ollie would decide that Ben would be his best choice to keep the records. Toe smiled to himself as the other men left the barn for the night.

It was Thursday, and Ollie worked a late shift because he picked up his chicken feed at the granary elevator in town before coming to work.

"Hey Ollie, is the work getting done with me going to high school?"

"I guess it is, ain't nobody complained. I heard you may be leaving after you graduate from high school?"

Toe hesitated. "No, nobody said nothin' to me.

Ollie spit a wad of tobacco into the gutter. "Just in case Dr. Helmsley has a plan of one kind or another, what you gonna do about the herd records?"

"Yeah. I was thinking about that. You got anybody in mind?"

"Me, no!"

"Ben knows a lot about the herd. I thought you might decide Ben would be a good one for me to train."

Ollie scratched his jaw and searched Toe's face, then laughed an insidious laugh. "I guess he won't be a-tellin' anybody."

"Yes." Toe smiled back. "He's a good secret keeper."

"You think he can do it?"

"I'll give him a try if it's okay with you."

"Toe, on a good day, you know how to pick 'em, cows and Home boys."

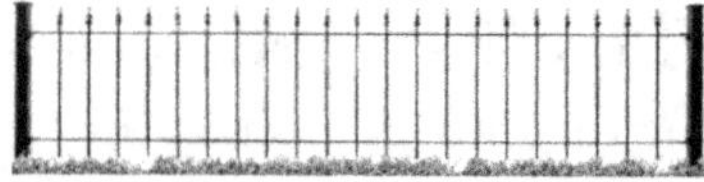

After his conversation with Ollie, Toe shared Ollie's plan with Ben. He wanted to tell Ben about Ollie's literacy without Ben being tempted to mock or ridicule Ollie if things went bad. Ben could not expose Ollie without endangering himself. They talked in the closet long into the night until Toe was assured Ben understood. When they passed the window to go to bed, they could see Ollie sitting on a bale of straw outside the barn door and Toe surmised he would be listening to the radio. Shep was racing around the bale of straw and back and forth toward the corner of the barn.

Probably a coon in the corn shed, Toe guessed. Ben was standing beside him.

Ben signed, "Hope he ain't chasing a skunk.

They watched as Ollie turned out the barn lights and the taillights of his truck disappeared down Farm Lane.

Kaye couldn't let her mind wander to the thoughts of getting caught; she had to concentrate on getting away. Her mind raced to Toe. There wasn't any way to leave a message. Besides, why would she want to after what he'd done?

A mass of black and white came bounding toward her.

"Shep! Shep!" Kaye whispered and crouched down. Please don't bark! The dog submitted, lowering his head for her to pet him. She nuzzled against him, then urged "Go back, Go back." She pushed his haunches away. He ambled toward the barn. She must keep moving. Ollie's truck loomed in the shadows.

Kaye swallowed the lump in her throat.

"Goodbye, Toe!"

She had to run away—now!

Kaye climbed over the tailgate of Ollie's truck, slid her foot down inside the tailgate, and pulled her other leg over. She knew the bags would be heavy but if she could tug them, maybe she could move them aside enough to make a space. She worked in the middle of the load, pulling first the corner of one bag, then tugged on the corner of another, pulling both bags in opposite directions, creating a cavity. Pushing one bag toward the cab and another toward the tailgate she created enough room to snuggle her body inside.

She struggled to prevent any bags falling off the truck. It was a large load. From inside the shallow cavity, she pushed the grain with her feet, and created a deeper space. She pulled the bag near her feet up and a bag from above her head down to hide the opening. In the dark probably Ollie wouldn't notice the bags were moved unless he climbed up on the load.

Kaye heard Ollie call "Shep" and close the barn door. He was coming toward the truck. She snuggled deeper into the opening.

"Jesus, please let me get away. Please help me." Tears fell down her cheeks. Her body trembled in fear, smothered in her tiny cavern. Kaye listened; the truck door opened. The motor started and the truck jerked and bounced toward the gate on Farm Lane. With each breath, the powdery dust from the grain filled her nose and lungs. At the gatehouse, she stifled a sneeze, then a second, burying her face into the deep crevice of the bags. She heard muffled sounds of the guard as he walked around the truck talking and slapping the bags.

"Just your grain, Ollie?"

"Yup, just my grain, Pete."

"Better hurry up if you're thirsty, the watering holes are closing."

"Yeah, I know, but I close Dunkin's Pub every other Thursday," Ollie laughed.

"Okay Ollie," he called. "See you Friday."

The old truck groaned under the load and bounced down the dirt road toward the highway.

Something from the grain bags pushed through her clothing, burrowing into her skin, and causing it to itch. The truck movements made the load shift. Soon it felt as if insects were crawling everywhere on her. She couldn't reach to scratch the itch. She wiggled her arms inside her sweater sleeves, fearful any movement could cause a bag to fall off the truck and she would be discovered. Her body trembled; her hands were wet with sweat. Perspiration ran down her chest and back. She ouldn't move, she couldn't risk a bag falling off the truck.

This was the worst of the worst rules to break. Rumors were that terrible things happened if you tried to run away. Most of the patients didn't try to run away because although they didn't know much, they knew they didn't have anywhere to go. Some wandered away, but most just stayed year after year. Kaye wasn't sure what punishment she might suffer for running away, but everything she imagined was severe. She could be locked in the building for bad kids. She'd heard about the basement cells. She would never be trusted to work in the nursery again. In a strange way it was a comfort to know that Jessie was with Jesus now. She missed her terribly, but at least Jessie wouldn't think she had left her. Never again would Jessie be harmed or be afraid.

The truck motor rumbled and lurched as Ollie changed gears. It heaved forward again. The heavy load bounced down the road. Kaye was carried along between the bags.

The motor of the truck stopped. Kaye struggled to awaken and orient herself. She heard hollering and laughing. Pushing the edge of the bag off her face, she blinked to see blue and red lights flashing alternately into the night. Tires squealed on the highway and a vehicle spun through the parking lot, pelting stones of loose gravel against the trucks. Men started hollering and another truck left the parking lot spinning out onto the highway. As silence filled the night air, she pushed the bag further away from her face. She could read the letters on the sign: B-A-R. A spotlight shining on the sign flashed from red to blue and back to red again.

She couldn't ride in the truck to Ollie's house. If he discovered her, he'd have to report her and take her back. She didn't know where she was, but she knew she had to get out of Ollie's truck and get as far away from the Home as she could. Hopefully Ollie would be in this place long enough for her to run and not be seen. The parking lot remained silent. Kaye slid the top bag up and pushed the lower bag away with her feet. She slid out from her dark hole and onto the bags, trying not to make any noise. Away in the distance she heard the whistle of the train. She could go toward the train. If she followed the tracks, they would take her to the water, just like Toe said. She rolled to her stomach, clutching her shoes, and wiggled over the load toward the back of the truck, inching across the bags until her legs passed over the tailgate. As she slid down toward the ground, her dress rolled up and circled her waist, exposing her bare legs, until her feet touched the earth.

She wrestled to pull her dress down over her legs.

An old man shuffled toward her. "I liked it better the other way, Missy." Drool glistening from his whiskered chin, he stumbled over his feet and fell. Kaye crammed her socked feet into her shoes and bolted across the parking lot, crossing the highway. She ran up a steep bank until she crashed into a thicket and tumbled to the ground underneath hoping no one else saw her besides that old man. She continued crawling on her hands and knees, pushing forward deeper into the brush as branches and weeds scratched her face and twigs caught on her hair. Beyond the underbrush, she dropped flat onto the ground. There were no sounds except her own panting. She covered her mouth to muffle the gasps that escaped her lips. Crawling back up the bank, she moved several branches away from her face, hoping to look down toward the parking lot. Ollie's truck remained parked in front of the bar and there was only one other car and something big near a tree. The drunken man, had he passed out when he fell, likely wouldn't remember seeing her. Then the thought struck: she had not put the bags back in place. Ollie would know, when he unloaded them, someone had been there. It was dumb not to think of that. Maybe he'd think the load had bounced around. No, Ollie could be mean, but he wasn't stupid. He would know someone had been inside that load of grain. He'd tell. They would think it was someone from the barns.

Kay lay under the brush until the bar closed and the spotlight turned dark. The old man climbed onto a tractor and chugged down the road. Ollie came out, got into his truck and pulled back onto the highway. The lights of Ollie's truck disappeared. The dark night loomed around her.

Her tongue clung to the roof of her mouth and her stomach growled. She was hungry. Thoughts of food filled her mind. Maybe at that building they had thrown some food out into those garbage cans by the back door. Kaye pushed her way out of the thicket and headed across the highway. First, she'd try to find some food, and then she'd follow the railroad tracks toward the sunrise. If she could find the water, Toe would come.

Chapter 22

Toe could not repress the memory of the night he left Ollie in the gutter, covered in blood from #84. It was the first time he had ever faced his own rage. He could have killed the man. In the nights that followed he would awaken, covered in perspiration, and filled with fear that he had harmed someone. Although someone had done evil, the fear of his own inability to maintain control created a secret terror.

Toe's hatred for Ollie encircled him like a serpent waiting to strike. The things Ollie had said about his mother and father remained deep in the recesses of his mind, but never in his consciousness. He had learned suppression is vital to living in an institution; survival is paramount. Survival exceeds every personal desire and buffers every affront. Don't react, don't cause trouble, don't show any loss of self-control or you'll pay the consequences. Daily, Toe faced his own vulnerability.

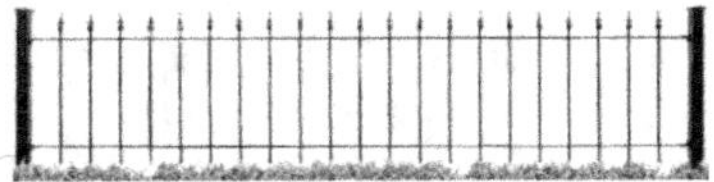

When Kaye was not at school the next day, Toe found Margo. She told him Kaye was not at the bus stop and she was supposed to move into her building but didn't show up. She figured Kaye would be in school on Monday.

Toe didn't see Kaye on the following Monday. He waited two more days. On Wednesday he stopped by the nursery after chores. He carried up two jugs of milk and knocked on the back door.

"Is Nurse Heusted working?"

"Yes, but you're not supposed to be here."

"I brought the milk," he said, handing Dottie the two jugs. "Will you ask her if she'll see me."

"She's busy."

"Please ask her."

"You're a persistent, young man. I'll ask, but if she says no, you better skedaddle, or I'll call safety."

Toe waited, shoulders slumped, leaning against the building, and tugging at his fingers, popping his knuckles.

Lucy Heusted came to the door.

"Oh, hi, Toe."

"Hi, thanks for seeing me." He straightened to his full height. "Have you seen Kaye?"

"No, she told me she was going to be busy for a few days and wouldn't be working so I didn't expect her. They moved her to another building."

"She hasn't been to school."

"Really? She loves school! She mentioned you had a spat. Perhaps she's still upset and avoided you. I'll let her know you stopped by if she comes to work."

"Thanks, Nurse Heusted."

Toe left the nursery hopeful.

When he reached the end of the building he turned around and went back to the door and knocked again. Lucy Heusted answered.

"Toe, do you need something?"

"Can you come out for a minute? I'd like to talk."

His voice cracked and his eyes filled with tears. This ordeal with Kaye, the ugliness with Ollie, his concerns for Ben, and the pressure of graduation, the talk of wanting to send him to college. It was all becoming too much. He was breaking.

Nurse Heusted came outside, closing the door behind her.

"Toe, what is it? I know Kaye cares a great deal about you and I know things will work out. It's difficult when you're young. She'll calm down and talk with you. I saw her that day and I know she was upset."

"Nurse Lucy," he turned away. The light over the door showered a dim gleam into the trees.

Toe turned and punched the wall with his fist. The explosion of his anger belied him. His shoulders trembled. Nurse Lucy reached out to touch his arm. He pulled away and continued to move his head from side to side, murmuring "No, no, no." He had nowhere to go, nowhere to make the ugliness of Ollie's words untrue and if they were true, that made him part of something terrible and ugly too.

"Toe, we have to trust God and pray for Kaye."

"It's not just about Kaye, Nurse Lucy—it's about a lot more." He turned. "Nurse Lucy, is there… a female in the nursery named Jackie Thomas?"

"Hush, Toe, lower your voice. I can't tell you that."

Toe scowled at her, his jaw fixed, his eyes black with rage.

"Who can you tell, Nurse Lucy? Her family?" His words hissed through clenched teeth. He grabbed Nurse Lucy's shoulder. He wanted to shake her until she told him the truth.

"Toe, —don't—hurt—me." She separated each word with a commanding tone.

He searched her face and his grip relaxed.

"Nurse Lucy." He began to tremble. Silent sobs racked his body, and his muscles shook and quivered. "You can tell me. If what Ollie said is true, I'm her son and my father… is a rapist." The words fell from his lips. His whole being filled with both the knowing, and not wanting to know. Despairing, he began to weep.

"Oh Seth," Nurse Lucy reached up as the boy-man received her embrace. His sobs burst forth confronting years of emptiness. A childhood of wanting to belong to someone and now discovering he is from a woman who was victimized by a man with no moral conscience.

Nurse Lucy could not hold back her compassion for him. It was more grief and loss than any one person should bear, let alone someone so young. Sometimes the pain inside this fence threatened to destroy her. They wept in each other's arms, Nurse Lucy's tears soaking his shirt, his tears pouring over her hair. After several minutes, she moved away. "I must go back inside. I must go to work." She released him. Her heart ached for a young man. She prayed for both Toe and Kaye, not knowing where her prayers might find them.

Walking back toward the dairy barn, he heard the train whistle miles in the distance. He had the answer to both his questions, but they were answers he didn't want to hear. The earth trembled beneath his feet as the train thundered nearer.

No one knew where he could find Kaye, and yes, Jackie Thomas was in the nursery, and Nurse Lucy knew Jackie Thomas had a child, born at the Home. He knew it was true because he watched her face when he asked. Everything Ollie said was true. His father was a rapist and his mother an imbecile. Why was it even important now that Kaye was gone? He stopped abruptly as the train whistle blew at the crossing fifty feet away. If Kaye knew about his mother having a baby boy, she must have found out while working in the nursery. If she thought he knew, that would explain why she was so upset. He replayed their last conversation over and over.

He had to find her. There were so many buildings and so many people.

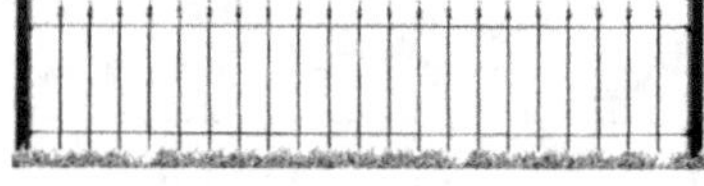

Toe waited another day until he saw Pete, the one safety guard he trusted, and asked him to see if he could find out any information about a girl named Kaye O'Shay.

For the next two days Toe attended school. He also paced and worried. The third day Pete stopped by the barn.

"Hey Toe, got a minute?"

"Sure." Toe left the barn and walked with Pete toward the road. "Did you find out anything?"

"Well, not much. Yes, there was a girl named Kaye O'Shay who lived in cottage #30. She worked in the nursery; other workers saw her there. She never showed up at cottage #25. The funny thing is her file is gone too. They probably have a registration file of her admission in the office but nothing else. No history, nothing. She's gone and so is her record."

"How does that happen?"

"Got me. If she ran, no one sent out a bulletin about her missing. Maybe it's because they can't find her file. They'd look pretty silly. If I were you, I'd be quiet. She's safer if you just don't say any more about her. I don't think I stirred up anything by asking questions because no one wants to look incompetent."

"Humm. Thanks."

"Do you think she can take care of herself out there?"

"Yeah… I hope so. She's pretty smart." Toe remained troubled as he worried about where she might find help. She kept the pearl necklace. He hoped she had it with her.

It's the only thing we have between us that's ours.

From the west thundered the eight p.m. eastbound train. The engineer sounded the whistle at both road crossings. Toe felt the tremor of the earth under his feet and watched it journey into the distance. Occasionally a passenger waved. They would ride all the way to the water.

The water? He and Kaye had talked about going toward the sunrise and to the water. He paused. If Kaye went toward the water maybe he could find her.

Chapter 23

For three days, Kaye followed the path along the railroad tracks. Having nothing to drink caused her tongue to cling to the roof of her mouth. Her palate had a foul taste. She smacked her chaffed lips. They were numb from the sun and early spring breeze. The extra clothing weighed her down during the day, but could not be discarded because it kept her warm through the night.

The afternoon brought occasional light rain showers. She waited until dark and crept into a chicken coop. When she entered, the chickens squawked at first, and made buk-buk-buk sounds. They quieted down as she remained still. It was comforting to be inside where it was dry. The warmth inside the building from the hens surprised her. She attempted to sleep resting on top of the waist high laying-boxes attached to the wall.

Kaye awakened predawn to the rooster's crow, and before leaving, she removed one sock and dumped the grain from the feeding tray inside. She tugged an empty feedbag down from the rafters and removed the folder from her undershirt. She placed it inside the bag, wrapped it into a flat bundle, and tied it with a piece of twine. Taking the long end of the twine she tossed it over a nail, then over her shoulder, backed up to the bag until it lodged against her back, took another piece of twine and anchored it in place, and then redressed. When a fat biddy hopped off her nest Kaye snatched two eggs and opened the door just wide enough to exit. Peeking around the corner of the coop she could see there were no windows from the house offering a view of the coop door. Hopefully, no one had seen her, and even the dog at the house had not barked when she entered or left the coop. The windmill stood between the house and the barn. Kaye sighed. It was the only water available, but she couldn't risk going near.

The dry chicken feed did not help her thirst. Back on the dirt road leading alongside the tracks, she cracked the end of an egg and sucked the liquid into her mouth. She ate them one at a time. The eggs made the crushed corn into dough; the lump became difficult to chew and swallow.

Kaye stopped to scrape the heavy mud from her shoes. The sun was rising in the eastern sky. She adjusted her socks and re-tied both shoes. Her thoughts turned to the importance she'd placed on wearing clean and matching socks every day at the Home, washing them each night and drying them on the radiator. She made sure Jessie had clean and matching socks every day too. Thoughts of Jessie were painful. How frivolous her sock concerns appeared now, as she removed the burrs and stickums from her clothes and rubbed the scratches on her legs. She should have grabbed a pair of overalls. There hadn't been time to plan. It was then or never. It's strange that Hannot scheduled her transfer and the trip to the hospital on a night Ollie would be working afternoons and his truck would be loaded with bags of feed. When Kaye saw Ollie's truck, she knew she had a way to leave. Only one person could have known how everything would line up to help her escape. Without faith, even Toe would have difficulty explaining this.

The blurred glow of the sunrise continued to move higher in the sky. It didn't pierce the cloud cover as it rose. The glow behind the clouds gave the area an eerie grayness. Continuing her journey, Kaye became more aware of changes in the sky and noticed there were no small animals scampering about. The temperature grew warmer. She shed her coat and sweater, carrying them in her arms while the bundle on her back pricked through her undershirt, chafing her skin. Moisture of her salty sweat burned in the scratches. The humidity increased until steam rolled across the small shallow pools of water beside the tracks. She followed the tracks, avoiding any intersections circling away and crossing the road at a distance and then weaving her way back again. She rushed into the thickets whenever she heard the rumble and whistle of another approaching engine. Fear called to her with every tremble of earth. Anyone her size and female seen walking along the tracks would be suspect. If the sighting were reported to the police, she could be returned to the Home. Kaye waited under the cover of the bushes as another train passed.

Noon had come and gone. The earth fell silent. Resting on a warm flat rock, Kaye could see the highway through the branches of a tree. She watched the automobiles move along a nearby road. Early spring bees hummed searching for blossoms and insects inspected the pussy willows near a bog. Kaye inched down the bank and followed a path around a bend toward a gas station/grocery store displaying a sign that read, *Tony's*.

A bread truck with red, blue, and yellow circles painted on it pulled off the highway, stirring up a puff of dust as it cruised around the building and pulled up in the back.

Kaye approached the store moving from one large tree, then another. She watched the man unload two wire racks of bread and carry them into the back door of the store. She rushed to jump inside the truck, pulled a loaf of bread from a rack, and scurried away hiding behind a storage shed, her heart pounding and her legs trembling. She hoped the cellophane wrapper wouldn't make a noise. She pushed the bread inside her coat and worked to pull the wrapper open. The driver returned to his truck, and she heard him slam the door and start the engine. As the seal on the wrapper opened, she inhaled the aroma and grabbed two slices of the soft white bread pushing them into her mouth. Never had plain white bread tasted so good. Someday she would pay for this bread. It's not stealing if she intended to pay for it.

She heard a wooden door slam. Someone came out of the store wearing heavy boots and stomped toward the shed. The door of the storage shed opened, and she heard the sound of heavy scraping, then the clinking of glass. The shed door slammed, but she didn't hear a latch close. Perhaps the door of the shed didn't latch. Carefully and curiously, she inched along the sidewall, around the corner. She tried the door. It moved. She opened it ever so slightly and eased her body inside.

In the dark, she found a small rock with her foot and placed it against the door, holding it open a crack. Light filtered in around her. Stacks of wooden boxes containing bottles lined the walls. Kaye removed one brown bottle, replaced the rock, and closed the door.

She hurried back toward the tracks with her bread and brown bottle. She stopped behind a tree and tried to pull the top off the bottle. The sharp edges of the metal cap gouged into her hand, and it started to bleed. She had nothing to pry off the cap. Holding something to drink in her hand made her thirst even worse. She would have to break the bottle to open it. Hopefully glass wouldn't get inside the bottle. She couldn't be sure someone was not within hearing range even if she didn't see anyone. She went to the tracks and looked at the rails and the spikes. She wedged the bottle top between the rail and a spike. She pushed the end of the bottle down. The top popped off, spinning into the air. White bubbles fizzed out and rolled down the sides. She carried the bread and brown bottle back to the cover of a thicket and tipped the bottle up. The liquid touched her lips then rolled onto her tongue. She gagged but resisted spitting it out. She swallowed it and took a deep breath. She ate another slice of bread and looked at the bottle. Maybe the bread would keep her stomach from tossing the awful liquid back up. It was wet, hopefully it would quench her thirst. She sipped another drink and forced herself to swallow, ate more bread and drank from the bottle until it was empty, and then curled up on her coat. The food, the drink, and warmth of the day lulled her to sleep.

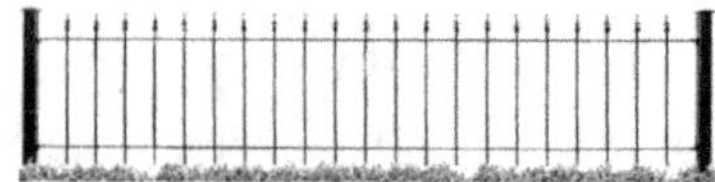

Kaye awakened, startled by a death-like stillness. Her head ached. The sun remained behind the clouds. She could not discern the time of day. Something about the stillness haunted her. Not a blade of grass quivered. She looked across a bog; not a cattail moved. She slowed her breathing to not disturb the death-like stillness that hovered. Not a bird was singing or a cricket cheeping. The whole earth appeared ghostly still. Kaye started down the footpath again. Her stomach cramped. She tasted the sour liquid and doughy bread in her throat and retched; her stomach ousting its contents. The sky above began to open. High clouds rolled to her right, and the low clouds rolled to her left. Rose pink clouds tumbled high across the horizon, while below foul chartreuse clouds swirled and formed column-like pillars. They were vertical, shadowing over the pink clouds. The whole earth was getting sick. Her stomach continued to churn as she swallowed, determined not to wretch again. All around her nothing moved. Fear coursed through her body; her senses conveyed danger was eminent, but she had no shelter, nowhere to hide. She heard a roar, a roar so deep and loud it hurt her ears. She started to run. Trees were bending and she stumbled as she ran. Brown dust filled the air. Ahead appeared the outline of a bridge over the railroad tracks. The bridge had high arches of concrete. Her chest ached and it was hard to breathe. Something was sucking the air out of her body. Terror filled her heart. Her legs wobbled as she ran, seeking shelter away from the roar and the thick cloud of dust. She stumbled up the bank. Without looking left or right, she ran across the road seeking refuge on the other side of the bridge, away from the wind. A car screeched to a stop.

A woman screamed, "Here, here!" Kaye turned. The woman heaved a blanketed bundle into the air toward her. Kaye lurched into the wind and grabbed at the untethered bundle. The wind whipped at it, unfurling the blanket and spiraling it up into the turbulent raging wind as Kaye clutched the leg of an infant child. She pulled the baby against her chest, circling her arms tight around its small body, sheltering it with her own. The child made no sound. She patted the baby's back and prayed, "Breathe, baby breathe." She pressed her back tight against the concrete wall of the bridge and slid down onto the grass. The woman appeared, skidding down the grassy bank, holding a small child, head first, under each arm. Their eyes closed against the blowing dirt. Both women pressed their bodies together, sheltering the children. The deafening roar encircled them. The earth trembled.

A whistle sounded. The headlight of a train engine pierced the dark cloud of dust. Kaye glanced up to see the woman's car careening into the air, disappearing into oblivion. The train burst forth from under the bridge. In moments they heard the roar of the storm, then the sound of churning and twisting steel as railroad cars collided against each other, whipping zigzag off the tracks to the left and right. Screeching sounds of steel against steel as the railroad cars collided behind them and echoed raging twisting protests. The roar of the wind lifted. Smells of smoke and sounds of crackling fire filled the air. Pockets of blazes burst forth along the tracks. The women tried to cover the children's eyes and ears. Men called out. People screamed. Torrents of rain pelted down, muddying the ground, soaking the people, and drenching the fires, sending clouds of smoldering smoke up from the earth.

The wind stilled, the rain stopped, then, it was over. Kaye looked at the baby in her arms fearful the child did not survive. The baby was panting, shallow quick breaths. It began to move its head. Kaye brushed away the cover of brown dust, as the infant struggled to open its eyes. She pulled it against the crook of her neck and murmured, lulling sounds as she checked the other children.

"We're safe. It's okay now. We're safe." She tried to comfort them. They were frightened and huddled together, but not injured. She looked at the mother; her eyes were vacant as the baby started to cry. Kaye lifted the infant toward the mother, but the woman did not respond. The baby continued to cry, and Kaye watched the front of the woman's dress dampen as the child wailed. She took the woman's hand as she would a child. She must get them away. The children should not watch this scene of horror.

"Come," Kaye urged. She held the baby and pulled the woman to her feet. Kaye turned to the older of the children, a boy about four, and kneeled to look into his eyes and spoke softly. "Mama needs your help.

Take her hand and follow me." The younger child, a girl of about two, clutched the mother's skirt, and together they struggled up the bank toward the road.

Away from the sight of the train, Kaye urged them to sit down on the grass at the side of the road. The sounds of sirens echoed in the distance. Now seated, she unbuttoned the bodice of the woman's dress and placed the child for nursing. The woman's arms remained flaccid at her side; she was listless and inattentive. Kaye held the nursing infant until the baby turned away from the breast. She re-buttoned the woman's dress and held the child.

Police cars raced past them, one returned. A policeman offered them a blanket. Kaye pulled the children against her. They huddled together, exhausted. With her free hand she wiped the dirt from the children's faces.

Together they took in the scene. They watched ambulances and fire trucks speed toward the accident. A chicken scurried across the road, featherless. Debris lingered everywhere, a tractor lay upside down in a field, and sections of a barn, now pieces of slab wood, littered the field. Kaye heard voices, people calling out from the train cars.

The policeman talked into his radio and returned. "The Salvation Army truck is coming. They'll have coffee and blankets. Just stay here." He continued directing ambulances and fire trucks toward the scene and ordering other traffic to turn around.

It was dark when a bus pulled up and the door opened. A man held the baby as Kaye urged the children inside. The mother of the children remained unresponsive sitting in the grass.

The little boy pushed his way back down the bus steps and pulled her hand. "It's okay, Mommy, it's okay. Come with me." She struggled to stand and follow him, her footsteps obedient, her mind detached from their course.

Kaye sought to take in all that had happened. Throughout the bus ride her memory was a blur. They arrived at a building and were directed inside to a high school gym. Kaye saw several people dressed in navy-blue uniforms moving about the room setting up cots and carrying cups of coffee, others offered blankets.

One of the workers approached her, a woman. "Hello, my name is Ann Marie." She too wore a navy-blue uniform and her hair was tied back at the nape of her neck. She had beautiful light blue eyes and a warm smile. She reached down to touch the children, giving each a friendly, reassuring pat.

"Is there anything you need?" She looked at the small family. Without waiting for an answer, she left, but returned moments later with a small tray. Two cups of coffee, cups of milk for the children, two bologna sandwiches cut in half, and four cookies. Kaye and Anne Marie fed the children. When the task was completed, Ann Marie sat down on a cot across from Kaye.

"You're safe here." She smiled. Her efforts to reassure them were comforting. "Is there anything you need?"

"I want my Daddy." The little boy pouted.

"We'll find your Daddy. Can you help us care for your Mommy?"

"Un-huh." The boy settled into a spot near his mother and between his sisters.

Kaye hesitated. "Would it be possible to get a needle and some thread. I have a couple buttons off my coat."

"I think I have a needle and thread in my first-aid kit. It has several strands of different colored thread. Does that matter?"

"No, that would be fine. Thank you."

Ann Marie returned with the kit and a second cup of coffee for Kaye.

"Can you stay with the children while I use the restroom?"

"Of course." Ann Marie snuggled the children near her and started to tell them a story.

Kaye entered the restroom wearing her coat. In the stall she removed her coat and blouse and untied the bundle on her back. She used the twine to secure the manila folder. She would discard the burlap. After sliding the folder inside her coat sleeve, she returned to the area where her newfound family waited.

After Ann Marie left to help the people arriving, Kaye slid off the cot and onto the floor. Using the tiny scissors from the kit, she carefully ripped out a section in the back of the coat hem and wrapped the matching thread around a piece of paper. She pulled the file out from inside her coat sleeve and slid it into the back of her coat between the fabric and the lining. She stitched up the hem with the black thread from the kit, and then made delicate stitches at the corners of the folder, securing it in place with thread that matched the fabric. How handy it is to know how to sew. The stitches were not noticeable. She had to protect the folder. There was no safe place to dispose of it here.

When Ann Marie returned, Kaye's task had been completed.

"We're trying to identify all the people in the shelter," said Ann Marie carrying a clipboard. "I need to fill out this form. Can you give me your names and your addresses? There were several storms tonight. People are searching for family members. I'm glad you're safe." She patted the children's knees and removed a cap from her ink pen.

Kaye was embarrassed, because through all that had happened, she did not know the children's names.

"I can't help you. I don't know these people. We just met during the storm."

"Maybe you can help me, little man." Ann Marie turned to the oldest child. "What's your name?"

"I'm Andy. Are you going to find my Daddy? His name is Tom."

"I'm going to try." Ann Marie attempted to reassure the child.

Andy continued as he pointed his finger at each introduction. "That's Susie, the baby is Molly, and she's Mommy." He was proud of his work.

"What's your other name, your second name?" Ann Marie asked.

Andy wrinkled his brow.

"My bad-boy name is Andrew Charles."

Kaye and Ann Marie shared a smile.

"Were you folks on the train?" Ann Marie asked.

"No, they were traveling in a car," Kaye said. "When the storm came, we went to the bridge for cover." At once Kaye realized the direction of this conversation. She had not thought about the danger of revealing her own identity.

"Car-all gone!" Andy lifted his hands into the air.

Suddenly, the children's mother let out a blood-curdling scream. Kaye thrust the baby into Ann Marie's arms and rushed to her. She placed herself behind her, wrapped her arms around the woman, and pulled her onto the floor. She slid down behind her, splayed a leg on each side, and clutched the trembling young mother tight against her chest. She held her the same way she had been taught to hold a hysterical child at the Home. She continued to hold the woman throughout her shouts of anguish and agony. The woman's body arched; her arms flailed. Kaye turned her head to protect her face from injury. A man rushed up.

"I'm a doctor. I have something that will help." He pushed a filled syringe against the mother's arm. "Hold her until she starts to relax, then you can lay her down. She'll sleep for a while. She's in severe shock. That was amazing, the way you protected her. How did you know what to do?"

Before Kaye could mumble an answer, he helped her place the woman on a pallet on the floor and covered her with a blanket. The children pulled away from Ann Marie, huddled close to their mother, and both started to cry a tired whimper into the woman's skirt. The baby, too, cried in response to the children's outburst. Kaye started to put the child to the mother's breast.

The doctor cautioned. "No, she can't breast feed. You'll need to feed the baby a bottle until late tomorrow. No breast milk while the mama has the medicine in her body." His eyes were kind but his voice stern.

Kaye placed the children one on each side of their mother and tucked them in with the blankets. The baby rested on a nearby pallet.

"Where will I get a bottle?"

"I'll find one and some formula." Ann Marie dashed away. When she returned, she was carrying a warm bottle for the baby and a sandwich for Kaye.

Kaye bowed her head to pray. Ann Marie placed her hand on Kaye's. "Amen," they said in unison.

"Let her rest," Ann Marie urged. "Maybe Mama will eat later. This has been a terrifying event. The poor woman probably thought she'd lose her whole family. The children will help her by being near." She folded back another page on her clipboard and uncapped her ink pen. "Back to my task. What's your name?"

"Maureen."

Ann Marie started to write. "How do you spell it?"

"M-a-u-r-e-e-n." Kaye spoke each letter, biding time to think. She looked up to see a woman filling saltshakers on the table from a blue box of salt, a picture of a girl on the box wearing a dress and the word Morton. She couldn't say Kaye O'Shay.

"Maureen Morton. M-o-r-t-o-n," she said. "My friends call me Maury."

Ann Marie wrote Maureen Morton. "Your address?"

Kaye covered her mouth with her hand and rushed to the bathroom, physically ill. When the retching stopped, she returned to the little family. Anne Marie had moved to another group of people and continued making notes on her clipboard.

She had to get out of there before they found out she was a runaway.

Chapter 24

"*I* gotta find her, Nurse Lucy!"

Toe stood at the nursery door holding two containers of milk. He had learned he could go almost anywhere at the Home if he carried two cans of milk. They didn't have to have milk in them; the two containers kept anyone from stopping him.

"You want me to take those?"

"No, they're empty. You didn't request milk, did you?"

Lucy Heusted laughed and patted his shoulder. "No, Toe I didn't request milk. It looks like you wanted to see me."

"Yeah," Toe nodded. "It's about Kaye."

Nurse Lucy shared her concern. "I haven't seen her, and no one seems to know anything."

"Yeah, I know. I think she tried to run away. I'm worried. I can't sleep, I can't do my schoolwork." He was wringing his hands and pacing.

"Toe, I don't think she would run away. Where would she go? She didn't have any reason to run, did she?" Nurse Lucy scowled at Toe accusingly.

"No, nothing happened like that. We never did nothin'. She got all upset if I tried to hold her hand for fear someone would see us and tell."

Nurse Lucy smiled. "Yes, I'm sure she would. But I can't help you."

"What can I do?"

"You could pray."

"Pray! Do you mean that?"

"Yes, I do, I've been praying ever since I learned she disappeared. Haven't you?"

"No. I don't believe in God."

"What do you believe in?" She waited for him to reply. "Look at you. You're a mess of fear and imaginings. You might want to think twice about saying, 'I don't believe in God.' If you think Kaye is out there somewhere and feeling frightened and alone, don't you think she's praying? I know Kaye and I know she loves God. You better believe she's praying."

Toe squatted on his haunches. He did know Kaye, and she would be afraid, and Nurse Lucy was right, Kaye would be praying.

"Do you believe God will protect her?"

"Yes, I do, Toe, and I believe He would like to hear your prayers too."

"I'm not happy with God. Kaye's gone. Look at my life! Your God wants me here? Do you know how many times a *Bible* thumper has walloped on me over the years? Some of those men are a mean lot."

"I'm sorry, Toe. I can't explain why things happen. But I know God loves you."

"If I don't believe in God, how can I pray?"

"You ask him to help your unbelief and to help you pray."

"Nurse Lucy, I'm gonna ask God to help me find Kaye, and if he does, then I'll know He's real and not something people make up in their heads. Good night."

Toe headed back toward the barns. The night had grown dark. Spring was in the air. On the edge of the potato field, he sat on a tree stump and looked up at the sky.

"Yeah, I said it and I meant it. I'm not sure you're really a God who takes care of people, but if you are, please watch over Kaye and help me find her. Amen."

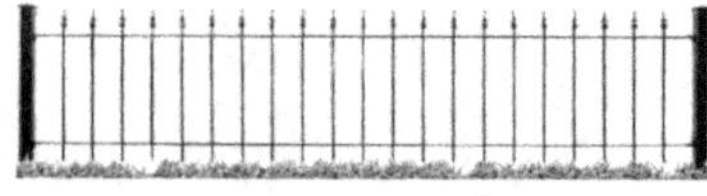

For the next two days, Kaye huddled with the children and their mother, keeping a vigilant eye on them. The children remained mute except for occasional outbursts of anguish. Kaye played games with Andy and some other children, making puppets from their socks, and telling them stories. Sometimes she let them help her make up the story and they acted out the animals or gestures.

Just before she tucked the children into bed on the evening of the third day, a tall handsome man with dark hair threaded his way through the maze of people, his face terror-stricken, his eyes darting, and searching. Kaye saw him before he saw them. There was no mistaking this adult version of Andy, unshaven, his eyes shadowed in dark circles of sleeplessness.

"Daddy, Daddy!" Andy ran toward him. Susie sucked her thumb and held her mother's dress with a clenched fist.

The man scooped Andy up into his arms and approached them. His body visibly trembled as he tried to maintain composure. He knelt and hugged Susie. Tears of relief rolled from his eyes and flowed down his cheeks as he took Molly from Kaye's arms and hugged her into his neck. He moved toward his wife, circling her with his other arm and kissing her on the cheek. She did not look at him or respond. He picked up her hand and kissed her palm. Her hand remained limp in his. He observed her. His face stricken with both panic and uncertainty; he turned toward Kaye.

"Who are you? What happened to my family?"

"Daddy, dis is Maury." Andy tugged at his Daddy's pant leg. "She finds us cookies."

Tom scowled. His accusing remark shocked her. For three days she had a family. She had risked her life to protect them from peril. She had sheltered them, hugged them, loved them, fed them, and cared for them. Now, reality scorched her like a branding iron, they were *his* family. She could hear her own words spoken to Nurse Lucy, "They are not your children." The same way she told Toe, "They are not your cows." This was not her family. These children she had loved and cared for were not her children. Love had a way of claiming ownership. Her heart writhed in pain.

The man waited for her answer. It was impossible to explain to this broken man all that had happened.

"There was a storm. A bad storm. Then the train—."

"Tom." He interrupted her. "My name is Tom, Tom Butler, and this is my family."

Reaching from deep within for words that would not come, she gasped and tried to reply. "I don't know, Mr. Butler. She, your wife, was like this after the storm. The first day here, she cried and was inconsolable, even though she was with the children. The doctor gave her medicine and she slept. Most of our time here, she's been asleep, but she hasn't talked."

"That's all. No one's tried to help her?" His fear and anger tumbled out.

"Yes, Mr. Butler." Kaye lowered her voice the same way she observed some workers did when speaking to one of the children at the Home if they became distressed. "Everyone has tried to help. They've helped me care for her and the children. Ann Marie, the woman over there from the Salvation Army has helped get formula for the baby and diapers."

Kaye felt desperate. She had no explanation that would satisfy him.

Tom looked at his wife. He held Molly in his arms. A grimace appeared on his face as he struggled to understand.

"Susie, take Daddy's hand. Andy, you take Mommy's hand. We're going home."

Andy took his mother's hand. Kaye urged the mother to her feet; she faltered and sat back down on the cot without looking at anyone.

Ann Marie approached, her uniformed presence bringing order to the chaos.

"I see you found them." She glanced at her clipboard. "Tom, is that correct? Are you folks going home now? Here let me help you." She took the mother's arm and assisted Kaye, and together they encouraged her to stand. "I'll walk with you to your car."

Kaye's stomach lurched as if kicked by a boot as she watched the family depart.

They were near the door when Andy turned to look back at Kaye. He wiggled free from his mother's hand and bolted toward her. "Come on, Maury. We're going home now. You come too."

Kaye looked at Tom.

He watched as Andy tugged Kaye forward. Then spoke abruptly. "Andy, stop, the lady has her own home to go to. Come on. It's late."

Andy refused to let go of Kaye's hand and continued pulling. "Daddy, she loves us, she said so. Didn't you, Maury? Don't you want to come to our house?" He was near tears.

The man observed her, his face gray with exhaustion and worry.

"She wants to come, don't you, Maury?" Andy's tears now surfaced.

Terror seized her. She had nowhere to go. These beautiful children had comforted her in ways they could never know. They were not hers, but she had indeed grown to love them.

Tom nodded as she and Andy neared him. "Do you want to come? Are you really willing to help us?"

"More than you could ever know, Mister Butler." She held out her arms. Tom surrendered Molly to her and placed his arm around his wife. Andy took Susie's hand.

"Here," Ann Marie handed Kaye a piece of paper. "Let's make a Molly sandwich." She laughed and reached around Molly to give Kaye a hug and whispered, "If you ever want to reach me you can call this number."

Kaye received the hug and slid the note into her coat pocket.

Chapter 25

Lucy Heusted worked late that warm spring night. She stepped outside to check the weather. Buds were forming on the trees and freshness filled the air. In the night sky countless stars flickered.

Her legs ached from hours of walking, and her arms ached from lifting the children. Everything she had to give, the work took, and left her empty without the satisfaction of a job well done. It left her emotions raw, and her heart wrung out like a twisted sheet. Doing her best and praying over the children and staff did not stop the gnawing questions she could not suppress. Knowing she had no right to ask did not bury them either. She tried to tell herself she made the day better for each child. Today, one child passed and three more were admitted. Tomorrow loomed ahead.

"Good night, Heusted," Maxwell called out. "You calling safety?"

"No, I don't want to wait. I'm tired. I just want to go home."

"You know what that memo was about. We're supposed to call for an escort after dark. I'll call. You get your things together."

Lucy Heusted tidied up the office and sat down in the desk chair to wait. She paged through the time sheets. It was the third night this week she had worked four hours or more over her shift. The hours at her own home were becoming sparse. There was only time to do essential things. Pot meals were prepared in bulk. She had no time to help with farm chores. Every part of her life evidenced neglect as she paid homage to the time clock at the Home. She rubbed her forehead. A headache? Had she eaten dinner? The previous hours blended into multiple tasks without recall. Time to go home. She had to stay awake for the forty-minute drive. Her gold wedding band glistened on her finger. "In sickness or in health," the preacher said. It was no wonder vows didn't say, "In fidelity or infidelity." Lucy mumbled. She had remained a faithful wife. Her sanctimonious pride carried her on through the days and years of her marriage into the majesty of her martyrdom. Other women admired her stalwart attitude; some told her so.

A tap sounded on the office door. "I'm here. Do you need something?" Earl Lance, from the safety department waited with one arm resting on the door jam. His mustache trimmed, his hair slicked back, and his uniform neat with a military press.

"Yes. Thanks, Earl. They insist we have an escort now after hours. It's a bit of a bother, I say. I hope I didn't call you from something important."

"No Ma'am." Earl's smile slanted slightly at Maxwell, who entered the office. "I can't think of a thing that's more important than escorting you, Nurse Lucy." Lucy caught Maxwell's glance as Earl's gaze passed down Lucy's uniformed body and back up again to her face. Lucy ignored his flirtations and gathered up her coat and purse.

"Maxwell, I'm leaving now."

"Okay. Ouuuwee!" Maxwell called over her shoulder as she fanned her face.

Lucy ignored her gestures, secured the door behind her, and followed Earl toward the distant day shift parking lot where she had left her car early that morning. In the dark, the tree limbs moved like giant arms, casting shadows from intermittent clouds passing over the moonlit sky. A gentle breeze stirred the promise of spring. Haloes of porch lights glowed from the cottages. As they entered the darkened area of the parking lot, Earl nudged against her.

"Oh, sorry. I was watching something moving." He pointed toward a boulder bordered by a tree and several shrubs.

Lucy stopped. "Is someone over there?"

"No, it's okay. I'll check it out later. Probably a groundhog or a rabbit."

Lucy searched in her purse for her car keys. Finding them, she fingered the key to make sure she had the grooved side in position and bent to insert it into the lock.

Earl reached over her head with his left hand and pressed against the top of the door, preventing her from opening it.

"It's almost time for me to punch out, would you like to meet at the Tavern, maybe for a drink?"

"I have a husband." Lucy turned her head, meeting his eyes with a stony glare. He was standing very near. She smelled his aftershave, the deep pungent fragrance of leather and spice, so contradictory after hours of creosote and fecal odors.

Earl whispered, "Well, from my observation, it's a sure enough thing he don't appreciate the fine woman he's got. A woman like you is special."

Lucy caught her breath. "Earl, your lingo is annoying. Don't let me keep you from your work," she snapped, urging him away as she opened the car door.

He stepped away.

He held the door open as she slid into the seat. He smiled with a knowing smirk. "It's okay. I know you'd like to meet me." He pushed the door closed until the latch snapped, then he walked away.

For the first time in several years, she felt a longing. A desire. Every muscle in her body was tense. She tried not to watch as Earl walked away. A chill swept through her. What had kept her from yielding to him? Years of waiting and longing mixed with her anger and rage. She drove toward home weeping, wiping her face with her hands and struggling to see the road through her tears.

Kaye had been right in what she said that night before she disappeared, telling Lucy she was wrong to preach forgiveness while she herself refused to forgive. Kaye said lying to oneself is worse than lying to other people.

Lucy longed to be home, in her house, with her husband. She had been so stubborn. The years she had wasted in anger prompted tears of frustration. The years of her anger had cost them both. She missed being held in his arms. How many wounds until love is too damaged, too mangled, when love is totaled, and written off as beyond repair?

Lucy turned into the driveway. The light was on in the living room. Her stomach tightened. Thoughts raced through her mind. Something dreadful had happened. It had to be something bad for him to be up so late. She rushed toward the house, tripping up the steps. She opened the front door. The click of the latch had startled him. He struggled from his chair to awaken, rubbing his eyes without looking at her.

"Is something wrong?"

"No, everything's all right. I've been up with a new heifer calving. When I saw it was past time for you to come home, I waited up."

"You waited up?" Her surprise and pleasure were not concealed.

"Yeah! And you're home now, so guess I'll go to bed" His gaze avoided her eyes. He turned off the light beside his chair and left the room.

Lucy listened to his footsteps ascend the stairs. She laid her keys on the hall table and hung her coat in the closet. She went to the kitchen to turn off the light and she saw the vase of roses.

The card read, "Twelve years and twelve roses. Happy Anniversary."

She had forgotten their anniversary. After years of her anger toward him, he still wanted to celebrate their marriage. It was love that had protected her an hour ago. The promises they made and God's love.

Lucy climbed the stairs, tears streaming down her face. Verses of scripture tumbled through her mind. "Remember not the former things, neither consider the things of old. 19 Behold I will do a new thing; ... I will make a way in the wilderness and rivers in the desert." (Isiah 43:18-19 NIV)

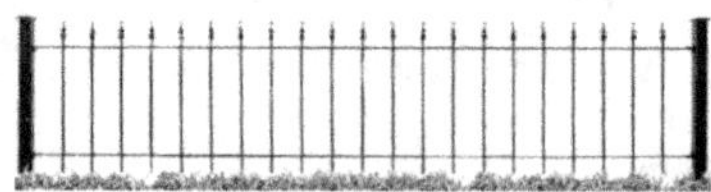

Toe stretched in his bed and listened as the train passed. The sounds droned on and on. The whistle sounded in the distance once, then again. He tried to estimate how far the train would travel until the miles would silence the whistle. Ever since he came to the barns to work, and lived in this cottage, he had played guessing games about the trains. The huge engines thundered past as sparks shot from the wheels. Some men tried to run. Few made it out and others took a step onto the track because it was the only way to stop the hell of their life.

Thoughts of Kaye had tormented him since the day she disappeared. He had searched everywhere he knew, and asked everyone he could safely ask, seeking information about her. If she was at the Home, they wouldn't or couldn't tell him, but all indications were she was not there. If anyone knew, Nurse Lucy would, and she confessed nothing. If Kaye was outside the Home, she was alone, all alone with no money. Someone could threaten to turn her in. He feared what she might be forced to do. He couldn't think about that; he had to do something, and he couldn't do it here.

Ben slept in the next bed, the bed he commandeered when he first arrived. Ben, though bigger, was the little brother Toe never had. All Ben's difficulties did not stop him from trying to entertain the men. When he found out he could make other folks laugh and have fun, he'd found his mission. The only man in the loft who could not laugh made everyone laugh with his antics. His temper was so well known and his strength, displayed in numerous contests, left him without challenging foes— except for Ollie. Toe smiled thinking about his solution to teach Ben the record keeping for the herd. Things had worked out well. He wouldn't have to worry about Ben and Ollie now, because Ollie needed Ben and they both knew it. There could be trouble if Ollie started drinking again, but that was better lately as well.

The bundle of clothing Toe had knotted in a belt lay tucked at his feet under his covers. He remained awake. There would be another train in two hours. He would be waiting. A man got up and went to the bathroom and returned. Other men stirred in their sleep. Within minutes, sounds of sleeping men filled the room with snores in varying pitch and rhythm, joined by groans, thrashing of legs, occasional pounding of a fist. Dreams colored by frustrations, limitations, and pressure to comply. Bodies tired from hard work. Some men had to be stopped from overworking and some men would lie down in the field on the first row of beans. Eating was the only activity all the men agreed on and they ate. The cook handled arguments over food, and she had a way to make any man regret "causing a commotion," as she called it.

The clock chimed downstairs. An hour had passed. Two o'clock. He had to try to catch the three o'clock train. The night watchman left his station before three and clocked off his checkpoints. No one would be watching the tracks. Any later and the men would be getting up.

He moved out of his bed, adjusting his body to avoid the one bed-spring that squeaked when he sat up. He slid his left leg out and held the frame, lifting his body up from the middle of the bed. He tiptoed down the stairs in his stocking feet, and stepped on the outside edge of the treads, avoiding the two boards that creaked. He picked up his shoes beside the back door. He turned the knob and released the lock with his penknife. The door opened without a click, and he eased outside.

He was almost at the stable when a stick cracked behind him and he turned to see Ben walking in his stocking feet and carrying his shoes.

Toe sat down on the grass and pulled on his shoes. Ben followed, mimicking Toe's every move. Toe patted Ben's arm and shook his head, "No." Ben shook his head, "No." Toe sighed. He stood up and walked toward the train tracks and crossed to the north side. There was always a possibility someone from the farm side might see him. Here no one could because the trees shaded the tracks from the buildings. He put his hand on the rails. He could not feel a tremor. He put his ear to the rails. Yes, the train was coming. He had to make Ben understand. Toe pulled Ben toward a tree and urged him to climb up. Ben obeyed. When Ben was up on the tree limb, Toe walked back to the tracks only to find Ben behind him again.

"No. Go back. No," Toe urged. Ben tugged at Toe's shirt, pulling him away from the tracks. Toe shrugged off Ben's grasp and pushed him toward the tree. Ben walked away, his head down.

Toe watched as Ben climbed up into the tree. He hated leaving Ben. He wished he could make Ben understand he didn't want to leave him. They were more than true friends; they would give their lives for each other.

Suddenly a flash of light appeared. The watchman was coming down the path. Toe rushed toward the tree and lay flat on the ground in the grass. The watchman walked past patrolling the south side of the tracks. Soon he would be back at the guard shack near the paved road. The one paved road that connected the front of the compound to the back. Toe waited until he heard the first whistle of the train. He crawled toward the tracks, pulling his clothing bundle. First the engine passed, then several cars of coal. He needed a car with an access step. The sounds changed. Passenger cars rolled by, and then empty cars. He lifted himself up and started to run alongside the train. He grabbed the bar beside the step with his right hand and held his bundle in his left. *Run, Seth Thomas. Run.* His legs pumped up and down; his shoes slid on the rocks that rolled under his feet. He struggled to hold his grasp and gain speed. He pushed off with his left leg and jumped, pressing every muscle into action, and using all his strength, reaching, hoping to land his right foot on the step! He missed. His body whipped forward, then his right leg disappeared into the churning wheels of the train.

Ben watched the dark shadow of Toe's body twirl into the air and land in the grassy ditch. He dropped from the tree and ran as fast as he could. He scooped Toe into his arms. Toe's body was limp. Ben was filled with terror. He could smell blood and grease and grass. Ben clutched Toe against his chest and ran toward the watchman's shack. Oh, if only he could yell. If only a sound would come out, he could get help. His tears flowed as he laid Toe on the ground outside the guard shack and pounded on the door.

Chapter 26

Outside the gym, Kaye followed Tom and his family to his pickup. He opened the door for his wife and turned to look at them.

It didn't look like there was room for six in the cab of his pickup.

"Okay." He paused, glancing around at the waiting faces. "Janie, you get in and sit next to me. You'll have to straddle the gearshift. Andy can ride on my lap, Susie, you sit on Mama's lap and Molly—what's your name again."

"Maury, Daddy," Andy chimed in, pressing Kaye's hand against his face.

"Yeah, Maury." Tom lifted Janie into the truck seat. He rushed around to the driver's seat carrying Susie, placed her behind the steering wheel, then lifted Janie's leg over the gearshift and seated Susie on her lap. "Come on, get in."

Maury, it is, she thought, glancing back at the school and down at Andy still hugging her hand. For this delightful little boy who offered her genuine love, and for this family, she could be Maury. Maury would be happy to love them in return. Her mood changed as thoughts emerged. There was no one—not one person—who would care who she was, or that Kaye Maureen O'Shay disappeared at the train, and no one to know exactly when Maury Morton arrived.

Kaye climbed into the truck holding Molly wrapped in a blanket. Tom returned to snatch Andy up into his arms and assumed the driver's seat. Kaye slammed the passenger door shut. Janie continued a low murmur, a sound between a moan and a hum.

Andy wiggled in his tight space. Tom started the engine and struggled to turn the steering wheel toward the exit.

"You've got to sit still, Andy. Daddy has to drive." Tom paused as he pulled out onto the road. "If you sit real still, I'll let you help me drive, like I do when you ride with me on the tractor." Andy stretched his body up to see out the windshield. Tom had his full attention now.

Susie wiggled to snuggle against Janie, who folded her arms across her chest, resisting Susie's attempts for comfort. Susie sat upright on Janie's right knee, holding onto the dash until she grew tired and slumped over against Kaye's arm. During their exit Ann Marie had given Kaye a warm bottle wrapped in a diaper. They had been riding for several miles when the baby started to whimper. Kaye snuggled the child near and unwrapped the warm bottle. The baby ate, and then slept.

"How long will it take us to get to your home?" Kaye asked.

"What?"

"Your home, how long will it take?"

"That's what I was just thinking about. I don't know what roads are still closed. It should only take an hour, but with all the detours, I don't know."

"Detours?

"Didn't you hear? There were five tornadoes that touched down that night. There's trees down and roads closed everywhere."

"No, we only knew that people kept coming into the gym."

They rode in silence as Tom maneuvered around a tree and followed detour signs and resumed travelling on another road.

"I was wondering when I'd need to feed the baby again. I only had one bottle."

"Bottle? Janie breastfeeds her babies. You didn't give Molly a bottle, did you? Janie'll have a fit."

The truck cab became silent again except for Janie's humming.

Tom was upset. Again, he thought she'd done wrong. First, he thought she hadn't got proper care for Janie and now the baby. If she told him Janie wouldn't feed the baby, maybe he'd blame her for that too. If she told him Janie could not nurse because of the medicine, he might be mad about that. He could stop the truck and tell her to get out. She had no idea where they were, and it was ten o'clock at night. No, he needed her to hold the baby. Her thoughts were interrupted by Tom's command.

"Give the baby to Janie and take Susie," Tom ordered.

"She can't, feed the baby." Kaye paused, anticipating another burst of anger. "The baby is sleeping now. Maybe Janie will feel better when she's at home and she'll nurse the baby there."

Silence.

He's still thinking about the route, the detours, and the downed trees. The children were quiet, lulled by the constant low humming from Janie. He must have realized she hasn't responded to him, not at the school gym or here in the truck.

After several detours, they arrived at Tom's farm. It was nearing midnight.

Tom carried the children to their beds. Kaye waited with Janie in the truck. Tom returned, lifted Janie's leg over the gearshift, and pulled her from the cab, easing her down from the seat. He attempted to help her stand. She raised her arms and slid through his grasp, her legs folding beneath her, and her head curved onto her chest, landing in a heap onto the ground.

Maybe she was sleeping.

"Janie, Janie, stand up," Tom urged, but she remained on the ground.

He bent down, lifted her into his arms, and carried her into the house the way he had carried the children. Kaye followed with Molly in her arms.

"Bring Molly upstairs. Her cribs up here." His voice growled with impatience and exhaustion. He gestured toward a door and disappeared down the hall and into a room with Janie.

Kaye turned on the lamp. The wallpaper was pink with teddy bears wearing tutus, seated at tables, having a tea party. Pink fluffy curtains hung at the window. Kaye changed Molly's diaper and covered her with a soft pink blanket from the foot of the crib.

Tom returned to Molly's room, carrying sheets, a blanket, and a pillow.

"Okay if you sleep downstairs tonight? Tomorrow, I can move Susie in with Molly, and you can have a room." He descended the stairs to the living room and placed the linens on the sofa. Kaye followed.

"That's fine. I don't need a room. We can wait and see how things work out."

His response was passive, again he was thinking of other things. "Oh, I'm working days for another week. That means I'm up at four. I'll try not to wake you."

"That's okay. The baby'll probably be awake anyway."

"Janie'll want to take care of the baby. You can sleep."

It was late. He still didn't understand. Kaye dismissed clarification. She didn't want to see him upset; he only had a few hours for sleeping.

"Thanks for the blanket. Good night."

Kaye opened the sheets and made her bed. Bottles—she had forgotten to make up formula for an early morning feeding. She went into the kitchen. On the counter was the bag Ann Marie had packed containing cookies for the ride and a container of powdered formula. She found a measuring cup, washed out the bottle she had used on the ride, rinsed it with boiling water, and prepared a bottle for formula. They had babies in the nursery at the Home who needed formula. Thank goodness she knew how to prepare a bottle.

The kitchen was both foreign and familiar. The appliances looked sort of like the ones in home-ec. Blue-checked ruffled curtains hung at the window over the sink. She rinsed a couple cereal bowls and wiped off the counters while she waited for the teakettle to boil. When she returned to the living room, there was a pair of women's pajamas on the coffee table. Amid all the chaos, Tom had realized she arrived with only the clothing she wore.

Tomorrow Tom would ask questions. Kaye went to sleep trying to piece together a believable story, one she could recall and that would stand up to investigation without revealing she had run away from a state institution. It wouldn't be right to tell him a lie after he had taken her to his home, but she couldn't tell him the truth. At three the baby cried, and Kaye hurried upstairs. Tom was at the crib in his pajama bottoms, picking up Molly.

"I'll take her to Janie."

"Tom, Janie has not responded to any of the children since the storm. Why don't we let her sleep and try later?"

Kaye held out her arms. Tom, half awake, surrendered Molly. Kaye carried the baby toward the kitchen. At 3:30 she heard water running upstairs. Tom was up for the day.

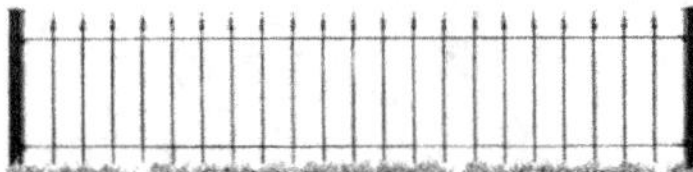

He left for work before sunrise. At six, Kaye made coffee, dressed, and prepared food for the children. At seven, Janie refused to nurse Molly. Kaye followed the directions from the doctor at the shelter and continued the formula feedings. Janie required care for dressing, eating, and direction for any activity. As the day progressed, Kaye found herself responding to the calls of "Maury" from the children. Watching Andy and Susie play she could not help thinking of Jessie. How she wished Jessie could have been as healthy as this little girl. The children surprised her, they were so independent at bathing, eating, dressing, and playing. Every part they have works, and they *have* every part.

During brief moments Kaye glanced at the newspaper. It had not published names of survivors or victims, stating they were notifying families. People were still missing. The article asked anyone with information about people displaced due to the storm to contact the local Emergency services. There remained multiple questions about the passenger list for the train.

Tom and Nate had shared rides to the plant for several years. But, for the first week after the storm Tom remained silent, preoccupied, and burdened.

The end of the week Nate asked, "How are things going at home?"

Tom could no longer contain his fear and frustration. He began talking and by the time they arrived at Nate's house, Tom was still talking.

"I can't let Janie's Mom know how she is. She's not getting better. Nate, she's not talked. She has this humming thing she does. It's my fault I didn't watch. After Andy was born, she got real sad and slept a lot. I had a woman come in for a couple months. After Susie, the Doctor said she had what was called the baby blues, but it didn't last, and she got better. So, after Molly, I thought she would be all right, but maybe I didn't see it. Then she was alone with the kids in the storm and the train wreck. I should have paid attention. I should have been there sooner. She walks around moaning and humming. The kids look at her and walk away. I don't know what I'd do without Maury."

"Maury?"

"That's the girl. Maury… Maureen… Morton. Anyway, she's good with the kids but she can't cook. She tries. She makes sausage gravy and biscuits."

"Is it good?"

"It's good. Last night, when I came in from the barn, she was busy with the kids, and sausage gravy was bubbling all over the stove. I could hear the kids racing through the house, Janie was walking down the road, and Maury was out there carrying the baby, trying to talk Janie into coming back to the house. When I got the gravy mopped up, I smelled the biscuits burning so I took them out of the oven and cut the bottoms off. The gravy had scorched but I saved enough for everybody to have some. When she came in with Janie, I had the food on the table. It's a mess, Nate. She can't keep doing it all, she's only a teenager. She says she's twenty-one but that can't be true."

"So, she makes good sausage gravy?"

"You got it. After the kids went to bed, I asked her."

"Where's she from?"

Tom's eyebrows shot up in surprise.

"Where she's from? No, I asked her if she could only make sausage gravy. I told her it was good sausage gravy. I didn't want to hurt her feelings, but Nate, I've eaten white gravy with beans, white gravy with potatoes, white gravy with chipped beef, we're eating white gravy for every meal."

Nate laughed. "Good thing it's good gravy. All those meals of bad gravy would be rough."

"She can't."

"Can't what?"

"Can't cook."

"Oh. What're you gonna do?"

"What can I do? I don't have time to cook. I can't call and ask Janie's mother to come from Tennessee. I can't ask my mom. She's so crippled with arthritis she can hardly get her own meals. She feels bad enough she can't help with the kids. I don't know what to do, Nate. I can't keep doing this." Tom turned his face away.

Nate sat quiet as Tom regained his composure. "Tell you what. You go home and tell Maury that Martha and I are bringing supper over tonight. It's Friday. We'll swing around by the lodge; we usually go there for fish supper. We'll just pick up dinner and bring it over. We'll be there after the chores. I bet Martha would lend your Maury a hand for a few days and she's a good cook."

"Bringing supper's okay but don't oblige Martha, I'll figure out something."

"Yeah. I hear yah! See you after chores."

The days were so busy. The following Monday, Andy returned to kindergarten, leaving Susie very lonely. The baby settled into the bottle. The morning routine stabilized. In the morning Kaye bathed the baby and Janie. Each night after supper Tom bathed the children and got them ready for bed as Kaye washed the dishes. The second morning Tom had encouraged her to sleep in, saying he preferred cold cereal for breakfast. Kaye ignored him because, as she said, she was up with the baby anyway, so it was easy to make him breakfast. His days were long as well. At first, she didn't understand that he worked in the factory, and wondered why he left every morning and wanted a lunch packed. After he switched to afternoon shift so he could work both the fields and plant, he told her, he worked in the factory so he could raise the kids on the farm.

They didn't talk much. Tom tended Andy and Janie. Kaye was busy with Susie and baby Molly. When the dirty clothes piled up, he spent Saturday morning doing the laundry. Kaye watched him sort the clothes, fill the washing machine with soap and hot water, and move the clothes through the wringer and into the two tubs of rinse water, putting them through the wringer each time. When she could, she helped by hanging the clothes on the clothesline. They had two lines of hand-made diapers.

On Sunday, Tom prepared the children for church and Sunday school. Janie started screaming when she saw Andy and Susie dressed and leaving. Tom could not quiet her, so Kaye circled from behind and slid to the floor, holding her the same way she had at the shelter. Janie struggled briefly.

"We'll missed Sunday school, but we can make church."

"You go on. We'll be okay."

Tom rushed to the car.

Janie calmed down and went to sleep in Kaye's arms.

That evening Kaye heard Tom tell someone on the telephone that he had a babysitter, and everything was fine. He thanked them for their concern and returned to the living room.

"Maury, you should know there might be some folks talking gossip about you living here, so don't be upset if someone is rude. Some people are stupid."

"Why would they be rude? I'm here helping your family."

"You're pretty, and they're people."

That was a curious thing for him to say. Pretty. She didn't have time to wash her face let alone curl her hair. She didn't feel pretty.

The days were long and hard. Everything was piling up, until Martha and Nate came that night and brought the fish supper. When Tom told her they were coming, she set the dining room table for seven, and a place at the kitchen table for herself.

Margo had told her some of the rules of working for folks. "You don't ever eat at their table. No matter how nice they are, don't forget you're the help. You don't eat with them."

Kaye wished she had worked outside the Home more than one day. There was so much she didn't know about a house. It was good she had taken the home economic classes. At least she could make béchamel and biscuits. She could mend the children's clothes and sew on buttons. The kitchen was a mystery. So many items she had never seen. She'd only baked biscuits in the oven and had never used the button on the stove marked broiler.

When Nate and Martha arrived that night, the baby had soiled her diaper, Andy and Susie were pulling apart a stuffed toy, and Tom came into the house with dirty boots, carrying a pail of eggs with chicken poop on them. Disgusting! Martha's arrival was an answer to prayer. She introduced herself saying her family was from Sweden. She had lovely blond hair she braided and twisted up the back of her head. She was slim and slightly taller than Nate. Her cheeks were a rosy pink. She wore a housedress and arrived with a basket of cookies and a bright red print apron folded on top. She hugged each child and held Janie's hand as she said hello. Janie pulled away and left the room. Martha patted Tom's shoulder.

As they washed the dishes together, Martha said, "Maury, you don't have to eat in the kitchen when we're here. We're friends. Tom didn't ask you to, did he?"

"No, he didn't say where I should sit. I know the kitchen is where the help eat and I'm working here."

"You certainly are working here." Martha said with a smile.

Kaye grinned. Only another woman would understand how hard she was working.

"I was wondering if I could come over tomorrow. I've got a few flowers from thinning out my garden. We could put them over by the fence."

"Sure, I think Tom would like that. He said Janie likes flowers."

And that's how it began. Martha came before lunch and planted the flowers, they baked cookies, and planned supper. When she left there was a roast with vegetables in the oven, potatoes waiting to be boiled, and a pie on the counter. Kaye was astounded how efficient Martha was in the kitchen.

"Where did you learn to cook?"

Martha pointed to Janie's shelf of cookbooks.

"From books?" Kaye had been so busy, she had not noticed the shelf of cookbooks. Kaye pulled the largest cookbook off the shelf.

Martha continued, "My mother taught me her favorite recipes but I wanted to make different foods, so I learned to use the recipes in the cookbooks."

That night Kaye started reading Janie's cookbooks. There were notes written on the recipes, notes with dates and people's names and comments about adding ingredients or lines through other ingredients, eliminating them. It was amazing. In home economics they were given single recipes, not cookbooks. There were recipes and directions for folding napkins and setting the table. In the back near the index, she found conversion charts and substitution tables. She loved it.

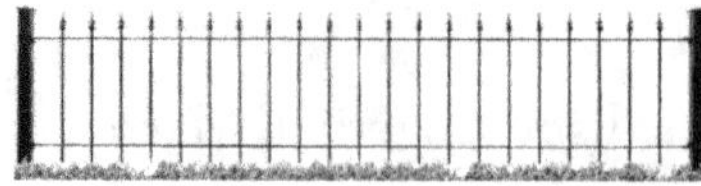

In the garden Tom planted, everything was growing well until the day Andy came running into the house crying.

"Maury, Maury! Mama's ripping out the garden!"

Kaye ran outside with Molly in her arms. Janie was down on her hands and knees, covered with soil, moving down the rows pulling out every plant. Her hair lay matted against her face from the sweat and dust.

Kaye watched Janie flailing at the plants and flinging them away. Too much damage had been done. She pulled Andy near and stroked his hair.

"Andy, it's okay. She doesn't know. She's trying to get the weeds out of her flowers. It's okay. Don't cry."

"But we planted it! Daddy and I. Tell her to stop."

"No, Andy, she won't stop until she's done. Then she'll be tired and need to rest. Come inside. You can have some milk and cookies, then you can read me a story."

That night at dinner Andy remained sullen until Janie left the table and resumed her place on the porch swing.

"Daddy, did you see our garden? Momma ripped out everything. We won't have any vegetables. Everything is gone."

"All gone!" Susie lifted her hands.

Tom beckoned Andy to his lap. "Andy, sometimes we can't make things better. We can only start over. Next year we'll have a bigger garden, you'll see. Next year will be better." He stroked the boy's head and held him close until his tears subsided.

For days, Janie would be quiet and sleep much of the time. Then something would alarm her, and she would scream, terror-stricken, so frightened Kaye had to hold her to keep her from running away. It was only when Tom was around that she became violent, but never when he was away.

"I'm afraid she's going to hurt someone, the kids, herself, or you," Tom said. "I can't be here all the time. I'm afraid for you."

"We'll be okay. You've been here for her worst times. I think she's afraid of something we can't see or understand. I'll tell you if I think there's any danger for us. I'm not frightened. I've seen people afraid like Janie."

"How…" Tom scowled. "How do you know about these things?"

"I worked in a school once where there were kids with problems. That's how I know to hold her when she goes out of control."

"You've never shared much about your past."

"I don't have much of a past. At least nothing worth talking about, and I'm not inclined to talk about it. Enough said!"

"It's your business. I'm glad you're here."

Evasiveness didn't work so easy on Martha; her questions remained persistent.

Kaye was not about to trust anyone with the truth of her past.

Toe moved, wrestling the sheets surrounding his body. The Train whistled again. The sound of the roaring wheels pounded in his head. Familiar with the mild tremor of the earth as the trains passed, he would not have been awakened by those sounds. Even the lonely echo of the whistle would not have disturbed his sleep. He rose up from the pillow. His gaze absorbed in the room. Patches of dimmed lights cast eerie shadows on the walls. Someone's moaning had awakened him.

His dreams were filled with Kaye. He could see her sitting on the gray tombstone. They were talking, but he couldn't hear her. She was walking away from him toward the school. He heard her laughing at Ben. He heard footsteps. A sudden spasm surged through the muscles of his right leg. His foot knotted and twisted behind him as his body contracted with a shudder. He struggled to push his right foot toward the foot of the bed to straighten his leg to ease the spasm. It continued to twist, tighter and tighter. The throbbing ripped through his muscles until he heard a scream. A door opened, light flooded into the room along with a woman's voice.

"Seth, it's okay now. I'll give you something for pain and you'll sleep again. Hush!"

A hand touched his arm. His body continued to shake in response to the torture of the twisting leg.

"Stop it! Make it stop!" he cried out. Beads of perspiration burst across his forehead; his jaw trembled. A straw touched his lips, and he sipped the water. It bubbled in his mouth and ran down his chin as the pain continued. It raged through his body. "Pull my leg down. Don't twist it like that. Please! Stop!"

"Seth, I must change your bed. The sheets are wet. You've been sweating. Here, put this cloth between your teeth until the shot starts to work. Here, bite it. That's good. Just hold it tight." She rolled him to one side, then another. While he was on his side, she rubbed his back and his buttocks, trying to relax the twisted muscles that refused to respond.

Toe's body continued to shake and tremble. She finished making the bed. The fresh sheets felt cool. He shivered. She placed a clean pillow under his head. Unconsciousness washed over him. The spasm of his leg lessened but the twisting of his foot refused to release its grasp. He slept fitfully.

Morning came. Sunshine filtered through the blinds. Footsteps never ceased to traverse the hallway. Trays and equipment passed, the metal wheels on the carts clunking and squeaking. People talked in street voices greeting one another and chatting, their voices echoing. Toe knew he was in a hospital, but the days tumbled together. He had been here a while. He touched his face. Stubble rubbed rough against his hand. He stroked his fingers through the mass of his curly hair. It was longer than he ever let it grow. His body felt weak and frail. He tried to think what could have happened to put him into the hospital, a fall out of the haymow, a kick from a cow or horse. Maybe someone had cold-cocked him in the barn. No, it was his foot that hurt. He reached for a drink of water on the table beside his bed and rolled on top of something. A buzzer sounded.

Within seconds, a woman with curly gray hair appeared beside his bed.

"Well, good morning, Seth. Welcome back to the world. Did you call?" She tucked his sheets in around the foot of his bed, and then touched his forehead. "Good, the fever broke. You'll feel better now."

"What happened? I feel like I got kicked by a mule."

She closed the door, pulled a chair near to the bedside, and sat down.

"Seth, you didn't get kicked by a mule. You got hit by a train."

"A train?"

"Ah-hum." She took a deep breath and continued. "We're not sure how it happened, but it appears you had a train accident."

He ignored the first part of her statement.

"What kind of an accident?"

"Your foot was crushed…the doctors had to amputate."

Toe studied her face. She wouldn't make up a story like that.

"They cut off my foot?" His words came in gasps.

Toe grasped the sheets, trying to fling them away to see. "They cut off my leg?"

"Seth, they had to— so your leg could heal. Your foot and lower leg were crushed." Her expression did not change. "Do you want to see the bandages?"

He rose up as she lifted the sheet, he touched the bandages, and then he flopped back onto the bed, and closed his eyes.

"That's that. No leg?" He whispered.

Her words were firm, but her voice kind. "So many people have come to visit you. You have a lot of friends. Look, there's a bouquet of wildflowers on the windowsill. A big heavyset boy brought them yesterday. Some boys brought him. He cried but he wouldn't talk. He's very upset about your accident. They called him Ben. I know he'll be glad to see you're awake. Some boys come every day. I'll let them know when you are ready for visitors?"

"No. No." He couldn't walk. He had only one foot. Would he have to use a wheelchair? He'd never be able to farm. The limitations and depth of being crippled magnified into anger.

"Take those flowers and your happy face and get out! And the next time you take a step, think about my foot somewhere in a bucket. Get out!"

"I'll go. Seth, I'm not taking the loss of your foot lightly. I've nursed you for days through a very serious time. You almost died. We all prayed you would recover. You've every right to be angry. But I didn't do anything to hurt you." She picked up the flowers to leave.

"I'm sorry I yelled at you. Don't take the flowers. It's a lot, you know."

She placed the flowers on the table. "It is a lot. I'll bring you a pain pill and a milk shake."

Toe tried to sleep. The nights remained long, filled with what they said was *phantom pain.* The medication decreased his conscious awareness of the spasms and stirred his subconscious longing for Kaye.

He asked his visitors about Kaye. Everyone said she had not returned to school. Not knowing where she was or if she was safe worried him. News from the farm and about the herd was sketchy. When a couple men from the farm came with an attendant, Seth cautioned them to watch over Ollie, and to make sure Mort and Hank didn't over feed their cattle.

Nurses came into his room to get him out of bed and into a chair. They helped him bathe. Their chatter annoyed him. Food trays came three times a day. He ate all the food he wanted. He didn't have to be concerned someone down the table might not have enough to eat. The milk shakes softened his spirit.

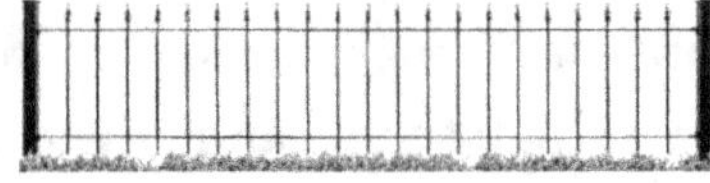

A few days later, Mr. Kent visited with two boys from his class. They joked about the most recent field trip and how the drag races were dull now.

After they left, doctors examined Toe's stump and commented on the healing. At the foot of his bed, they discussed plans for his discharge. They didn't introduce themselves or talk to him. They talked to each other, over him. Toe suffered this annoyance until they discussed his discharge.

"So, gentlemen, are you making a plan?" He asked.

The older doctor with graying hair smiled, surprised to hear Toe had a question. The younger doctor glanced up from the chart he was holding "Yes we are, are you interested?"

"Where did you go to college?" Toe asked.

The man lifted his chin. "I did my surgical residency at Mid-Michigan University."

"That's too bad." Toe shook his head and paused. "I've always understood that medical school graduated only proctologists?"

The older man gasped and laughed until he had to sit down. It took a few minutes for the younger physician to appreciate his patient's humor. He forced a responsive smirk. "And where will you study?"

Toe grinned, eyeing both men with amusement.

"My plan is to study mechanical engineering. I've had letters of acceptance from three colleges."

"Ahem!" the younger man cleared his throat and opened the chart to the first page, furrowing his brow.

"Are you re-reading my address?"

Embarrassed, the physician glanced at the older man. Toe watched the exchange.

"It's not good to make assumptions." Toe searched to balance his anger and wit. "I do live at a State Institution; I have lived there my entire life. However, fate has arranged for me to one, lose my right foot, and two, to graduate from high school and attend college. I am grateful for your good care. Now that you have presumed on my life, perhaps you wish to make an appointment with your colleague to have your head removed."

The old man stood and reached out to shake Toe's hand.

"Young man, I think you have a splendid career ahead of you, whatever you choose. We're planning for your discharge from the hospital in three days. You need some physical therapy to use crutches, and then you're on your way. Come on, Dr. Clancy, he'll be fine."

Later that night when Dr. Clancy was on call, he returned to Toe's room with a chessboard.

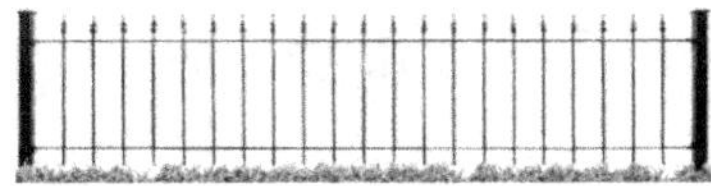

Toe scanned the hospital room, standard color, standard equipment, but he was different. This experience had changed more than his appearance. The twisting pain occurred less often; his leg was healing. All his life he had been labeled by a defect he could not correct and now that defect was gone. He couldn't be Toe because the toe that tripped him and caused him to eat dirt throughout his childhood was no longer a part of his life. From today on he would be Seth Thomas with a straight foot, when it arrived—and he trusted it *would* arrive. Someday, Kaye would see him standing tall and walking with his chin out and his shoulders back. Someday he would take her where she could wear a beautiful dress, he would hold her in his arms, and they would dance. He must succeed. He had promised her a prom. Seth Thomas was not a man who would break a promise.

The physical therapist arrived at the door of Seth's room. He parked a cart of equipment in the hallway and was reading the chart when he entered.

"Do you talk?"

"Yes."

"Good, I'm going to teach you how to walk using crutches. Have you ever used crutches before?"

"No."

"Do you know how tall you are?"

Without a pause, Toe moved off the bed and stood up.

"On which leg?"

The physical therapist paused then saw Seth's face beaming with jesting humor.

"My apology. My name's John."

Seth introduced himself and held out his hand. He sat back down on the side of the bed and decided they were going to get along just fine.

Seth's upper body was strong and once he achieved balance and control with the crutches, he was discharged.

Chapter 27

Martha became a faithful Tuesday visitor. Kaye came to relish Tuesdays. Martha helped her get caught up on the laundry, the house cleaning, and prepared the supper meal before she left. All the other days were chaos.

Kaye's daily race began when Tom got up for work. She held the baby on her hip as she prepared his breakfast and packed his lunch. When she got the baby fed and put her back down to bed, Andy and Janie were up. Some days Janie sat in the living room and stared out the window. Other days she followed Kaye from room to room without any indication of what needed to be done or where anything should be placed.

"What do you want this morning, Andy? Oatmeal pudding or eggs?"

"Maury's Oatmeal pudding with honey." His cheerful reply brightened the room.

"Oatmeal pudding it is. Janie, would you like oatmeal?"

Kaye, accustomed to no reply, waited for Andy.

"Mama wants oatmeal pudding with raisins." Andy patted Janie's hand and tried to place a spoon in her fist.

Kaye dished up the breakfast, toasted bread, poured juice, and rushed up to get the baby before she woke Susie.

Time for Andy's bus. Time to feed Susie. Time to bathe the baby and dress Janie and Susie. The days filled with guarding Janie, guarding the toddling baby, and guarding Susie. Some days Kaye couldn't remember going to the bathroom or taking a drink of water.

Every meal turned into a process of getting Janie to eat, helping Susie, cleaning up the baby's highchair, and mopping the floor under the table. Sometimes Janie would eat with Andy's encouragement, sometimes with Tom's. She wandered around the lawn, sat in a chair for hours, and other times she slept. Her activity could not be trusted. Once she stripped off her clothes and bathed in the cow's trough. Another time she tied the dog inside the hen house. After the garden incident, Kaye realized she must be always vigilant. Even the nighttime required watchfulness. Tom slept so sound he didn't know when she left the bed. Most nights Janie slept on the floor beside their bed. Kaye preferred to sleep on the sofa downstairs instead of in the bed Tom had moved into Susie's room for her. If Janie left the upstairs Kaye would hear her come down the stairs before she could leave the house or disturb things in the kitchen.

One night in early August, near 9 o'clock, Tom entered the kitchen as Kaye finished the dishes.

"The little ones are down."

"Good work. Janie is out on the porch. I put the baby down early. I hope she doesn't wake up in the middle of the night."

"She probably won't. She was yawning during supper." Tom picked up a dishtowel and started drying the dishes. When he finished, he set the towel on the counter.

"I don't know what I'd do without you here," he said. He left the kitchen and headed toward the barn. Kaye scrubbed the sink and watched him through the kitchen window. Her feet hurt, her back ached, and her heart hurt for the burdens he carried. She loved this family.

But she could hear the echo of her own words to Nurse Lucy and Toe: "They're not yours."

Seth waited at the front door of the hospital, sitting in a wheelchair, expecting a car from the Home to pick him up. He was not prepared when Mr. Kent drove up with two boys from ag class. They jumped from the car. Both boys were laughing.

"You should see the look on your face!" Chuck picked up a paper bag containing Seth's clothes and placed it in the back seat as Larry angled the crutches and slid them in the back.

Seth asked, "Why are you guys here?"

"We thought you wanted to leave so we're here."

"I can't go joy riding today. I've got to go back to the Home."

"Get in, Seth. Sit right here." Mr. Kent patted the passenger seat as Chuck and Larry climbed into the back.

"You're sure this is all right?"

"Yep. We got the okay from Dr. Helmsley himself. He said we could pick you up today."

When the car pulled out of the hospital and turned in the opposite direction Seth became alarmed.

"You're going the wrong way."

"It's a surprise." Mr. Kent adjusted the radio to the popular rock and roll station. The boys in the back seat bobbed back and forth, snapping their fingers to the music.

Mr. Kent pulled up in front of his house, stopped the car, and turned to Seth.

"Seth, you're staying here with us until graduation. The steps at the Home farmhouse are too steep and narrow for you to go up and down with crutches. The farm managers were concerned about you not being able to do your share of work, costing them a man, so you're staying here for a while. Come in, we've got another surprise."

They entered the house where Mrs. Kent had a chocolate layer cake on the table with *Welcome Home* written on the top in white icing.

"Sit down, boys." Mr. Kent pulled out a chair. "Can't waste good chocolate cake. We've got a celebration."

Seth pulled himself up to the table, manipulating his leg to avoid bumping his stump. He laid his crutches on the floor. Mrs. Kent, a petite woman with shoulder-length brown hair and a plaid dress, sliced the cake and placed wedges on each plate, while Mr. Kent poured tall glasses of milk.

They had just started to eat when a knock came at the front door.

"I think we've got company," Mrs. Kent said, and scurried to the door.

Seth heard Dr. Helmsley's voice. "Hello, I heard Seth is here."

"Come in, I'm glad you could make it," Mrs. Kent said.

"I didn't want to miss this!" Dr. Helmsley removed his hat and coat and sat down in the chair Mr. Kent placed at the table for him. He readily accepted a piece of cake and a cup of coffee. After a bite of the cake and a sip of the coffee he wiped his mouth with his napkin.

"Wonderful cake, Mrs. Kent. Welcome home from the hospital, Seth," he said, handing Seth a long envelope.

"What's this?" He was confused.

"I think it's what you need to get on with your life."

His thoughts immediately turned to Kaye, but he knew he shouldn't ask. To ask could lead to trouble for him. They might suspect that he knew something about her disappearance. Pushing Kaye to the back of his mind, Seth opened the envelope and a hush fell over the table. Mrs. Kent stopped pouring coffee as everyone waited for him to read the letter.

"Is this real? Honest to goodness real?" Seth's eyes searched each face. Larry and Chuck were not laughing. Mr. and Mrs. Kent waited. Dr. Helmsley was smiling.

"Yes, Seth. It's real. You're emancipated, no longer a ward of the State of Michigan. Mr. and Mrs. Kent have agreed to sponsor you until you are twenty-one."

"I can go anywhere I want? I'm really free?"

Mr. Kent placed a hand on Seth's shoulder.

"Almost, Seth. When Dr. Helmsley asked if we would be willing to sponsor you, we wanted one thing— we want you to continue your education. You have a gifted mind. That's all we ask."

"I never thought this could happen. I mean, all the talk about college? I didn't think it would happen. I thought someone would pull the rug out from under me. I didn't dare even hope."

As everyone started talking, his thoughts rushed to what his leaving the Home would mean to Ben.

"No." Seth placed the letter in the envelope and handed it back to Dr. Helmsley. "Thanks, it was nice of you, but I better go back. There are guys depending on me and… I can't leave Ben."

Mr. Helmsley lowered his voice, choosing his words. "I understand, Seth. Those men have been your family for eighteen years. But the truth is many of the men need to be there. They would be lost outside." He finished his cake and held his coffee cup in his hands. "Many could not manage outside, and Ben is one of them. I've checked on him while you were in the hospital. The boys here took Ben to visit you, but he got so upset they didn't take him again. He's back to cooperating and doing his chores now. He works in the kitchen every afternoon helping cook. It's a good place for him and he seems happy."

Seth had to know.

"The dairy reports. Is Ollie turning in the dairy reports?"

"I saw the farm reports for April, the May ones are due next week. There were not any problems I heard about."

Seth took a deep breath, perhaps his first in several minutes. He read the letter again.

"Can I go outside for a few minutes?" He slid his chair back and picked up his crutches.

"Sure. It's been a busy day. I'll save you some cake for later." Mrs. Kent placed a wedge of cake on a clean plate and headed for the kitchen.

"Come on, guys, I want to hear what's been going on."

The three boys went outside.

When they were a safe distance from the house, Seth asked, "Hey, you guys heard anything about Kaye?"

They looked at each other, unsure what to say.

"No, Seth. Nobody's heard anything. She didn't come back to school and since your accident all the talk is about you."

"I want to know she's okay." Seth poked at the grass with his crutch.

"I heard she broke up with you." Larry questioned.

Seth shook his head. "She did. That doesn't mean I broke up with her."

"Well," Charley stroked his jaw. "I always say there's plenty of fish in the sea, probably one waiting for you to ask her out this very minute." The boys nodded in agreement.

"Come on, fellas. Look around." Seth's tone lightened. "I haven't been emancipated long enough for them to start lining up."

The boys snickered.

Seth was back.

Seth waited in the room of the school counselor, Mrs. Jennings. His summons came during English class. This meeting could be about his not graduating because he missed so much school. Nothing had changed in the office, it still looked like paper chaos. He'd tried to prepare; he'd gotten used to things going good and then going bad.

Mrs. Jennings bustled in carrying more folders.

"Hello, Seth. I hear you're doing very well." She smiled.

Being summoned to the office was never an indicator all was going well.

She placed her armload on another stack and removed a folder from the top of a file cabinet.

"This is your academic record." She thumbed through the pages. "When you entered high school, you entered as a sophomore. You've done well but you're a few credits shy. I think taking those sample placement tests improved your scores for the college entrance exams. We've received notification that you must complete a few more academic credits before they can accept you for admission." She pulled a pencil from a cluster of curls on the back of her head and used the eraser end to shuffle the papers.

"Here, see this?" She slid a paper around for him to view.

Seth reviewed three columns highlighted with a check mark. "Yes."

"That means you don't have enough credits for those requirements. You have enough credits to graduate, but you're going to have to do academic work this summer to enter college in September. Six weeks of summer school will slide you in with no problem. Just sign here." She whipped another form across the desk.

"That's the whole summer."

Mrs. Jennings scowled. "Seth, one summer in a lifetime is not too much. Sign *here!*" She pointed to a blank line.

No way to argue his way out of this. She would not take no for an answer, and he really didn't want to turn the offer down. She was right, one summer was not too much to ask for all he wanted to someday give Kaye. It was for them, summer school and college. Their dream if he could only find her.

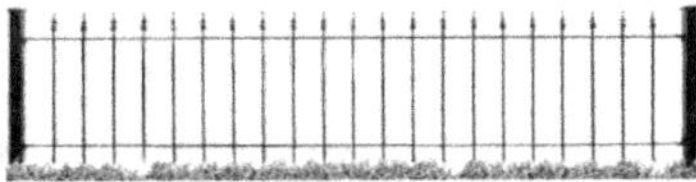

The morning of graduation day Seth strapped on his first artificial leg. The industrial arts classes and ag group sponsored spaghetti suppers, the local Farm Bureau groups organized events, and two civic organizations helped raise funds to pay for the prosthetic leg and foot. It felt good to be standing. After practicing, Seth was ready to walk across the stage to receive his diploma.

Graduation was held in the high school gymnasium. The temperature was high for June. Parents and family members, dressed in their Sunday best, came to sit on bleachers and listen to the State Representative, the Valedictorian, the Salutatorian, and the Superintendent of Schools. Seth walked in the procession, receive his diploma, and moved his tassel to the left side of his mortarboard with the other students of the graduating class. Seth knew Dr. Helmsley was in the audience.

If only Kaye could have been there too.

Chapter 28

"There's about two weeks between haying and grain harvest," Tom said. "A farmer must watch the storms this time of year. You'll see, Maury, the wind that dried the hay gets stronger sometimes and then the storms come early. We need the wind, but we need it gentle. Those wheat heads get heavy. It's the same way when the sweet corn gets ripe, the night before we're planning to pick it the coons come. That's what happens some years to the wheat. The storm winds just pound it down so low we can't combine." Tom stood at the kitchen sink gazing across the fields as he talked. Over the last few weeks, he had shared more and more about the crops and the process of farming.

"We haven't had any rain," Kaye added. "Martha calls it dry showers when it looks so near storming and doesn't. She says the clouds stay high."

Tom left the kitchen, chewing on a toothpick the way he did when he wasn't smoking a cigarette, and carried his empty milk pail back to the barn. That must be all he's going to say until supper. Kaye turned on the burner under the kettle of potatoes and set the table.

Molly mumbled and rolled around in the playpen. Kaye resorted to using the playpen for Molly when she had to rush outside periodically to stop Susie from chasing the chickens. Andy was home all day since school ended. He could be trusted, but Susie was three going on four and was very independent. Kaye's days were so busy she feared dozing off if she sat down.

Janie would wander away, although she usually remained in the living room rocking chair or on the porch swing. It had been three months since the tornado, and still she had not spoken. Her face became thinner and more drawn. Her eyes gave no recognition, nothing but an empty stare.

Tom returned from the barn carrying both Andy and Susie on his shoulders.

"Fee fi fo fum," Tom roared. The children giggled. "I smell pudding of some kind." He placed the children on the floor, telling them to go wash for supper. They rushed off eager to please. He washed up in the utility room before coming into the kitchen and scooped up Molly.

"Let's eat, Molly." Tom sat down. Janie remained in the living room. Kaye left the kitchen and returned with Janie.

Supper was noisy and kept her busy, cutting portions, feeding Molly, and encouraging Janie to eat as she stared blankly at the bowls of food or out the window.

Kaye tried everything she knew to reach Janie, but nothing stirred a response. There could be no way to know how much she heard or how much she understood. Nothing and no one could encourage her participation.

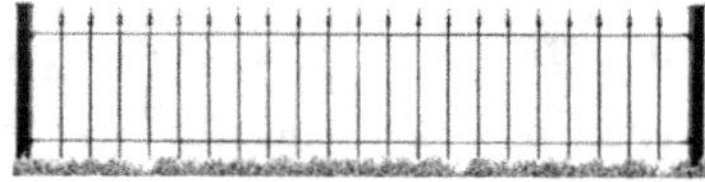

One Tuesday, Martha arrived as usual, and they worked to complete their chores. After lunch Martha opened her basket.

"I brought you something."

"You already do more than I can ever repay."

"This is different. It's for you."

"Me?" Kaye looked up.

"Yes." Martha smiled. "I started piecing a quilt." She unfolded the fabric.

"Oh, that's beautiful." Kaye traced the circles of fabric with her finger.

"I'm making it for you. If you choose which color you like best, I'll make the backing that color."

"This one, the rose color. It's like the wild roses growing along the fence."

"Rose it is."

Martha folded the pieces of fabric and placed them back into the basket.

"I'll get the diapers off the line." She grabbed the laundry basket and headed out the door toward the clotheslines.

They worked together folding and sorting clothes as the children napped. When they finished Martha packed up her things, checked supper in the oven, and bade her goodbye.

Around three o'clock the clouds started moving in. The house darkened and Kaye turned on the dining room light. The girls awakened at their usual time. Andy rushed through the house exiting out the front door with a cookie in each hand.

"Andy, you didn't ask!" Kaye called after him as the screen door slammed against Susie howled and bolted outside behind him. Kaye rushed upstairs to pick up Molly, who was crowing baby sounds from her crib.

A clap of thunder boomed nearby.

Kaye thought, *I should have gone after Susie. I'm never in the right place at the right time.*

She rushed downstairs to close the windows and counted 1, 2, 3, 4, 5, another clap of thunder. The storm was close. Suddenly she heard Andy and Susie screaming. Even when they had been injured, she had never heard them scream with such terror. She rushed to the porch. Janie had scooped a child under each arm and was running toward the road. Kaye paused, unsure if she could catch her carrying Molly. The thunder clapped again. Kaye ran to the phone and dialed the operator.

"Help, I need help. Send the police to 5447 Weister Road. Hurry, please."

"Do you have a fire?"

"No, I need help. Send the police."

Kaye hung up the phone, placed Molly in the playpen, and ran out the door. Her heart was pounding. She called out to Andy and Susie.

"Maury's coming! Maury's coming!" Janie was on the dirt road and nearing the highway. There was no way to anticipate what Janie might do. The children continued to cry out. Trucks and cars passed on the highway. Kaye heard a siren in the distance.

"Oh God, please let it be someone coming to help."

Cars pulled off the road to let the police pass. When Kaye got to the police car it had pulled over to the side of the road. Janie had fallen into the ditch. Her face buried in the deep grass, she was still holding the children against her with all her strength. Andy and Susie sobbed and held each other's hands. It thundered again and lightning zigzagged across the sky.

"What's this all about?"

"Are you the police?" Kaye asked as she trotted up to the officer.

"I'm the constable. Name's Bart Cotter."

"Maury! Maury!" Andy and Susie screamed. They struggled against Janie, and she released them. The children ran to Kaye, their faces scratched from the fall. She kneeled to pull them closer.

"It's all right now. You're all right. We're going home." She turned to the constable.

"Will you help me take my family home?" Kaye tried to remain calm, hoping she wouldn't have to explain everything.

"Who are you and who is she?" Bart Cotter scowled, as Janie remained sitting in the ditch. Grass stuck in her hair and her dress covered with dirt and stains.

"I'm their babysitter and she's Janie, their mother."

The officer pushed his hat back off his forehead as if trying to understand this situation.

Rain began to fall, and wind whipped around them. Kaye tried to shelter the children with her arms.

"Please help me take them home."

He opened the door of his car and the children popped into the back seat. Kaye pulled Janie up from the grass and helped her into the seat next to Andy.

"This nice man is taking us home. We'll be fine now." Kaye climbed into the seat, urging Janie to move over. "Please hurry, officer, I had to leave the baby."

He pushed the red light on the top of his car toward the middle of the roof and turned on the siren. "We can hurry now," he shifted his bulky body in behind the steering wheel.

"Listen to that." Andy jumped around in the back seat as the siren shrieked. Janie lunged for the door. Kaye grabbed her arm.

Officer Cotter turned to back up the car and observed Kaye's alarm.

"She can't open that door. The handle's off."

Kaye sighed with relief, catching Janie's flailing arms and holding them. As they pulled into the driveway, Tom's truck roared in behind them.

The constable stopped the car and turned off the engine. He opened the back door.

Facing the constable, Tom yelled, "What's going on?"

Kaye rushed toward the house to get baby Molly, leaving Tom and the officer to hear the explanations of a five and a three-year-old. Tom carried his children toward the house as the rain pelted down, but Janie stood beside the car, shaking in the rain, refusing to move. Leaving the children on the porch, Tom went back, scooped Janie into his arms, and carried her into the house. Her hair and dress were drenched and muddy. Unable to find the Afghan, Kaye pulled the tablecloth off the dining room table and wrapped it around Janie, guiding her into her favorite chair. The officer urged Susie and Andy inside.

They talked at the kitchen table; the children spoke of Mama running toward the road.

"That's why we were yelling, Maury. Daddy said he would spank us good if we ever went near the road." Andy began to cry as he talked. Tom pulled him into his arms.

"It's okay, little man, you didn't want to go in the road. It's not your fault."

"Why did Mama take us... road?" Susie sobbed, rubbing her nose with her hand.

Kaye wiped Susie's face with her apron.

"I don't know how to write this up." Bart fumbled with his pen and paper.

"There's not much to write. A lady took her kids for a walk down the road. It started to rain, and the babysitter was worried so she called the police. Simple as that."

"Are you sure?" Bart looked at Janie sitting in her rocking chair, her face soiled, she was patting the grass stains on her dress and humming and rocking back and forth.

"Yep, that's all, simple as that." Tom rubbed his hands together.

"Well, if you're sure."

Tom walked toward the door. "Thanks for your help."

In the driveway, the constable paused to remove the portable light from the roof of his car, and then drove away.

When his car left the yard, Tom turned to face Kaye. "I knew it, Maury. Somebody's gonna get hurt." Tom's face was flushed, and his fists were clenched.

Kaye gathered the children into her arms for a quick hug.

"You go upstairs and wash your face and hands. Maury's got a surprise for you before supper."

The children scrambled upstairs.

"Tom, we must talk about this later. They've had enough excitement for one day."

"I think we all have." He looked toward Janie rocking in her chair. She continued rocking and humming. "Except Janie. What am I supposed to do? I have to work." He sat down at the kitchen table, covering his face in his hands.

Kaye served up small dishes of berry cobbler and set them at each place on the table.

"Let's eat dessert first. Dinner will be a little late."

Andy and Susie bounced into the room and climbed up into their chairs. After they finished the cobbler, Kaye turned to Tom.

"Can you change Molly? I'll put on dinner."

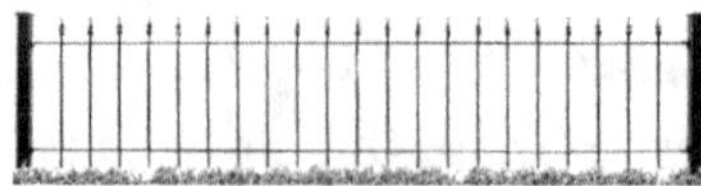

Tom returned to the kitchen after reading to the children and placing them in their beds for the night. He paced back and forth across the kitchen. "Do you have any idea what I was going through when I saw that police car with its lights and siren? Which of the kids? What had happened? What had Janie done? Had something happened to you? I didn't know you were in the car. Everything… I thought of everything possible in those minutes."

"I had to call for help. You weren't here. The children were afraid."

"I'm not blaming you." He was almost shouting. Dropping into a chair, he lifted his hands into the air. "I don't know what I'm supposed to do."

"Tom, everyone is safe now. The children understand Janie is not well. I don't know how but children know things like that."

"We can't go on this way. I learned that today. I'm going to bed. I've got to do something different, even if I don't want to. The doctor said we might have to put Janie in a mental institution. This isn't safe for any of us. I worry every day, whether I'm working in the fields or at the plant." He urged Janie from her rocking chair and directed her up the stairs.

Kaye couldn't bear the thought of Janie living away from her children in an institution. There would be no chance of her ever recovering away from them. She understood Tom's dilemma, but somehow there must be another way. Kaye tidied up the kitchen, then rested in Janie's rocking chair. Fatigue blanketed her body. Today was her fault, she must be more vigilant. Somehow, she would find more strength to care for this family and keep them safe.

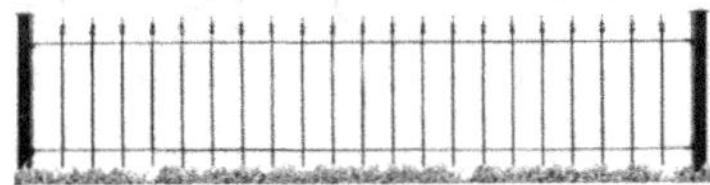

"Mr. Kent, it doesn't seem right to be going to school every day when there's work to be done."

"You are working, Seth. You're working on your future. There'll always be farm work, that's the nature of it. But you must think past what you know how to do, to what you're going to learn. The industry of automation is moving by leaps and bounds."

"You could have gone into industrial work, what with all the farm machinery and everything, but you went into teaching agriculture. I think you really like farming, too. Did you ever want your own farm?"

"I did at one time. But so much has changed. I think teaching is a good way to encourage farming. It's the best of both worlds for me."

"I miss the guys," said Seth, sitting down on the porch glider. "I don't understand why I can't go over there and see them. What's the big deal?"

Mr. Kent went into the kitchen and returned with two glasses of iced tea. "You must respect Dr. Helmsley's request. The guys might not feel so good about your opportunity to leave. It's not like it was. He said they had quite a time with Ben after your accident. It's better to do what he suggested. Don't go, Seth. Please, don't go. You could put yourself in harm's way. You don't know how some of the guys might feel."

"It's wrong that I can't see Ben."

"It may be wrong but that's the way it is, and you have to accept it."

Seth bundled his books together. The beautiful days of summer called to the boy in him. Walking home from school to Mr. Kent's house after his sessions gave him time to think because he couldn't walk as fast as he used to. Maybe that was good. The walk didn't help the sore developing on his stump from the prosthesis. He didn't mind having time alone after a full day of books and tutors.

It was between crops on the farms. Most farmers would have their second cutting of hay in the barn, and the straw would be baled as well. Seth wondered, what would they be doing at the Home. Probably hoeing in the eighty-acre garden. That work never ended. There was always the milking too.

He missed the cows, the barns, and the men. He missed Ben. He agreed with Dr. Helmsley that it might upset Ben to see him, but it would just as likely upset Ben not to see him. Some rules don't make sense. Ben was stubborn. He wouldn't understand no matter how they said it. He would think the worst. Maybe, that he didn't care about Ben anymore.

It had been almost two months at Mr. Kent's house, and Seth realized no one asked how he felt about being away from the Home. It was the only family he'd ever known. Ben was his brother. He'd taught Ben not to fight. He'd taught him to observe situations. He'd taught Ben how to read and write and do math and the procedure for the dairy records so he would have some protection. Now they think he should be grateful to not ever see Ben again.

A car zoomed past, whipping dust into the air, and stopped a few yards ahead of him. Butch jumped out from behind the steering wheel.

"Hey, Seth, want a ride?"

"I'm just going to Mr. Kent's."

"That's okay. Come on, hop in."

Seth walked toward the car favoring his prosthetic leg. Larry and Chuck popped their heads out through the back windows.

"My very own three stooges," Seth chuckled.

"Hey there, schoolboy. Doesn't look like Mr. Kent's giving you much of a summer."

"Nah, they set up tutoring so I can catch up. I lost a few weeks after the accident."

"Then what?" Butch shifted the car into gear and spun back onto the road.

"College. What did you guys decide to do?"

"Me—" Larry slid forward so Seth could hear. "I'm going to Michigan State in ten more days. Look out, college girls, here comes Larry!"

"Sure, big college man. Those girls will scare you silly. You've never even had a date."

"And you, Butch, I suppose you have your girl at home waiting for you to take her to the movies tonight?"

"As a matter of fact, I do." Butch laughed.

"So, what'd you decide, Chuck?" Seth turned in the seat to face him.

"Navy. I'm going to sail the seven seas and see the world."

Butch pulled into the gravel pit driveway.

"Let's catch a swim. It's hot."

"I don't know how to swim."

"You don't?" Two of the boys yelled in unison.

The three boys burst from the car and shed clothing all the way to the bluff that overlooked the icy water.

"Last one in buys at the root beer stand tonight," Chuck yelled and jumped in, holding his nose.

Seth shuffled down the trail, passing shirts and pants hanging from the bushes.

"Come on, Seth."

Butch burst up from the water and splashed the other two.

"Seth, follow the path and go down to the shallow water. Come in there. At least get wet."

"Naw, that's okay. You guys go ahead."

He didn't want to undress and unstrap his leg in front of the guys. They'd probably make a smart remark—like wood floats. Some days the jokes didn't bother him. Other days he wanted to punch them out. None of them knew about walking with a gimp, using a crutch, or strapping on your leg. They didn't understand anything in his life. They joked and had cars. They danced with their girlfriends and held them in their arms. No one asked about Kaye anymore.

They had it all. Some days despite everything he had now, compared to living at the Home, his life was something someone else had decided for him. Opportunities they created, goals they set, and he was supposed to show up and measure up.

He wanted to walk home but his stump was raw. The prosthesis didn't fit right, but he said nothing. He didn't want to complain. He'd figure something out. He couldn't walk that far without his crutch. He shouldn't have left this morning without it.

The boys returned, tugging their clothes on over their dripping bodies.

"It's okay, Seth." Butch paused and looked at Chuck. "You probably don't want to see the chicks and drink root beer."

Seth laughed at the boys, their damp hair standing on end, and their shirts twisted around their bodies. They were hopping around brushing the sand from their feet and trying to put on socks and shoes without stepping down into the dirt.

"I like root beer."

"Don't nothing bother you, Seth? I just insulted you."

Seth wasn't paying attention. He was thinking about Kaye.

The boys climbed into the car. Butch backed out of the drive and headed toward Mr. Kent's. "Really, Seth, don't nothing bother you? You haven't had a fight all through school. I've heard the kids call you names. Don't you get mad?"

"Yeah, I get mad, and I can fight. But I think a man should seek to change what angers him, not be controlled by it, and even if you're right, a fight won't make a fool believe you."

Chuck leaned forward.

"What the heck is that all about?"

"Got me," Butch replied. "You ask some admiral when you get in the Navy and come back and tell us."

"Naw, the Navy won't teach that, I'll ask at M.S.U." Larry offered.

Seth sat quietly in the front seat, thinking. These were the best friends he had on the outside. They were all going in different directions in two weeks. Might as well say it.

"Yeah, something bothers me."

Butch turned down the radio and the boys silenced.

"It bothers me that I can't see my buddy, Ben, at the home. He's deaf. I don't know what they told him when I didn't come back. I'd sure like to see him, they said he saved my life."

"So why didn't you go over there? It's only a mile from school." Butch asked the question for all three.

"Dr. Helmsley, from the Home told me not to go back. He said Ben came to the hospital and got real upset and they didn't want him getting into trouble 'cause he saw me."

"What kind of trouble?" Butch held the lead.

"You wouldn't understand how it works out there… He's a big guy… it could be bad if he got upset and started a fight or something."

The remainder of the ride the boys were quiet. When the car pulled up to Mr. Kent's house, Seth climbed out.

"Thanks, Butch. Thanks, guys. Sorry about buying the root beer."

"Listen, Seth," said Butch. "How about we pick you up on Sunday afternoon and we take a ride over to the Home? We could go in the back drive if we have to. Maybe we can find a way you could see Ben. Wanna try?"

"I'd sure like to see him."

"We'll pick you up about two."

"Thanks, Butch."

There were always visitors at the Home on Sunday. Butch pulled up to the front gate. Seth sat in the back seat and turned his face away from the guard.

"Just want to visit my cousin Ben. He's out on the farm." Butch spoke as if he visited every Sunday. He drove the car back toward the barns. There was a baseball game in progress, lots of yelling and hooting. Four guys were pitching horseshoes and other guys lined the benches to watch. They found Ben sitting alone on an empty wagon, looking across the fields. The boys waited by the trees and let Seth approach Ben alone. Seth pulled himself up onto the wagon to sit beside Ben. At first Ben didn't pay attention, then he turned and jumped to the ground, grabbing Seth, and hugging him, lifting him up into the air. Seth pounded on Ben's shoulder to let him down. If Ben could have made a sound everyone for miles would have known Seth was back.

Ben grinned from ear to ear, patted Seth's head and shoulders, then reached down and pulled up his pant leg.

"Hey, stop that." Seth tried to pull away. Ben had a hold of his prosthesis and wouldn't let go. Seth landed on the ground with a thump. At once Ben was on the ground beside him, mouth wide open, slapping his knees, and pointing to Seth's face. Seth's three stooges joined in the laughter and sat down on the grass.

Ben made gestures about Seth eating supper. Shaking his head, no, he would not be staying for supper. Seth continued to explain he came to see Ben for *today*. But there was no way to explain for today. Dr. Helmsley had been right. As Seth tried to explain that he was going away to college, Ben became more upset gesturing that Seth was leaving him, and nobody cared about him here. He had no friends. No friend like Seth. Ben began to cry. Seth continued trying to explain, but nothing he said would stop Ben's tears. When they both stood, Ben pushed Seth's shoulder, gesturing toward the car. As Seth turned away, Ben kicked him in the butt. Seth struggled, lost his balance and crashed against the front fender of the car. Ben stood a distance away, shaking his fist and weeping.

Seth slid into the front seat. He couldn't stop his own tears as he watched Ben's anguish. Nothing in his future, no success he would ever achieve, could erase this memory of Ben's agony and pain.

Kaye was the only one who would understand him and Ben, because she had Jessie.

Chapter 29

Kaye scoured the cast-iron skillet, wiped it dry, and placed it on a warm burner on the stove.

Tom came downstairs and entered the kitchen. "They're all tucked into bed and waiting for their story."

"You'll have to read the story tonight, I have to wash Janie's hair and cut her fingernails. I wait to do it when you're here in case I need help. She's easier when you're here."

"You think she knows when I'm here? Come on, Maury, she's so far away!"

"No, she's different when you're around. Maybe it's your voice. Who knows."

Kaye continued sweeping the floor and straightening the chairs.

Tom's silence hung heavy as he leaned against the doorway between the kitchen and the dining room. Amid the sounds of the scraping chairs against the linoleum they heard Janie's soft humming and the squeak of her rocking chair.

As Kaye approached the side of the table near Tom, he reached out, circling his arm around her waist and pulling her toward him.

"Tom!" Her rebuke was sharp as she pulled away. "No! That is not *proper*."

He raised both his arms, imitating a gesture of surrender, still smiling.

"I'm… sorry." He left the kitchen with his hands in the air.

Twice within the last three weeks he had made comments about how much he appreciated her being there. She sensed him watching her as she cared for the children, prepared the meals, or cleaned. He was quiet and polite. So far, he showed respect for her, but sometimes she worried. Once he put his arm around her reaching for the baby. He was ready to leave for work and his skin smelled of aftershave. His face became more tanned as the summer went on. He was a handsome man. Her love for this family and these children continued to grow daily. It would tear her heart out to leave them. She had nowhere to go, they needed her, and she loved them all so much. Even caring for Janie in some ways was an extension of caring for Jessie. Caring for people was all she'd ever known.

It was Andy who brought her here. The truth was she wanted to come, and Tom needed her. By the end of the first week, Tom stopped trying to talk to Janie or show affection toward her. Kaye's days were busy, and at night, she was so tired she only thought about Toe. When she saw other men with their wives, she wondered what Toe was doing and if he still thought of her. She made him a promise. He said he loved her. No, as handsome as Tom was, and as lonely as she felt, Tom and Janie were married, they were a couple, in the same way she hoped someday she and Seth would be a couple. It would not be right to think of Tom in any way other than as Janie's husband. If she never saw Toe again, it still wouldn't be right. She had no place to go. She had to do what she knew was right.

She went to the living room and coaxed Janie from her rocking chair. They passed the front door and Janie pulled away. Sometimes she liked to sit on the swing on the porch, other evenings she wanted to walk her path around the yard. Kaye stepped through behind her and, taking Janie's hand, they walked the path she had worn around the perimeter of the yard. Sometimes Janie picked up one of the children's toys and placed it back in the sandbox. Other times she remained distant, humming, or moaning and walking. Tonight, she stared far off into the fields and tripped twice paying no attention to the ruts or to where she was walking.

Janie was distant, preoccupied in her thoughts. Kaye had grown to be perceptive of Janie's moods. She talked to Janie as they walked, the same way she had talked to Jessie. She would tell Janie what the children did that day or chat about the chickens or crops. If Janie pushed her away, Kaye stopped talking, leaving Janie in her private, quiet world. Tonight, Kaye didn't feel like talking; her mind was filled with ambivalent thoughts of holding the children in her arms and the fear of never seeing them again.

When they returned to the house Janie compliantly went upstairs to the bathroom, stepped into the bathtub fully dressed, and sat down.

Kaye entered the bathroom and helped Janie undress, but Janie would not leave the tub. Kaye prepared the bath and washed her hair, but Janie battled against having her nails cut.

"Maybe tomorrow night." Kaye sighed. When they finished Kaye took Janie's hand and urged her to the bedroom.

Tom was in the children's room reading stories and mimicking animal sounds. The children were laughing.

Kaye removed the spread and laid it over the quilt rack. As she turned, Janie was standing directly in front of her. In her hands she held her wedding picture. She had removed it from the bedside table and was gesturing with it, toward Kaye.

"Yes, I've seen your wedding picture." Kaye smiled. "You were beautiful!" She stepped to one side to move around Janie, but Janie stepped also and aligned herself in front of Kaye again, thrusting the picture toward her. Kaye paused, then took the picture into her hands, watching Janie. For the first time, Janie's eyes met hers. Janie did not look angry, but her expression was hopeless emptiness. As quickly as it appeared, it vanished. That single moment of connection was gone. Kaye turned to see Tom standing in the doorway, and Janie waiting at her bedside, unsure what to do next. And there stood Kaye, holding their wedding picture. Kaye gave the picture back to Janie, touched her arm, and shook her head.

"Your Tom."

She placed the picture on the bedside table and helped Janie into bed. Returning to the bathroom she closed the door and locked it. She scrubbed the tub, running the water to shield the sounds of her sobs.

She had come so close to having a real family and loved them so much. She could not take advantage of Janie's fate to justify her own happiness. She washed her face with ice-cold water and dried it, tempering the magnitude of her broken heart. Entering the children's rooms, she tucked them into bed, and kissed their foreheads. Andy was still awake.

"Night, Maury. I said my prayers. Daddy heard them. Do you want me to say them again?"

"You're a good boy, Andy Pandy." Kaye used her pet name for him and ruffled his hair. Andy giggled and snuggled down into his covers.

Kaye went to the room she shared with Molly, closed the door, knelt beside her bed and folded her hands in prayer. Only God could help her with this heartbreak. Only God could help her when she had nowhere to go and no one to trust. After her prayers, she lay down on her bed. Sleep would not come tonight. In a few minutes she was up. The night-light provided enough light for her to move about the room. She would start packing. She folded her two dresses. One apron would be sufficient. She removed her coat and laid it on top. No need for a coat in August but winter would come. Patting the back, she traced the border of the folder she had placed inside months before. She folded one sleeve, then checked the pockets. One contained a slip of paper; the paper Ann Marie had handed her the night they left the gym. She unfolded it.

"If you ever need to call me, you can reach me at the Salvation Army. Call this number. If I'm not there, I'll call you back as soon as I get the message.

God's blessing, Ann Marie Yu 7-2728"

Her answer had come. Tomorrow she would go to Port Huron, call Ann Marie, and ask for help. Ann Marie hadn't asked questions at the shelter. But that was an exceptional time. She could trust Ann Marie. Somehow it would work out. Somehow it had to work out.

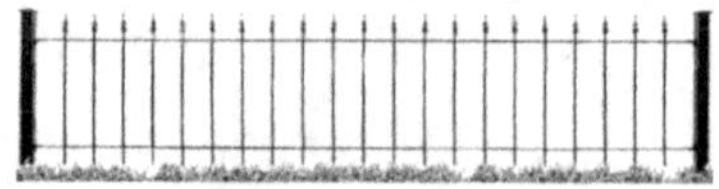

The next morning, Tom was reading at the kitchen table when Kaye entered carrying Molly.

He looked up.

"And how's our baby girl this morning?" Molly heard her Daddy and lifted her arms and squealed.

"Happy as usual." Kaye smiled and snuggled Molly against her shoulder. She prepared a bottle and placed Molly in the playpen. Kaye sat down across the table from Tom. "Tom, I've made a decision. I'm going away."

"Kaye, for heaven's sake. I've apologized for my actions. It won't happen again."

"You don't understand. Even if it didn't happen again." She sighed, shifted in her chair, and looked him in the eyes. "Sooner or later, I might want it to. Last night Janie picked up your wedding picture and brought it to me. She insisted I take it. The look in her eyes… for that moment she was saying something."

"I saw that. She probably thought she was giving you a gift." Tom's frustration and sarcasm parlayed in his voice.

"No, for a moment she wanted to speak and then it was gone. On some level she knows you are her husband. And we know it too. I'm going away because it's the right thing."

Kaye stood to leave the room. Tom jumped from his chair.

"You do that, you run away."

His words pounded against her. Yes, she did run away. She had run away before she came to his home. Kaye wasn't sure if he was ranting because she could have run away, but he couldn't. His words panicked her and yet they confirmed, leaving was her only option.

"You go, then. We'll be fine. I don't know how, but we'll be fine." He left the house, slamming the back door behind him.

After chores he returned for breakfast. They ate in silence. The children scampered off to play.

"Will you take me to the bus station?"

"Today? You're going today?"

"Yes, I told you."

"I didn't know you meant today."

"I've helped you the best I know how. Martha will be here at ten. She could take me to town if you'll stay with the children."

"Why the rush? Can't you wait until I can find someone, a housekeeper?"

"No, I must go today. Please understand."

"Well, I don't."

Kaye cleared the table. Tom watched her move back and forth across the kitchen. His face grew red with vexation. He went to the phone.

"Hi, Mom, it's Tom. Can you come over for a couple hours this morning? Yeah, everything's okay, I need some help with the kids, that's all. Sure, in about an hour, thanks." He hung up. "Call Martha and tell her not to come today. I'll be back in when Mom gets here and drive you into town."

"Martha was—" The back door slammed.

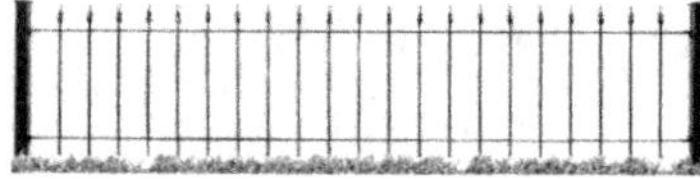

Kaye was crying when she placed the call to Martha.

"Hi, it's Maury. Tom asked me to call you and tell you he has some plans for today and ask if you could come another day."

"Is everything all right? You sound different, are you sick?"

"No, it's not something he expected to do, but it works out, it needs to happen today."

"Well, all right. How about Thursday?"

"I'll check with Tom and have him give you a call."

"Check with Tom? Are you sure everything is okay?"

"Yes, Martha, everything is going as it should. Thanks for asking. I've got go."

Kaye hung up the phone as Tom's mother entered the kitchen.

"Hi, Maury, is someone sick? I didn't change my dress or anything. Tom sounded like it was urgent."

The back screen door slammed, and Tom entered the kitchen.

"Hi, Mom, thanks for coming." He kissed her on the cheek as she poured a cup of coffee.

Kaye picked up two brown grocery bags, one containing her few clothes and the other her brown coat, the one she brought. She started toward the front door.

"For heaven's sake," Tom grumbled. "Put those down. I'll go up and get a suitcase. Go tell the kids goodbye. I told them you're taking a vacation."

He stomped up the stairs, his heavy boots thumping on each tread. Janie walked through the house humming, moving her head back and forth, her arms straight down tight against her body.

"Where's she going?" Tom's mother expressed more anxiety about staying with Janie than the three busy children.

"She'll probably walk around the house and then sit in the porch swing. There are bottles in the refrigerator for Molly. There are sandwiches for the children and Tom's lunch is packed."

"Maury, you're a wonder. What's this about you going?"

Tom reappeared, carrying a navy-blue suitcase with white vinyl trim.

"Here, you can use this."

He placed the suitcase on the sofa; a key on a keychain dangled from the handle. He placed the two paper bags on the sofa.

"Maury, go tell the kids goodbye." Tom removed Molly from his mother's arms and put her into the playpen. "Mom, will you pack Maury's things in the suitcase?"

Maury wasn't used to Tom's commanding tone.

"Thank you."

She refused to cry and upset the children. It would be best to follow his orders. No need to make him angrier; she needed a ride.

Kaye stopped at the playpen to hug Molly, then outside to hug Andy and Susie.

Tom came outside, carrying a paper bag and the suitcase. He placed them in the truck and handed Kaye the suitcase key. Molly started screeching, and Tom's mother carried her toward the house. Kaye ran back up the porch steps to kiss Molly's cheeks, dodging to escape the baby's clutching grasp at her hair.

"Have a nice cation!" Andy called.

Kaye scurried around the truck and climbed inside.

They rode to town in silence. Tom parked on the street in front of the gas station. He started to turn off the engine and hesitated.

He put the truck in neutral and set the brake.

"Here." He handed her a twenty-dollar bill. "I'm sorry it's not more, it's all I've got."

Kaye couldn't look at him. She reached to take the money. "I wouldn't take it but…. I'll pay you back when I get a job."

"Yeah, you do that, and I'll send you a check for working twenty-four hour days for five months." His words were still abrupt.

"I appreciated living at your house and helping your family. Thank you." Kaye looked around. "Do you know where the bus station is?"

Tom pointed toward the entrance to the gas station. "It's a small town, Maury. Go inside the gas station, the bus counter is in the back on the left."

Tom heaved a deep sigh, pulled her suitcase from the truck bed, and carried it toward the bench in front. When she returned, he asked, "Where are you going? Do you have family somewhere?"

"I'm not sure. We all have family somewhere, don't we?" She smiled. "Goodbye, Tom, and thank you."

Kaye reached out to take the suitcase and glanced across the street to see Mrs. Carlson, a neighbor, waving at them. "Tom." She pointed toward the neighbor.

"Hello," Tom gestured a brief wave. "What time does your bus leave?"

"Soon."

"Okay, I'm going home." He took a couple steps toward the truck and turned back. "Maury, I don't know what's ahead, but somehow, I hope you're in it."

The knot in her throat pulsed and tightened. Kaye took a quick breath to hold back her tears. A picture of Janie crossed her mind, Janie rocking and humming, her beautiful golden hair swinging against her shoulders, her empty eyes, and empty arms, refusing to hold her babies or to touch them. The loneliness of her presence and her absence tortured her family, and in Kaye's heart, she knew her being there risked deepening Janie's wound. She must go. Port Huron. The name sounded safe, as if she were entering a harbor.

Sometime during her thoughts of Janie, Tom drove away. Kaye sat down on the bench to wait. In two hours, a bus would deliver her to a place of refuge.

Her life was becoming a collection of memories of people she had loved. Kaye wasn't sure she could remember what Ann Marie looked like, only that she was kind and willing to accept there was more than Kaye wanted to explain. Kaye hugged her brown paper sack to her chest. It was there in that sack, her identity. Someday she would look at those papers. Now it was enough to know they were with her. She clutched the change from the bus ticket in her hand, nineteen dollars and four cents. She'd never held that much money before. She must be careful to spend it only if she needed to.

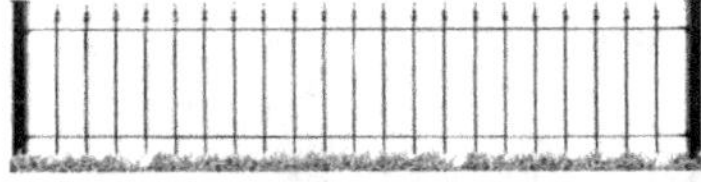

Seth asked, "Mr. Kent, why don't you use your tractor in the barn?"

"That was my Dad's. Hasn't run in years. I don't want to get rid of it."

"Things that don't run don't have a purpose."

Mrs. Kent smiled. "I've been telling him to get rid of it, but he wants to keep it around. I guess he wants to watch it rust."

"I could fix it for you."

Mr. Kent rocked back in his chair. His supper was finished, and he waited for a piece of the pie Mrs. Kent was slicing at the counter.

"Why do you want to do that?"

"I got nothing else to do. I need to be busy. I can tinker almost anything."

"He fixed the lock on the back door yesterday." Mrs. Kent smiled. "I wonder what he's fixed upstairs since he moved in." She placed a piece of pie in front of Mr. Kent.

"I've been thinking, Seth, you need a car, but I don't have the money to get you one. Tell you what, you get that tractor running, we can sell it and see what kind of a car we can get you."

"I don't have a license, and anyway, I can't drive with one leg."

"I thought you told me you can fix anything. Are you lying to me?'

"No sir." Seth blinked startled to be challenged with a lack of integrity.

"Well, if you can tinker, I'm sure you can put a hand throttle on a car."

"I could. I know I could." Seth couldn't contain his excitement. A car. A car he had earned and one he could drive.

"You start on that tractor tomorrow and I'll check around and see if I know anyone who wants a tractor that runs like a top and see if I can find someone who has a car to sell."

"Mr. Kent, you're terrific. Can I use the tools in the shop?"

"You sure can. If you need help with something heavy, I have a winch and a chain we can hook up to the truss."

Night and day, every spare minute he had, before and after summer school, Seth worked on that tractor. Within two weeks he had it running. Mr. Kent negotiated an arrangement with Jimmy Sutton of Sutton's car dealership to trade for a 1952 Chevy with an automatic transmission.

The first stop for the tractor was the paint bay at the dealership. When Jimmy met Seth and found out he had restored the tractor he offered him a job in the garage. Mr. Kent was right, in no time, Seth had converted the gas pedal to a hand-operated accelerator.

"Mr. Kent, I haven't received my letter from the engineering college. Classes start on August 20. Have you talked to Mrs. Jennings or Principal Saunders? Do you think it went to the Home?"

"No, Seth, this is the only address they have. I thought it was all set if you finished your summer classes. I forgot you needed a letter. I'll give her a call."

Next day, Mr. Kent placed a telephone call to Mrs. Jennings. That evening he reported the conversation to Seth.

"She said she'd made arrangements last February with a former student Thaddeus Portus. He works at the Saginaw plant. He agreed to sponsor you. She's waiting for a call from him. She'll get back with me tomorrow."

The next day Mr. Kent received a telephone call from Mrs. Jennings. He was glad Seth was upstairs. He wanted to talk with Florence. He lowered his voice.

"Hello, Florence, any word on Seth's letter?"

"Hi, Fred, I should say so. You tell Seth, he'll have his letter tomorrow. I'm driving up to Saginaw to get it myself. Tell Seth I'll pick him up at 7:30 in the morning and we'll hand deliver the letter to the engineering school on our way back. It took a little shuffling because Thaddeus said he had forgotten he agreed to sponsor Seth. I think he got wind that Seth was from the Home and an amputee. He didn't want any part of that. Ridiculous. I want him to meet Seth. I should have done that first, but I thought he'd know I wouldn't recommend someone who wasn't capable. I'll take care of all that tomorrow. He agreed to honor his previous commitment to me. It's all taken care of. Tomorrow our boy heads to a degree from one of the best mechanical engineering colleges in the nation and I know he can do it."

"Florence, there are some things that worry me."

"What things?"

"I know he can do the academic work because he's willing to study hard, but I worry about the other things. Sometimes the things that are normal stuff for us he doesn't know. It's like he's lived in a closet all his life. About his leg, shouldn't we be concerned other students will try to stop him from participating on projects, or ridicule him? How will he climb the scaffolding in the plants, those are huge machines."

"First, he's not been in a closet, Fred, he's been in an institution. Being confined alters people. Give him time, he'll catch up. He's very intuitive. Yes, his accident does leave him vulnerable to prejudices. We can't protect him from everything, and we can't stop him from having a future because it's going to be difficult. Ford started hiring veterans after WWI. By now I would hope all automotive plants have a hiring policy. He's got us and he knows we'll help him. What more can we do?"

Mr. Kent paused. "You're right. It's just that I've seen his frustration and embarrassment."

"You've done a fine job keeping his eye on the goal and getting him a car. His grades from the summer sessions are very good. He can do this. He must have the chance."

"Thanks, Florence, for following up on it. We'll see you tomorrow morning."

"Goodbye, Fred."

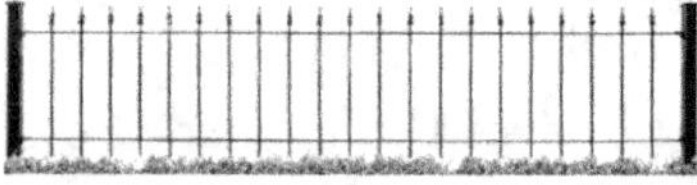

From the landing on the stairs, Seth overheard Mr. Kent's contribution to the conversation. Some of what he heard was painful even if it was true.

Chapter 30

Kaye tapped her suitcase with her toe and hugged her coat in the brown paper bag. The bus pulled up to the curb and the doors opened with a sucking swoosh, then folded back toward the inside of the bus. She stood up from the bench and the bus driver exited the bus, nodding to her as he passed. She waited, unsure if she should get on when he wasn't there. Another woman passed her and boarded. The steps were steep and high. Kaye picked up her suitcase and stepped up, but the next step caught the corner of her suitcase. She faltered, grabbing at the hand bar to keep from falling backwards. The money stuffed in her left shoe had altered her balance.

The bus held a few people. Some were moving around inside as others edged past her and exited. She found an empty seat in the front of the bus behind the driver and sat down. A lady across the aisle leaned toward her.

"Honey, the driver puts your suitcase in the compartment under the bus," she said in a kindhearted way. "You don't have to hold it."

"Oh."

"Just set it outside and he'll load it when he comes out."

"I want to keep it." Kaye hesitated. It contained only a few clothes, but they were all she had. She didn't want the suitcase to get lost or stolen.

"Suit yourself, honey." The women smiled and didn't seem upset. "Say, where you headed?"

"Port Huron."

"I'm going to De'troit. That's my town. I was up to visit my sister but those fields and sticks. Whooee! That's just empty land up there in that thumb. Do you like the thumb?" The lady was rather plump, wearing a printed summer dress and white shoes. She had red circles on her cheeks and red lips. Her hair was curly, the color of a rusty car.

"It's all right."

"I'm just saying a hello before I take out my book. It's a romance. Once I start reading, I'm just into my story. Don't think I'm rude. I like my stories."

Kaye smiled at the lady and moved over to the window seat, stowing her suitcase next to her feet, and crunching her brown bag on her lap. It was comforting to have her coat. As old and worn as it was, it did keep her warm and her folder was inside. She crossed her feet and looked at her shoes that also served as her pockets. The stitching on the inside of her right shoe was tearing loose. She had tucked the note from the Salvation Army lady in that shoe, hoping it wouldn't slide out. The heel of her left shoe flopped sometimes. She had tacked it twice in Tom's workshop and one tack had worked through to poke her heel. She hoped she could find new shoes soon. She moved her feet under the seat conscious of how worn and old they looked.

The bus rolled past fields of grain and corn. They were a blur of green and gold as Kaye's thoughts tumbled in her mind. She knew this day was coming the day Tom brought home the four quarts of strawberries from Martha's. The events of that day rolled through her mind like a movie reel.

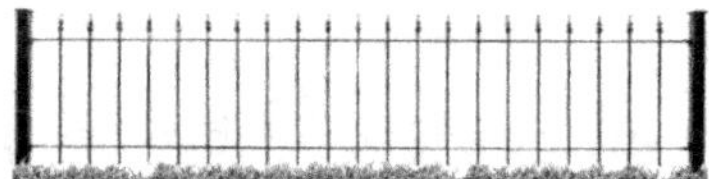

Tom had arrived home in the afternoon and breezed through the door with a box in his arms.

"Hi, Martha picked strawberries today and gave us four quarts. I thought maybe we could have shortcake for supper with some of those fine biscuits you make."

She didn't look at Tom, only picked up the box of berries and placed them by the sink. Angry thoughts rushed through her mind. Thoughts of pioneer women she had read about. *Sure,* and she'd dress a chicken, dig some taters, and knit a pair of socks before supper. Her tongue pressed against the roof of her mouth. He didn't have any idea about her day. He didn't even ask.

When Tom came in from milking the cows, he set his pail of milk on the floor near the sink and began washing his hands. Kaye placed the bowl of washed and hulled strawberries on the table. The room echoed with silence. Tom eyed his family seated at the table: Janie in her chair wearing an apron, the ties of the apron securely knotted around the back of the chair; Andy and Susie, too, were tied in their chairs with aprons; Molly was secured in her high chair, new to sitting; padding had been placed on each side of her small body, propping her upright. Kaye sat with her hands folded, looking down.

"Maury," Tom scowled. "Why is everyone tied into a chair?"

"Strawberries, Tom," Kaye could not conceal her anger. "There's only one way I know of to wash and hull strawberries in time for supper with a teething baby, a toddler, an inquisitive little boy, and a confused woman who wanders. And… there are no biscuits. Excuse me while I go for a walk."

The screen door slammed behind her.

When Kaye returned, Tom was holding Molly on his hip and trying to wash dishes with one hand. Molly's eyes were red from crying. She was gnawing on her fists as she clutched pieces of bread with melted cheese oozing from between her fingers. Pieces of bread crusts from leftover grilled cheese sandwiches remained on the child-sized plates. Two empty tomato soup cans lay on top in the waste basket.

"Want me to take Molly, or wash dishes?"

Tom stepped away from the sink. He was wearing an apron with a lace-trimmed ruffle across the top of the bib.

Kaye burst into laughter; Andy and Susie careened into the kitchen. Tom had looped the skirts of their aprons over the waistbands, dwarfing the garments to fit the children's small bodies.

"You all look…" She glanced at the children's expectant faces. "You look like good helpers!"

Tom surrendered Molly to Kaye's waiting arms.

"Guess I can't feed soup."

"You can learn," Kaye smirked, as she removed Molly's bib, wiped her face, and placed her in the playpen.

Tom tossed his apron onto his chair. He came toward her, his face grim, his eyes cold and hard. "You can't tie people to chairs, Maury."

"I can't?" Kaye's hands went to her hips.

"You can't. What makes you think that's okay?"

"Well… that's how you do it."

"You… do it?"

"You keep them clean, and you keep them safe." Kaye continued to clear the table. Tom stepped in front of her.

"You mean where you worked before?"

Her body trembled. She couldn't talk about that. Tom was more upset about tying the children to their chairs than if they had gotten hurt. At the very least he should appreciate she'd kept them safe. And there would be no conversation about where she had lived before.

"I'll check on Janie."

Tom grabbed Kaye's arm.

"Janie is fine, listen." They could both hear her humming and the creak of her rocking chair. The children raced out the back door.

Kaye stammered. "I guess I got upset. I'm doing the best I can." She sat down in the nearest chair as tears tumbled down her cheeks, her body aching from fatigue and her mind racing to stay alert. Between the tears she told Tom about her day. Trying to do the laundry, her search for Janie in the middle of the day, and Andy finding her asleep under the grape arbor. Janie had eaten something, berries of some kind, and she had three episodes of diarrhea. Kaye had to clean her, and the third time, she had to give her a bath. She still had two loads of laundry to hang when Tom came home with the strawberries.

"It's all I could do to get them prepared in time for supper."

Tom paced the kitchen.

"I'm sorry, I didn't know."

"You didn't ask."

"I don't know what to do!"

Kaye stood. "Until you have another plan don't complain about mine." Never in her life had she spoken to anyone in such a tone and with so much anger.

Tom moved in, his face now inches from hers. "Don't tie up my kids!" he shouted.

Kaye scooped Molly from the playpen and handed her to him. Instantly the child's wails pierced the air.

"Tomorrow is yours!"

Kaye went to her room, angrier and more hurt than she had ever been. Sitting on the bed her tears flowed. Silent tears of fear, dread, shame, and anger. Her body quivered. She came from a place where human beings had to be tied to chairs, secured in beds, fed, and diapered, people from birth to 3, to 33, to 53. He had no idea about cleaning them, getting bit by them, and loving them. Maybe she did belong behind the fence. Maybe she should go back. Maybe this was too hard. Hannot was right, she should never have children of her own. She didn't know how to take care of healthy normal children. All she knew was the kids in her building and the nursery.

The next morning everything changed forever.

Kaye awakened to a tap on her door.

"What time is it?"

"It's nine, your breakfast is on the table if you're hungry."

That was Tom's voice. She hurried to dress, noticing Molly's crib had not been used last night. Kaye went to the kitchen, unsure what to expect.

Janie was on the porch swing, wrapped in a blanket. How long would she stay there? Andy was pulling Susie and her doll in his wagon up and down the driveway. Tom set a plate of scrambled eggs and toast at Kaye's place at the table. He poured himself a cup of coffee and sat down across from her.

"I'm sorry about last night." His hands circled his cup. He didn't look up.

Her mind raced toward duty.

"What day is this? Shouldn't you be at work?"

"I didn't go. I called in sick."

"Tom," her voice sounded alarmed. "That's a *lie.* That's a *sin.*"

"Yup, Maury, it's one of many I'm sad to say."

"If you have a job, you must do it. You must go to work. What will happen?"

Tom scowled a puzzled frown.

"Why are you so concerned?"

"Won't you get punished?"

"They won't pay me for the day if I don't work. I get a smaller check. I guess that's the punishment."

Kaye turned her focus to the eggs. She had said too much again.

"You missed work because of me."

The eggs tangled in a lump as she tried to swallow.

"No, Maury, I missed work because I have a family who need me. You're part of my family. I got upset last night. We could have talked about it. Maury, tying someone to a chair is mistreating them. You cannot tie people up, children or adults. If certain people heard about it, they could investigate and possibly take my children away from me. There are some people already talking about Janie being dangerous to the children."

"What?"

"Yes, if Andy's teacher stopped by and saw the children tied to their chairs or Andy went to school and told the teacher or anyone he gets tied to his chair, I could lose my kids. I worry because I don't know what Janie will do next. Maury, the bottom line is from now on I want you to play with the kids, watch Janie as best you can, and I'll do more to help. I know how to cook and do laundry. I can clean too. I'll lease the fields out and only work in the plant. That will give me more time at home. We were both right in the wrong way."

Her body tensed; she tried to focus on her plate. She didn't want to look up. She knew the risk. When her gaze moved from the table to his chest, his chin, and up into his eyes… she knew. He loved her.

Feelings she couldn't explain welled up within. She couldn't look away. They stared into each other's eyes, their longing punctuated by Janie's humming and the rhythmic creak of her rocking chair.

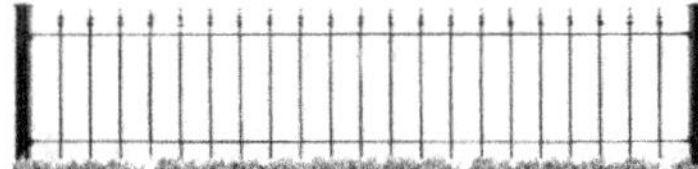

The blur of the passing scenery slowed to identifiable shapes, forming trees and buildings. The bus rumbled and groaned, jerking in an attempt to halt. Passengers struggled to stand upright, grasping the backs of the seats ahead of them, staggering to the pitch and roll of the moving vehicle. They attempted to organize articles and belongings to exit. Kaye waited. Having no destination, she had no need to rush. People shuffled from the back of the bus forward. She watched them moving tighter together, preventing anything or anyone from intersecting to cause a delay in their departure. Kaye watched the lady across the aisle. The large flowers on her print dress adhered to her backside, held there by her perspiration from sitting in the vinyl seat. Her book was secured into her handbag. With two elbow jabs and one "Excuse me," she acquired her position into the column of people filling the aisle. Resisting the surging force of the other passengers behind her, she braced her forearm against the seat ahead, nodded to Kaye, and waved her hand.

"Come on, Honey. Isn't this your stop?"

The man behind the woman scowled. "Keep it moving. What's the holdup?"

Kaye jumped up, tugging at her suitcase that instantly wedged itself between the seats. In her effort to dislodge the suitcase, she dropped the brown bag. It landed upside down on the floor ahead of her. She clutched her suitcase with her left hand, fearful it would slide under the seats if she dropped it. She reached forward clutching the bottom of the paper bag. Its contents spilled out onto the bus floor, a bundle of burgundy wool.

"Here, Honey, I'll get it." The woman reached down, grappled the garment into a mass, and proceeded to stuff it into the torn sack.

Kaye stared at the burgundy wool looping around the woman's hand.

"I got it," the woman announced. "You just come along."

Kaye wrestled her suitcase loose, scurrying in ahead of the woman. They rushed to catch up with the exiting passengers.

Kaye's mind raced in thoughts about her brown coat while her feet swept her in the direction of the exiting people. Inside the bus station, the woman placed the brown bag on a bench.

"Here's your bag. I guess you don't need that heavy coat today, riding a bus in this heat. I have another hour yet to ride."

Kaye studied the bag beside her.

"Ten minutes," the bus driver called. "Back on the road in ten minutes. Next stop Detroit."

"I've got to hurry, honey. Don't want to miss my ride. Nice meeting you." The woman rushed off in the direction of the restroom.

Kaye spread her fingers across the slats of shiny dark brown wood on the bench and struggled to pull her mind back to the present. She was in Port Huron. It was August, like the woman said. It was Friday. People passed by, the doors of the station opened and closed. The exhaust of the bus choked her each time it gushed in through the doors. Her arm pressed against the soft paper of the bag. All day she had clutched that bag as something precious. Tears pooled in her eyes. She wiped them away. It wouldn't do any good to cry. It was gone, her coat and her folder. Her personhood. Who she was, where she lived, what she had done for sixteen years! She had not read the contents. Without the file folder Kaye Maureen O'Shay did not exist. Numbness filled her body. Her hope for refuge in a city named Port Huron lingered amid her disappointment.

Nobody knew her. *K, Kay, Kaye Maureen O'Shay, Maury Morton,* the names echoed in her mind.

"Honey, you all right?" The flowered-dress lady returned, interrupting her thoughts. Standing in front of Kaye, she tugged at the rumpled skirt of her dress and struggled to release it from her moist body. "Somebody coming for you?"

"Thank you. Yes. They'll be here soon." Kaye urged a smile of appreciation toward the woman, now outside the door and out of range to hear. She fluttered a wave. Kaye waved back. The bus roared away. The bus station grew quiet. Kaye pulled the collar of the burgundy coat from the top of the sack. She was tempted to throw it into the garbage. What was wrong with her, someone wanted her to have a nice warm coat. Maybe it was his mother. No, Tom would do that. He would buy Janie another. They would not save her old worn coat. Someone would probably burn it. Emptiness filled her. She pushed her thoughts away.

A woman sat down next to her on the bench and unwrapped a tuna sandwich. The smell of fish filled the air. A man in soiled work clothes paused and took a seat to her left. The odor of perspiration was more pungent than the tuna and bus exhaust hung in the air. He opened his newspaper. People smelled. They all smelled different, but they smelled, and adults had different smells than children. People boarded buses and people exited and arrived at the bus station. This was her first time in a large city. Automobile and truck traffic increased as horns honked, and the sidewalk filled with people. The afternoon sunshine moved on toward the tall buildings of the city, casting shadows, inviting its residents to go home. She watched the men and women. Everyone had a purpose, a destination, someplace to be. Women wore skirts and blouses; some carried a jacket or sweater over an arm, wore high heels, or carried a handbag. Kaye had seen pictures of shoes and handbags in magazines. There were women in summer dresses and white shoes, carrying shopping bags with handles. Men and women dressed in fine clothes and others in working clothes. She watched them dodge each other, avoiding physical contact. The cacophony of sound and human beings formed an intricate dance to which everyone was in step, yet uninvolved and oblivious. Kaye removed the note from her right shoe and read the message one more time.

"Salvation Army of Port Huron, Telephone Yu 437-2728, Soldier, Ann Marie."

She did say, "If you ever need anything, you can call."

"Yes, Ann Marie." Kaye caressed the card with her fingers. "I need …" Kaye took a deep breath. The clock said 4:30. She had been sitting here in the bus station for over two hours. Crunching her paper bag with its errant contents against her body and carrying her suitcase, she approached the clerk at the ticket window.

"I'm looking for the Salvation Army, can you tell me how to get there? There's a lady named Ann Marie."

The man at the counter pulled a small map from his desk and circled a spot.

"I don't know about any soldier named Ann Marie, but I can tell you how to get to the Citadel." He turned the map toward her.

"You're here." He scratched an X. "When you walk out you want to go right. It's not far. It's a big building, there's a sign on it. Be careful and stay on the street. Don't go down any alleys or side streets and get lost. The streets intersect at an angle because of the river. Keep watching the street signs and stay on Huron. The Citadel is a big building. You could use the telephone over there and call. They might have someone who would come over and meet up with you, being you're carrying that suitcase and all."

Kaye looked at the telephone booths. She had never used a phone that looked like that.

"I don't think I should call…" She hesitated and turned to the man. She glanced around; no one was nearby. She leaned in toward the ticket window. Her voice was low. The man cupped his hand to his ear and leaned toward her to hear, "I don't know how to do it. The telephone?"

"You just wait there, Missy. I'll close this window a minute and help you." He slid a piece of cardboard across the window and disappeared.

At once a man appeared beside her. She trusted it was the man from behind the counter because he was still wearing his visor. He was short. He must have been standing on a box or sitting on a stool behind the ticket window. He barely reached her shoulder.

"Follow me." He hurried toward the row of telephones. "Do you have money?

She nodded.

"Okay, you can call from this telephone. Just put your money in. Do you have the number?"

"Yes." She bent down and removed two, one-dollar bills from the arch of her left shoe. How unreasonable, men's clothes had pockets and women didn't.

"Here." She handed him the dollar bills.

"Can't use that," he said and removed a dime from his pants pocket. "We'll use this. Now, you step inside so you can talk." He dropped the coin in. "What number?"

Kaye produced her slip of paper and read the number. "Ann Marie, Yu7-2728."

"You put the coin in here, always a dime. That'll get you the operator. She'll ask the number and tell you how much money to put in these holes. If it's a local call you just put in the dime, here, and dial the number. Like this. The man dialed the number and handed Kaye the receiver.

"Gotta go, Miss. Good Luck." A clock up on the wall chimed five o'clock.

The phone rang.

Kaye didn't know what to do.

A voice came on.

"Salvation Army."

"Anne Marie?" Kaye asked. She didn't really know how this worked.

"No, can I help you?"

"Oh, I need to talk to Ann Marie."

"I can take a message for her."

"She gave me this number after she helped me during the tornado. She said I could call her if I ever needed help."

"One moment."

Kaye waited, trying to keep her suitcase and coat as near as possible. All of a sudden, the bus station was a mass of people, but most looked too tired to steal.

"Hello, this is Ann Marie."

"Hello." Kaye struggled to make herself clear. "You may not remember me; my name is Maury Morton. I was in a tornado last spring, and you helped me."

"Yes, …I remember… you were with some children and helping their mother. Is something wrong?"

Her voice was kind and her questions sincere. Kaye started to cry. "I need…I need to talk to you."

"Where are you now?"

"I'm at the bus depot. I arrived this afternoon. I'm not sure how to find you." Kaye stopped talking, but she couldn't stop the tears.

"It's all right, I'll come there. It may take a few minutes. Sit down and wait for me. I'll come as soon as I can."

"Thanks, Ann Marie." Kaye hung up the phone and waited near the door. She would have to tell Ann Marie, she needed everything.

"It's all loaded." Seth stood beside his car, using his shirtsleeve to remove a speck of dust from the polished fender. Mr. and Mrs. Kent peered in through the car windows.

Mrs. Kent moved from window to window. "These windows are so shiny I can't see inside. You let me know if you need anything else."

Seth placed the bag of cookies she handed him on the passenger seat. "You've done more than enough. It's only one room."

Mr. Kent circled the car. "Press the brake pedal so I can check the taillights. Your tires look pretty good, lots of tread. You should make it till spring on those."

Together they had scoured the attic, the garage, and the basement for things Seth might need. They also solicited contributions from a few neighbors and friends. Packed inside his car, Seth had two crates and a board for a desk, a chair, lamp, typewriter, paper, ink pens, erasers. His drafting teacher gave him a drafting board. Mr. and Mrs. Kent had provided clothing in addition to his customary shirts and blue jeans. He had new dress pants and dress shirts, along with a sweatshirt, a jacket, boots, winter coat, and gloves. Seth packed and repacked his belongings, amazed to own so many items.

Mrs. Kent went into the house and returned with a long box. "I saved this to give you today. Go ahead, open it."

Seth kneeled down on the grass and opened the box. Folding back a sheet of tissue paper he saw the quilt. He had watched her work on it in the evenings after supper.

"I made it for you. I think it has the things you like."

He unfolded the quilt, unable to hide his excitement. She had used prints with cows, farm animals, apples and fruits, vegetables, and she had embroidered a drawing of the high school. Every block contained something he liked or was important to him.

"Mrs. Kent, thank you! I know you put a lot of time into this."

"You're welcome. It's our agreement, Seth. You live in our home, and you go to college. We're so proud of how hard you've worked despite many obstacles. We hope you'll always think of our home as your home." She started to cry. "I want you to go but I hate to see you leave. Isn't that silly!"

"No, I feel like that way too. I'll never forget what you've both done for me. I know I was not always easy to be around. Things moved so fast this summer. I wasn't sure this is what I wanted, but I'm willing to try. That's all I can promise, I'm willing to try."

A car turned off the road and into the driveway, throwing dust into the air. When it stopped three boys piled out, laughing, and shoving each other toward Seth. Butch slapped Seth on the shoulder.

"You're first one of us to leave, so we came to send you off. We're going to follow you to the county line. We want to make sure you leave town." They all laughed again.

Seth turned to Mr. and Mrs. Kent.

"My very own Three Stooges."

"Yes, I'd say they qualify." Mr. Kent laughed at the boys' antics.

"Oh, we bought you something to help you remember us," Butch said, turning to Chuck and Larry.

"It's in here." Larry crawled around inside Chuck's car and returned. He handed Seth three items as he named them. "An empty root beer mug, 'cause you don't need a full one, an empty package of cigarettes, cause you don't smoke, and a rubber band and spit wad, cause you always wanted to shoot one but left it up to us. Here, now don't forget us."

"I gotta get outta here." Seth chuckled and shook his head. He hugged Mr. and Mrs. Kent and got into his car. He was ready.

His three stooges followed to the county line.

During the entire drive, Seth only thought about Kaye. How different today would be if she could have helped him pack his car, and if he could have held her in his arms and promised her their future. He wiped a tear from his cheek. From somewhere deep within he had hope.

Chapter 31

Nothing about Ann Marie had changed. Her warm and friendly reception confirmed Kaye's hope that Port Huron would be a place of healing.

"First things first." Ann Marie circled Kaye's arm with her own. "Let's go to Dexter's. It's a restaurant down the street. We'll get something to eat. I've worked all day and I'm hungry too. They have good soup and sandwiches. Is that all right?"

"I'm not fussy about food, but I'm hungry. I do have some money; I can pay for my food."

They walked toward the restaurant. Kaye dodged people on the sidewalk. "This is a busy town. There are people everywhere."

"Port Huron is sort of a hub. We have the river for boats, tracks for trains, and streets for cars and buses." Ann Marie continued, "People coming and going and crossing the bridge back and forth to Canada."

Kaye interrupted, "Where do the trains come from?"

"Detroit, the thumb, from all across the United States."

"Do they come from Lapeer?" Kaye tried to keep her voice calm.

"Yes, and from further away. They come from Chicago and farther west."

"Is this where the trains stop? I mean do they end here?"

"No, there's a tunnel under the river. They go on to Canada."

Kaye had more questions but decided now might not be a good time to ask. She was here, beside the water. Now she knew Port Huron is where the trains go to the water and the sun rises.

Ann Marie opened the door to Dexter's and their conversation about Port Huron ended.

During the meal Kaye shared news about the children and Tom. She talked about the berries she picked and of learning to can vegetables. She paused. "Janie didn't get better."

"I'm sorry to hear that. No one knows why, but sometimes, something terrible can leave a person devastated. We can keep praying for her."

"I prayed." Kaye offered. "I've prayed a lot. I used to go to church and Sunday school." She halted. It wasn't good to talk about her life before the storm. She had to be more careful.

When they finished their food, Ann Marie settled back into her chair with an expression of concentration. The maturity she displayed alerted Kaye's instinct of suspicion. Ann Marie wasn't as young as she first thought.

"Maureen, I have to ask a couple questions."

"*Maureen.*" So many thoughts flooded Kaye's mind. The tornado, the blue saltbox with Morton printed on it, her boldness to make up a name. Ann Marie knew her as Maureen Morton. It wasn't true. The Sunday school teachers had been right. One lie did lead to another. Every Sunday school teacher said truth was always better, even if it involved punishment. This involved more than punishment. Telling the truth could destroy everything.

"I don't mean to pry…" Ann Marie paused. "Do you need something?"

Realizing she had been *wool gathering,* as her teachers used to accuse her. Kaye scrambled in her chair. "I need to use the bathroom."

"Yes, of course. It's down that hallway. Ladies on the right."

"Thank you."

In the restroom Kaye locked the door behind her, turned on the faucet, and looked in the mirror. The girl who looked back was pale and frightened. Her heart pounded in her chest, and her hands trembled. Liar, liar! She was fearful Ann Marie could see her confusion and would be concerned she was not telling the truth. Ann Marie talked about Jesus. She would never believe there could be a time that telling the truth would not be best. The truth. If she told her, Ann Marie would have to tell the police and they'd send her back to the Home. Then she would probably live there for the rest of her life.

Kaye washed her face and straightened her dress. The right thing to do would be to not involve Ann Marie in her lies. That would be the right thing to do, but having no place to go altered her decision. She would have to be Maureen Morton a little longer. Perhaps later she could leave Port Huron and Ann Marie wouldn't find out. She faced the girl in the mirror.

"Maureen, we're going to do this. There's no other way. Please, God, you know I always tell the truth. Please help me." She closed the door behind her and returned to the table and Ann Marie.

"Do you feel okay?" Ann Marie asked.

"Better now. Thanks."

"They give me money to help people. I'll pay the bill and the tip."

"Tip?"

"Yes, you know, the tip. Money you leave for the waitress."

"Yes, of course." Kaye watched Anne Marie put down two quarters beside her plate.

"Thank you for the food. It's been a long day. The city is so big and there are so many people. I've never been in a city this big before. Do you live here?"

"My family's lived here since I started high school. Someday I'll travel if that's what the Lord has planned. For now, I'm happy to be here." She placed her fork across her plate, sipped some water from her glass, and put the glass back on the table. "I hope you understand I have to ask some questions so I can help you."

Kaye nodded. Her heart was not pounding as it had been. The restaurant was not as busy as when they arrived. No one was seated near them.

"Is there anything you want to tell me about your situation?"

Kaye took a deep breath and tried to avoid looking at Ann Marie.

"I decided to come to Port Huron, it sounded like a safe place, Port Huron... like a harbor. I once heard a man talk about a harbor being safe. He said captains take their ships into port if a storm is coming. They're kind of the same, aren't they? Harbors and ports? I'm a good worker. I couldn't stay with Tom's family. I loved the children and cared for Janie...." Kaye's gaze moved from Ann Marie's face, toward the floor.

She didn't want to explain about Tom. "It wasn't the right thing to do. I know about rules. Do not steal. Do not kill. I know about the rules in the *Bible*."

Ann Marie continued her steady gaze.

"Maury, are you in trouble?"

Kaye didn't answer.

"Have you committed a crime? Are you expecting a child?"

"Oh, no, ma'am," Kaye looked at Ann Marie. "I don't make babies and I haven't hurt anyone, and I didn't steal anything. I don't have any place to stay because I can't go back to Tom's. And where I lived before, I can't go back there. I don't have any place to go. I understand if you can't help me. I'll get by." One glance at Ann Marie's face and she knew it wasn't right to involve someone as nice as Ann Marie in her lies. "Thank you for the food."

Kaye left the restaurant, turning back toward the bus station. It might be open all night, and she could sit there until she had another plan. Ann Marie caught up with her on the street.

"Maury, I told you, I must ask those questions. I'll help you. I know a place where you can stay for a few days until we have a plan. You can come to the Citadel and help me during the day. I called the lady while you were in the restroom. She said she'd give you a room for a few days. Please, come with me."

Kaye struggled. If she went with Ann Marie, it would involve her in the lies. If she didn't go, Ann Marie might think she'd done something bad, something she had to run away from. The streets were getting dark.

A horn let go a loud blast. Kaye jumped back, pressing her body against the building.

"What's that?"

"It's a freighter entering the bridge approach. You'll get so you don't even hear them."

"That's too loud to not hear it." The noise reminded her of the train echoing through the bridge the night of the storm.

"They are loud, and they blast a lot when it's foggy. Then the air is heavy. It's the music of the port." Ann Marie's smile conveyed a devotion to the sounds of her city.

"We turn here. There's a lady who lives in the third house by the name of Myrtle Dombrowski. Everyone calls her Mrs. D. but it's by invitation. Until… you call her Mrs. Dombrowski. "I think you'll like her. She does have rules."

When they arrived at the house, Ann Marie explained the architecture.

"It's called a four-square, the house. Mrs. Dombrowski has lived here a long time. She's so good about helping girls."

Kaye observed the vast front porch that held a swing and several chairs. They climbed the steps.

"Come on. After you're settled in your room, I'll have to go. It's past suppertime but there are dishes to do at the Citadel." She knocked at the door. Mrs. Dombrowski answered the door and smiled.

"Come on in! And I imagine this is the young lady you spoke of on the telephone. I just got home. I had a quick errand. I'm glad I didn't keep you waiting."

Kaye wondered if she had been working, and, if so, what kind of work required her to wear a suit on such a warm day.

"This is Maureen Morton," Ann Marie said. "She arrived today from the Thumb."

"Welcome to Port Huron." Mrs. Dombrowski's smile was warm and inviting. "Have you been here before?" She wore her hair in a braid, coiled low on the back of her head. She was tall and her heeled oxfords added another inch and a half. The uniform fit her no-nonsense demeanor.

"No, ma'am."

"You appear to be a nice young lady." Her assessments were forthright. "Is that all your things?

"Yes, ma'am."

"Would you excuse me for a minute?"

They entered the house. Ann Marie closed the door behind them as Mrs. Dombrowski disappeared down the hall.

Ann Marie waited, gazing out the window at the activity on the street. Kaye regarded the furnishings of the house. The wood glistened and the mirrors and windows were so clean they were almost transparent.

"It smells like lemon." Kaye whispered.

"Everyone I know uses lemon wax on the furniture. I like the smell, do you?"

"Yes, it's nice."

"What kind of polish did your mother use?" Ann Marie's inquiry posed a passing attempt at conversation.

"We just dusted. We used vinegar on the windows." Kaye wrinkled her nose. "These windows are clean, but I don't smell vinegar."

To the right of the front door, two steps raised to a landing. On the landing there was an oval window with a stained-glass border. More steps ascended to the second floor. The banister and the stair treads were dark wood. A red patterned carpet covered the middle of the stair treads. Kaye could see hardwood floors from the dining room. Beautiful carpets sectioned off seating areas. She could only get a glimpse of the kitchen. A dark red-patterned vinyl covered the kitchen floor. White cupboards with grooves lined the walls. To her left, in the living room a maroon-colored sofa and two chairs stood clustered in front of a fireplace. A table separated the two chairs. The room beckoned her in. Along one wall, a long wood table holding several books was positioned in front of a large window. A wooden chair, with round spindles up the back and with wooden arms, stood open and waiting. Kaye wondered about the view from the chair; outdoor scenes enticed her. The fireplace screen had painted panels, but she couldn't see the details. She didn't enter the room. She found it difficult to imagine living in such a grand house.

"Is this the work you do? Finding homes for people who have no place to go?"

"No, yes, sometimes. My work is dependent on what needs to be done today. I don't make a schedule on a calendar. Each day has its needs and its blessings. I show up and do whatever needs to be done. Today it was Maureen Morton, and I've had a pleasant afternoon. I must confess, I wasn't sure I'd ever see you again. I'm pleased you called."

Kaye recognized sincerity in Ann Marie's voice. Her own longing to belong somewhere caused her voice to falter.

"I have nowhere to go." Those were hard words. No place to go wasn't completely true. She did have a place to go, but it didn't offer her a life of her own choosing, only the life of a servant. There she could never have a husband, or a family, no home of her own to clean or polish. As much as it hurt to say it, she believed with all her heart she did not have any place to go. *The Home.* She hoped she would never hear about The Home ever again, yet it lingered like a stain she could not remove. She moved away from Ann Marie and approached the China cabinet. The glass doors sheltered numerous pieces of glassware and dishes. Kaye was viewing the delicate flowers on a fine porcelain dish when Mrs. Dombrowski reappeared wearing a plaid dress and an apron.

"That's an old habit," she laughed. "My mother always made us change our clothing when we came home from school. We had to back then because clothing was passed down to younger family members. Some of us always want our mother's approval."

"My mother made me change when I came home from school too. I understand," Ann Marie said.

Mrs. Dombrowski turned to Kaye.

"I see you admire pretty dishes."

"I've never seen anything like these!"

"Most of them are from my family. I've collected a few. I have friends who painted China and gave me some as gifts. That cabinet is pretty, but it is a chore to clean."

"Mrs. Dombrowski, I don't mean to introduce you to Maureen and run, but I must go back to the Citadel." Ann Marie reached for the doorknob.

"Of course. We'll be fine. You run along."

Ann Marie rushed down the sidewalk and toward the main street, leaving Kaye and Mrs. Dombrowski standing in the foyer.

"Are you hungry?" Mrs. Dombrowski asked.

"No, thank you. We ate before we came."

"Then you're ready for a rest. Follow me, your room is this way." Mrs. Dombrowski ascended the stairs with the speed of a woman twenty years younger than she appeared.

"I like these stairs. They keep me in shape," she chuckled when she reached the top. "Down this hallway. You're on the end. It's a small room and it's the farthest from the bathroom, but it's been the practice that the newest girl gets the smallest and farthest room. Seniority has its place." Her good-natured humor brightened Kaye's mood. She opened the door to a shallow room wide enough for only a single bed, one chair, a small window, a two-drawer dresser with a mirror above and hooks on the wall. Kaye counted the hooks: ten.

"There's no closet. They didn't build these old houses with closets. Just the essentials."

"This is very nice; I don't have many clothes." White organdy curtains bordered the window; white chenille spread covered the bed, the wallpaper displayed pink roses and garlands of green ivy. A colorful rag rug at the bedside brightened the gray painted floor. Kaye touched the soft puffs of the chenille spread. Mrs. Dombrowski opened the window.

"We probably should let in a little fresh air. This small room gets stuffy. You can close it when you like. Now I best tell you the rules right off. There are *no* men allowed in this house except my brother who does maintenance work for me, and my two sons who visit when they're in town. I mean it. Absolutely no entertaining. There is a signup list in the kitchen, you can sign up if you want to bake something, but you are responsible for the ingredients and for cleaning up the kitchen. The bathroom has a list on the door. That list indicates which day of the week is your laundry day and what day each person is responsible for cleaning. The laundry room is in the basement and the clothesline is off to the side yard."

"Don't I have to pay to live here?"

"When you can. The Army pays me until you can find work, or as long as you donate time at the Citadel. There's plenty of work to do there. Ann Marie said you were still in school. How old are you?"

Kaye inhaled.

"I'm seventeen, ma'am. I'll be eighteen in March."

"I guess so. You look young for your age. It doesn't matter to me as long as you obey the rules. Now, as for the neighborhood, we do get our share of sailors in town, so you have to be alert. Stay off the street after dark unless you're with someone. It's just a good idea. There hasn't been any trouble for years, but I like to keep my girls safe."

"How many girls live here?"

"Today I have five and you make six. I can put up a couple more, but it gets crowded. There's a bathroom downstairs but you must be fully clothed to come downstairs. No robes, pajamas, that sort of clothing. I give each girl a shelf in the kitchen so you can eat breakfast here at the house if you want. No one cleans up after you." She scowled, emphasizing her point.

"Yes, ma'am."

"I think that's all for now. You go ahead and unpack. Are you in for the night?"

Kaye's head tipped a nod. "Ann Marie said she would stop by tomorrow if I needed help to enroll in school and maybe find work."

"Good night then." Mrs. Dombrowski smiled and closed the door.

Kaye sat down on the rug next to the bed. The cool breeze felt good. It was getting hard to keep lying to nice people. She closed her eyes and took a deep breath.

"Hooonnnk." A freighter's horn sounded again, startling her. It would take some time before she'd no longer jump at each blast. She untied her shoes, although they were stretched enough that she could remove them by kicking them off. Still, she had been taught to untie them properly and a rule is a rule. Her socks had holes in the heels and the cuff stretched wide on her leg. It would be nice to get some new socks. She opened her suitcase. It was almost full. Startled, she jumped up and turned on the light. Yes, the suitcase was filled with clothing. She removed two sweaters, two dresses, a brassiere, four pairs of socks, a slip, four pair of panties, a pair of pajamas, a hairbrush, a can of talcum powder, not full but not empty, two barrettes, a comb, a hand mirror, and a toothbrush. *Oh my goodness!*

Tom's mother must have packed the suitcase. The clothes were Janie's. She recognized them. Her own ragged underwear and dress were not in the suitcase. That was kind. Kaye began to cry, unsure if it was about being away from Tom's family, Janie's clothes, being alone in a big city, or lying to nice people who were willing to help her. The tears flowed until late into the night. It was cold when she closed the window, removed her clothes, pulled on Janie's pajamas, and crawled into the narrow bed.

Chapter 32

The leaves turned colors and fell to the sidewalks before Seth had time to look outside. The crisp days and chilly nights arrived with the harvest moon, but his schedule started with his course books before sunrise and ended long after the moon crested the eastern sky. The weekends offered little reprieve from academic demands.

On Fridays, some of the guys headed out for a date or home to see their girlfriends. The price turned out to be high for the engineering students who were less than gifted. Mr. and Mrs. Kent understood Seth's need to remain in Flint and study on the weekends. He wrote them every Sunday afternoon. Next term, he would be in the plant, and they were running twelve-hour shifts, six and seven days a week. Other students had warned him the rotation into the plant would be as rigorous as his academic schedule. The students rarely spoke of the dropout rate, but it was apparent as seats became empty in the classrooms. The first week of class the instructors reiterated the dropout rate. They tried to spur the students on to completion, but sometimes the statistics threatened them with a constant, overriding sense of impending doom.

This weekend he planned to go to Port Huron and search for Kaye. Planning the trip had not been easy, but it was coming about with minimum expense. The railroad had a special for this weekend only. He didn't have enough money to stay overnight, but he did have enough for a round trip train ticket. He'd spend a Saturday in Port Huron searching for Kaye and return on an evening train. As the weekend approached, he began to hear his own doubts. After six months making her own way, she wouldn't be standing at the water, waiting for him. She could be anywhere in the city, or any other city. He might never find her. The whole idea of searching for her might be foolish to anyone else, but if he didn't go, he would always wonder. He had to try.

Saturday morning, he arrived at the train depot ahead of the scheduled departure. Wearing khaki pants, a plaid shirt, a navy jacket, and carrying books in a canvas valise, Seth's student status was evident. The train ride would provide time for him to study. People gathered in the depot. The porters called out the departing trains and destinations and announced the times of arriving trains. Seth remained engaged in his studies. When the porter called "Port Huron," he startled. His book fell to the floor, bringing the attention of the people around him. He clutched his notebook, picked up his textbook from the floor, and headed toward the departure gate. He moved along the platform following the flow of the Saturday crowd. Another train approached from the opposite direction. The wheels of the moving train rumbled, their steady rhythm pounding the ground with the force of heavily loaded cars. The sounds magnified by the train's proximity to each other echoed louder and louder. Seth struggled against the tide of the people. He remembered the stories Louie told about the trains. His mind raced to thoughts of that night, of Ben and the dark. Pushing his way through the crowd, he reached the building and pressed his body against the wall. His left leg trembled, and the phantom spasms of his right leg contracted. His brain relived the terror, and his conscious grip could not contain his thoughts. He had slipped. His foot. His leg. Memories flooded his mind. Beads of sweat formed across his brow and ran down his neck. Ben running, carrying him, his head bouncing against Ben's shoulder. He remembered fragments of that black night. Screams. The hammering wheels of the train thundering on.

Still shaking, he couldn't board the departing train. Seth returned inside the depot and sat down on the bench he had occupied earlier. The train left the station amid the porter's calls and late arrivals rushing through the station. He crunched his ticket in his fist. Wasted money. This was not what he expected. Some of his emotions came from years past and others only had months to heal. Fear! Throughout his childhood, after years of falling, he had been afraid someone would push him in front of a train. The fears he had suppressed for years converged on him from the shadows of long ago. The shock of his reaction struck his core. As a young man, he had allowed no fears to surface. He was taller than most of the men, stronger and quicker; his defenses were wily, and they had not failed him until today.

The clock struck nine, then ten.

If he could refund his ticket, he could use the money for gas. He'd ask for a refund and drive. He didn't have to take the train.

He set his books on the counter and passed his ticket through the window.

"Can I get a refund?"

"You should have done that before the train left, son. Change of plans?"

"Yeah. Something like that."

The ticket master met his eyes and made the assessment.

"One of these days, you'll get on."

"What?"

"One day you'll get on."

What did he know? How could this man know how hard it was for him to board a train? With a glance, Seth questioned the man's sincerity.

"I saw your limp when you came in. Trains have different meanings for different folks. I've seen immigrants who couldn't get on. Trains took their family away. They've been places, seen things. The war. I've seen it before. You take your time, son."

"Is there another train going to Port Huron?"

"Not until noon. You want a ticket for that one?"

"No… thanks."

"Here's your money. Don't give this morning much thought. It'll work itself out. You'll see, as you get older, some things you just have to give time."

Was it about looking for Kaye, or was it about the train? Probably both. He went home. Maybe the ticket master was right, it takes time.

Kaye filled her days working with Ann Marie at the Citadel, sorting clothing, and helping prepare meals.

Ann Marie passed by carrying a pile of children's clothing. "On Thursday, you can go over to the high school and see about registration. Do you have your school records?"

"No, do I need them to go to school?" Kaye searched Ann Marie's face for an answer.

"I don't know, I think so. Anyway, if you don't, we can get them later. Were you born in Michigan?"

"I don't know for sure. I forgot. I have to run an errand for Mrs. D. I'll see you on Thursday."

Kaye laid down the clothing she was folding and left without saying goodbye. This lying had to stop. Yet the lies keep growing. Now what was she going to do. Ann Marie will keep asking and she couldn't keep rushing away or saying things that aren't true. If she had her folder maybe there would be a copy of her birth certificate in it. She should have looked when she had it. Now, she'd never know.

Kaye sat down on the front steps of Mrs. D's house. Even if she had the folder, it could have something on it that said she belonged at the State Home. It wouldn't list her parents. They didn't leave their names. Ann Marie said a birth certificate. She'd have to wait until Thursday to ask.

Ann Marie stopped by Mrs. D's house on Thursday morning, and they walked to the high school together. They filled out the required forms, and Kaye signed her name as Maureen Morton. She had to think of herself as Maureen Morton.

"Mrs. Scott will see you now." The secretary pushed away from her desk, rolled toward a file cabinet, and waved them toward a door with a frosted glass panel that read PRINCIPAL.

"Ann Marie, I remember you as a student. I hope you're doing well?"

"Yes, Mrs. Scott, I'm doing very well, thank you. I came with my friend Maureen Morton, and she wants to enroll in high school. She hopes to complete her senior year and graduate in June."

"Welcome, Maureen. Why don't you sit down, and we can discuss your placement."

Their discussion of class selection included several of the classes Kaye had taken and several she would need to graduate.

"We will need the forms from your former school." The principal paper clipped three pages together. "I can mail these if you like, just give me the name and address."

"Can I get them for you? The schools merged and I'm not sure where to mail them."

Mrs. Scott hesitated.

"It's usually not done that way. Did you say you're from out of state?"

"Yes, Nebraska. We moved a lot. I'll get them as soon as I can."

"If you're sure, I wouldn't stop you from attending for back records, but it's helpful for your class placement."

"I'm a very good student and I'll work hard. You'll see."

"You said you're equivalent of a senior status."

"Yes ma'am."

"We'll see how you do. Academic achievement is challenging when you must change schools," Mrs. Scott said, her voice skeptical. "Take these with you and see if you can get them returned to me as soon as possible."

"Maybe I could find some of my old report cards. Would that help?"

"No, I need your academic record. Especially your high school records. That's all."

She ushered them from the office.

As they walked back toward town Ann Marie asked, "Maureen, what's the problem with getting your school records?"

"I don't want to talk about it. I'll see what I can do. She said I could attend school."

"Yes, but you can't graduate without evidence you accomplished the required credits." They continued in silence. At the corner, Kaye paused, fearful Ann Marie was angry. She wanted Ann Marie to trust her.

"Do you want me to come back to the Citadel to work? I still have the afternoon."

Ann Marie frowned. "No, I have to meet with someone. Come by tomorrow afternoon."

Kaye worried throughout the walk back to Mrs. D's. She didn't have an answer for Ann Marie or Mrs. Scott.

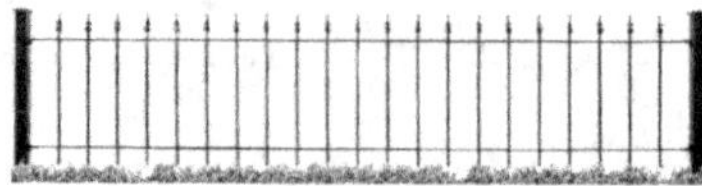

By Thanksgiving Kaye had a part-time job after school and weekends at Dexter's restaurant, but she still hadn't gotten used to being called Maury by adults.

"Maury, your order's up." Danny banged his fist on the counter. "What's wrong with your hearing? I called you three times. If I have to deliver the food myself then they don't need to pay you."

"Sorry, I didn't hear you."

"The restaurant is not that noisy. What's with you?"

Kaye placed the coffee pot back on the warmer.

"I said I'm sorry." She grabbed the plate of eggs, added two pats of butter on top of the toast, and carried the order to the table. It wasn't the first time she had ignored someone calling her Maureen or Maury.

It was hard to focus on the food orders and whether she would get enough time this afternoon to do her homework at the library.

She was only working at the restaurant on Saturdays now, because she had added another class to her schedule. She couldn't study at Mrs. Dombrowski's because it was too noisy, and when she was there, Mrs. Dombrowski frequently had errands for her to run or needed help in the kitchen. Ann Marie was watching for an apartment Kaye could share with another girl, but it hadn't worked out yet. Ann Marie needed help at the Citadel, and they were paying her rent. She had to help when they asked. Her schoolwork was piling up. Not enough time to read the assignments. Not enough time to reread her papers to avoid errors.

After her shift at Dexter's, Kaye rested on the bench outside the library. She had to go inside. She had to study. The cold seeped through her coat and her sweater. Her shoes were wet, and her socks were frozen against her legs. Ice had formed on her shoes. Numb and cold, she moved around the corner and through the doors. Inside, the building was warm. She approached her favorite table next to a heat register, sat down, and slipped off her shoes. For a minute she would put her head on her arms and rest.

"Miss, we're closing now."

Kaye was startled awake. "What time is it?"

"It's nine. We close at nine."

"Oh yes." Kaye bundled up her books and papers, slipped into her cold damp shoes, and hurried out the door.

Why had she registered as a senior instead of a junior? She thought she would be able to do the work. All her high school grades were excellent. Now she questioned if the teachers had graded her as a Home student and not on the regular grading scale. Stumbling over the crusted snow and ice toward Mrs. Dombrowski's, she started talking to herself. "English, you can do English. Math, you can do math. Algebra is math with symbols. It's like a story problem. All you have to do is figure out what the symbol means. Government, it's the words, those long words and what goes with what. Now, Chemistry, that's a real choker." She arrived at Mrs. D's, placed her bag of books on the porch, grabbed the broom, and started sweeping the snow away.

If she hurried, she could finish before her toes froze completely.

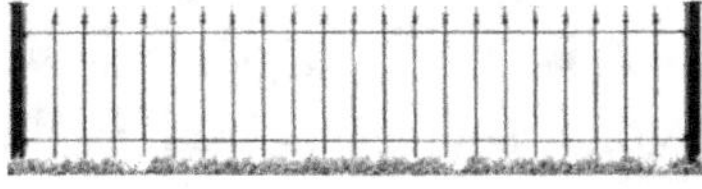

Sunday after church Maury slipped on Janie's coat. She had a pile of homework waiting to be done before Monday morning.

Ann Marie stopped her at the door. "Maury, can you stay for a bit and help us serve the dinner? We don't have enough help."

"I have a lot of homework, and I helped peel the potatoes."

"I understand." Ann Marie returned to the kitchen.

She shouldn't refuse after all Ann Marie's done for her. From the second story window Kaye watched the snowflakes tumbling down. Winter had arrived. She did have homework, lots of homework. From this view she could see the people drifting toward the Citadel. They were coming for shelter and a meal, poor people, lonely people, and hungry people. Kaye removed her coat, the one she would forever know as Janie's, placed it on the coat rack, hurried to the kitchen, and donned an apron.

Ann Marie gave her a quick hug and handed her a soup ladle. The people filed through one by one. Today there were several children. These children were sullen and sad, so different from the children at the Home. Even with their deformities and even when their laughter was inappropriate there was some laughter. She had learned hungry children do not laugh.

"Now, come back if you're still hungry when these are gone," Ann Marie urged as she scooped mashed potatoes onto their plates from a kettle big enough to stand inside. Her warm and welcoming smile urged smiles in return.

Ann Marie scraped potatoes from the sides of the kettle hoping for enough to serve one more person. He came through the line, always the last to be served, the man in a long, worn gray coat, and shabby gray felt fedora hat. Curls of gray hair tumbled down over the collar of his coat. He passed through the food line, his chin down, and his face shielded from view by a neck scarf and the brim of his hat. Kaye had seen him before. She tilted her kettle, unable to fill the ladle.

"Sorry, the soup is gone," she apologized. He lifted his hand in a gesture, palm down. She wasn't sure if he meant he didn't eat soup and it was okay, or it didn't matter, or he knew he was late. His nonverbal reply piqued her interest. He didn't walk like an old man all hunched over, but moved like someone tired, very tired. He wasn't greedy because he always came last and ate what was left without complaint. Each time, he carried his tray to the far side of the room and placed it on a single table, along the wall. He would move one chair and place it at the table facing the wall. There he would eat his meal in solitude, speaking to no one. He would leave as he arrived, alone.

Kaye carried her empty soup kettle to the kitchen, following Ann Marie.

"Ann Marie, does that man come to every meal at the Citadel?"

"Most, I would say. Maybe not every meal."

"It's sad that he's always alone."

"Don't bother him," Ann Marie warned. "He doesn't like to be around other people. We've invited him to sit at a table with others, but he ignores any invitation. He knows his ways. Better to respect him than to bother a man who has troubles."

Kaye placed her soup kettle on the worktable and removed her apron. Without further discussion with Ann Marie, she made her decision.

"I think I'll try." She returned to the dining room, aware Algebra, Chemistry, and an English theme awaited her attention. Maybe she was avoiding her homework, but this man's loneliness bothered her. She carried a chair to the man's table placed it at the side of the table and sat down, avoiding eye contact.

"Mind if I join you?" she asked.

He waved his hand, indicating he preferred she go away.

Kaye ignored his gesture, choosing to remain. She lowered her voice to a soft melodic tone she used with Jessie, speaking only loud enough for him to hear.

"I saw the snow falling before I came to the dining room. The weather report said it would snow about three inches today. It surprises me how pretty it is as the snow falls onto the water. I'm new here...." She gazed at the table, imagining a snow globe. "Did you ever see one of those round things that you shake, and it looks like the snow is falling?"

The man continued eating. He did not respond. He ate his meal with his teaspoon, deliberate movements, and small portions.

"I'm in high school, my senior year. I have a lot of homework. It's my fault, I got behind last year and now I must catch up. It's second year algebra and chemistry that's causing me fits. Oh, and the theme about *Macbeth*, due on Friday." She waited. The man continued eating. His pace was so slow his food must be cold. The gravy setting up on his potatoes had formed a skin and congealed to a shiny glazed pool. He must be used to eating cold food at this pace. The room was clearing of people. Chatter and clatter tumbled from the kitchen, as the help washed the table dishes and the pots and pans. A man came in with a broom and began sweeping the dining hall, avoiding the area where Kaye sat with the gray man finishing his meal.

Respect and love, that's what she learned about the people of the Salvation Army. Even though he was late, ate alone, and now delayed their leaving, he was a guest, sent by God, and thus they would treat him. She had learned that first from Ann Marie.

"I don't want to fail my classes. I have to try harder, I guess. I've prayed too. Pray and work hard, that's what Ann Marie says. Do you know her? She's the one who scoops the mashed potatoes. That's her favorite food to serve." Kaye waited until he had finished his meal before she spoke again. "I hope you come back again. Would it be all right if I sit with you when I'm here?"

He finished his meal and carried his tray to the counter. He didn't have to scrape his plate because nothing remained on it. He returned to the table and removed a pencil and a piece of paper from his pocket. He sat down and wrote.

"*I will help with your schoolwork. Come back in 1 hour. Bring books! OK?*" He tapped the OK and handed her the pencil.

Kaye circled the OK and thrust the pencil toward him.

He secured his scarf over the lower portion of his face with his left hand, looked up for the first time and nodded.

"Thank you. I'll be back." Kaye smiled at his kind eyes.

He left the building, his hat tilted into the wind.

Kaye rushed to tell Ann Marie. "The gray man, he's offered to meet me here in one hour to help me with my homework."

Ann Marie paused.

"There will be some workers here all afternoon, but I'll come back too. I have lessons to prepare for tonight. You can work in the Sunday school room. I'll work in the corner. I won't bother you. That was kind of him. Did he share his name?"

"No, but I do know a little more about him… I know he has a hare-lip and maybe a cleft palate. That's why he eats alone. He doesn't want anyone to see his face. His eyes are friendly."

"A cleft palate?"

"Yes. He must eat small, slow bites. He probably can't eat soup. Soft, thick foods are easier to swallow."

Ann Marie tilted her head, giving Kaye a sidelong glance.

"You know some interesting things, Maury."

"Just life. You learn things as you go along." Once again, she had said more than she intended. She rushed home to gather her books, the list of her assignments, and returned in less than one hour.

The man in gray waited at the front steps of the Citadel.

"We can go inside. Ann Marie said we could study in the Sunday school room." They moved up the steps and into a small classroom with a window. Kaye pulled a table toward the window and placed a chair on each side. The man moved his chair around to her side of the table. He pointed his first finger down and moved his hand back and forth, indicating it would be better if they worked side by side. He removed his coat and laid it over the back of a chair. His neck scarf remained around his neck. He did not remove his hat. They faced the street. Snow continued to flutter to the ground as they worked. He did not speak but used a pencil to point out the directions in her books, occasionally writing a note on her notebook paper. As she worked on her problems he waited until she could not work a segment of the problem, then referred her back to the place in her textbook that taught that concept. They finished the Algebra and Chemistry problems.

"Bring your Macbeth theme on Wednesday, after school and I will look it over," he wrote.

"You'd do that?" Kaye wanted to give this stranger a hug. God answered a prayer she had not prayed. She had her homework done and had helped with the Sunday meal too. The homework problems were difficult but now she understood how to do them and wouldn't be afraid if the teacher called on her to show her work on the board.

"Thank you!" Kaye gathered her papers and placed them in her notebook. "I don't know your name. Mine's Maury, that's short for Maureen."

He motioned with his hand. The same gesture as before. She assumed it meant, "It doesn't matter."

"It's all right. I'll just call you *My Friend.*"

He checked his neck scarf, making sure it was secure. He looked up, his eyes crinkled at the corners. They were cornflower blue. His face was tanned and weathered, what she could see of it. He wore a blue cotton work shirt and a heavy cream-color fisherman's sweater. His pants showed areas of mending, patches added with tiny stitches. His work shoes were dark from the wet snow. The laces of his right shoe had several knots.

"See you on Wednesday. I'll come before church, at about five. Is that all right?"

He put on his coat, looked out the window and up at the sky to check the weather. Then he nodded and left the building.

Isn't that strange, a man who knows chemistry and algebra so poor he eats in soup kitchens? He probably knows Shakespeare too. She'd find out on Wednesday.

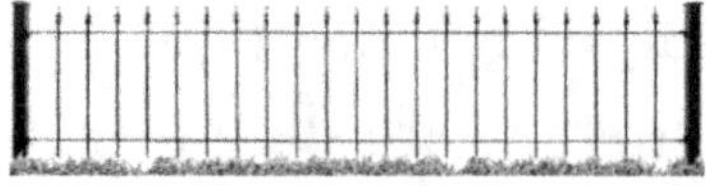

Wednesday

Kaye hurried toward the Citadel. The temperature had turned even colder, and gusts of wind brought bursts of sleety snow against her coat. Snow caked on her shoes making them heavy as she walked. Boots, she needed boots. She saw the man dressed in gray huddled in the entrance, blowing on his hands. They must be cold. She'd try to find him some mittens or gloves before he left today.

"I'm here. It's almost done." She gestured toward her binder containing the pages of her theme. They stepped inside the foyer. He sat down on the second step of the stairway, opened the binder, and removed the pages of paper. Kaye leaned against the wall and waited as he read, head down, engaged in his task. After he finished, he removed a red pencil from his pocket and lifted it up seeking, permission to mark the pages.

"Sure. Anywhere you can see that needs correction make a mark."

He inserted punctuation, noted places for clarification, and drew lines through redundant phrases. At the top he wrote *Word count?*

"Yes," she replied. "It has to be five hundred words… It looks like I've lost some." She sighed. Troubled, she would have to write more, possibly a lot more.

He read the paper again from beginning to end. He added simple words over sentences, words like, *how, why, where, describe, summarize.* Handing her each page as he finished, she read them; there were several areas where she could write and make the paper more interesting.

"You're like a fog cutter." Kaye let go a chuckle. "Are you a teacher?"

He wrote a note, "*Good start, keep up!*"

"I won't see you again before I have to hand it in." Kaye struggled to suppress her panic.

He wrote, "*You know what to do now. OK?*" He looked up, his lower face covered and nodded.

"Will you stay for church?"

Without an answer, he headed up the stairs toward the balcony. Kaye waited for Ann Marie to arrive.

"Ann Marie, do you believe God answers prayers?"

"Of course I do, Maury."

"Do you believe God sends people in answer to prayers before you've prayed?"

"I don't begin to understand how God works. The *Bible* says, *His ways are not our ways*. We don't have to understand to believe."

"I didn't even pray about help with my homework. I worried about it, but I forgot to pray. I think God sent the gray man to help me. Do you think that could happen?"

Ann Marie removed her coat and placed it on a hanger on the coat rack. "Maury, other people have prayed for you too. Yes, I believe God answers prayers in many ways, not always the way we expect. Are you staying for worship?"

"Yes."

The service opened with prayer. When the band started playing, Kaye's heart lifted to the balcony, and she prayed for the gray man, thankful for his help.

Mittens. Kaye leaned over to Ann Marie, "I forgot to mention the gray man doesn't have any mittens. Is it all right if I run down to the clothing room and see if I can find some?"

"Check the box just inside the door. It's full of gloves and mittens."

Kaye hurried to the clothing area and returned to hand them to him as he left worship.

Before they prepared to leave, Kaye handed Ann Marie the marked pages of her theme. Look what he did to help me."

"I must apologize for telling you not to disturb him because he preferred to eat alone. Leave it to you to find a way. You're very interesting, Maury. I believe God has blessed you. Continue to follow where He leads."

Walking home, Kaye speculated about God answering prayers, and what Ann Marie said about other people praying for her. God had never answered her prayers to be adopted into a family. He did make it possible for her to go to high school. He did protect her when she ran away. God did use her in answer to Janie's prayers. She caressed her pearl button necklace. She had to believe.

Chapter 33

"Why aren't you ready? I told you 6:30!" Marvin checked his tie in the mirror in Seth's room.

"I'm not going," Seth signed.

"You can't do that! I promised Nancy we'd pick 'em up at seven and we'd better be there at seven."

"You take 'em."

"Come on, Seth. You've been stuck in this room studying for weeks now. I told the guys I could get you out. It's only one night."

"I told you; I've got a girl."

"So, I heard that before. So, when did you see her last?"

"A few months back." Seth picked up his roommate's shirt and threw it in the laundry. "It's a full-time job studying and picking up after Joe."

"You're changing the subject. Tell me about this girl of yours. Does she have a name?" Marvin plopped down on Joe's unmade bed.

"'Course she has a name! Her name is Kaye."

"So, you haven't seen her for months?" Marvin crossed his right leg over his left knee, gripping his right ankle. "Why is that?"

"I don't know where she is."

"You have a girlfriend, you haven't seen for months, and you don't know where she is, but you can't go out for an evening with a few friends? Get your coat. I've heard enough." He grabbed Seth's jacket and threw it across the room. "Come on or I'll drag you out."

"I don't want to go."

"My mother said doing what you don't want to do builds character. It's my mission to help you build character." He slapped Seth on the shoulder and started toward his car.

Seth followed, thinking only of Kaye.

Marvin raised his eyebrows and nodded toward the girls.

"She's pretty. Didn't I tell you she's pretty?"

"Oh, Cheryl you mean?" Seth wasn't above trying to irritate him.

"Of course I mean Cheryl. Nancy is too, but she's my girl and don't forget it."

"You won't let me." Seth sipped on his pop as the girls returned from the ladies' room.

Marvin rubbed his hands together. "Are we going to bowl or sit and watch?"

"My score's better if I sit and watch. You go ahead." Seth gestured toward the lanes.

"What size, Seth?"

"Do I have to wear shoes to sit here?"

"No, you need shoes to bowl."

"Marvin, what part of *no* don't you understand? I'm watching tonight."

"Okay, okay, I tried." Marvin turned toward Cheryl, shrugged his shoulders, and lifted his palms in surrender.

Seth watched them change into bowling shoes and select their bowling balls. The three hovered at the ball rack. He was sure they were talking about him refusing to bowl. So what if he didn't want to bowl? He didn't want to come along, but there he sat.

Cheryl stepped up to the lane, took three steps, and bowled her first ball. Pins scattered, leaving three pins standing. She picked up the spare with her second ball.

"Shoot!" Marvin muttered. "That's why they wanted to come bowling. I could use a little help here. Can you bowl?"

"Don't know." Seth shrugged.

"What?"

"Never bowled. I said, I'll watch tonight."

Seth noted their approach, how they held their shoulders and how some people turned their hand as they released the ball. The alley's dim lighting directed everyone's attention toward the pins. Two small table lights hovered over the tilted desktop where score sheets were clipped in place. The three took turns writing in the scores. They finished the first game and bowled a second.

"That's it!" Cheryl rolled up the score sheet and grinned. "I won." She unlaced her shoes and slid into her brown loafers.

"You always win," Nancy said, taking the girls' shoes back to the desk.

Marvin followed her. "What, you didn't offer take my shoes back?"

"Whew! No! Nancy told me about *your* feet!" Cheryl jeered at Marvin with a friendly smile.

Seth stepped out from behind the table where he had been sitting. His right toe caught the corner of a chair leg. He reached for the railing and missed. His body pitched forward, his left foot missing a step up to the main level, causing him to twirl before his head smacked the floor. The carpet smelled of ancient dirt, years of stomped-in grime.

Marvin rushed toward him. The bartender, sensing a fight, hit the overhead light switch and vaulted over the bar.

Marvin kneeled, reaching out. "You okay? What happened, man?"

"I tripped. That's all." Seth brushed his arm with his other hand.

The bartender, twice the size of either of them, seized Marvin by the collar, pulling him to his feet.

"Let go of me, we're friends!" Marvin yelled.

The girls scurried around the bartender. "What happened?" asked Nancy.

"Ewww!" Cheryl yelled and pointed toward Seth's leg as she stammered," "What's? What?" She covered her mouth with her hand, her eyes opened wide.

Seth's glance followed hers. His pant leg lay flat, ripped open, exposing his leg and lower straps that anchored his wood and flesh colored prosthesis. His foot had twisted, causing his shoe to be angled backwards.

The bartender released his grip on Marvin, who helped Seth to a nearby chair as Cheryl bolted to the exit with Nancy in pursuit.

Seth re-adjusted the angle of the prosthesis as best he could.

"I'll need an arm to the men's room."

In the restroom Seth readjusted the thigh straps and re-angled the prosthesis. He bent a twisted buckle back into a useable shape with his pocketknife and pushed his pant leg down past his knee. He couldn't repair the flapping pant leg. Nothing to do now but leave.

Outside, Cheryl was crying, and Nancy was trying to calm her.

Seth heard their discussion as he passed.

"It's not a big deal. People have accidents." Nancy tried to explain.

"Sure, he's not your date. You could've told me!"

"I didn't know."

"I'm going home," Cheryl said, sniffing.

As they reached the car, Marvin climbed into the driver's seat and Seth into the passenger seat. They waited for the girls.

"We'll give them a few minutes. I've got an idea."

Seth leaned against the passenger door, unsure what to do. Marvin called to the girls, huddled near the entrance to the bowling alley.

"Let's go get something to eat."

Nancy came over to the car.

"Cheryl called her dad; he's coming to pick us up. I'll go with her. Call me tomorrow. Good night." Nancy kissed Marvin's cheek.

Seth didn't want to say goodbye to the girls. No loss. He didn't want to say hello to them either.

Marvin pulled out of the parking lot.

"It's a bit of a shock, you know. Well, for the girls. How long you had that?"

"A long time."

"I knew you had a limp, but I thought it was a bad knee, I figured probably from football. I mean, I didn't—I wouldn't have suggested bowling. I wish I had a beer."

"Yup, possession and a drunk driving charge would make everything better."

Marvin turned to face Seth.

"You could have told me."

"Why, so you could pick something a crippled person could do? So, you could tell the girl ahead of time before she even meets me, that half of me is fake? You didn't know because it's none of your business."

Seth's anger burst from a place deep within. The tone of his voice shocked him. He couldn't stop his fervor. "I'll do my classes and I'll do my shop time and missing a foot won't stop me."

Marvin continued at highway speed. "Any objections to having a pop at my apartment?"

"No thanks."

"Don't you care about how she reacted?"

"No, I won't. That's it. I won't care, but she did make me think. The last time I saw my girl was before my accident. Now I wonder, will she feel the same way? I hadn't thought of that."

The car rolled on; silence filled the space. When they reached Seth's rooming house, he climbed out of the car. A streetlight cast a beam revealing his torn pant leg. Marvin came around the car.

"Need any help?"

"Not now. It was back there," Seth smiled searching for his former good nature. "I've got it from here. Thanks, buddy." Seth slapped Marvin on the shoulder and went inside.

As Marvin pulled away from the curb, Seth leaned against the door casing and moaned. Grief gripped him. He should have thought of how Kaye might feel. Pretending he was still the same wasn't going to help. If him having an artificial leg mattered to one girl, a girl he didn't even know, it could matter to the one he loved.

By November, Kaye had come to the attention of the school counselor, Mrs. Duncan, a plump woman with short bluish hair. She peered out from between two small mountains of file folders on her desk.

"Maureen, I was notified by the office that we've not received your records. I made a note here after we first spoke that you would retrieve them and bring them in."

Kaye didn't know whether to run away at that very moment or die. She could feel the heat of her face, it must have been turning beet red. Her heart was pounding so loud it boomed in her ears. She took a deep breath; it wasn't likely she'd die there on the spot, not at her age.

"I'm sorry. They haven't arrived just yet." She tried to keep her voice even, although fear paralyzed her.

Mrs. Duncan moved her chair around the corner of the desk, ignoring the stacks of paper between them. She opened a file. It contained a few papers, unlike the other students' files that contained four years of history.

"You have very good grades so far, Maureen, and you've taken difficult subjects: Chemistry, College English, and Algebra—what are your plans after graduation?"

She had registered as a senior but without her records she had no evidence she had completed three years of high school. The truth was she had not completed her junior year, but she thought if she could do the work, it shouldn't matter. It did matter. Her lies were adding up. She probably couldn't graduate without getting her grades from her previous school, and that was impossible. Her mind continued to race, trying to justify what she knew were lies.

Mrs. Duncan scowled, annoyed upon not receiving a response. "Maureen, I mean that seriously. What are your plans?"

Kaye swallowed the lump in her throat. She had plans and dreams.

"I want to be a nurse someday." The words came out in a whisper.

"Did you say a nurse?" Mrs. Duncan leaned toward her.

"Yes, I've had experience caring for people. I'm good at it. Several people told me so. I want to help people."

"Maureen, this may be your lucky day." Mrs. Duncan removed some pages from a long envelope on her desk. "I received this information last week. There's a new program available. Due to a nursing shortage, the federal government has started a program to subsidize practical nursing students, and the curriculum we have at our local college meets the criteria." She sorted through the few papers in Kaye's folder. "I can give you an application today. You take it and fill it out and I'll work on getting a transcript of your previous school records. You don't have enough classes from this year alone to get you accepted."

"Could I take more classes?"

Mrs. Duncan searched Kaye's face.

"You have a full class schedule."

"Isn't there something we can do? What if my transcript doesn't come?" She worried about sounding desperate, and that Mrs. Duncan would think there was something wrong. Her thoughts raced. *Don't cry. Believe it's possible.* "Can we find a way?"

"Well, you could attend night classes next semester. It's possible you could have enough classes completed by the time the program starts. There's a chance there might be a waiting list. If that happens you would have more time to take extra classes."

Kaye waited.

"Let me look into it." She opened a file drawer and removed four pages clipped together.

"Here's the application. Bring it back to me and I'll add a letter of recommendation. Do you know anyone else that would write a letter for you?"

"Yes, Ann Marie would, and I'm sure someone from the restaurant." Kaye took the application. "Thank you, Mrs. Duncan, thank you for helping me. You won't be sorry."

"Maureen, I know already I won't be sorry. You have a busy semester ahead."

"I'll bring this back tomorrow." Kaye rushed out the door. She was holding her dream in her hands.

The excitement of her future took her thoughts to Toe. She wanted to believe he would come. Someday they will build their lives together.

On Saturday afternoons she tried to find time to walk down to the river. Winter so near the river had brought the icy winds of the northeaster storms. Kaye walked the path along the river. The lights outlined the bridge and sparkled on the ice-crested water. Today, she believed with all her heart that Port Huron was a city of promise, a harbor where she could safely rest, and a place where her dreams could come true. Everything about Port Huron echoed their promise to each other. Amid all her fears and anger, she could not forget his words the day he held her in his arms and told her he loved her and said, "If we are ever parted, we'll meet at the water, where the sun rises and brings the new day."

Chapter 34

Snowflakes sprinkled the windshield as Seth cruised M21 headed to the Kents' for Christmas. The windshield wipers whipped the feathery flakes away, leaving two semicircles outlined in white on the glass. Classes had ended at six p.m. for a holiday of ten days. However, his assignments would require him to return after four days. He would need the engineering library, which remained open every day except Christmas.

The town was decorated for December. It had been nine months since he had left the Home. Everything in his life had changed. Coming back to the Kents' for Christmas hadn't occurred to him until Mrs. Kent wrote that she had his room ready and to please let them know what day to expect him.

This year he would celebrate Christmas in a family home. He had always celebrated Christmas with a lot of people over the course of his life. He couldn't explain to anyone the fear of not knowing what to expect. He tried to refuse the invitation until Mr. Kent called and asked that he reconsider, explaining that Mrs. Kent had planned meals with his favorite foods, and had been baking for days.

The colored lights on the porch were visible from the corner stop sign. A tree was framed by the picture window, but it had no lights; Mrs. Kent said they would decorate it together. As soon as his headlights flashed across the front of the house, Mr. and Mrs. Kent appeared on the porch.

"Merry Christmas, Seth!" Mrs. Kent called from the steps. "We're glad you decided to come."

Mr. Kent rounded Seth's car and helped with his bags.

"Right this way." Mrs. Kent opened the door to Christmas decorations scattered everywhere. Candles on the table surrounded by a wreath of greens. A garland hung over the fireplace; a nativity scene rested on the mantle. The aroma of cinnamon permeated the air.

Seth asked, "What's baking?"

"Just like a growing boy to want to know what's cooking," laughed Mr. Kent.

"Apple crisp. Are you hungry? We waited dinner."

"Oh yes, I'm hungry. I'll take this upstairs to unpack and wash up to help."

"No bother!" Mrs. Kent called from the kitchen, already moving food from the oven onto the table.

"It's plain food tonight, Seth—roast beef, mashed potatoes, and so forth."

Suppertime was filled with catching up on Seth's assignments, the rotations, student friends, factory assignments; Mrs. Kent's activities with the library and church; Mr. Kent's agriculture classes, and activities.

"How did the auction go this year?" Seth inquired of Mr. Kent.

Mr. Kent finished chewing his food. "You mean the one from the Home?"

"Yeah. Did they get good prices?"

"Oh, yes they did. The same fellows were there to bid up the stock. I think it went very well."

"Did you see Ben?" Seth paused, holding his fork in midair.

"No, I didn't. I asked, but the boys said he didn't want to come."

"Did they say if he was okay?"

"I don't recall anyone saying anything more. Sorry, Seth."

The room fell into a silence. Seth found it hard to swallow his food. He didn't feel hungry, remembering how upset Ben had been the last time he saw him, and how upset he was every year about the selling of the stock. Ben would weep for days. He always did.

"The stock looked good, Seth. You'd be proud."

"Anybody mention production records?"

"Only individual ones for the cows that were for sale. Those were good."

"I heard Traverse City is selling their dairy herd."

Mr. Kent passed a glance toward Mrs. Kent. She stood from her chair and started toward the kitchen.

"I've got apple crisp all ready. Seth, would you clear the plates and I'll get the bowls and spoons."

Seth could tell they weren't going to answer about Traverse City. Mr. Kent had to have heard the discussion about discontinuing the farming operations at the State institutions. Rumors weren't always right but rumors start somewhere.

Seth's thoughts went to Ben and the other men, and what would happen to them if the farming operation closed, but that was out of his control like everything else at the Home. He had lived there long enough to know the people in control didn't begin to understand what the work meant to the men, how they loved and cared for the animals, and the pride they took in the crops.

"Do you want more dessert?" Mrs. Kent asked.

"No, that sure was good. Nothing like that at school." Seth forced a smile and sequestered his thoughts.

"Let's go decorate the tree." Mr. Kent pulled a tangle of lights from a box. "Here, Seth, take this end and walk toward the kitchen.

"Looks like I could walk all the way to the barn."

"The missus likes lights," Mr. Kent said laughing.

They put the lights on the tree while Mrs. Kent cleaned up the kitchen. Then they worked together to put on the decorations. They had just finished when a clatter sounded on the porch.

"Reindeer?" Mr. Kent questioned, as Mrs. Kent peered out the window.

"No, it's Seth's three stooges." She opened the door, laughing. "Come on in, boys."

"We came to kidnap the college boy," Butch said.

"This college boy is not going anywhere. Don't you listen the weather warnings?" Seth said groaning.

"You don't know what you're missing. We got some nice plans," Hank prodded.

"Why don't you boys stay here and play some penny ante," Mr. Kent said, perceiving Seth's weariness. "Besides, it looks like it could get slick out there."

"Now we could consider that." The boys nodded to each other.

Mrs. Kent removed the tablecloth from the kitchen table, and Mr. Kent found two decks of cards. Seth carried the jug of pennies from the hearth and emptied it onto the table. Within minutes the boys were laughing and pushing stacks of pennies toward the middle of the table. Mr. and Mrs. Kent played two hands, and then retired to the living room. It was after eleven when the boys surrendered their pennies back to the jug and left for home.

"You boys are welcome to go to Christmas Eve service with us," Mr. Kent offered.

"No." The boys nodded in agreement. "You go ahead." They left as Mr. Kent pulled the car out of the garage.

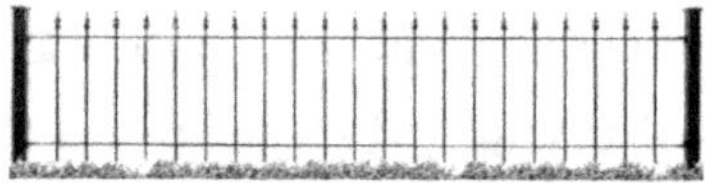

Seth rode in the back seat as Mr. and Mrs. Kent chatted about Christmas on the way to church.

"Did you have Christmas Eve services at the Home?" Mrs. Kent asked.

"We had concerts and stuff all during the season." Seth didn't want to be reminded of his friends back at the Home, especially not on Christmas. What would it be like to go to church on Christmas Eve with a family? He had never thought about it happening for him. Some people came and took their family member home for Christmas, but no one ever came for him.

He missed much of the service, sitting in the pew, watching Mr. and Mrs. Kent. It would be great to go to Christmas Eve service with Kaye.

Christmas morning after their gift exchange, Seth sat on the floor surrounded by shirts, boxes, wrapping paper, and ribbons.

"I've never had so many clothes."

"It might look like a lot but I'm sure you don't have a lot of time to do laundry with your studies and all." Mrs. Kent spoke with a compassionate tone.

"That's true. But I don't have anything for you folks."

"Yes, you do." Mr. Kent held up the card Seth had brought home reporting his grades. "This is the best gift of all, to see that you're doing so well. That's a difficult school, Seth, and this shows us you're working hard. We're proud of you."

"Thanks. I'll have money next year. I start working when I get back." Seth paused, eager to change the subject. He placed his gifts in a pile and gathered up some of the wrapping paper.

"I was wondering if you see the kids from the Home at school, Mr. Kent?"

"No, I don't. They didn't continue the program this year. The new administrator didn't think it proved to be a good plan with two students running away." Mr. Kent filled his pipe.

Seth stopped his activity. "Who ran away?"

"Well, the O'Shay girl ran away last spring. They didn't put it in the paper; there were rumors that somebody inside helped her, although no one admitted it. Then Margo disappeared over the summer. Word had it that she ran away with Sonny because they both left town about the same time. Sonny's folks said he headed west to California. Nobody knows for sure if Margo went, but everybody suspects it."

"That's too bad. Didn't the new administrator see the opportunity it gave me?"

"Yes, but that's one plus, and two minuses." Mr. Kent tapped two fingers on the table.

Seth couldn't hide his concern. "Do you think Kaye had help from the inside?"

"Funny, Seth, that's what I was going to ask you."

"Me? No, I wouldn't know about any help from the inside. She told me off good, the night before she left. She was gone for two days before I even knew. I'm still not convinced she isn't inside somewhere." He clinched his fist.

"It doesn't sound like it. I'm glad you didn't have anything to do with her leaving. I know you liked each other."

"That was then... I don't have any idea where she is now." Seth settled back in his chair. "But I have to admit, I'd sure like to."

"Isn't it funny? A girl tells you off royal and all you want to do is find her again. I know about that, don't I, Mrs. Kent?"

Seth watched them exchange an amused glance.

"Yes, you might say you know about that, Mr. Kent." She replied.

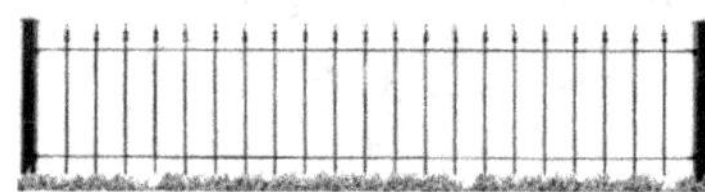

"Maury, can you help me prepare the Christmas program?" Ann Marie circled around the room at the Citadel, distracted. "I know they're here. We set them out last week."

"What are you looking for?"

"The books—the *song* books. They're the newest ones, covered in navy blue cloth. I didn't check the basement, just the music center. I'll be right back."

A knock came at the door. Kaye answered, opening it slightly and peeking through. "Can I help you?"

"Just checking on the time for the program. My sister's in town with some friends and she wants to come."

"It's at seven, and there'll be cookies and punch after," Kaye offered.

"Thanks, lady. We'll be here. All five of us."

Kaye closed the door and removed her chemistry element chart from her purse. Top row, second row, and third row. She tried to memorize the elements. It was the bottom row that became so convoluted in her brain.

Ann Marie returned with the books on a large cart.

"Put these out on the chairs on the stage. What have you got there?"

Maury stuffed the chart back into her handbag. "It's some homework I study when I have time."

"What kind of homework?"

Kaye groaned. "Chemistry. It's the elements chart."

"I can help you with that. I made up a limerick when I was in high school. I'll see if I can remember it. Nothing like a rhyme to help you memorize stuff."

"What's that?"

"A limerick. It's like a simple little ditty or several lines of a rhyme. You make up something silly using the first letters of a word, then you can remember the order of the words."

Kaye cast a sideways glance at Ann Marie.

"A limerick?"

"Sure. It works."

"Here come the men to set up the chairs."

The Christmas concert was a success. The band played, the chorus sang, and the audience joined in on several songs. The people gathered in the great room for punch and cookies.

A voice called out, "Kaye!"

Kaye turned to see Margo racing toward her.

"Oh my gosh, you're here and you're all right. I worried, we all worried." Margo's words fell out all at once.

"Shush!!" Kaye grabbed Margo's arm. "Stop."

Ann Marie passed carrying a tray of cookies. Kaye pulled Margo toward the kitchen door. No, she couldn't take her in there. Outside, that was her only choice. Everywhere there were people who knew Maury, but not Kaye.

When they reached the side door, Margo halted.

"I'm not going outside. It's cold—"

"Shush," Kaye urged. "Just for a minute."

They slid out the door, through the narrow opening, to avoid producing any noticeable draft entering the room and drawing attention. Outside, Kaye hugged Margo.

"How did you get here?"

"I came with a group of women from Romeo."

"I'm glad to see you. I really am. But there's a problem." Kaye glanced right, then left, and pulled the door closed behind them.

"Oh, my, you didn't break a rule, did you?" Margo giggled. "Everyone knows Kaye always obeys rules."

"It's more than that. I broke a lot of rules. I've lied about my name. I lied about everything. I'm asking you, please, please don't tell. I'm going to high school, and I have a chance to go to nursing school. If you tell anyone the police can come and take me back. Promise me you won't tell."

"Really, Kaye, you can trust me. I won't tell. I'm getting emancipated. Next month I'll be eighteen. At first the lady I worked for in town said she'd be my guardian and sponsor me and I could work for her."

"For how long?"

"That was the catch, for as long as she wanted. Then Sonny told me he was going to California, and I could go with him. I worried about getting him in trouble, me being a minor, so I said no. Then Sonny asked his aunt in Romeo to help me, and she agreed. She signed papers for guardianship. She said I could live with her temporarily if I enrolled in school. I'm living with her until June when I finish high school. Sonny said he's coming back then and maybe we'll get married."

"But you're not illegal. I am. I'm a runaway."

"That doesn't matter anymore, you're almost eighteen."

"It does matter, and eighteen's not twenty-one." I don't have a guardian. I don't know anything about being emancipated or whatever you call it."

"So, what rules did you break?" Margo sounded delighted with the thought.

"If I tell you then you'll know, and you could get in trouble."

Margo leaned into whisper. "If I told you the rules I've broken, you couldn't shake a stick at yours."

"I'm Maureen Morton now."

"You don't say!"

A tap came on the door.

"Is Margo out there? They said she went outside." Someone called.

"I'm here. I'm coming in."

Margo hugged Kaye.

"Your secret's safe with me, unless I forget, then who knows." She flitted back inside, fluttering her red fingernails, leaving Kaye stunned. She knew Margo would keep her secret, even if she teased she might not.

"If you'll help me clean-up we can go back to my house for a snack," Ann Marie said, gathering the books into her arms as Kaye arranged the chairs and put the room into order.

"The children liked the popcorn balls." Kaye was pleased she had worked several hours helping make them.

"Not so good for their teeth, but a sweet treat is nice at Christmas. Let's go. Mom has some hot chocolate waiting and I have a gift for you."

They walked the few blocks to Ann Marie's house, singing Christmas carols.

A different Christmas, and a Merry Christmas!

The lights of Kaye's twig Christmas tree blinked intermittently. The silver balls of various sizes turned ever so slightly on their strings. It did brighten the corner where it stood on an orange crate. She huddled in the rumpled overstuffed chair and waited for the lights to blink again.

She was lonely. Seeing Margo for those few minutes brought back so many memories. She was lonesome. She had shopped for gifts for Tom's children, but to send them would mean contact with Tom, and that wouldn't be good. Sometimes she dreamed about the children. There were times she woke up thinking Janie was standing beside her bed holding their wedding picture. On those nights, she couldn't go back to sleep. The dreams were just too vivid.

Tom had never held her in his arms. When she dreamed of being held, it was always Toe. She would love Tom's children forever.

Children, thoughts of children, always took her back to her cottage at the Home.

All the questions she wanted to ask Margo would go unanswered.

The days continued to hold their torments, both real threats and those imagined. Kaye didn't know which were worse.

She touched the pearl button on the braid around her neck. Each time she touched it she remembered his promise they would have a real home and a family.

Chapter 35

On Monday morning, a foreman took Seth to the break room and introduced him to the crew with whom he would be working for the next six weeks.

"Oh yes, we like's those engineering boys a lot. They's always so knowledgeable." The men laughed, joining the tall journeyman leading the team.

"That's Jack. Don't let him get the best of you. He's a joker, and sometimes his jokes aren't funny, but most of the students survive." He turned from Seth. "You don't get this one, Jack. I'm assigning him to Henry."

Jack shrugged and left the break room mumbling about brains and sweat.

"Henry, take Seth out and show him where the problems are on line two. He'll work your schedule and follow you for the next six weeks. Seth, Henry's a good journeyman, and you can learn a lot from him."

Henry nodded, without reply. Seth perceived that Henry's relationship with the foreman was one of a workingman to a superior. Not friend to friend.

The others left the room. Henry poured a second cup of coffee and sat back down at the picnic table. He was short, only up to Seth's shoulder. He didn't carry any fat. Kind of a wiry guy, is how Mr. Green would have described him.

"You drink coffee?" He gestured toward the coffee urn.

Seth was caught off guard as he wondered if this short man would be the type to fight… maybe in his younger years.

"Oh, yeah!"

"Get a cup and let's started on the right foot."

Seth poured a cup of coffee and smiled. He was sure Henry didn't know Shakespeare had used the term the *better* foot. Starting on the better foot was his only option. Seth was concerned about climbing the scaffolding and the catwalks. No feeling in his foot made climbing more dangerous. He knew there were accidents in the plants every day. People were killed and were carried out with the line continuing to move as the men shuffled to cover the vacant job. He'd heard the stories from the students who returned from plant rotations. This couldn't be worse than the Home, when he had to watch over his shoulder for Ollie and his pitchfork.

"Now, we got about ten minutes to sort this out. Then I have to get to work, and you follow me. Where you from?"

"Lapeer. I know farm work."

"Lapeer. All I know about Lapeer is there's a loony place there. Good you know about farming, that'll help. You know how to work then. The first thing you gotta learn is to be smart. You ever been in a plant before?"

"No, sir."

"Henry, call me Henry. It's noisy and sometimes you can't hear. Pay attention. You're working with me, but I can't mother ya. Sometimes you'll be on your own. Pay attention. Equipment that's moving don't stop because there's a man in the way." Henry grabbed an empty cup and spat. "I climb sometimes. You don't have to. You still need good work shoes. Keep your laces tied and your pant legs snug. You afraid of heights?"

"No, sir. No, Henry."

"Seth." Henry stood up and looked down at him. "I don't like swearing. I don't like fighting and I don't gamble. You want to do that you call the foreman and tell him you want another journeyman. If this sounds all right to you, let's get to work."

After months of study and books, walking all day on concrete took its toll. Spots on the floors were oil covered and footing was slippery. Henry's pace offered Seth opportunity to learn the layout of the lines and machinery. Henry did a lot of pointing, but Seth couldn't hear over the machines. At the end of the first day, Seth sat in his car and looked at the dark stain on his pant leg. His stump was bleeding. How would he ever make six weeks at this pace?

The next morning Seth waited for Henry in the break room.

Jack smirked from the other side of the area. "Henry probably won't be in today. You wore him down to a frazzle yesterday with all that walking. He ain't covered that many miles since 1946." The men joined in and laughed together.

Seth leaned back against the wall and sipped his coffee.

Henry arrived smelling of liniment.

"Today we're going to work on line three. Did you figure out that gaff I was telling you about?"

"Yeah! I talked to the night shift this morning and I have an idea." Seth pulled out a piece of paper from his shirt pocket as Henry sat down across the table.

"Can't wait to see what the engineer boy figured out." Jack smirked toward Seth. "We been waiting for months to see what some student engineer would think up."

"Go to work, Jack. You should know everybody doesn't make it through." Henry's voice was surly. He pulled Seth's paper over to have a look. After the men left, Henry slid the paper drawing back toward Seth.

"That's an idea worth considering. Just a shift in the angle, is that what you're saying?"

"Would it work?"

"You asking me?"

"It's your machine, isn't it?"

"Engineers usually don't ask somebody working the machine what they think." Henry lowered his voice. "Those boys all seem to come out with an attitude. That's what you're up against. You're different, Seth. I could see that yesterday. We've tried the angle thing but not a combination shift with that left corner. Jack… he didn't make it, you know. That's why he's so snarly. Most guys don't know he tried, but I know. He'll lay for you if he gets a chance, so watch him." Henry spat into his cup.

"I will."

"Did you get the line layout yesterday?"

"Yeah, I started to draw it up last night." Seth pulled out a pad of paper.

Henry thumbed through the pages.

"Good. We'll focus on line three today. I can't cover that much ground every day. You sore?"

"A little stiff."

"Me too. Let's get started."

The weeks passed without incident. Jack stayed away from Seth, probably because Henry never left Seth alone. Henry's crew liked Seth. They noted his limp, but no one mentioned it to him. There were guys with fingers missing and fellows with war injuries. Seth could see there were enough different kinds of jobs if a man had a mind to work. It was also evident danger lingered everywhere.

Seth's idea for the machine on line three didn't work but it did start other ideas rolling. It was the man who used the press during the night shift that suggested a possible solution. Teamwork that was what Seth took away from his first plant experience. It took a team to know the equipment, the needs, and how to get the best production. His next paper outlined the importance of team building and its relationship to production. It wasn't new; he had seen Mr. Green accomplish that at the Home. Seth didn't realize it then, but what he had witnessed was the assembling of a team of men with different capabilities. Mr. Green put the team of workers together, his goal was to have a healthy herd and increase production. It had worked there, maybe it could it work in a production plant.

Seth managed to care for his stump and padded it enough to make it through the six weeks without having to use his crutch. Full-time work would be different if he had to walk the plants. He couldn't worry about that now, he had to get through the courses first. One thing at a time.

1958

Winter brought snow, freezing rain, and ice to the river. The Department stores advertised their white sales. All the seasonal businesses closed for three months, awaiting the thaw and warm weather.

"It's quiet here in the winter," Ann Marie said. She had stopped by to walk to the Citadel with Kaye. "I can hear the snow crunch. It's nice, don't you think? I look forward to the slow season. Time to catch up." Ann Marie's scarf whipped against her face and muffled her reply.

"Did you say catch up? With what?"

"Everything. We work planning the next year's activities. There are summer camps to schedule; the mending room is in full swing. The trucks arrive with the after-Christmas donations. There's lots of sorting and stocking to do, and there's planning for emergency supplies to aid in home fires, preparation for the spring storms."

"I hear people talking about tax time, what's that?"

Ann Marie laughed.

"It's when we pay taxes to the government. The money goes to the military, to roads, to all sorts of things the government runs."

"Nobody who mentions it is happy."

"Sometimes people don't count their blessings. Maury, are you working Saturday? You could help me sort clothes."

"I think I'm busy," Kaye wrinkled her nose. "You know some of them really smell."

"That's why we sort them, and you can be a part of the party." Ann Marie slipped her arm over Maury's shoulders. "Look at it this way, you can sort them dirty or mend them after they are clean. Your choice."

"Mend, hands down."

"You know how to mend clothes?"

"Hand me a hole and I can patch it."

"Another skill I didn't know."

When Kaye arrived at the Citadel on Saturday, Ann Marie pointed her toward a room with sewing machines and women sitting on chairs mending clothing and linens. Kaye found a chair near the window and introduced herself to the woman seated next to her, who in turn introduced herself as Hilda.

"What would you like me to do?"

"There's the pile of big and there's the pile of little." Hilda gestured left and then right. "There are buttons to sew on, zippers to replace, and patches to put on. Just pick something and start working. Thread, needles, and scissors are on the workbench, thimbles too if you need one."

Kaye worked throughout the morning mending by hand, sewing on buttons, and basting patches to the knees of pant legs.

At lunchtime Ann Marie invited the women to lunch in the kitchen.

"Your new girl, that Maury? She knows her way around a needle," Hilda remarked as she spread peanut butter on a slice of bread.

"She amazes me," Ann Marie offered. "Do you know how to sew on a machine, Maury?"

"I have, yes," Kaye replied, avoiding any reference to her level of skill.

The day ended. The women stood, loosening their shoulders with stretches.

"Don't realize how stiff you get just sewing all day," groaned one woman who looked near forty.

Kaye too stretched her arms lifting them over her head, then down. She walked to the window. "It's still snowing."

"Forecast is six inches tonight," Hilda offered.

Kaye didn't hear Hilda's reply. She was staring out the window at a woman leaving the Citadel wearing a brown wool coat. A coat that looked very much like her old brown coat. Very much. She ran down the hall to the coatroom.

"Ann Marie!" Kaye called out. "Did you just give a woman a brown coat?"

"Yes, I did. Poor dear. She needed it, too. Said she has five children."

"Where did it come from?"

"Out of the donations from the thumb area. Why?"

"Ann Marie, give me a coat the same size. Please."

Kaye ran to the coat racks, searching for a coat that would fit the woman.

"Maury, what are you doing?"

"Ann Marie, I can't… this one, can I take this one?" Kaye snatched a blue coat from the rack, the hangers tangling as she struggled to tug the coat free.

"I guess so," Ann Marie said hesitantly.

Kaye rushed from the building, carrying the coat and trudging through the snow, searching for the woman. Not sure if she walked or came by car. Kaye ran checking the alleys and store doorways.

"*Wait! Wait!*" she called as she watched a woman approach a car down the street. The woman ignored her and opened the car door.

"*Please wait!*" Kaye called. Her chest pounded, snow covered her head and shoulders, her feet were wet, and she slipped as she tried to run on the icy street. She wrestled with the coat she carried struggling not to drop it in the slushy piles of snow.

The woman turned and scowled. When Kaye neared the woman, she held out the blue coat as she gasped to breathe.

"Please ma'am. Would you exchange that coat for this one?" Icy droplets of tears streamed down Kaye's face. She could feel her nose running and wiped it with the back of her hand as she pushed her tears away.

"This here's my coat. A lady at the Salvation Army gave it to me. Why are you running down the street and hollering at me like I stole it? I didn't take nothin.'"

"I'm sorry, I know you didn't take it. It's just that it's a coat I had a long time ago and … it was taken from me and … it has special meaning to me. I know you didn't take anything. This, this blue coat, it's a nice coat, real heavy and warm."

A bulky man in a plaid shirt bellowed from behind the steering wheel.

"Iris, take the blue coat and get in the car. "He leaned forward to look at Kaye.

"Lady, next time just ask, don't come yelling down the street like a banshee."

Iris removed one arm from the sleeve.

"A person could freeze to death in this weather. Is there something wrong with you, girl?" She shucked off the brown coat, handing it to Kaye, and slipped on the blue one.

"No, I'm all right. I'm sorry to trouble you. Thank you."

Iris climbed inside the rusted green Ford. Kaye tried to close the door, but it sprang back, knocking her into the pile of snow on the curb. The man climbed out from the driver's side and stomped around the car.

"I gotta shut it. You all right? That spring's wadded up and don't work right." He pushed the door closed pressing his bulk against the resistant metal.

Kaye pulled herself up from the snowbank, tired and worn as the car lumbered away.

Preoccupied, she carried the coat, and walked the six blocks to her room. Her sweater was white with snow, and she shivered from the cold. She removed her shoes in the foyer, pulled her wet socks off, and carried them both up the stairs. In her room she placed her socks on the radiator, and her shoes under, on a newspaper. She removed her sweater and replaced her wet clothing with a pair of flannel pajamas and then hung the garments up to dry, but the coat lay in a pile on the floor. Was it there? She hadn't dared to look for the folder. If it was there, she had a lot of questions she hoped it would answer. She pulled a blanket from her bed and curled up into the over-stuffed chair beside the window. It was almost dark. Few cars passed. The streets were blanketed in fresh snow, quiet and still.

The doorbell rang. Who would be calling on Saturday night? Most people were at home or downtown. Maybe it was Ann Marie. Kaye hadn't gone back for her coat or purse. Tomorrow was worship, would Ann Marie put her things away until tomorrow? From her window Kaye could see Ann Marie leave the porch and walk toward the main street. She must have just checked to make sure she was home. Ann Marie was one in a million, she wouldn't ask questions. She trusted. That made it harder for Kaye to tell her lies.

Kaye fell asleep in the chair and awoke before dawn. She picked up the coat to place it on the chair and got into bed. The corner of something firm bounced against her shin.

It was there.

It was still there.

Chapter 36

It was quiet in the hallway of the rooming house. Seth stepped up to the pay phone, dropped a dime in the slot, and dialed.

"Please deposit twenty-five cents for the first three minutes."

He placed each coin into the proper slot and waited. He could hear the connections taking place amid the jingle of the coins sliding to their destination.

"Hello?" Seth took a breath. It was Mrs. Kent. He didn't want to talk to her. He didn't want to tell her. His hand was moist as he held the phone and gathered his courage.

"Mrs. Kent, it's Seth. Is Mr. Kent at home?"

"Seth, what a surprise! We were sure you'd come home for your birthday. Will you be coming home soon? Is everything all right?"

"Yes, it's fine. I need to talk to Mr. Kent."

"He isn't home from school yet. He gets home late on field trip days. Today they went to a tool auction. I'm sure he'll want to tell you about it. Can I have him call you when he gets home?"

"No, I'm using a pay phone. Can I call him, say about seven?"

"Sure. Wait a minute I think he just drove in."

"Please deposit another twenty-five cents for three minutes."

Seth could not hear Mrs. Kent in the background. He deposited the coins and listened as they clinked through.

"Thank you." The operator confirmed his payment.

He heard another click and Mrs. Kent was back.

"Seth, Seth, can you hear me?"

"I'm here."

"Here's Mr. Kent."

In the background he could hear Mrs. Kent explaining it was Seth calling and that no, she did not know why he was calling.

"Hello, Seth. Good to hear from you. How's everything?" Mr. Kent sounded out of breath and his voice moved away from the telephone. Perhaps he was taking off his coat.

"Mr. Kent, I want to talk to you about—not being here."

"Oh, do you mean you want to be somewhere else?"

"I'm going to quit school. I wanted to tell you first."

"Quit? Is that what you said?"

"Yes." Seth's voice broke as he struggled to stifle his panic and pain.

"Humm! Well, Seth, why don't you come home? Tomorrow's Friday. You didn't quit yet, did you?"

"No."

"Can you come home tomorrow for the weekend? We can talk about it."

"There's nothing to talk about. I'm not an engineer. I'm a Home kid. I don't belong here. I don't belong in a place where I'm supposed to be the one who knows. I belong with my cows and the guys."

"Seth, do you have gas money to come home?"

"Yes."

"Then we'll see you tomorrow night. After supper we can catch the basketball game. I'll tell Laura. What time will you be here?"

"Six, I suppose."

"Then we'll see you at six."

For the next eighteen hours Seth worried how he was going to explain to Mr. and Mrs. Kent in a way they would understand that this is not what he wanted to be doing. He had no desire to graduate from engineering college and work in the plants as someone who had the answers or could figure them out. There was no way he could make them understand he had to leave and find Kaye.

Two weekends he drove to Port Huron on Saturday and did not see a glimpse of her. The first thing after quitting college, he would spend more time looking for her. He might find someone who knew her or had seen her. If only he had time.

The door opened as he turned off the motor of his car. Mr. Kent came down the front walk and carried Seth's bag into the house. "Laura, our boy's here. Let's eat."

Mrs. Kent smiled as she placed the platter of roast pork on the table. She returned to the kitchen for the bowl of mashed potatoes and a server of brown gravy, adding vegetables and dessert. After supper they cleared the table together, and the men went into the living room and sat down, Mr. Kent on his big easy chair with his humidor and pipe, Seth across from him on the sofa.

"I want to explain why I'm quitting college. I've already decided, but you helped me a lot and it's only right I give you an explanation."

Mr. Kent packed his pipe with tobacco and lit a wooden match. Soon, smoke curled toward the ceiling. He held his pipe in his hand and looked at it as if it had an answer to a question that hadn't yet been asked.

"I have one question. What is it you plan to do after you quit college?"

"I miss the cows. I miss the guys. I don't want to complain, but these past months have been hard."

"Lonely?"

"Yeah." Seth fumbled with the crease in his pants. "Lonely, that's right. All I can think about is being back with the guys. About the cows and the production records, breeding for the herd. That's who I am. Not some book learning guy. I don't fit in with the guys at college, they all have homes and families. They have plans. They want things I don't care about. I'm a Thoreau kind of guy. I enjoy the simple life. You probably find it hard to believe, but I miss the Home. I know it sounds strange to you but that's the truth.

"Seth." Mr. Kent laid his pipe in the ashtray and leaned forward. "Let me tell you something. I wanted to farm, but farming is changing. It's a major business now. Machinery is growing bigger and more expensive, fields are expanding. It would take years for you to get enough money together to finance a farm." He paused. "Seth, is farming the real reason you want to quit? Your grades are excellent. You have a gift. Your brain works like an engine. What are you going to do if you quit college? Going back to the Home is not an option. You've been emancipated since your eighteenth birthday."

Seth squirmed in his chair. Mrs. Kent came into the room and picked up her knitting basket. She glanced at him. "May I stay?"

"Sure, you're all the family I got." Seth didn't look at either of them.

Mrs. Kent sat down. "We are your family by choice, Seth. We love you and we want you to do work that makes you happy." Mrs. Kent placed her knitting in her lap.

"It's Kaye," Seth blurted out, his voice trembling. He brushed his eyes with his hand to wipe away the tears that were forming. "I love her. We made a promise if we were ever separated, we would meet at the water. I've driven twice to Port Huron to look for her. I know she'll come. I want to be there when she does. Soon, it'll be one year since she left the Home, and I know if she can she'll come."

Mrs. Kent moved to kneel in front of Seth.

"Oh Seth, we didn't know you've searched for her. I'm sorry."

Mr. Kent cleared his throat. "Seth, I know it looks like a long time to wait, but it isn't. Four years will go by fast. You can go to Port Huron on your vacations and breaks. Think about what you'll have to offer her when you have your degree. You have an opportunity to guarantee a future for both of you."

Mrs. Kent interrupted, "Fred, I know you're right, but what if she's searching for him, too?"

"Then I'm telling you they'll find each other." Mr. Kent's practical nature pressed on until he looked at their faces. "When is the anniversary of her leaving?"

"It's the weekend after St Patrick's day," Seth said.

"That's next weekend." Mr. Kent paced toward the front door.

Mrs. Kent offered a solution.

"If you'll stay in school, Mr. Kent and I will do everything we can to help you find her. Next weekend we'll come and pick you up and we'll all drive to Port Huron together."

Mr. Kent made no reply as they waited for Seth's answer.

"Can I sleep on it? When I came here today, I had my mind made up. I know what you're saying is important. I want to quit. Maybe I'm using Kaye as an excuse. I don't even know if she still cares about me." Seth placed his elbows on his knees and his face in his hands. After several minutes of silence, he rose from his chair. "I'm going to my room. I'll give you an answer in the morning."

All night he tossed and turned. His dreams were filled with train sounds, splashing water, and images of Kaye. He couldn't decide to wait three years longer.

Once a week was all the pain Kaye allowed herself. Every Friday for weeks she removed the suitcase from under her bed, placed the brown wool bundle on her lap, and opened it. Two of the three buttons on the front of the coat did not match. Someone had replaced them. The cuffs too had been turned and re-stitched. How well she knew the color, the feel, and the smell of that coat. Sometimes she held it to her face and cried, remembering. She was wearing this coat when she told Toe that Jessie had died. He held her and told her he loved her. She remembered her friends at the Home, Margo, and the others from high school, then the children in her cottage, and the children in the nursery. Her memories were scrambled. She wept for Andy, Susie, baby Molly, and Janie, Tom's family. There weren't enough tears to wash away her heartache.

Ann Marie never asked about the coat or even if she traded the blue coat. That was like Ann Marie, always respectful. She would wait until Kaye offered information.

A year ago yesterday, Kaye rode away from the Home in the back of Ollie's truck. Today she would remove the folder and today she would read it, every page. The coming year would be a year of knowing.

The weeks since she had found the coat were a time to process what the contents of the folder would mean in her life. Kaye, the girl, remained in the ditch at the train wreck, while Maureen, the woman, assumed responsibility for another woman and her children, nurturing and caring for them the only way she knew how, with her whole heart.

Inside the back of the coat she inspected the stitches she had placed around the folder. It remained in place between the two fabrics of the lining, protected by the brown wool. She snipped the stitches one at a time. She would not remove the folder until all the stitches were removed. She would make a ceremony of her heritage. The sunlight dimmed from the window. Evening shadows crept down the street while traffic moved at a gentle pace.

Kaye turned on the overhead light and returned to her chair. In the silence she hummed "What a Friend We Have in Jesus," and snipped. When all the stitches were removed and the pieces of thread stacked in a neat pile on the desk, she removed the folder of K. O'Shay with trembling hands.

The folder remained the same, its original manila cream, the edges frayed from wear, and inside the sheets of paper were crinkled but intact. There was information on the inside flap of the folder and on the inside of the back, graphs with signatures and dates, indicating the areas of residence and duration. She shuffled through the pages, a portion of them for education. A page documented immunizations and medical care. The top paper, most current, was a form for a surgical procedure, signed by a physician and a judge, days prior to her leaving. One page had brief notations, "observed encounters'" and dates. They must be the dates someone reported seeing her with Toe. She read other observations of her behavior, conduct, and progress. There were symbols she did not understand. The word "moderate" was noted throughout the chart. Under behavior disorders/discipline someone had written "temper tantrums typical for age-specific" and "rapidly responds to discipline." Stapled to the back of the chart was a notation from someone titled Supervisor. She could not read the name, only the title. The note directed: *K. O'Shay is not to be placed into day worker status. K. should remain inside the Home. For her to gain social exposure could cause severe disturbance and confusion.* Stapled over that notation was a directive: *K. O'Shay is a candidate to attend high school, recommended by two classroom teachers and the nursery supervisor, Nurse Lucy Heusted, where K. has worked for two years.* It was signed by Dr. Helmsley. Nurse Lucy had recommended she attend High School. She'd never told her.

Under all the other papers in the back of the folder was a copy of her birth certificate, faded and barely readable, with so little information that the word unknown filled in more spaces than any other item, and her legal name, K. O'Shay, a letter, not a name. Still, one letter for a name was better than a number on the front that identified her within the institution.

Was there another folder somewhere with her original birth certificate? She studied the pile of papers. She could burn them, and no one would find them, or she could continue to keep them in the coat. She could show the folder to Ann Marie and explain why she had lied for months. She wanted to believe Ann Marie would understand.

In the morning Kaye placed the papers back inside the folder, tucked it into the lining of the coat, put it inside her suitcase, and slid the suitcase under her bed. But by noon she knew it was futile to pretend. A lie was a lie, and she was really hurting herself.

Later that day she went to the Citadel and found Ann Marie working alone in the clothing room. "Hi," she said. "I came to see if you needed any help."

"No, I have two more boxes, then I'm done. You're not working today?"

"No, Patsy gave me the day off. I helped Mrs. D. clean this morning and went to the store for her."

"Homework?"

"I'm headed to my books and desk now if you don't need me."

"You run along."

Kaye hesitated. "Ann Marie, have you ever had anyone you really trusted lie to you?"

Ann Marie stopped folding clothes and turned to look at Kaye. "Yes, now that you ask, I have to say, I have."

"Did you forgive them?"

"The person never asked for forgiveness, but I did forgive him. Why?"

"I wanted to know."

"It's always better to forgive. Un-forgiveness festers like a sore. I've learned the hard way it's not worth it."

"You've learned? I thought you— I thought."

Ann Marie smiled. "Maury, do you need to forgive someone?"

"I need it both ways, I need forgiveness and I need to forgive."

"That's a bundle to carry. I'm sorry that burden is troubling you."

Kaye took a deep breath eager to change the subject. "I have to have my homework ready for the gray man tomorrow afternoon."

"I know he'll be here waiting. Work hard and don't worry about the things troubling you. God loves you and He will help you through it."

"Ann Marie, I've—" Kaye stopped, she must tell Ann Marie.

She left the Citadel with her burden. Yes, God did know what was troubling her and He did understand her pain and loneliness. Still, she felt very alone.

The next day was Saturday. Since she'd arrived in Port Huron, even if she worked on Saturday, she would try to find some time to walk the river path. Today the path was snow-covered with patches of blue-gray ice. The snow on the banks had been sprinkled with black soot carried on the wind from the foundries. Undaunted by the weather, whatever the season, she came. She would sit on one of the benches and watch the freighters and the white caps. Sometimes her gaze followed a piece of wood or a seagull as they bobbed down the river riding the rapid current. The water calmed her, and the bridge came to mean *a way*—a way to go from one country to another, a way to go from one life to another. The bridge also helped her believe that Toe would come.

Chapter 37

On Sunday morning, Mr. and Mrs. Kent picked Seth up at college, and the three of them headed for Port Huron.

"I packed a picnic lunch. I thought maybe we could have a picnic at one of the overlooks."

"There are overlooks?"

"Oh, yes there's several up the shoreline from Port Huron. North." Mrs. Kent handed Seth a cookie from the basket.

"What's south?" Seth looked at the map Mr. Kent had laid on the seat.

"There's Algonac and Marysville, lots of little towns."

"I drove up to the tip of the thumb one Saturday and stopped at a couple restaurants. I thought she might have found work." His voice trailed off.

"Seth, I'm glad you decided to let us help you. Thanks for including us."

"I guess it was a combination of lots of things. It was hard with the other guys seeing their girlfriends. When you said I couldn't go back to the Home, I hadn't thought about that, it was always in the back of my mind; I could if I wanted to. I don't. It wasn't like I remembered it. There were bad things there too. I'm going to finish college. I started helping a couple of other guys out with their homework. I didn't know they were having trouble."

"You made a good decision, Seth. Someday you'll thank us for being firm about your staying in school." Mr. Kent's ever-present pipe bloomed with clouds of smoke and the fragrance of cherry tobacco, Mrs. Kent's favorite.

They rode in silence until they saw the bridge looming on the horizon.

"Do you know where you want to look? Anywhere specific?"

"We knew the trains went to the water, that's it. We didn't even know the name of the town where it went. The guys talked about Chicago the other way, so we decided we would meet where the sun rises over the water."

"Fine, fine. Yes, indeed, at the water," Mr. Kent mumbled.

"Now stop," Mrs. Kent scolded.

"All I'm saying is there's a lot of water to…"

"Seth, you just go where you want, and we'll meet you at the car." Mrs. Kent looked at her wristwatch. "About 5:30?"

"Yes, I'll be here." Seth started off down the river path, his gait hopeful, and his spirit light.

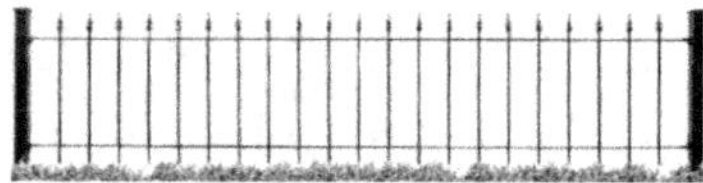

He returned to the parked car at 5:30, crestfallen and his mood heavy. He climbed into the back seat without a word.

"One Sunday, Seth. It's one Sunday. We can come back. Did you ask anyone if they had seen her?

"No."

"I did," Mrs. Kent offered. "I stopped at a corner store and asked if anyone had seen a girl named Kaye O'Shay. No one knew of any girl by that name. We'll keep trying, Seth."

"Needle in a haystack," Mr. Kent muttered.

"Do you want to come back next Sunday?" Mrs. Kent asked. "Or should we wait a couple weeks?"

"If she's not here today, I don't know what to think. I was sure she would come."

"Two weeks, we'll come again in two weeks."

"No, that's okay. I can come alone. I have to come on Sunday because if we don't work on Saturdays, we have class."

"Can you stop by for Sunday dinner? It's on the way," Mrs. Kent said.

"Sure," Seth said grinning. "I can do that."

He would go again any Sunday he could.

The brass plate on the door read, Counselor. Kaye knocked.

"It's open," came a reply.

Kaye turned the knob and peeked inside.

"Maureen, it's good you stopped by. I planned to send you a pass to come and see me today. I reviewed your records. Come in and sit down."

Kaye closed the door behind her and edged around a file cabinet, stacked with folders, and topped with a tray and a cupcake, probably a gift from the Home Economics class. Mrs. Duncan moved her coat from the chair and stuffed it into the open cubicle of a bookcase. The office was little more than a closet. A narrow window high on the wall opposite the door allowed some light. The window was composed of three glass panels glazed with a sickening yellow-gold paint that had flaked around the edges of the glass. Mrs. Duncan's plumpness required delicate maneuvers around her desk to avoid a paper avalanche. Her customary smile was enhanced with a light touch of blush and dusted with face powder. Her perfume smelled like sugar cookies.

"I had hoped to avoid this, Maureen, but it's near graduation and we've not received the transcript from your previous school. You cannot graduate without that transcript."

"I understand. Mrs. Duncan, I can't get it." Kaye couldn't hide her sense of hopelessness and didn't want to look at the kind lady who had helped her not only to enroll in high school, but also to apply to the adult education-nursing program.

Mrs. Duncan frowned at her with a whimsical glance that said, "Fess up, I've heard it all."

"I guess I won't graduate." Kaye stood up, intending to leave the office. Her mind raced between thoughts about the lack of the transcript and not graduating to concerns that if she did achieve graduation the name on her diploma would be a lie.

"You're enrolled in the nursing program," Mrs. Duncan said, checking her copy of the catalog, thumbing through the pages until she found the Nursing section. "Classes start the Monday after graduation." Mrs. Duncan scanned Kaye's face. "What's your plan?"

Kaye waited, her hand resting on the doorknob.

"I went to the admissions office a couple weeks ago. The clerk said I could write an admissions exam and, if I passed it successfully, I could go into the practical nursing program. She said I might qualify for a Merit scholarship."

"I've had veterans do that. How did you find out about the test?"

"My tutor. I told him I didn't have enough credits to graduate, and he told me to go to the admissions office and ask about the test."

Mrs. Duncan's face flushed. It was obvious she'd overlooked that option. "I'm sorry, Maureen, I have a lot of students. I was waiting for your transcript. Did you take the test?"

"Yes, two weeks ago. I worried I wouldn't have enough credits for graduation. I took as many extra classes as I could."

"I understand. When will you hear the results of the entrance exam?"

"I should hear today or tomorrow. They said they would hold my spot in the program until this Friday."

Mrs. Duncan clasped her hands together and, using both forearms, parted the stacks on her desk, allowing her to see Kaye.

"Please, sit down. Don't you want to participate in the graduation ceremony?"

"I had hoped... I'd be able to." Tears filled Kaye's eyes. She should have left the office when she got up the first time; too much talk could create more problems.

"Do you have anyone coming to graduation?"

"My friend Ann Marie said she would come and a man, I call him 'the gray man'. He's been helping me study."

"That settles it." She smacked her palm on her desk. "I'm going to recommend you attend graduation and go through the ceremony. You'll receive a blank diploma, I can't help that, but you will receive one. Are you aware you've achieved academic honors?"

"I have?"

"Yes, and it's only right for you to get recognition for the work you've done. You go down and order your cap and gown, you don't want to disappoint your friend Ann Marie and your tutor."

Kaye left, eager to accomplish her errand and end the discussion about Maureen Morton's graduation from high school. She scurried down to the office to order her cap and gown and pick up two invitations.

Graduation was everything she had hoped it would be. The dark blue robe swished around her legs and billowed out in the breeze. From a dress shop on Pine Street, she purchased a white summer dress with a tucked bodice and found a pair of white pumps her size at the Salvation Army store. Her mortarboard and tassel wobbled on her head. Her brown hair tumbled on her shoulders in soft waves.

The graduation program had an asterisk beside her name, denoting her grade point. Her name was also listed in the recognition section. *"Maureen Morton the academic award in English/Literature."* She traced the places in the program where her name appeared.

She searched to find the gray man and Ann Marie. They were seated together, smiling and waving. Ann Marie was wearing a yellow summer dress, with a white jacket, and a small white hat trimmed in yellow.

Kaye's thoughts bubbled and she began dreaming. Next year she would graduate from nursing school. Dreams were possible.

"Let me see your diploma," Ann Marie said after the ceremony.

"It's just a piece of paper. We'll look at it later. I'm hungry."

"Let's go somewhere special," Ann Marie suggested.

The gray man shook his head and smiled at Kaye with those beautiful kind eyes. He didn't speak, but he was pleased. Today he wore a gray suit and a white silk dress scarf around his neck covering the lower third of his face and chin. Kaye was sure Ann Marie had found him a suit at the Salvation Army store. Probably the nice scarf too. His shoes were worn, but he had polished them. He pressed a piece of folded paper into Kaye's hand, nodded, and walked away.

Kaye placed the paper inside her purse. She'd look at it later. It wasn't money: he didn't have money. A note would be all he could afford to give her, a note small enough to fit into her palm.

Kaye turned to Ann Marie. "He's a nice man. I wish I knew more about him. I still don't know his name."

"Respect and kindness are rare gifts. I think you've given him something too. I would say I know two special people who shared time together."

"That's the way he wants it… I've never heard his name. And yes, he is kind."

They watched him depart down the street.

Ann Marie and Kaye had dinner at Dexter's. The menu special was meatloaf, Kaye's favorite. The staff at Dexter's insisted on treating Kaye, in honor of her graduation. The cook decorated a small cake that read, "Congratulations Maury." After dinner Ann Marie asked to see the diploma again.

"If I show it to you—" Kaye hesitated.

"You've worked so hard. I'm proud of you. And now you're off to college on Monday. Whew! You're taking the world by storm, as they say."

"No, I'm not." Kaye glanced around to see if anyone might overhear what she intended to say. "No, I'm not taking the world by storm." She laid the diploma on the table and opened it. Ann Marie looked at the blank form.

"What … I don't understand. You just graduated; I saw you."

"No, I didn't. I participated in graduation. I couldn't graduate because they don't have my transcript for my other three grades of high school."

"You won't graduate? Not at all?"

"That's correct, I didn't, and I won't. Ann Marie, this is difficult. I have something to tell you— I don't know what will happen when I tell you the truth. I don't know what you will have to do. I'm afraid, Ann Marie. I am really afraid." Kaye swallowed the lump rising in her throat.

"Do you want to think about it and maybe tell me another time?"

"No, I want it to be over. I feel so bad about lying to you. You're good and honest and you love people. You trusted me, and I deceived you. I'm truly sorry. I have to tell you—" Kaye hesitated but decided to just blurt it all out.

"There is no Maury, Maureen Morton isn't real."

Ann Marie's eyes opened wide.

"You're telling me you're someone else?"

"I — it's complicated—"

Regaining her composure, Ann Marie attempted to filter this new information.

"Were you Maureen Morton before the tornado?"

"No. That's when I first used that name. If I had received a diploma, it would have been Maureen Morton's diploma, and if I start nursing school with this lie, my license will be a lie. I couldn't live with that. Can you come to my room? I want to show you something."

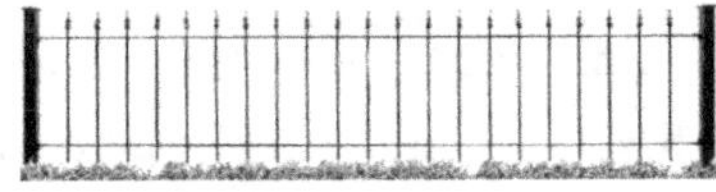

They walked together, in silence back to Mrs. D's house. Upstairs in Kaye's room, Ann Marie sat down in the big chair and waited as Kaye pulled the suitcase from under her bed and removed the brown coat.

"Is that the coat I gave the lady that day when you came into the store so upset and wanted another coat to give her?"

"Yes, this is my coat. I'd lost it several months ago. No, that's not true, when I left Tom's family, he or his mother put another coat in the bag in place of mine. Apparently, someone put mine in a Salvation Army donation box and it's found its way here. I had to have it back. This is why."

Ann Marie watched as Kaye unfolded the coat and carefully removed the folder. "It's my coat. Do you remember, after the storm, at the shelter I asked for a needle and thread?"

"Yes, I think so." Ann Marie frowned.

"This is my folder. I took it when I ran away from the place where I was living. I had tied it around me under my clothes. At the shelter that night I stitched it inside my coat for safekeeping. I didn't want to throw it away. It's all I know about me."

She handed Ann Marie the folder and waited, sitting cross-legged on the bed as Ann Marie read the pages. When she finished, Ann Marie looked up.

"Your name is K.?"

Kaye took a deep breath. She leaned back against the wall. "My real name is K., a letter. My last name is O'Shay. I was born on St. Patrick's Day, March 17, 1940. For whatever reason they, whoever they were… I refuse to believe my parents would discard me so I refer to them as *they*. They decided the day after I was born to leave me at the entrance of the State Home. I attended school at the Home. The school only goes to the sixth grade, but one teacher encouraged me to study on. When I was fourteen, a new administrator came. He started a program for some students to attend high school, and I was one of six students selected. When I started high school, I changed my name from K. to K-a-y-e M-a-u-r-e-e-n O'S-h-a-y. That's the name I wrote on everything in high school."

She moved off the bed and sorted through the papers and found the court form.

"This—" She shook the paper in front of Ann Marie. "This is why I ran away. They were going to send me to the hospital. The doctor and the judge decided I should never be able to have my own children. I didn't have a choice, Ann Marie. I had to run away." The tears burst forth. She slid to the floor, rocking in anguish as sobs shook her body.

"Maury, Maury." Ann Marie sat down on the floor next to her and held her in her arms. "It's all right. I believe you. Tell me everything."

Kaye rubbed her eyes with her sleeve. Ann Marie pulled a handkerchief from her purse and handed it to her.

"I don't understand the surgery, or why. Did they do surgery on every girl?"

"No." She removed the page of notations of encounters. "It's because of this. I'm not lying anymore. I had a boyfriend; his name is Seth. We went to school together, and to high school, too. Some people must have seen us together and decided I was at risk to get a baby. We didn't do anything, Ann Marie. There is no reason. But then I found out about him, and I got mad because I thought he knew about his mother. I didn't want to have a baby like the babies I took care of in the nursery."

"You worked at the nursery in the Home? Help me put the pieces together."

"Yes. I started working there when I was twelve. In my cottage, I took care of Jessie. That was my job. Jessie was like a sister to me. When she went to the hospital, they couldn't get her to eat, so I snuck in and when they found out I was good with her they let me come every day to feed her. After she was well, I was old enough to work in the nursery, so I worked there whenever I wasn't in school. Then, while I was in high school, Jessie died. Ann Marie, I feel so bad. I couldn't be everywhere. After Jessie died, Hannot, the supervisor of my cottage, decided I should move to the older girls' building. One day, when I came home from the nursery, Hannot told me I was going to the hospital the next morning, and then after the surgery, I would move to the older girls' building. One of the workers told me about the surgery. She said they were doing me a favor. I was angry with everything that was being decided for me."

"So, you ran away?"

"Yes. I waited until late that night and climbed inside Ollie's truck. He gets chicken feed on Thursdays, so I crawled in under the bags and rode away."

"Do other people run away?"

"Where would they go?"

"How old were you when you ran away?"

"I'd just turned sixteen. That was last year. I'm seventeen now. But I'm not twenty-one, and I don't have a family or a guardian. They teach trades there. Sometimes people find work outside. Others live their whole life at the Home."

Ann Marie moved back into the chair and sorted through the papers, reading each form, line by line.

"We must look at this objectively, item by item. You have two names. You have a copy of a birth certificate, with your legal name. Let's call K. O'Shay your legal name. You went to high school and changed your name to Kaye Maureen O'Shay. You ran away as a minor. After you ran away you changed your name to Maureen Morton, using the nickname Maury. You graduated from high school, but you didn't earn a diploma. On Monday you are to enter college as Maureen Morton. Have I got it right so far?"

"It sounds simple when you organize it like that."

"I must organize information. That's how I deal with it."

"What will you do now that you know? Will you call the police?" Kaye's gut churned. She watched Ann Marie's face trying to anticipate her reaction.

"Maury, do you want me to call you Maury or Kaye?" Ann Marie hesitated.

"It doesn't matter, now that you know the truth."

Ann Marie took another deep breath. "Let's go for a walk down by the water. It's not dark yet, and we can sit on a bench and watch the bridge light up. It helps me to be near the water. I think we both need some fresh air."

Kaye folded the brown coat around the folder, placed it inside the suitcase, snapped it shut, and pushed it under the bed. They left the house and walked toward the riverfront. Several other people were enjoying the warm June evening.

"I didn't know water moved that fast down a river," Kaye said, pointing toward a gull bobbing along on the rapid current.

"It's fast all right, and there's a strong undertow. This river looks narrow because you can see Canada, but let me tell you, it's taken its share of lives."

They sat down together on a bench, waiting for the bridge lights to come on.

"Have you decided what you're going to do?" Kaye asked. The rules part of her wanted to know, the fear part of her hoped for the impossible.

"I've been praying, and I think I have to see someone about your legal rights. I must protect us both. I can't do that without the correct information. But first I have to know if you trust me enough to not run away."

Kaye couldn't hide her surprise.

"Where would I go?"

"Anywhere, I suppose."

"That would be another lie. God wouldn't like that. No, I'm not running away. If it's bad, then it's bad."

"We're not going to look at the bad. We're going to look at trusting God."

The bridge lights flickered on, sparkling in the dusk. Headlights of automobiles and vehicles traveling to and fro on the bridge blinked on in response.

It was dark when Ann Marie and Kaye walked back to Mrs. D's house.

"See you in church tomorrow."

"Oh, yes. What's Sunday without worship and the band?" Kaye struggled to smile.

"Indeed." Ann Marie gave her a reassuring hug and strolled toward Main Street and her home.

Alone in her room, Kaye sat in the dark and looked down on the street. She wanted to trust God. Now that the truth was known, she felt a sense of peace. Kaye turned on her radio to the most popular male singer crooning, "It is no secret what God can do." The music filled her room and her soul. She agreed with every word as she prayed "Thank you."

Chapter 38

Mr. Kent drove his tractor into the barn and closed the door. The clouds hung heavy in the sky. Another day of rain was in the forecast.

Seth pulled into the driveway and hurried toward the barn. "Sorry I could only stop by today. I wanted to get home and help bring in the hay." He cast a glance toward the sky. "Looks like it's been raining here."

"It's been raining all right. It'll have to dry a spell before we can get any second cutting. Come on in and have some iced tea. Laura's got cookies, too."

The men walked together toward the house and entered.

Mrs. Kent poured iced tea and set out a plate of cookies. "Hi, Seth. You're looking good. Are you home for the weekend?"

"I planned to help put in the hay, but it looks like I'm too late for first cutting and too early for second."

"If you could get on the field you could cultivate. That's not likely today." Mr. Kent sighed.

"Every year's different. That's what keeps farming interesting." Mrs. Kent removed her apron. "I'm taking this pie over to the Smiths. Seth will you be staying?"

"I can't stay for dinner; I need to get back. I have homework to finish.

"Have you been to Port Huron today?"

"Yeah," he wrinkled his forehead. "I keep hoping."

"It'll happen. I'll be right back and start dinner." Mrs. Kent carried her pie to the car and drove away.

Mr. Kent went into the living room and returned with his pipe.

"Let's go out to the swing. Maybe the rain will hold off for an hour or two."

From the lawn swing perched on a knoll behind the house, they could see several of the fields. Mr. Kent puffed on his pipe. The air hung heavy with his thoughts; things Seth should know.

"I want to tell you something, but first let me say Ben is fine."

"Why are we talking about Ben?" Seth's tone immediately became defensive and belligerent.

"There was an accident at the farm."

"What kind of accident?"

"I don't know the whole story. I don't know who does. But, one morning last week, Ollie was found in the bull pen."

"What in the…."

"He was dead, Seth."

"Well, that stands to reason, considering the size of those bulls. Why would he be in the bull pen?"

"They aren't sure. It appears that he was pitching hay down the shoot from the mow and slid down into the bullpen. Pitchfork and all."

Seth's eyes shifted, searching Mr. Kent's face for more information.

Mr. Kent continued, "I know you said you were concerned about Ben, working for Ollie. Looks like you don't have to worry about that."

"You said Ollie was in the bullpen with his pitchfork?"

"That's the story I heard."

"Was there anything in the paper?"

"Oh, no." Mr. Kent shook his head. "It's considered Home business."

"Yeah, I know about that. So, who told you?"

"Paddy."

"He's honest. What'd he say?"

"He came up to me when I stopped to arrange a field trip for the class. He pulled me to the side and asked if I'd be seeing you. I told him not often. He said he wanted to tell me about Ollie so I could tell you. He thought you'd feel better about Ben. He said, 'Tell Toe they found Ollie in the bullpen with his three-tined pitch- fork.'"

"He said that?"

"Yes, that's exactly what he said to tell you."

"Anything else?"

"Paddy said he didn't want it to get out. He told me the night Ollie fell, Ben came to him with a hole from a fork tine clean through his thigh. He and Ben cleaned it and put a bandage on it. They agreed not to tell anybody. They're all talking about Ollie dying with his pitchfork."

Seth remained quiet for a long time. "Ben's all right?"

"Yeah, saw him yesterday. Walking pretty good. He's pitching baseball today."

"No investigation?"

"I don't know about that, it seemed pretty evident when they saw that the grate was off the hay shoot just above where he fell."

"Yeah," Seth nodded. "He wasn't a bad guy, you know. He could be a lot of fun. It's the bottle. He couldn't handle the bottle. Paddy said Ollie shouldn't drink. He said some folks get crazy and shouldn't ever drink."

"I've heard that. I saw Ollie a couple times when he was a little wet."

"Wet?"

"Yeah, had a nip or two."

"I'm sorry he died that way."

They sat together, the swing moving only a gentle pass forward and back. The clouds gathered overhead, and the wind started to blow.

"We better go in." Mr. Kent stood.

Seth remained on the swing, staring across the fields.

Mr. Kent filled his pipe.

"Let's go in, Seth. It's getting late." Mr. Kent stopped the moving swing with his arm. "You headed back to Flint?"

Aroused from his disturbing thoughts, Seth followed him toward the house.

"Classes start too early to stay over. I'll call you on Friday."

Mr. Kent watched Seth drive away. Tonight, Seth would not be thinking about classes. Tonight, he would be thinking about Ben.

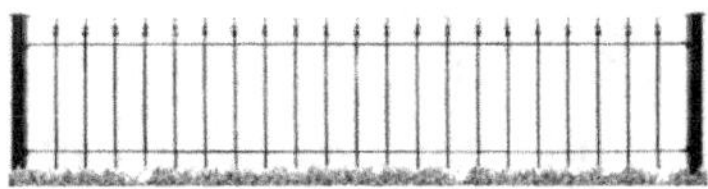

On Monday, Kaye entered the Nursing program. She found her way to the administration office and picked up her schedule. Next stop, the bookstore. Her books were listed in her syllabus. The clerk, also a working student, helped her find the ones she needed for first semester. Orientation started at ten in the auditorium. Kaye pulled a map out of her school catalog, turned it until she was sure where she was, and started off. When she reached the creek at the bottom of the map, she sat down on a bench in tears. She could not make it to the auditorium in time. Late the first day! She hated not doing things right. Nothing to do now but "the next thing." Oh, Nurse Lucy, that's what she said when they were working in the nursery and things got overwhelming. "Do the next thing." The next thing was to go in the opposite direction she had come.

A young man stopped his bike and smiled.

"Lost?"

"Not now, but I have to hurry. I'm already late."

"Where you headed?"

"The auditorium."

"Hop on, I'll give you a ride."

"In a skirt?"

"Here," he slid back on the seat and pointed to the bar in front of him. "Come on, it'll be fun— if we don't crash into a tree."

Kaye laughed and climbed onto the bike. Crashing into a tree might be the next thing.

When they arrived at the auditorium, students were still entering. The president was wrapping up his welcome, and the teachers were seated on the stage awaiting introductions.

"What's your name?" Kaye whispered.

"Rick... Richard... I *prefer* Rick. What's yours?"

Kaye choked a cough.

"Maureen," she whispered back.

She and Ann Marie decided it would be best if she continued to use the name Maureen Morton until they could seek legal counsel. For right now, Ann Marie would meet with her superior, and Kaye was to continue with her education.

After orientation, the students went to their respective classes. Kaye followed some other students to the science building.

The instructor was talking when Kaye entered.

"Find a seat," the instructor admonished the students. "My name is Miss Turpen. I am as old as I appear, and I have been teaching that long. You will have a very busy year—*if* you complete the program. There are those among you who will not. If you finish, you will know the art of nursing and you will understand how to work. If I ask you a question, and I will, I expect the correct answer. I take my teaching as a serious endeavor. We will meet every morning this week at six, in the lab next door. We will begin in the hospital the following week. Arrive tomorrow morning in uniform with your shoes polished, nails short, hair pinned up. Your assignment tonight is the first five chapters of your Nursing 101 textbook. There will be a quiz on Wednesday covering the first five chapters, and an exam every Friday on the lab assignments. A passing grade is required to continue. If you have any questions don't ask them until you have completed your reading assignment. I will see you tomorrow morning. I do not accept tardiness."

"Whew!" The student beside Kaye gestured as she wiped her hand across her forehead. Miss Turpen responded with a scowl.

Kaye turned to leave the room. She noticed Rick going out the door on the other end of the room.

During the afternoon Kaye found her way to the other four classes on her schedule. The classrooms were familiar but the anatomy lab with its skeletons and bones, dismembered joints, and posters of tissue, muscle, and organs, were a bit overwhelming.

At each classroom she saw Rick. He nodded but they didn't have an opportunity to talk until the next day, when he shared that he was attending school on the GI bill and had been a medic in the Navy.

The next two weeks passed in a blur of activity and study. Kaye attended worship on Sunday. She spent every waking minute deep in her books, coming up for air only to eat and sleep. Miss Turpen was exactly as she presented herself. No nonsense and no allowances for tardiness. She inspected shoes, stockings, and uniforms for hem length, hair, and nails. Her tests were ruthless and exacting. On Monday morning of the third week, in the restroom of the lab building, Kaye scoured the bottom of her purse for another bobby pin to secure her hair. She could find only three, and three were not enough. Removing her wallet and other items, she found one more bobby pin. Wedged between the prongs of metal she found the note from the gray man. She'd forgotten about it since graduation day. Placing it on the edge of the sink, she wet her hair, split it into two sections, braided each, and twisted them into a secure position, anchoring them with the four bobby pins. "Stay," she commanded, staring into the mirror.

"Does that work?" Another student asked as she wrestled with spirals of curls.

"I hope it does, or Miss Turpen might just jerk me baldheaded!" Kaye offered some humor, trying to ease the tension. She picked up her purse, grabbed the note, and scurried toward class. Arriving a few minutes early, she opened her textbook and her notebook. It wouldn't hurt to look prepared. She placed her pen on the notebook and opened the note.

> *Dear K. O'Shay,*
>
> *Congratulations on your graduation and achieving honors.*
>
> *May you achieve your dreams.*
>
> *Zeke*
>
> *The donut man.*

She reread the whole note and gasped. It was addressed to K. O'Shay. She read it a third time. Zeke! The Gray Man was Zeke, Ezekiel from the bakery at the Home. When she was young, she would take Jessie past the bakery. Jessie loved anything sweet, and she loved the smells of the breads and donuts. It was a treat if he saw them because he would place two donuts dusted with powdered sugar, for them on a napkin, on the windowsill. He wore a white cloth like a scarf around his neck and covered his nose but as a child she never thought about him covering his face. The nurses wore masks sometimes and the cooks wore nets on their hair. It didn't seem strange that along with his baker's cap and white apron he wore that white cloth.

Everyone loved Zeke's donuts. Years had passed since she'd had eaten them. As she grew older, going to the bakery was no longer as important as going to see Toe play baseball.

The students clattered into the room, interrupting her reflection on the past. She folded the note and placed it inside a pocket in her purse as the room silenced, announcing Miss Turpen's entry. The focus today was bed making, square corners, firm sheets with no evidence of a wrinkle, and a pillow placed in the case with a one-hand method. Efficiency and detail held equal value. Miss Turpen measured the drop of the sheet on each side of the bed. Any error resulted in her snatching the bedding off the bed and redirecting the student to perform the task according to the textbook directions. After the details were accomplished, Miss Turpen removed a stopwatch from her pocket and proceeded to time each student. Hands trembled, sheets were dropped, pillowcases twisted, and frustration mounted. The third time Kaye made the bed she passed both procedure and timing. Exhausted from the experience, she left for her other classes. Rick joined her, pushing his bike.

"How'd you do?" he asked.

"I passed. How about you?"

"I passed too. She sure gets caught up in detail."

"It's important. People can get bedsores from creases in the sheets."

"You seem to know a lot about nursing."

"Not really. I've taken care of some people, and I learned things. Now onto biology class."

"Yah, see you later." Rick didn't enter the classroom, but walked over to a tree and sat down in the grass and closed his eyes. She shared his need to be still, but biology was the next thing.

Kaye walked home thinking about Zeke and the note. There were bakeries in Port Huron, and places where a baker could work, especially someone as skilled as Zeke.

Working on her homework, she prayed for the other students. They were becoming a tight group, encouraging each other, and studying together.

She had to hope because hope was all she had.

Chapter 39

"Hi Seth! You're home a week early," Mr. Kent called from the porch steps.

"Did you know about this?" Seth waved the newspaper.

"Now don't get all upset, Seth. Some things we can't do anything about. It's the state making the decisions."

"Mr. Kent, they can't do this. You've seen the farm! You know what it means to the men. You've seen the herd. Stop them, somebody's got to stop them."

"Come inside, Seth."

"I don't want to come inside; I want to stop this."

"Come inside and sit down. I'll tell you what I know."

"No politics during supper," Mrs. Kent cautioned as she placed the food on the table.

"Then it'll be really quiet after grace," Seth mumbled.

Supper was indeed quiet. Mrs. Kent cleared the table and cleaned up the kitchen. Seth and Mr. Kent talked until late into the night.

"They can't just sell off the herd and put the men in the cottages all day. Who thought up something like that?"

"It's not seen as gainful employment. The social scientists see it as forced labor. There's more than one point of view."

"Who speaks for the men's point of view? How much they love caring for the animals and harvesting the crops. It's what they do. The orchard, the gardens, the melons, and strawberries, everybody eats it. We raise our own beef and pigs, even the guys that feed the chickens have pets."

"Seth, times are changing. Farming is an industry now. I told you when you wanted to quit college that the machinery is getting bigger, and the farming operations are getting scientific."

"Mr. Kent, you know it's not right. You know it."

Nothing Mr. Kent could say would change Seth's mind or relieve his frustration and concern for the men at the Home.

The next morning Seth left early. "I got to be to the plant by seven. I'll call if I can come next Sunday."

He pulled out of the driveway onto the road. If Seth couldn't understand, surely the men at the Home couldn't understand. Now, day after day, they would sit in the cottages. As he drove past the entrance gate, his heart ached for the men.

Miss Turpin called the class to order tapping her pencil on the blackboard.

"Assignments are posted on the board. You have been through orientation and know your way around the hospital. Rodgers and Morton, you are going to OB today. A primigravida"— she paused and scowled at the nursing students. "Miss Morton, would you clarify for the class?"

Kaye swallowed the lump in her throat. "A first-time delivery."

"Very good. Yes. She's been laboring all night. Two other women delivered before morning. The doctor expects her to deliver within the next couple hours. You'll be our first students in OB, so I expect you to conduct yourselves accordingly. You will be reporting to the class in post-conference. Submit your written observations tomorrow morning."

Pairs of nursing students wearing gray starched uniforms, their backs ramrod straight and their faces pale with anxiety, checked the assignment board and dispersed to their locations. Freckle-faced Linda Rodgers rushed down the hallway beside Kaye.

"Have you ever seen a baby born, Maury? Why the hurry? If we slow down, maybe the baby'll be born before we get there."

"That's what I'm afraid of, I don't want to miss seeing a real human being come into the world all pink and smiling. It's got to be cute!"

"Cute?" Linda's eyes opened wide in alarm. "They're so little. It's frightening."

"They won't let us do anything. We only watch. We're students, Linda."

"I've been doing lots of things I didn't think students did! I'm not all that thrilled about Turpin's *learning opportunities.*"

"Better to get the experiences now than later when there's no one to ask."

"Maybe nursing isn't what I should be doing," Linda said. Her brow furrowed with worry.

"It'll be fine. Stay with me." Kaye pushed her way through the double doors.

"Students, Rodgers and Morton, right?" A stocky, middle-aged nurse in a green scrub gown and cap, her mask pulled down below her chin, welcomed them. Kaye decided she appeared less intimidating than Turpin but cut from the same cloth.

"That's us," Kaye offered as Rodgers huddled behind her.

"Right this way. I'm Nurse Davis. Our mama's down here in room B. She's been laboring all night; it's her first. She said it's fine to bring in a student nurse or two because she's a nurse." Nurse Davis breezed into the room. "Good morning, Mrs. Heusted. These are the students I told you about."

Kaye paused midway into the room.

The patient lay amid twisted sheets and gasped for air. She hollered and grabbed the side rails of the bed. "Hand me that!" Her cheeks were red and puffy. Beads of perspiration trickled down the sides of her face. Her eyes were wide with fear.

Kaye handed her the flashlight type canister dangling from a strap on the bedrail. The woman clutched the canister, fit the black rubber area over her nose, and closed her eyes.

Nurse Davis adjusted the mask on her face. "Breath deep, Lucy. That's good." She turned to Kaye and Linda. "This is called Trilene." She tapped the canister. "It's a light analgesia, very good during childbirth."

When the contraction subsided, the woman removed the small mask.

It was Nurse Lucy. Kaye gasped. She was having a baby. Her own baby! Would she recognize her? What was going to happen if Nurse Lucy realized she was here?

Nurse Davis observed the contraction as an expected activity and continued with her duties.

"You stay here with her and introduce yourselves. She's a little older for a prima but a sweet girl. I must get things rolling. I don't think we'll have much longer."

As the contraction subsided, the woman rolled her head, shifted her body, and took a deep breath. "That's one more done." Ignoring them, she turned toward the door. Is Dan out there?"

"I'll look." Kaye opened the door. "Dan?" She opened the door wider. A man of about thirty-five, wearing a red plaid shirt and blue jeans, hurried into the room. She'd never pictured Lucy's husband. Lucy had said he was a farmer. He was handsome. Dan rushed into the room, his appearance disheveled. That's probably how a man appears after spending the night at the hospital, with his wife in labor.

Lucy and Dan huddled together reassuring each other everything was progressing and soon they would have their baby.

Linda Rodgers tugged on Kaye's sleeve.

"Let's go. We shouldn't be here."

Kaye scowled at her.

"Where would we be? We're the nurses."

Linda gulped, attempting to step back far enough to disappear into the wall. Kaye pulled her forward.

"Hello, Mrs. Heusted, we are your student nurses." At that moment Maury caught the full attention of her patient. "My name is

Maureen Morton, and this is Linda Rodgers. Is there anything we can get for you?"

Another contraction started. Lucy pulled the canister to her face, waved her husband to go away, and focused on the contraction.

Nurse Davis came in and examined her.

"It's baby time," she announced. "Let's move to the delivery room."

Davis motioned Linda and Kaye to go through the next door.

The room they entered had a wall with sinks and a rack of scrubs. It had been less than a week since they had learned to scrub in, but they knew how.

Davis entered from the Delivery door. "Grab a sink and start washing. There's the timer. I'll be right back."

The girls executed the procedure with the precision demanded by their instructor. Soon they were garbed and headed into the delivery room.

Between contractions, Lucy Heusted sounded euphoric as she chatted with the doctor and nurses.

"I'm so excited to see my baby." She glanced toward Linda and Kaye. "It's my first baby."

"That's wonderful." Kaye stepped up to the head of the delivery table, confident the mask would hide her identity.

"My husband wants a boy. I told him I want a girl because I want the baby to be welcome no matter what." She lowered her voice to a whisper. "I'd like a boy for him. A farmer wants a son—"

Lucy yelled out again with another contraction, her cry echoing around the room.

Someone in scrubs placed a mask over her nose and mouth. "Breathe in. That's good, just like you have been doing."

Kaye didn't hear much as she stared at the woman on the table. Lucy Heusted is having a baby, and I'm here to see it happen. Tears rolled down Kaye's cheeks behind the mask. She began to pray. "Dear God, please watch over Lucy and the baby, please make everything go well. Amen."

"It's coming! It's coming!" Lucy called out, her face round and flushed as she strained.

The staff worked together in synchrony, ignoring the students, each knowing exactly what the other was doing.

The doctor entered the room, arms up in the air, as a nurse assisted him with a gown and mask, and then held the gloves for him to apply. He stepped up to the table, lifted the drape, and nodded toward them.

"Come down this way, girls. Student nurses, right?"

Nurse Davis ushered them toward the delivery drape.

"Don't faint. Are you both okay? There's a stool if you need to sit down."

Kaye questioned whether it was proper for her to be here for someone she knew without her permission. However, Lucy didn't know it was her. Kaye considered all that had happened since she last saw Nurse Lucy and now, they were together to share this moment. Her thoughts were suddenly jolted by the sound of a baby's wail.

"Baby boy Huested has arrived. A beautiful boy. Look how strong he is!" The doctor announced the baby's arrival with the same pride as if it were his very own. "I think he's going to be a good farmer." The doctor chuckled with delight as he held up a squirming little pink baby.

"Oh, he's, he's—!" Lucy cried out again.

The nurse grabbed the canister that dangled from Lucy's wrist and placed it back on her face.

"Here," the doctor shouted as he quickly handed the baby boy to the nearest nurse and moved behind the drape again.

"Wonder of wonders, and here comes another one. A little girl. Ah, she's a wee one."

Kaye couldn't hold back the tears. Twins! Two babies.

The babies were held near Lucy so she could see them. Tears streamed down her face. "Aren't they beautiful, so beautiful," she crooned, and reached out to touch them. "Are they all right? Tell me they're all right?"

Lucy's anxiety was taking hold of her emotions.

The staff didn't pay attention to Lucy's pleas, but Kaye knew what she was asking, and she knew no one could reassure Nurse Lucy until she held the babies and examined them herself.

Kaye and Linda followed the babies to the nursery. According to their textbook, the nursery nurses would weigh and measure the babies, check them over carefully, wash them, diaper them, and place them each in a bassinet, and roll the bassinets out to the viewing window where Daddy could admire his babies.

Kaye watched both babies carefully, imagining any possible danger that could lurk nearby or harm them. "Please be careful," she prayed, watching anxiously as the nurses performed tasks so routine to them.

Later, Kaye and Linda passed by Lucy's room. She was resting and waiting to see her babies. Linda tugged on Kaye's sleeve.

"We have to go."

Kaye didn't want to leave; she wanted to hold the babies and talk to Lucy. She wanted to tell Dan how happy she was for them. She wanted to know the babies' names. By hospital rules, probably her being here for this event was wrong, and yet it was so right. So beautifully right.

Chapter 40

Today was the day Seth had been waiting for: his last day in this plant. His next assignment would be at the technology center. All the engineering students rotated through the prototype-design area, but it wasn't the design of the automobiles that excited Seth, it was the engines. To be an automotive engineer, to explore the design, the materials, the energy sources, the challenges, and the opportunities. Engines were why he stayed with the program. He had to admit Mr. Kent had been right when he challenged him to consider what the automotive industry could offer for his future.

Seth arrived early and waited in the coffee room for Henry. Several men were playing cards at the picnic table while Seth poured a cup of coffee and took a spiral-bound notepad out of his pocket. He reviewed yesterday's notes.

Jack brushed against Seth as he passed.

"Don't you have an office somewhere, Engineer Boy?" he sneered.

"I wanted to talk to you about the cable before the line starts."

"You don't know a cable from your armpit. Get out of my way." Jack jostled against Seth a second time and pretended to avoid spilling coffee on him.

Several of the men chuckled in amusement.

Henry entered as Jack walked out. "Trouble in paradise, Seth?"

"Not much longer. Today's my last day for a few weeks."

"Sorry to hear that. I've enjoyed knowing you." Henry nodded and stirred his coffee.

"Thanks, Henry. I've learned a lot from you. Is it always this way? Do they ever accept the engineers?"

"It takes time. Some of the engineers survive, but others don't want or care to. They see themselves as better, so it makes for hard feelings."

"I sure wish we could work together."

"I've seen it happen but it's rare. The engineers don't want to listen to the worker, and the worker won't look at a new method or way that might cost someone a job. It's economics for them."

"Yeah, it happens everywhere. It's happening in farming too, bigger machines and fewer men. I'll be back here in a few weeks. I'm rotating through the prototypes next. There's some innovative stuff going on there." Seth paused. "Say, Henry. I've tried to talk to Jack about that cable on #842. He won't listen. I know it's thick, but until we find out what's shearing it, we don't know how much wear it'll take."

"They've had that machine shut down for almost two days. Production won't be happy to shut it down for an inspection when we don't have any specific reason. I know what you're saying, though. Let's go take a look."

Henry and Seth examined the powerful press. They looked the machine over like a physician assessing an ill patient: timing, brake, electrical cables, and hoses.

"Any ideas, Seth?"

"There's a novelty, an engineer with an idea," Jack mocked.

Zing.

Seth looked up to see the rear cable skyrocketing toward the roof. "Look out!" he yelled, reaching out to grab Jack by his shirt collar, pulling him back and away from the front of the machine as the top part lifted from its anchor bolts and began to swing toward them like a giant pendulum. Those seconds seemed like a slow-motion time lapse. Jack pulled away from Seth's grasp, while hoses ruptured, more cables sheared, pounding metal and screaming men chorused in a cacophony of sound. As the noise subsided, the ballast of the machine swayed above them. The men had scattered. When Jack pulled away from Seth, he fled in the wrong direction.

Scurrying under the swaying machine, Seth found Jack huddled into a ball his arms protecting his head. He had panicked.

"Jack, come on, I'll take you out." Seth pulled Jack to his feet. A gash on the side of Jack's head was bleeding. "Come on." Again, Jack crumbled to the ground. Seth bent down, his face inches from Jack's. "I said get up." He grabbed the front of Jack's shirt and pulled him to his feet.

A siren sounded. They had seconds.

Jack's body went limp. Seth turned; wedging his shoulder under Jack, he pulled him onto his back, half carrying and half dragging him toward the exit. The siren continued to wail.

Seth stumbled out the door, piling into the group of men. Together they heard the thunderous crash behind them. Henry pulled Jack off Seth's back and lowered him to the ground. Jack huddled, rocking with terror.

Seth sat down on the pavement. His pants were torn, his shirt bloodied and covered with oil.

"How'd you find him, Seth?"

"I know what some men do when they get scared. They run toward the danger. I've seen it before. I looked there first."

Henry pushed his hat back on his head. "Well, I'll be." He looked down to see Seth's pant leg open, exposing a leg that didn't look real. "Well, I'll be."

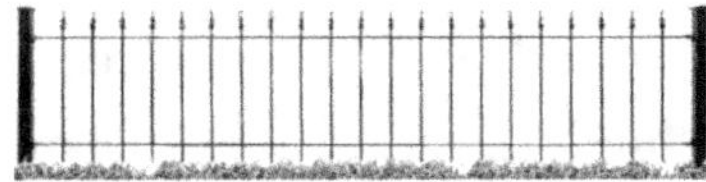

Maury marked another week off her calendar. Each Saturday she noted the weeks completed in her nursing program.

At five a.m. she removed her flannel nightgown and slipped on the plaid uniform she wore to work at Dexter's restaurant. The uniform wrapped around her waist and puckered at the belt. The demands of her studies and the constant worry about her emancipation were reflecting in her weight loss. Saturday was the only day she could work.

The work she did at the house for Mrs. D. reduced her rent by half. She also picked up groceries and ran errands for Mrs. D whenever she asked. She was standing at the front door as Kaye came down the stairs preparing to leave.

"You're up early," Kaye remarked.

"Yes, I am. I'm worried about you. You study all the time and try to work too. I think you're getting thin. Don't forget to take care of yourself."

"'I'm fine, Mrs. D. The courses are hard but I'm passing. Will you be home when I'm done working today? I want to tell you about my OB experience. The lady had twins."

Mrs. D. laughed aloud, delighted to share Kaye's excitement.

"I can't wait to hear."

"See you later." Kaye stepped out into the early morning light, eager to meet the familiar faces at the restaurant. Saturday morning brought several regulars.

"Hey, Maury," Johnny the cook called, as she entered through the back door and into the kitchen. "You got a secret admirer you haven't told us about? There's a letter for you at the cash register. It came on Wednesday."

Kaye placed her purse in the locker, removed a clean apron from the closet, and tied it around her waist. The restaurant would be open in ten minutes. She hurried to arrange the dining area and then checked the menu on the chalkboard above the pass-through to the kitchen for the specials. The smell of coffee brewing accented by the sweet smell of warm cinnamon rolls filled the restaurant. Kaye immediately thought of Zeke and sprinted toward the kitchen.

"Johnny, the cinnamon rolls smell wonderful. Have you ever made donuts?"

"Donuts? No. Folks get their donuts at the bakery. They come here for food."

"Don't be testy, you know I love your cinnamon rolls." Kaye pulled a warm roll from the corner of the tray, tore off a portion, and placed half on a napkin, tucking it away toward the back on the counter. "Johnny, if a baker made terrific donuts, where could he find a job?" She nibbled on the soft buttery cinnamon roll.

"Do you make donuts?"

"No. Do I look like a donut baker?" Kaye swallowed. "I'm a nurse. Well, I'm going to be." She washed her hands to remove the sticky sugar and cinnamon.

"You're also going to be an unemployed waitress if you don't unlock the front door and start pouring coffee. If you're waiting on Peggy, she called and said she'd be late."

Kaye darted toward the front door, unlocked it, welcomed in the first two customers, and hurried back to the kitchen.

"Johnny, I was serious about that person who makes donuts."

"So, you know someone who can bake?" Johnny shook both pans on the stove and stirred the bubbling oatmeal.

"I don't know about baking, but he can make the best donuts of anyone I know."

Johnny pointed toward the dining room and sighed. "I'll talk to Patsy. I could use some help, but I don't know if she'll hire. I'll let you know."

"You'd talk to the manager? Johnny, you're a pal."

He pointed to the door of the dining room. "Coffee, go pour coffee."

Kaye scurried out to the customers. Sully, a city policeman on duty was behind the counter pouring his own coffee.

"You're cute, Sully, but you're cutting in on my tips!" Kaye laughed and tugged him toward the counter stool.

The morning vanished in a maze of plates of scrambled eggs, hash browns, sides of bacon and ham, platters of sausage and biscuits, and bowls of hot oatmeal. Lunch started early. Kaye was on the step stool, erasing the breakfast menu from the blackboard, when Johnny came out of the kitchen carrying a slip of paper with the lunch menu.

"What'd Romeo say in his letter?"

"Oh! I forgot all about it."

"Poor Romeo." Johnny chuckled. "Patsy stopped by, and I asked about your baker. She said she would think about it. It wouldn't be many hours at first."

"Thanks, Johnny." Kaye finished the menu, put the step stool away, and made sure everyone's coffee mug was filled before looking for the letter. It was stuffed between two vinyl dinner menus and a pile of mail, addressed simply *Maury*, the address Dexter's Restaurant, 618 Huron, Port Huron, Michigan. The handwriting was done in block letters with black ink. She didn't know anyone who wrote in block print letters! There was no return address. Kaye tore open the envelope and removed a single sheet of folded paper. Two photographs dropped onto the counter. She picked them up; three chubby smiling faces beamed back at her.

Maury,

My Aunt and Uncle stopped by and said they ate at a restaurant called Dexter's, in Port Huron on the 4th of July weekend. They said their waitress's name was Maury and they described you. I don't know if you'll get this.

We miss you. I'm sending you Andy's school picture and a snapshot of Susie and Molly. I'm coming to Port Huron on Saturday, October 18. I'll make reservations at the Inn by the bridge for 8 p.m. I hope you'll come.

Tom

Maury folded the letter and looked again at the pictures.

"Some cute kids! Nieces? Nephew?" Johnny was peering out from the pass through.

"Were you reading my letter?"

"Tried but couldn't see it." He raised his eyebrows up and down on his forehead like Groucho Marx and tapped his finger as if he were holding a cigar. "And I say guess the pictures rule out a Romeo."

"Yes, Groucho, it rules out a Romeo."

"Did I see something about the Inn?"

"Johnny, you were reading over my shoulder!" Kaye stormed into the kitchen.

Johnny held up an empty frying pan. "Work, Maury, we got work to do."

Two customers at the counter were laughing at their antics when Peggy yelled from the dining room, "If you two are going to play games, I'm going home early."

Johnny and Maury exchanged glances and resumed their work.

On Saturdays the restaurant remained open late. After the lunch crowd left, Patsy, the manager, came out of her office and poured a cup of coffee.

"Maury, can you work through to seven? Peggy's son is sick, and she has to leave early."

Johnny was preparing to leave as Sessil, the late-shift cook, entered, donned his chef hat and apron, and went to work.

"She's been here since 5:30," Johnny said, speaking up for Kaye as he plopped his ball cap on his head.

"Well, she only works Saturdays and I'm asking." Patsy grimaced at Johnny's interruption.

"I was going home to study," Kaye said and sighed.

"I need the help, or I wouldn't ask," Patsy cajoled her.

"Besides, your date isn't until the eighteenth," Johnny called out as he ducked out the back door.

By the time Kaye rushed to the back door Johnny was waving from the far end of the alley.

Kaye returned to the dining room where Patsy was waiting. She didn't acknowledge Johnny's teasing Kaye.

"Johnny said you know a baker and would like to find work for him."

"He's a donut maker. I don't know if he can bake other things. I was just asking where he might go to find work."

"We don't usually serve donuts, but we could try them. After Johnny asked me, I thought about it; maybe it's something we could do on Sundays."

"We're closed on Sundays."

"That's right, but we could make donuts, take orders, and deliver them. There might be places that would like to order donuts for Sunday. It's worth a try. The kitchen wouldn't be tied up with meals that way. We could also offer donuts on Mondays. Tell your friend to stop by and we can talk about it."

Maury sat down on a counter stool. "Can't."

"Can't what?"

Patsy appeared puzzled because she had offered to help.

"He can't talk about it. He's a terrific baker," Kaye pleaded. "But he has a speech problem. It's quite severe; he can't talk. He's very smart. He tutored me all the way through my senior year."

"Well then, how can I talk with him?"

"If you could make it after my classes I could come with him. We write."

"I don't know if I could help him—if I can't talk with him."

"Would you just meet him?"

Patsy remained hesitant. "I could do that." She nodded.

"Wednesday. We could we come by after class, about 4?"

Patsy paged through a calendar at the cash register. "Yes, I can be here then."

"One more thing." Kaye paused. "He wears a scarf around his neck, and it covers the lower part of his face. If it were white, it would look like he's a baker covering his beard. He'll be in the kitchen making donuts. It won't matter."

Kaye knew she was treading on thin ice; cleanliness in the kitchen was a big deal to Patsy.

"I'll meet him. That's all I'll promise," Patsy said and headed for the door.

"You're terrific. Thank you. Thank you." Kaye scurried around, setting up the tables for dinner.

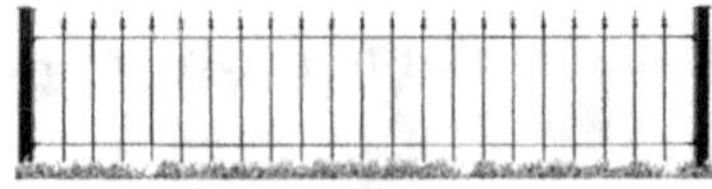

On Sunday, Kaye went to worship at the Citadel, hoping to see Zeke. She was excited to offer him the opportunity to work, especially doing something at which he excelled. She wrote a note explaining the job, and that she would go with him on Wednesday. He wasn't there before church started. He always sat in the same chair in the balcony. Kaye placed the note on his chair and took her seat in the band. The borrowed cornet offered her more joy than she expected. She had played in the band at the Home but didn't want to play in high school. She was surprised how much she remembered. At first, when they invited her to audition for the band, she was hesitant, but with practice, she improved enough to join. She warmed up her instrument as others arrived.

After church she hurried to the balcony. The letter was gone. She could only wait until Wednesday and see if he would come.

Ann Marie passed through the balcony picking up papers and rearranging the chairs.

"Maury, I've been looking for you." She glanced around, satisfied no one was near, she pulled Kaye to a chair in the corner and sat down.

"I want to tell you I've been working with someone, and I think we can achieve your emancipation. I can sponsor you and I have several letters of recommendation. Everything is going well. How are your nursing classes?"

"The teachers are tough, but I think I'll pass everything."

"I'm proud of you." Ann Marie patted her shoulder. "I'll let you know when I hear more." She left for the kitchen. There were always more people to feed.

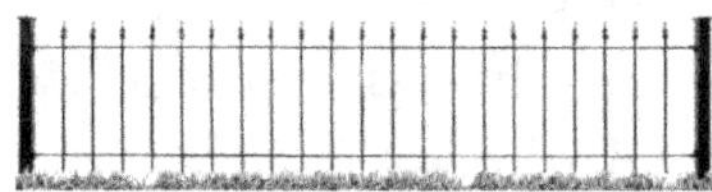

Concerns were piling up. Classes were getting harder. The student nurses had finished their fundamentals class with Miss Tursek. She was only an introduction to future instructors. There were the challenges of vocabulary and memorizing all the terms of anatomy. Kaye applied the anatomy terminology to her person and patted parts of her body, as she said the name of bone and/or muscle, and then spelled the words aloud to herself.

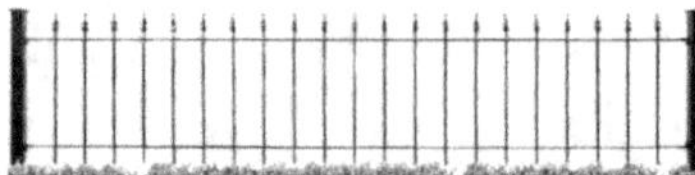

On Wednesday, Zeke was waiting on the corner at the bus stop. Kaye rushed up to him. "I'm so glad you came."

He shook his head.

"We have to try."

He removed a prepared note from his pocket and handed it to her.

"*Thank you, K. But if I go into a bakery, someone could find out I'm from the Home and take me back as a vagrant. I'm homeless. I don't ever want to go back.*"

"How old are you, Zeke?"

He took the paper and wrote 42.

"If you get a job, you can get emancipated."

Zeke rubbed his fingers together, indicating money.

"Yes, you're right. I have someone helping me right now but I' going to pay them back. If you're working, you can too."

He listened, nodding for her to go on.

"My court hearing is coming up. I'm working and going to school. I have letters of recommendation. The lawyer says I've proved myself."

He took the paper again and wrote. "*It's dangerous-doesn't always work.*" He pointed to his mouth.

They both sat down on the bus stop bench.

Kaye understood what he was saying, and it hurt to think about how much he had suffered because of his appearance. She swallowed the lump in her throat.

"Zeke, life is a risk. You are homeless. Lots of things can happen on the street. Wouldn't you like to have your own place to live, a job? Don't you want to try?"

He patted her shoulder and lowered his head. He was trying to make her understand his sorrow.

"I can't guarantee anything, but will you at least meet the manager? If she won't consider hiring you then I'll accept that decision, but if she offers to give you work, well, then we can go from there. Right now, you don't even have an offer. Couldn't hurt to ask, right?"

Zeke looked up and closed his eyes. He stood, reached for Kaye's hand, and together they walked toward Dexter's.

Patsy introduced herself, looked at Zeke's neck scarf, and began the interview. Kaye answered as many questions as she could for Zeke, and he commented in writing.

The trial baking session happened on the following Sunday, and it proved everything Kaye had touted about Zeke. Johnny was there too. He and Patsy pronounced the donuts feather light and delicious. Patsy scheduled donut baking to start the following Sunday.

One concern remained: establishing Zeke's legal independence. Until they were declared emancipated both Zeke and Kaye walked in the shadow of the State.

Saturday afternoon, Kaye's ritual included a walk to the bridge. It held hope and anticipation as she searched among the people for one man, a tall handsome dark-haired man with deep blue eyes that twinkled.

On the days when she went later in the day, she waited at the water's edge for the bridge lights to switch on before returning home. The lights twinkling on the water softened the day's disappointment. She couldn't tell anyone why she went every Saturday; they would laugh at her. Teenage love, they'd say. Many nights she tossed in sleeplessness, plagued with thoughts that maybe she had been wrong. Maybe Seth didn't know about his parents. Maybe Jackie wasn't his mother. She had jumped to a conclusion without knowing the truth. She was so sure then. If she could contact Lucy, she might know something about Seth, but if Miss Turpin heard she had done that she could be expelled from the program, and besides, if Lucy still worked for the Home, she'd have to report a runaway.

Kaye's concerns regarding Tom's letter continued. She had hoped the situation had ended when she left over a year ago, difficult as it was to leave. Now here was this invitation to meet him. She loved the children so much, but everything about falling in love with Tom would be wrong. It would hurt Janie. It would hurt them all. No, she would not go. The pictures he sent were a constant reminder. She could go and explain how she felt. No, if he did not hear her the last time he wouldn't hear her now.

Maybe by now, Toe had married. Kaye lifted the braided necklace from inside her blouse and stroked the pearl button against her cheek. Whenever she touched it, he was near. She could feel his breath against the side of her face, and she remembered.

<h1 style="text-align:center">Chapter 41</h1>

"Seth, I heard you're going up to the thumb today. How about giving me a ride home." Jason came down the hall pulling a duffle bag of laundry. His hair was standing on end, as if he had just crawled out of bed and he had not shaved.

"This place is just like living in a rooming house." Seth laughed. "How did you find out where I was going?"

"It's easy, I listened on the phone. I heard you tell somebody last night."

"I charge to haul dirty laundry."

"You'd charge a friend?"

"Yup, I would. Did you lose your razor too?"

"Just for the weekend. Okay, it's a deal. I ride free and leave the laundry here."

"And disappoint your mom?"

The guys bantered all the way to the car. Jason tossed his duffle bag in the back and climbed in the passenger seat. Seth slid in the driver's seat, started the car, and pulled onto the street. Jason was silent until Seth turned left onto M21 and headed east.

"I've never been in your car before. Did you engineer that set-up?" He pointed to the lever where Seth's right hand rested.

"Yeah. I have a problem with my right foot. It's safer to drive with hand controls."

"Oh, you never said anything."

"Nothing to say. Where are we headed to drop off this laundry?"

"Sebewaing."

"That sounds Indian. I usually go to Port Huron and drive north from there to Port Austin. Where's Sebewaing?"

"You go north on M24, that shoots you right up to the bay. Sebewaing is on the bay. Does your family live on the sunrise side?"

"Sunrise side? It's called that?"

"Sure, we live on the sunset side. Your family over there?"

"Family, no, I'm looking for a friend. We said we'd meet at the water, where the railroad tracks end. We did talk about the sunrise though."

"The railroad tracks don't end at the water Seth; the trains go under the water and through the tunnel into Canada. Besides, you could have a search trying to meet someone 'at the water' in Michigan, with five great lakes."

"I didn't know the trains went under the water. No, we agreed to meet at the water. I decided to go to Port Austin this morning and stop along the way down, coming in from the north. I'll be in Port Huron by late afternoon."

"Needle in a haystack, looking to meet somebody at the water." Jason mumbled. He slid down in his seat and dozed the rest of the ride.

In the silence Seth's thoughts turned to doubt. This was the first time he had come on a Saturday. He always thought he would see her on Sunday. To everyone else it was a high school romance, and they were young.

Seth tried to counter his doubts as he observed the scenery. The sky was a deep, October blue, and everywhere leaves of crimson and gold dressed the hardwoods. The evergreen trees were lush velvet green.

He thought about the trees changing color at the Home, and the freedom he felt today as he passed the miles and miles of autumn blaze.

A gas stop roused Jason, who handed him three dollars without opening his eyes.

"Thanks, buddy." Seth added the money to his own and filled the tank.

On the road again, Jason began to talk about his courses.

"It's getting harder for me, Seth. How are *you* doing?"

"I'm doing okay. There's a lot of terminology and math to learn. I guess I'm more of a tinkerer than an engineer. I like motors."

"I just want to get done and make money. I hear the girls like engineers. You hear that?"

Seth laughed as Jason continued to share the advantages their degree would offer.

"I'm wondering about that person you're meeting at the water?"

"What about her?"

"I knew it. It is a girl? Does she know you're going to be a Mechanical Engineer?"

"Jason, you should try to find a girl who isn't impressed with how much money you can make. You want a girl who cares about you."

"Is she pretty?"

"Who?"

"That girl you're trying to find. *Your* girl! She must be if you're driving all that way to find her. You can pull over by Doc's gas station. I live around the corner. My buddies all hang out there. There they are."

Seth pulled up to the curb near Jason's friends.

"Thanks for the ride." Jason pulled his duffle bag out and bounced it onto the street. "Good luck finding your mermaid."

"See you at school. You got a ride back?"

Jason held out his thumb. "It's slow going, but it's a ride."

"All right." Seth waved and headed toward Port Austin. The highway angled back and forth near the water, then away.

Signs with names of little towns to the right appeared: Pigeon, Bad Axe, Ubly. He drove on to Port Austin and circled through the State Park. Whitecaps topped the waves that swirled and bounced up and down toward the shore. A few teenagers frolicked in the water, eking out the remnants of summer.

This time he brought a picture of Kaye. Mr. Kent had asked the teacher from the yearbook staff for a picture. Mrs. Kent was sure someone, somewhere along the way, might recognize her if they saw a picture. Seth stopped at a few restaurants and a couple small stores. At an ice cream shop in Port Hope a lady thought she might have seen someone who looked like Kaye, but she wasn't sure. He drove on to Port Sanilac.

The stopping and questioning took more time than he had planned. He checked his watch and reviewed the map. It was four o'clock. If he drove on to Port Huron, he would be there by five, have some supper, and be at the bridge before sunset.

The sparkle of the water beckoned although his stomach growled from hunger. He parked the car and walked down to the shoreline path. The traffic on the bridge moved at a steady pace. Seagulls circled overhead, begging for a morsel. A freighter progressed along the river toward the lake.

A man standing beside him peered through a pair of binoculars. "Look at the size of that ship, riding low she is. She's carrying iron ore. Look at the flags a flying."

"She's a big one," Seth replied, as he watched the massive ship glide through the water. He continued along the walkway. The water offered a peaceful greeting. Seth sat down on the park bench and watched the people stroll past clicking pictures of each other with box cameras, pictures of the bridge, and the ships. His hopeful mood from the morning had all but diminished. Maybe an ice cream cone all day wasn't enough food. He hated to leave the water to eat. Usually, he brought a sandwich or a snack, but leaving so early this morning and rearranging his day to start from Caseville down had changed his route. He needed to find some food. He got into his car and headed south, passing through residential areas, weaving back and forth nearer the river, then away. In the south end of town he saw a building, elevated, about five steps, with a thatched roof over the entrance. The porch was surrounded with a crosshatch railing. A sign on the roadside announced *Sully's Crab Shack*. It had red lettering on a pale-yellow background. Fish netting had been draped over the upper corner and a lobster cage was nailed to the opposite lower corner.

Crab. He'd never had crab. Maybe they served fish. Crab might be expensive. There were several cars in the lot, and the noises emulating from the building sounded like people having fun. Rollicking fun would be more like it. He thought, *I'll get a take-out and go back to the park and eat. Nah, the sea gulls. I'll eat here then go back. Maybe the service will be fast so I could get back before sunset.*

Seth entered to the noise of the jukebox playing songs from the top ten hits. Two tables of teenagers clustered around the jukebox. A few couples were holding hands. That was a good thing. Today he felt a lot older than these kids and he felt alone. He found a table for two and sat down. A man came out from the kitchen wearing a white apron with the ties crossed in back and knotted in front.

"Menu's on the Blackboard. Let me know when you're ready to order." He placed a glass of water on the wood table. "Name's Johnny."

"Fish basket?" Seth asked, unable to see the menu with the man standing between him and the blackboard.

"Fries, three pieces of fish, and coleslaw. Pop or iced tea?"

"Pop," Seth replied.

Red-checked curtains fluttered at the cottage-style windows. A group of picnic tables formed a circle around a dance area where one couple hopped, held hands, and twirled in time to the music as the others laughed and sang along.

"What are you kids doing tonight?" Johnny called out from the kitchen.

"We're going to the drive-in," someone shouted.

"What you going to see?" He yelled to match the volume of the music.

"Something bloody!" a boy shouted back.

"You'll scare those girls to death," Johnny warned.

The music from the jukebox paused as another record rotated into place.

"We've already seen it," a girl assured Johnny.

"That's good, 'cause probably none of you will be watching anyway." Johnny laughed.

The guys paid the bill and they all filed out the door, piled into three cars, and drove away. As Seth finished his fish basket, Johnny came out to clean off the tables the kids had used. He wiped up the counter and refilled Seth's pop.

"Haven't seen you before. You from around here?"

"No, I come over on the weekends sometimes. I like it near the water."

"Don't we all."

"Is this your place?"

"No, I cook here on the weekends. The waitress called in with a migraine. I told her to stay home. It's sort of slow this weekend, end of the season. So, you come to town on weekends?"

"Yeah." Seth didn't want to explain. He had been explaining all day. Describing a brown-haired girl about eighteen, five foot five. There were a lot of them. Nobody had seen the girl he was looking for.

Seth pulled out his wallet, handed Johnny the money, bill and tip.

"That your girl?" Johnny pointed to the picture in the open wallet.

"Yeah, I hope so."

"Why so glum?"

"I can't find her. She moved away a couple years ago, and we promised we'd meet at the water. I come on the weekends when I can."

Seth closed his wallet and slid it into his back pocket.

"What's her name? Maybe I know her."

"Kaye. Kaye O'Shay."

"Nope, sorry. Wish you luck, though." He entered the kitchen, and then returned. "Hey, show me that picture again?"

Seth pulled his wallet out, opened it, and handed Kaye's picture to Johnny who dried his hands on his apron before taking it. Johnny studied the picture and looked up at Seth.

"This looks like somebody I know, but that's not her name. You don't know a Maureen Morton by any chance?"

"No." Seth reached for the picture and turned to leave, then returned to the counter. "Wait, did you say Maureen?" Seth stopped, frozen. Could it be possible Kaye was using the name Maureen? But Morton?

"If this isn't Maury, it's her sister."

Seth sat down on the barstool.

"Do you know where I can find her?"

"What time is it?" Johnny looked at the clock. "I don't know where you can find that Kaye girl, but I know where you might find Maury. At eight o'clock she's supposed to be at the Inn by the bridge."

"You don't know for sure?"

"Why don't you stop in and check? Can't hurt, can it?"

"No, I guess not." Seth returned Kaye's picture to his wallet. Knots started twisting in his stomach.

At the door he turned around. "Johnny, is the Inn a fancy place?"

"You need a jacket to go into the dining room, but you've already eaten. You can always go into the bar."

"I don't drink."

"Order a pop." Johnny laughed.

"Right." Seth shrugged. From the jukebox a new song started to play, one about love being cruel. Seth closed the door behind him and sang the lyrics all the way to the Inn.

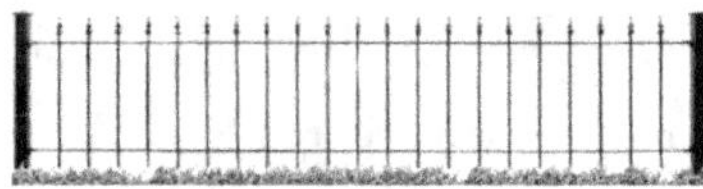

"Hair up, hair down?" Kaye gazed into the mirror over her dresser as she tried different up-do hairstyles, then brushed her hair until it glistened, and let it fall in gentle waves around her shoulders. She was talking to herself as she wrestled with the decision of going to the Inn and not going to the Inn. Kaye reread the letter. "This is trouble with a capital T," she mumbled.

Turning toward the window, she sat in the chair and wrestled with her decision. Questions overwhelmed her. She slid off the chair and kneeled in prayer.

"You know I don't know what to do. You know I don't want to make a wrong decision. If I don't go, it won't answer his question, and he will look for me again. If I go, I must tell him it would be wrong for me to return to his house under any circumstances. I've never been to a fancy place like the Inn. I've never worn such a pretty dress. I seek to do what's right. Please help me make Tom understand."

She cried as she prayed, smearing her make-up. She repaired her mascara and dusted her cheeks with powder. The dress she borrowed from Mary Ann lay on her bed, a deep emerald-green crepe de Chine; the color matched her eyes. Mary Ann had a room down the hall at Mrs. D's. She worked at an expensive dress shop off Main. Although Mary Ann was generous, Kaye asked with reluctance to borrow her nicest dress. I can't get a spot on this, Kaye worried as she slid the dress over her head and zipped the side zipper. The jewel neckline concealed her pearl-button necklace. Folds in the bodice flowed on a diagonal from the left shoulder across to the right secured at the waist. The skirt, cut on the bias, draped over her hips, emphasizing her narrow waist. She slid her feet into a pair of black pumps and checked the seams of her stockings. It was seven-thirty. Carrying a cardigan sweater, she descended the stairs, intending to reach the bus stop and catch the northbound seven-forty.

Mary Ann and Mrs. D. were in the parlor as she reached the landing.

Mrs. D. turned her gaze toward Kaye. "Well, my goodness, Maury, you must be going somewhere special tonight."

"I wanted to look nice tonight." Kaye couldn't hide her apprehension.

"You look very nice, yes you do. It's just that I've never seen you so dressed up."

"It's my dress, Mrs. D. I loaned it to Maury for tonight."

"I was invited to have dinner at the Inn…" Kaye searched their faces seeking affirmation or disapproval. She turned back toward the stairs.

Mrs. D caught her arm. "I didn't mean to hurt your feelings. You look very nice."

Mary Ann smiled and adjusted a tuck at Kaye's waist. "It fits perfect."

Mrs. D opened the front door. "You look lovely. Go along now and have a nice dinner. It's high time you did something special."

"You're sure I look all right?"

"More than all right." Mrs. D. smiled.

Kaye hugged Mrs. D. and thanked Mary Ann again, then rushed toward the bus stop. She could do this. "We've talked about this, you and me. I'm not alone." Kaye brushed her fingers across her pearl button under the bodice of her dress. I feel pretty. If only it could be Toe I'm meeting.

The bus rolled to a stop. Exiting, she paused, with one foot on the street and the other remaining on the bus step. Her grasp tightened on the handrail.

"Ma'am, you gotta let go so I can close the door.

If she let go, she couldn't get back on the bus. Kaye swallowed the lump in her throat, took a deep breath, released her grasp, and strode toward the Inn.

Chapter 42

As Kaye entered the mahogany foyer and stepped onto the plush carpet, she sensed luxury beyond any she had ever known. The hall clock chimed eight. A pedestal floor directory indicated the room to her left was the library. As a waiter wandered in and out of the room bearing trays of glasses, clouds of gray and blue smoke from pipes and cigars entered the hallway, affording the combined scents of various woods, spices, and peppery smells.

The waiter paused. "May I help you, Miss?"

"I'm… looking for the dining room."

"Follow me, please." The jacketed waiter spun to his right and moved swiftly down the hallway. Kaye hurried to follow, fearful she would trip, as the narrow heels of her shoes sank into the carpet. Beautiful oil paintings in massive frames lined the hallway.

On her left, the word B-A-R glowed through a leaded glass panel. An archway opened into the room where stools lined the bar and a mirrored wall reflected bottles and glasses. A couple people occupied barstools.

"This way," the waiter urged. Unaware she had stopped, she hurried toward another man, he was older, suited in an identical manner, standing at a lectern.

Her original guide disappeared as fast as he had appeared.

"Do you have a reservation?" The gray-haired man scanned a page on the lectern.

"I'm meeting a friend for dinner. Tom Butler."

Kaye struggled to peer around the man in search of Tom.

"Yes, I see."

The man knew she didn't belong at a place like this. She shuddered, wishing to disappear.

Another waiter appeared. "Henri, please seat this lady at table seventeen."

Henri's eyes danced as he smiled at her. "This way madam. Your host selected a table with a view of the bridge." He walked with his head held high and a towel over his forearm."

Tom was standing as they approached.

"Maury, you came." He didn't hide his apprehension. "Please, sit down," he urged, as the waiter pulled a chair from the table. Kaye's knees folded and the chair encased her trembling body.

"Would you like to order a beverage now, sir?"

"Yes." Tom glanced at Kaye and hesitated.

"We'll have two ginger ales."

The waiter smiled and did not look at Kaye. "Yes sir." He disappeared.

Kaye turned her gaze from the lights of the bridge toward Tom.

He reached toward her hand, but as soon as he touched her fingers, Kaye withdrew, and clasped her hands together in her lap. This was the wrong thing to do. He wouldn't understand why she had come.

He slid the thick linen napkin to one side. "I'm glad you're here. I had a hard time getting away from Andy when I told him I was coming to see you."

He told the *children?* She struggled to suppress her panic.

"You look wonderful. So, you found work?" His question drew her back into the present.

Kaye straightened her shoulders. She must control her fear. In a few months, she would be expected to make medical decisions that could involve someone's life.

"I'm studying nursing. I'll finish the program in the spring."

"I hoped you would do well." He removed several pictures from his inside coat pocket, and placed them on the table. Snapshots of the children; Andy playing with the dog, Susie carrying her pet chicken, and Molly gnawing on something with her new teeth, blond curls fluttering around her head.

Kaye smiled as she remembered endearing times with them.

The waiter appeared with their beverages. "Would you like to order?"

"Are you ready to order dinner?" Tom asked.

"No. Let's enjoy the view." She didn't want him to pay for an expensive dinner—then tell him she wouldn't see him again. That wouldn't be right.

Kaye sipped her drink as she and Tom shared happenings over the past year.

Their conversation diminished as the musicians returned from their break and started to play. One couple stepped onto the dance floor, then another. Kaye watched them glide around the perimeter, the ladies so graceful and the men so handsome.

"Would you like to dance?"

"I don't know how." Kaye mumbled her answer, sure that her inability would discourage him.

"You don't have to know how; I have to know how. I lead and you follow. It's that easy."

She hesitated. The music started again, and the dancers moved into each other's embrace.

"Come on, Maury," Tom said, as he stood and reached for her hand, urging her to join him. She followed to the dance floor. He turned and circled her, placed his right hand in the center of her back and clasped her right hand in his left. The delicate pressure of his fingers on her back stole her attention as they moved around the floor. Listening to the music, Kaye responded to his lead. She was dancing. She closed her eyes trying to halt the tears that refused to remain hidden. If only, if only.

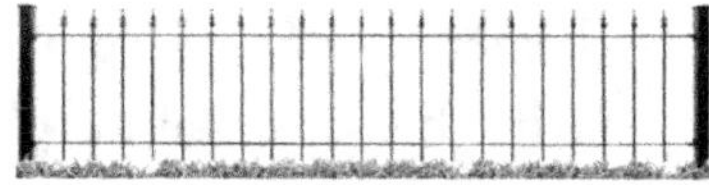

Toe entered the driveway to the Inn at seven forty-five. He glanced around, seeking the parking lot. There must be one somewhere, but the drive took him directly to the portico entrance. A parking attendant approached.

"Park for you, sir?"

"No thanks. My car has special controls. Is there somewhere I can park?"

"Certainly, sir. Are you staying at the Inn, or will you be dining with us tonight?"

"Just stopping by the bar to meet a friend."

"Sure, follow the drive to your right, that will take you to the south entrance. The bar is on your left as you enter."

Seth followed the attendant's directions, entered the bar, and selected a stool. He assessed the dining room. The view looking down on the water and the lights above from the bridge would offer a beautiful view. He could see areas of the dining room. To the right of the dance floor, a combo group with guitar, drums, and tenor sax, had just finished a set and were entering the bar. Laughter tumbled into the room as several couples passed down the hall toward a long table in the dining room. One couple clearly were bride and groom, as she was carrying a bouquet of flowers and wearing a small white hat with a veil.

"Well, sir, what'll it be tonight?"

Seth rubbed the glistening wood on the bar. "Root beer?" He murmured low to avoid any other patron hearing him.

"Simple up. I got it." The bartender reminded him of Mr. Green, friendly, and yet, all business. "That's black oak. The wood." The barkeeper tapped the bar.

Seth looked around trying to estimate how much a pop cost here. He should have asked Johnny. The way the people were dressed indicated expensive tastes. Seth spent the next several minutes taking in the paneling, lighting, the beautiful bar, and stained glass.

"Another pop?"

The bartender clicked Seth's empty glass on the bar, giving him a questioning stare.

Seth sighed. "Yeah, sure." He'd sip this one slower.

The bar emptied out as the music combo and some guests returned to the dining room. The bartender wiped down the bar as he moved toward Seth.

"So, I'd wager you're here to meet a woman, am I right?"

"How'd you know I was meeting anyone?"

"I know people. *You* wouldn't be here if you weren't meeting someone, and I don't think you would be that uneasy if it were a man."

Seth pulled out his wallet and removed Kaye's picture. "I'm hoping to see her."

The bartender wiped his hands and held the picture toward the light. "Pretty girl, Irish?"

"You're good."

The bartender laughed and pointed to the tip jar. Seth tossed in a dollar.

"Tell me, does she know you're going to be here? You seem edgy."

"No, she doesn't know." Seth lowered his chin. This had to be the dumbest thing he'd ever done, and it was going to cost him a fortune. "Say how much is a root beer anyway?"

The bartender pulled the dollar out of the tip jar and dropped it into the till. "We're even, you and I." He removed Seth's glass and refilled it with ice and pop.

Little rivulets of water dribbled down the sides of the cold glass as Seth traced them with his finger.

"I haven't seen her for a long time."

"How long?"

"Going on a year and a half." Seth wiped his hand on his pants and slid the picture back into his wallet. "She's probably found somebody else by now."

"You didn't. I bet she hasn't either."

"You're going three for three here and I'm out of tip money."

"I'm pretty good." The bartender watched the dancers move onto the dance floor as the music resumed.

"Do you see that girl in the dark green dress?" Seth followed the man's stare toward the dance floor. Kaye wouldn't know how to dance like that.

"I can add a little taste to that, and we could get rid of those jitters."

"No, I've got a long drive tonight."

"Hey, she's sat down at a table." The bartender leaned closer. "If you go to the restroom, you can get a better look."

"Two-fold journey. Save my chair." Seth slid off the barstool in search of the restroom. On his return he passed the dining room archway and paused for a moment. She looked like Kaye, but she looked different, taller, the same beautiful dark hair. He returned to the bar. "You're right, it looks like her, but she's with a guy. She's found somebody else."

"You're not as good as me, but if you keep trying you might get there."

"What?"

"The guy with her. He's older. He's got a wedding ring on. Your girl, she doesn't."

"How do you know that?"

"While you were gone, I asked their waiter."

"You're sure?"

"As sure as your next tip."

Seth reached for his wallet as the bartender laughed and shook his head.

"So, what now, Romeo?"

"I don't know. It's been so long. I've been to Port Huron so many times looking for her, but I never thought about what I'd do when I found her."

"You could ask her to dance."

Seth gulped. He felt his body tense. He wished his prosthetic shoe would stay on the ring of the barstool when his leg did that nervous tic. Dance! Another reason why he shouldn't be here.

Chapter 43

Kaye laughed as Tom shared anecdotes of the children. The farm flourished this year. His job helped support the farm. He didn't talk about the hardships, and he only referred to Janie once. Kaye knew Janie must still be at home or Tom would say otherwise. She didn't ask.

"We should order dinner." Tom picked up a menu and began reading, sorting through his likes and dislikes, urging Kaye to make a choice.

"Tom." She had to tell him. She couldn't order dinner. It was too expensive, and besides, she wouldn't be able to eat. Not tonight. "Tom, I have to tell you…"

He lowered his menu, peering over the top. "Can't it wait until after dinner?"

"No." Her reply was firm. "Tom, I won't see you again. I made the right choice when I left the farm. We both know that. You're married and I'm sorry, so very sorry about Janie. I know you love her, and she loves you. Tom, don't you see?"

The music started again.

Tom stood and pulled her toward the dance floor.

"This isn't the answer." Kaye said.

"Just one more dance, Maury, just one." He drew her into his arms. "I can go on if I know that's the way you want it to be, but I will think of you every day."

They moved onto the dance floor.

"Tom, I do care. It's not right and we can't make a wrong right."

Seth listened to the music. He knew the songs. He'd listened to big band sounds over the years and the newer hits he heard on the radio. He was trying not to watch the dancers. He didn't know if the girl was Kaye, but if it was, he didn't want to see another man holding her in his arms.

"So, you gonna make your move or what?"

Seth shrugged. "I don't know how to dance." He couldn't tell this guy he only had one good leg. That would be great. After all this time, he cruises out on a dance floor and falls on his butt. Nice!

"You don't have to dance, buddy, you ask her to dance. That's when she recognizes you. You have a lot to catch up on for a year and a half. She'll want to talk. She's a woman. The dancing will come later." He chuckled and patted Seth's shoulder.

"That's dumb, how do I ask her to dance and then not dance?"

"Listen up. You cut in when they're dancing."

"What? That doesn't have the sound of turning out well. Just cut in."

"Don't you know about cutting in?"

Seth's empty response answered the question.

"You go up behind the man when they're dancing and tap on his shoulder. Then, in your most polite voice, you say, 'May I cut in?' He'll turn to her to see if she objects. If she doesn't, he'll step away. That's how it's done."

"Just like that?"

"Just like that."

"And I don't have to dance?"

"Not after she sees you. She'll grab your hand and you'll be a goner. If she feels like you do."

"What if he says no?"

"Buddy, you had *no* before you walked in the door, now you have a chance at a *yes!*"

Seth glanced toward the table where they were seated. He watched the man stand and pull the woman to her feet. For a second it looked as if she might not…then, she was in his arms.

Seth's mouth was dry. His hands trembled. His heart pounded a drumbeat he could feel in his ears. His gut churned. They circled past the archway to the bar, her hand on the man's shoulder. Seth slid from the barstool. He could leave without seeing her. He turned toward the dance floor. Other couples were dancing now. Gripped with the desire to hold her once more, he approached them and touched the man's shoulder.

"May I cut in?"

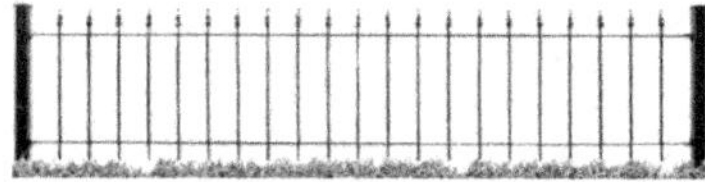

Kaye raised her eyes to meet his and caught her breath.

Seth presented his hand to Tom. "Seth Thomas. Pleased to meet you."

"*Seth?*" Kaye gasped.

Tom's gaze turned from Seth to the radiant smile on Kaye's face. He relinquished the grasp of her hand and extended his to Seth.

"Tom Butler. Do you know each other?"

Kaye struggled to find the words. "Yes. We know each other."

Tom passed a glance from Seth to Kaye and back to Seth. "Goodbye, Maury."

Kaye turned to face him. "Goodbye, Tom."

The music started again. Seth pulled her into his arms. The couples danced around them. He held her until her body stopped trembling.

Seth removed a velvet bag from his pocket and lifted out a strand of ivory pearls. "These are for you. I've found my pearl of great price."

"Seth, if you know that story then you know God brought us together."

"I bought the pearls because I had to believe I would find you."

"Thank you, Seth. They're lovely." Kaye reached inside the neckline of her dress and pulled out the horsehair braid with the pearl button. "But they'll never be as precious as my pearl button necklace. I haven't taken it off since that day."

"And you, my dear Kaye—" Seth said, holding her close, "you are worth more to me than all the pearls in the world."

Seth and Kaye shared a kiss as the other couples on the dance floor formed a circle, applauding and laughing.

Love had taken them on their journey to the water, and now, love would bind them with a three-fold cord. (Ecclesiastes 4:12 KJV)

About Nelle Cooper

Nelle Cooper is a retired registered nurse, speaker, and author. The daughter of a dairy farmer, she grew up in a seven-gabled farm home where one upstairs room was dedicated to antiques and ancestry, every item telling its own story. She enjoys cooking and believes that a recipe is a place to start. She enjoys gardening and will never plant flowers in rows. She collects seeds from year to year and hangs her laundry outside in the sunshine. She has long had a propensity to ask, "What if?" and this story born of driving through the land that was once the Lapeer State Home is no exception. After the children's chapter book Princess Lil, this heartfelt historical novel is her second book. Nelle Cooper shares a restored centennial farmhouse in Hadley, Michigan, with her husband, Ed, kitty Poppy, and Cavalier dog Miss Torrey.

Acknowledgements

First and foremost, I owe sincere appreciation to the team at Fresh Ink Group, for their skills and encouragement in bringing this novel to the reader.

To the residents and staff of Oakdale, The Lapeer State Home, who are the inspiration for this work of fiction.

Thank you to my first writing coach, Emily Gehman.

To Mary Vee, for her dedicated assistance through the reviews and redrafts.

To the Salvation Army of Port Huron for providing historical information.

To Arcadia Publishing for the history provided in the book *Oakdale: The Lapeer State Home*.

To Jan Gillis, for sharing the history of the Lapeer State Home, reading the original draft, and contributing essential information.

For the collaboration of everyone who shared information about the history of the State Home, with the request to remain anonymous. You know who you are. I am deeply grateful.

To my mentor and prayer partner, Ginger Miller, for her unwavering support.

To my husband, Ed, for listening, reading my chapters, and encouraging my creativity.

I will always delight in his response to my brainstorming, as he asks, "Is this about someone I should know?"

To my daughter, Deb, and my son, Bill, because they cheer me on.

To my readers. Thank you!

All Glory to my Savior.
"And whatever you do, whether in word or deed, do it all in the name of the Lord Jesus, giving thanks to God the Father through him." Colossians 3:17 NIV

Fresh Ink Group
Independent Multi-media Publisher
Fresh Ink Group / Push Pull Press
Voice of Indie / GeezWriter

Hardcovers
Softcovers
All Ebook Formats
Audiobooks
Podcasts
Worldwide Distribution

Indie Author Services
Book Development, Editing, Proofing
Graphic/Cover Design
Video/Trailer Production
Website Creation
Social Media Marketing
Writing Contests
Writers' Blogs

Authors
Editors
Artists
Experts
Professionals

FreshInkGroup.com
info@FreshInkGroup.com
Twitter: @FreshInkGroup
Facebook.com/FreshInkGroup
LinkedIn: Fresh Ink Group

Chapter book for kids!

Paperback

Ebooks

Audiobook

Princess Lil is a sad pony. Her little girl grew up and went away. Now Lil is in a scary place with lots of mean ponies. A fun furry farm-cat called Taffy and a nice roan horse named Pearly try to help. It even looks like Princess Lil might have a chance to cheer up special-needs children, too, but she is already too hurt and too sick. Princess Lil is about the differences between loyal friends and those who bully others. It shows the power of caring about ourselves and the people who look out for us. Is it too late for a sad pony in a scary place? The answer might just depend on how much we all love Princess Lil.

The Lapeer State Home has been a large part of the history of Lapeer County since its beginnings in 1895. After starting with three buildings and housing for 200 patients, the facility grew to encompass several hundred acres and, at its peak, accommodating over 4,000 patients. The history of the home includes a variety of memories from staff members, patients, and visitors who once walked its halls. Images of America: Oakdale: The Lapeer State Home provides a journey of this historic institution and attempts to bring some clarity to questions that remain about the home and its past.

Arcadia Publishing